A CHANGE OF LUCK

By Julia Markus

UNCLE
AMERICAN ROSE
FRIENDS ALONG THE WAY

JULIA MARKUS

For Laurie & Burt Langer,
with best Regards,
Julia Markus

A CHANGE

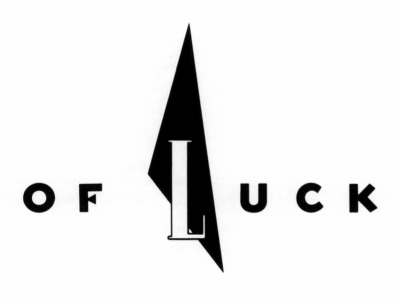

OF LUCK

VIKING

VIKING
Published by the Penguin Group
Viking Penguin, a division of Penguin Books USA Inc.,
375 Hudson Street, New York, New York 10014, U.S.A.
Penguin Books Ltd, 27 Wrights Lane, London W8 5TZ, England
Penguin Books Australia Ltd, Ringwood, Victoria, Australia
Penguin Books Canada Ltd, 2801 John Street,
Markham, Ontario, Canada L3R 1B4
Penguin Books (N.Z.) Ltd, 182–190 Wairau Road,
Auckland 10, New Zealand

Penguin Books Ltd, Registered Offices:
Harmondsworth, Middlesex, England

First published in 1991 by Viking Penguin,
a division of Penguin Books USA Inc.

1 2 3 4 5 6 7 8 9 10

Author's Note: This is a work of fiction. Any similarities to
persons living or dead is purely coincidental. Certain details
of local geography and recent history have been shaped to
fit the story.

Grateful acknowledgment is made for permission to reprint
an excerpt from *The Andy Warhol Diaries*. Copyright
© 1989 by Estate of Andy Warhol. Reprinted by permission
of Warner Books, New York.

LIBRARY OF CONGRESS CATALOGING IN PUBLICATION DATA
Markus, Julia.
A change of luck / by Julia Markus.
p.   cm.
ISBN 0-670-81414-8
I. Title.
PS3563.A672C46   1991
813'.54—dc20   90-50339

Printed in the United States of America
Set in Garamond No. 3
Designed by Francesca Belanger

To the Reader

"LUCK IS COMING OUR WAY."
(Chinese fortune cookie, variation)

Life really does repeat itself. The old songs come back in a new way and the kids think they're new and the old people remember and it's a way of keeping people together, I guess, a way of living.

ANDY WARHOL
The Diaries

*The author is grateful
to the Corporation of Yaddo for
a long summer stay that
supported and encouraged
this work.*

PART

ONE

O N E

Elaine Netherlands had a change of luck on the day she made a wrong turn in Danbury, Connecticut. It was early summer and she was sticky. Why hadn't she bought an air-conditioned car? Was it purer to be lost and sweaty than lost and cool? What happened to the road? She was on a perfectly good road when she simply veered off into this wood. Too hot to think, she thought, got out of the car, and looked around. She was wearing leather sandals, a pair of rolled-up jeans, and a Hard Rock Cafe, London, T-shirt cast off by her stepdaughter years ago. Where exactly was she? And, since she wasn't a great believer in accidents, why had she made a wrong turn? Had her stepdaughter Nola's reappearance set her off course? Nola, at nineteen, walking right back into her life. Hi, Elaine. Bye-bye three years of silence.

Elaine had called her old friends Peter and Judith, while she was still in shock. "Come on up," Judith told her. "Get some distance. We'll talk." Maybe jumping into her car the next day to drive to Connecticut wasn't a wise thing to do?

Walking into the shade of the unfamiliar trees, she stretched her arms to the breeze. Long, slim, muscular arms—she was in good shape. Why not? She had reached her late thirties at a time when the country had decided that forty, even fifty, could look as good as can be and when Joan Collins held out the promise of a whorish and gorgeous old age.

Elaine had very thick, dusty-blond hair that she wore close to her scalp. The curls were natural and the color almost was. Her nose was long, aquiline. Broken at the ridge from an early fall off a bike, it added a hawklike intensity to her good looks. Her light-brown eyes were remarkable for their intelligence. Something very clear shone from them. Usually. Right now she was perplexed. She'd driven from Manhattan past Danbury before, many times, and had never lost her way. She sighed, suddenly seeing her stepdaughter—her cool and careful eyes, her broad and vibrant face. Seeing Nola dredged up emotions. Not now, she said to herself. Calm down. Take a look at the forest, see the trees.

What she saw was a freshly cut path just where one finds new things, right under one's nose. Or, in this case, close to her feet. Her stepdaughter's T-shirt unglued from her back. Why not a walk through the woods? Who says you have to rectify a wrong turn immediately? She left her car on the hill and followed the path. After a while the woods soothed her. Slowed her down. Had she been running? Where was she rushing? She saw a tree stump and decided to sit for a moment. Collect herself. She picked up a stick and peeled some of its bark, scratched NOLA, then scratched a question mark into the ground.

The ring yesterday at Elaine's door. The Chinese restaurants and the Y slipped their announcements under it. Usually she didn't respond to a ring.

"Who's there?"

"Elaine, it's me."

Elaine, it's me. Three years had passed, but just as any child would, Nola simply rang her bell, simply expected her stepmother to be there when she needed her. She probably would have been bent out of shape if she hadn't found her at home, waiting. Elaine realized she was not surprised, she indeed had been waiting—since the divorce from Larry, Nola's father. She opened the door.

Nola in the doorway. Her hair short, jet-black, full in front, then clipped back. There was a red fringe all around it. She had on wonderful earrings: two big circles of red and gold. Black net covered her tight sleeveless scoop-necked red T and fell to the waist of her short black skirt. She wore a variation of the ballet slippers they used to call "slut shoes," tied up in a webbing of laces beyond Elaine's technical skills.

She looked great. But she wasn't a pretty girl, all vulnerable and smooth-skinned the way Elaine had been at her age. She had a broad face, some problems with her skin, which was porous and could break out at times. Her nose was small, though, and her grayish eyes were wide-set. They were mysterious eyes; they didn't give her away. Nola played with the way she looked, and the wildest thing about her appearance was how it could change.

"Oh, Nola!" Elaine exclaimed. "How wonderful to see you. You look so good! I can't help it, Nola, forgive me, but you're all grown up!"

Had Elaine opened her arms first? They hugged each other in the hallway. "Come on in," Elaine said finally. "You feel hot. It must be scorching out there. Want a Pepsi?"

"Diet?"

"Sure. What do you think, I used to stock it just for you?"

"Oh, Elaine." Nola pouted for a moment, like a little girl. "I've got problems. It's heavy," she said in her raspy voice. "I swear to God it's intense."

Nola sat on Elaine's old needlepoint couch, the one Elaine had inherited from her grandmother. Nola was rubbing her hand over the rough texture of the Provence pillow, reminding Elaine, poignantly, of—herself. Maybe Elaine had once looked as incongruous on that couch as Nola now did.

Nola talked. She had just finished her junior year at NYU, dean's list, just as Elaine had always been, and was now involved with a back-to-basics postpunk band, Second Hand. Not only was she going with the lead guitarist, a dynamite guy named Jimmy; she was writing his lyrics, and, get this, she was beginning to sing with the group as well. "You know, Elaine, I'm fine, just fine, the moment I get on the stage, but before that I can't believe what I'm about to do."

"You always could sing."

"That's 'cause you're tone deaf. And, anyway, it's not opera. To be honest, it's not the voice I care about at all, it's what's behind it."

"You're behind it."

Nola smiled. "I am, aren't I? That's just what I feel."

With great restraint, Elaine kept herself from continuing: You're behind anything you want to do. Anything you want to do, you can do, you can be. All you have to do is get behind it and do it.

She had no idea why her ex-husband, Larry, used to say she wanted to spoil Nola. Because she listened to the music Nola liked? She didn't really want to make it artificially easier for Nola; every person has to go her own way. She just wanted to make it more real for Nola, more honest than it had been for *her*.

What Nola wanted to do was to take a year off from school and tour with Second Hand.

"Your senior year, Nola?"

That's what her father had said too. Wait.

"It's good advice, don't you think? Isn't it better to finish one thing before you begin another?"

Nola shrugged. "I'll make it up."

"Where would you be going?"

"California, first."

" 'California über Alles,' " Elaine joked.

"Hey, you remember listening to The Dead Kennedys?"

"I have the cassette. But tell me, what's in California?"

"Oh, nothing," Nola said excitedly. "Only the chance for a small part in a movie. And a manager who can book us in clubs. Only first we have to get there. Silas says many start but few get there."

"Silas?"

"An old guy who lives over me and Jimmy."

"Wait a minute. You moved out of your father's? You're living with a boyfriend?"

"Yeah, for the last three months. On St. Mark's near Avenue A."

"What did your father say?"

Nola shrugged. "Not much."

"I can just imagine."

"Yeah. Well, anyway, let me tell you about Silas. He's done everything, been everywhere. Listen to this. He writes lyrics and he does puppet shows and cooks and he's been a standup comedian. You'd like him, he used to live in Italy. He's been in films over there. But he always kept this apartment in New York, you see, for"—and Nola sang it out—" 'Eighty-eight Dollars and Eighty-eight Cents'! But, man, he has connections. He told me he'd wave his magic wand—that's how he talks—and what happens but he's got someone who listens to our tape and says, Okay, tell them to come to L.A., Silas. There's no one like him in the world. You know what he calls himself, Elaine, though—"

"Silas Mourner."

Nola's eyes grew Orphan-Annie wide.

"I knew him slightly in Rome, maybe fifteen years ago. If he remembered me, it would be as Elaine Bright."

Nola looked uncomfortable.

"Not that he'd remember."

"No. I don't think he does. I mean, he knows you as my stepmother."

"So Silas lives above you. You're right about him. He's an original. It's a small world," Elaine said. "Be careful of people who live on nothing." She smiled. "Don't lend him money."

"I'm the one who needs money. If I can raise my share, three thousand dollars, California here we come."

"So you need money."

"For a van, Elaine. A really great one. It's ours. It's waiting for us. It would make the trip. I hate to ask you for it, Elaine. But you said, if I ever needed anything, to ask. We need some money. I'd pay you back, I swear."

"A van?"

"Hardly used. Big enough for us, our equipment. It's the only way to go. Don't look so worried. Three thousand dollars. I swear I'd pay you back."

"What I'm worried about is déjà vu. I don't want to be in between you and your father. I was there once, if you remember, and it wasn't a very comfortable position."

"I'm sorry, Elaine."

"I'm not asking for an apology."

Nola looked at her quizzically. She hadn't been offering a personal one. Why should she?

Elaine realized this. "I don't know what to say. I have to think about this, Nola. I realize your father is rather opinionated on certain issues. But he has reasons for wanting you to finish your education. You're such a very good student. That's why I always felt you should be allowed to go your own way. I don't remember anything you've ever done that's ever affected your grades."

"Remember when you used to help me with algebra?"

"You remember?"

"Sure. I couldn't believe all the stuff you knew."

Elaine looked at her. "Maybe I've helped you with your grades. That's nice to know. I've been of some use." Whoops, the edge of the three-year separation. The edge of anger. She controlled it. "I hate to think of you giving up college right at the end."

"I'm not giving up, Elaine. I'm postponing it. I can go back. But for Second Hand, if we don't do it now, maybe there'll never be another year."

"There'll be another band."

"I don't want another band. This is special. This won't come around again. This is something I have to do."

"And what does your father say to that?"

"If I do this, he doesn't want to see my face."

"He doesn't mean it," Elaine said, suddenly forced to pluck a classic from the air. "He's just very upset; he's . . . he thinks he's doing it for your own good."

"Don't you think I know something about my own good?"

"Definitely. But I'm not your father and I'm not your mother."

"You've been like a mother to me."

"Oh, please, Nola. Just don't try to manipulate me. I mean, I'm glad you've come to see me; I'd be happy to help you if I can. I used to think I was like a mother to you, at least at certain times. If not a mother exactly, a friend, someone who understood. Oh, I don't know what I used to think. But I did find out what you thought, what you felt. I was just your everyday wicked stepmother."

"I'm sorry," said Nola, who suddenly looked embarrassed.

"About what?" Elaine asked archly.

About what? Nola had nothing to be sorry about. Elaine, in the shade, crossed out the question mark with her stick. Nola had shown up at her door. What would Larry think of that? She came back. She talked with her. She asked for what she needed. A van. Elaine looked up, way up, at the undersides of leaves. Then she moved back on the stump so that her head rested against the bark of the tree behind her. Closed her eyes . . .

She started, opened her eyes quickly. When she got up she noticed a white sign posted to a tree to her right, with an artistically drawn arrow and the word OFFICE painted in green. She'd continue her walk, follow the arrow, get some directions.

The path led to a wide sweep of grass. In the distance she saw the blue glimmer of a lake. She turned and found herself standing on cobblestones facing—newly constructed townhouses. A cluster of eight. Quite well constructed with gray shingles and dramatically slanted roofs that had skylights cut in. Each bore a white sign with the name of a Lake: Erie, Como, Placid, Louise . . . LUCERNE, the corner townhouse, was used as OFFICE.

She opened the door of the Lucerne and walked into the gray-carpeted hallway, following it to the spacious living room, softly carpeted as well. Above her, on the second floor, a balcony under a cathedral ceiling. Light slanting in, adding the illusion of even greater space. The light and the space transported her.

A woman approached her. A cheerful-looking woman in a plain blouse and loose skirt, her hands thrust deep in her pockets. She had light-brown hair and brown eyes and a round face. She was shorter than Elaine and stocky.

"May I help you?"

Rather than asking for directions, Elaine found herself answering, "Just looking."

"Take your time. I'm here if you need me."

"Thanks." Elaine wandered into the sunlit kitchen.

The room was furnished with all the bright implements of modern life one missed out on in Manhattan. So much counter space. Built-in wall oven, built-in dishwasher. Built-in microwave. Was this planet Earth or a space station? Should there be a woman or an android in control?

"An electric stove?" Elaine called out.

"Of course," she heard from the distance.

Electric stoves. Who the hell had this dream? Not Elaine. She was a purist about gas—did you ever see a restaurant with an electric stove?

"The stove's a mistake," Elaine said as she walked back to the living room with its extraordinary swoop of space.

"The stove's a mistake?" the realtor asked, and looked up from the brochures she was placing on the big desk. Next to it were material samples, plans, price sheets. There was a huge ground plan for the completed complex on the wall.

"In my opinion," Elaine said, "I think a lot of people who buy here will want gas stoves. Can they be substituted?"

The realtor smiled kindly, as though Elaine were a friend. "No, that's not an option." She could say no. Elaine respected people who could be direct.

It dawned on Elaine that she was standing there in jeans and a T-shirt. A Sportsac slung over her shoulder. This townhouse had to be selling for much more than she made, even in a very good year. Yet the realtor, who certainly didn't look inexperienced or overeager, seemed to regard her seriously, as someone who might buy. It had been the same when she bought her Toyota. Of course, that time she was really buying. But the salesman went over the mechanics with her, opened the hood, and pointed out features, while she kept nodding knowingly, trying to look smart. And she realized that this man was not posturing, that he believed what he had been told at a recent sales conference: women were to be taken seriously. They, statistically, were paying with their own money.

"Why don't you take a look upstairs?"

Elaine found herself walking up the stairs like a buyer. She stopped at the balcony under the cathedral ceiling and looked down over the graceful living room and ample dining alcove. She turned from the balcony and made her way to the very large master bedroom. Before inspecting the attached bath, she saw the sliding doors and walked out to the terrace.

Oh, this was nice. A good view of the water, and the weeping willows bending branches toward the lake. There was a lounging chair near her—for the realtor?—and the sun felt good. At the same time it made her realize how unobtrusive the air conditioning of the Lucerne model had been.

For a few minutes the day absorbed her—sunbathing of the

unconscious. She did not think of anything. Then: The Lucerne model, she thought, looking around the terrace. It's bound to appreciate. It would be a nice place to be in the summer. She walked back in.

"What do you think?" the realtor asked when she came downstairs.

"It's very nice." Elaine walked over to the table and browsed among the floor plans. She found the Lucerne. Beneath where she was standing, this model had a two-car garage, and above her was a laundry room, which she had missed. It could be made into a darkroom, she thought involuntarily. Her ex-husband had been a photographer. She suddenly realized she'd speak with him about the van. Not now, she thought. She did not want to dwell on Nola now. She picked up a price list from the desk and moved to the dining-alcove wall where there was a huge, colored blowup of the architectural plan. Lake Acres was the name of the project.

Perhaps it was her mood, but the plan on the wall appeared as an idyllic landscape. The lake was nicely rendered in watercolor blue and bordered by the poignant light-green weeping willows. Then there were the woods leading away from the lake and up the hills. There was something alive about the Connecticut hills. Indian hills, she called them. These hills had been inhabited long before the white man insisted on his ways.

From the blowup it appeared as if the architects had understood this—the hills predominated, not the project. She didn't have to look at the price list to realize that such subtle nonobtrusiveness costs money.

The cluster she was in, the eight units of Stage One, was rendered in detail on the plan. The rest of the stages, fifteen in all, were skeletal outlines running up the hills. The outline of each unit included a number, and most of those numbers were tagged with red dots. Up to Stage Eleven, that is, where the red dots began to peter out. That stage looked as if it would be built near where Elaine's car sat in the woods. Stage Twelve was clean.

Price list, red dots—it was like an art opening.

"All those red dots," Elaine said. "Are they contagious?"

Pam smiled. That was the name on her badge. Pam Delaney, Prospect Realty. "Maybe so. Each one of them is a unit reserved. You see, the project was begun in September, less than a year ago. We had no idea that people would reserve units at such a rate. I mean, we've just opened Stage Eleven for reservations and, look, half have deposits on them, and we're talking completion in two, perhaps three years."

Elaine looked down at her price list. "The Lucerne, for example. Am I reading this right? Those in Stage One went for a hundred and five thousand dollars, and the ones that are being reserved in Stage Eleven are being reserved at two hundred thousand dollars?"

"That's right. And with that the builder is nervous. Who knows what the hidden expenses will be over the next two or three years, while they are being built?"

"He must be nervous all the way to the bank. You're saying a unit such as the Lucerne has had an appreciation of ninety-five thousand dollars in less than a year?"

"It's the location, you see. Location, location, location. We've got the only lake property in the area, and this expanse of woods. Yet we're minutes off the highway, three minutes from the airport, and you'll be able to walk to Danbury Fair."

"Danbury Fair! I must have just missed it, then. I made a wrong turn. It always brings back memories, that place. I went to the Fair when I was a kid."

"Oh, the Fair's gone."

"The Fair's gone?"

"Everything on the Fairgrounds was taken down and auctioned."

"Just like that?"

"There was some objection. But in the long run how can you object to progress? After all, we have growing pains. We're a corporate center now. They're building the Danbury Fair Mall. It'll be the biggest shopping center between Stamford and

Bridgeport. It will be like living in New York without the dis-advantages."

Elaine smiled. "I rather like the disadvantages."

"I thought you were from New York. I could tell."

"It's incredible, isn't it?" Elaine said. "Only in America. Well, goodbye, Danbury Fair."

"And hello, Macy's!"

"Easy come, easy go."

"Progress!"

The realtor was, of course, in a professional position, so let's hear it for the future. Elaine, former purist, could hardly admit to herself that she was factoring the Danbury Fair Mall in with the seemingly endless possibilities of Lake Acres' appreciation.

"Ah," Elaine said, tentatively, "how much of a deposit does one need to, say, reserve a Lucerne in Stage Eleven?"

"One percent. That would be two thousand dollars. You see, you have to be satisfied with your unit after it's built. The buyer is completely protected here in Connecticut. The whole amount is returnable to you at any time on written request."

"With interest?"

"No, no interest."

Elaine tried to look serious. Was it possible, Elaine thought, that Pam hasn't heard of a flip? Why, in Manhattan, people were flipping apartments instead of pancakes. Real estate, not death, was the great equalizer. The center of every conversation. What would a cocktail party be, what would a love affair be, what would a marriage be, without its inevitable referent?

Here's what was happening in Manhattan. If a rental building was going co-op, the landlord would offer the occupant of a rented apartment an insider's price to convince him not to oppose the conversion. He could buy his apartment for much less than it would be worth on the open market. Often the renter would buy his own apartment in order to sell it immediately at the higher price. Now, who's to say a Lucerne model wouldn't be worth much more than two hundred thousand dollars by the time it was built? In two or three years why couldn't it be worth three hundred or four hundred thousand dollars? After all, this was Fairfield County. What was to stop Elaine from finding someone who would want to buy at a price somewhere between what she could reserve a unit for today and the higher market value of the future? She could make a lot of money.

No wonder people were reserving units. What a small price, returnable without interest, to take a shot at progress, a gamble on the future. Elaine's brain was working—the way a brain works picking a horse, picking a stock. Instinct and gray matter and an American expectation. Her cheeks were flushed.

She followed Pam downstairs into the chalky cleanliness of the newly constructed basement. They inspected the two-car garage. Elaine tested the automatic door opener. They walked out. The day had turned balmy, and there were dense puffs of clouds in the sky. Pam led her to the cluster of townhouses that was currently under construction, and to the second floor of the end unit, showing her the thickness of the connecting walls as they climbed. This floor was half Sheetrocked, and they looked down at the lake through the walls that were not yet up. The realtor traced out an area with her pointed finger, conjuring up the clubhouse, soon to be built.

"You see, these units take time," Pam explained. "Once you buy, you have a chance to upgrade."

"Upgrade?"

"Certainly," Pam said, missing that Elaine needed clarification of the term. "Everything can be built to order. I'd say people are spending an average of twenty thousand dollars extra on adding skylights, more closets, different entrances—"

"Really?"

"Oh, yes. I'd say most people are going upscale on bathroom fixtures and fireplaces."

"Was that fireplace in the living room real?"

"Of course."

"Well, I'm not a fireplace person," Elaine answered, a bit

miffed. What was she doing here? Upgrading. The type of money that needs to spend more money.

"Why, there was one man," Pam said, "truly, he was a bit difficult. He wanted to have the living room placed where the kitchen was, and the kitchen where the living room was. We had the architect try to reason with him. He brought in his own architect. It took him some time to realize it wouldn't work."

"Some people are impossible. I don't envy you, dealing with the public."

"What do you do?" Pam asked before she thought, then qualified, "I don't mean to be nosy."

"Oh, I know it's not a credit check. I teach at Staten University, and I write as well."

"Anything I'd have read?"

"Well, I'm coming out with a book soon."

"What's it about?"

"It's about love." She felt compelled to add, "It's fiction."

"Oh boy," Pam said. "I've always wished I had the time to sit down and write. Could I tell a story! Maybe I could tell you and you could put it down."

"I think everyone has one book in them. Including me."

"But you've actually written yours. I'm going to look for it."

"Well, thanks. You know, my publisher has hopes for it."

"That's wonderful. What's it called?"

"The Passion and the Vow."

"Oh, that's beautiful."

"Hey, a bidet!"

"What?"

"I'm thinking of upgrading the Lucerne. Forget fancy fireplace fixtures, but definitely a bidet. That was one of the great things about traveling in Italy, the bidet."

"No problem," Pam replied. "But . . . when . . . when I look for your book, what's your name?"

"Oh! Isn't that funny? I thought I told you. I'm Elaine, Elaine Netherlands." She held out her hand and Pam shook it.

Then Pam looked around the half-done condo and out to the lake once more. She sighed. "It really is a great location. You know, there was once a famous hotel on this spot."

"I'm sure. History's an upgrade."

"Yes," Pam answered seriously. "I think you're right. Do you know the Hotel del Coronado in San Diego?"

"I do."

"The same architects. The very same. Why, The Retreat was the pride of the region."

"I've never heard of it."

"You will, you will. Lake Acres is a tribute to it." A gleam in Pam's eye. "The Retreat burned down in 1928. Of course, those were the days before fire coding."

"Of course."

"There's an old photo of it in our brochure. Let's go back. I'm going to give you one."

"Great. By the way," Elaine said with a smile. "How do I get back on I-84?"

Elaine sat in her car, her Lake Acres brochure beside her. She was staring past trees. Pam believes I have the money to live here, Elaine thought.

Why? Come to think of it, I didn't blink at the price. I asked about installing another sliding door. I thought the two-car garage a feature. I looked down my nose at the electric stove (they've made a mistake there: people who pay those prices understand gas). I lost points on the wood-burning fireplace; I asked if it was real. And then I said, cool as could be, "Well, I'm not a fireplace person." Well, I'm really not a fireplace person. I'm a working woman. I'm a woman on my own. Fireplaces aren't for me. The Lucerne's not for me. Or is it?

Elaine had been a child in the nouveau-riche fifties and had early equated money with airheads, ice sculptures, and women who spent their adulthood on shopping trips. She had gone to college to find the life of the mind diametrically opposed to money. Either/Or. A Kierkegaardian situation. She had opted for the life of the mind. But now was it only Lake Acres? Was it living on her own? She had made a wrong turn and was thirsty for something more.

She had been ahead of her times in believing she could subsist on her own, but it had never occurred to her to really live on her own—to cook real meals for herself, or buy a house. Then, in the mid-seventies, there was Larry, the marriage. She taught part-time, because she could afford to, and wrote her scholarly books. It had never occurred to her not to be free for his photography shoots, not to go along with him. But when she walked out on him, even though she didn't have a steady job, she didn't take a cent. She wanted to do more than walk out, she wanted to begin again.

Which she did. She was now full-time and tenured at Staten U. And with tenure at the university came some things she had known nothing of before, fringe benefits and a retirement fund. She began to look more steadily at the world around her. Every morning, breakfast out with *The New York Times* and *The Wall Street Journal*. And when she saw the latest issue in the supermarket, she'd pick up *Money* magazine. It seemed to her economics was exactly like life. Opinions, rumors, theories, and contradictions. Sudden shifts and swings puncturing expectations. She at times felt that humanity could be tracted simply by following the obits and the business news.

She had been raised in a family that believed no tragedy was greater than a woman being on her own. She had watched *Picnic* on her VCR the other night. There was Rosalind Russell, desperate. She had to get married to escape from teaching school. Either her boring boyfriend would marry her and she'd be able to live in his apartment over his store—salvation!—or she would have to live for the rest of her life as a boarder, sharing meals with three other old maids. There were no other alternatives, and Rosalind Russell knew it.

Could women get mortgages in those days? Elaine wondered,

looking down at her shiny Lake Acres brochure with its sepia photograph of The Retreat. Then she put the brochure down on the seat next to her, took a breath, and fastened her seatbelt. There was a Lucerne available in Stage Eleven.

She drove out of the woods, found the circle road, and then pulled into the complex, where she parked her car outside of the Lucerne.

"You're back!"

"May I use your phone? I have friends waiting for me in New Milford."

"Sure," Pam said, "it's a local call."

Afterward Elaine sat on a chair next to the small desk in Pam's private office, the den. She opened her checkbook. She couldn't believe she was doing it. Make a wrong turn in the road, get lost in the woods, follow signs, and take an option on a townhouse. Pam had offered her a Diet Coke, and they'd gone through the stipulations three times: once was never enough for Elaine when it came to business. They agreed she could postdate the check by ten days. That would give her time to transfer from her money-market fund and/or change her mind. She looked down at the yellow check, with her name and box number on it. She added the number where she could be reached.

Her hand trembled slightly as she wrote "Prospect Realty" and then "Two thousand" and drew a line. Signed her name. Entered the transaction. Tore out the check. "Here." Pam clipped the check to the form Elaine had filled out, then opened her desk. "For you," she said, handing Elaine a sheet with red dots.

"Oh, are we going to have a ceremony?"

"Why not?"

They walked out to the living room. "Are you sure this isn't pin-the-tail-on-the-donkey?" Elaine said, wavering.

"How could it be?" Pam asked. "Your eyes are open."

"So they are." Elaine stuck her red dot to her Lucerne, in Stage Eleven of the projection.

.   .   .

She couldn't resist walking down to the lake's edge. She'd phoned Judith; she had time. She could see the white sand and, beyond it, the calm blue expanse, which her parents had once told her was good for her eyes, if she just sat still and stared and stared. The first hint of clear golden light stretched flat over the afternoon. She mulled over her two-thousand-dollar option as she arrived at the lake. It really was a beautiful location. Not far from her a group of men congregated, workers, seven of them, their shirts off, their carpenters' belts slung around their waists. One, quite a handsome man, wore a brightly colored bandanna, pirate fashion, over a lot of hair, and they were all speaking, obviously joking, in a language she didn't understand. Some Eastern European language? she wondered.

She retreated to the shade of the nearest weeping willow and sat on an unopened sandbag. She watched the guys gesture and smoke, wishing she too had a cigarette. Look at the way the handsome guy with all that hair smoked, holding the cigarette suggestively, as if it were a joint, taking a drag that contained a thought, squinting, then flicking the lit butt into the sand. He was standing next to a taller guy, and slapped him on the shoulder. Whack, the wet sound of flesh. Then that taller one separated himself from the others. Also well built and very striking, he was holding a clipboard rather than a cigarette. He too had abundant dark hair, but his was short and curly. He spoke that foreign language, interspersed with English, as he motioned to the men, motioned to the development, then left, spreading out his free hand to them. Watching him walk toward her she thought, What a wonderful face. Broad, cleft chin, big blue eyes. When he saw her, he looked surprised and stopped.

There she was, sitting on a sandbag underneath a weeping-willow tree. She was looking up at him, noticing the muscles in his arms. Did he understand English? "What language were you all speaking?" she asked slowly.

He looked surprised again. "French."

"French? Well, I'll be. I thought it was some sort of Eastern

European language. But not Czech." She stopped herself from saying, Are you sure it's French?

But he undersood. "They're French from Quebec. They have their own ways."

"And you?"

"Me? No. Well, maybe. A quarter. My grandfather came from Quebec. I was married to a French Canadian once. I sort of picked up the language." There was a pause. For perhaps three seconds, he looked at her in an abstract way; he was thinking. He made up his mind, kicked over the other sandbag, and sat down.

"What's your name?" he asked.

"Elaine."

"I'm Mario."

"Mario?"

"Mario Picard. Is that so strange?"

"In a way. I almost married someone named Mario once. He was a Roman."

"No relation. I'm from Tampa Bay."

She laughed.

"How'd you meet a Roman, as opposed to a generic Italian?"

"In Boston."

"Figures. Why didn't you get married?"

"I chickened out, in Rome."

"Smart. It would have been smart in Boston too."

"Well, I could have done it better. Over there you marry a whole way of life, you know. I just got scared."

"They say it's smart to get scared sometimes."

"In a way. Haven't you ever been?"

"Sure, but never in time. Timing's everything, isn't it?" And he smiled at her. Then he said, "Elaine—that's a nice name. Can— no—may I ask you, Elaine, what are you doing here, distracting my workers?"

"Why, they never even saw me. I saw them."

"Want to bet? They saw you up there with Pam on the Erie. You stopped them, on my time too."

"You mean it's true what they say about construction workers?"

"Of course, they're men."

"Men," Elaine repeated.

"Are you going to work in the office? We've been watching them interview secretaries."

"Me?" She laughed. "No. I'm the victim of a wrong turn. No one told me they tore down the Danbury Fair since the last time I came by. I mean, no more gigantic statues of Paul Bunyan or Superman or Porky the Pig to let you now you're passing Danbury. I can't believe they tore them down."

"Oh, they auctioned them. The guy I rent from bought a small one. The American eagle."

"Really? They auctioned them? I wish I had known. Anyway, I must have gotten confused by all the new construction going on and landed up here. And I like it. It's new, it's pretty. The company's nice. Who knows, I might buy a place and never leave."

"It would be nice to have you here."

He said this and looked at her so directly that she became embarrassed. There was a sincerity in his eyes, almost a longing. For what? she wondered. His face was very expressive and he seemed smart. She felt a longing in him, that was the only way of putting it. A longing that reminded her of . . . herself.

"Where are you from?" he asked.

"Manhattan."

"I should have guessed," Mario said. "I like the City. But when I go with—see that guy over there?"

"The handsome one?"

"Yes. That's Wig. When I go with him, it gets real expensive. And I don't like to go alone. So I stay put. Stay home. Read. The quiet life. Like all my noise is behind me."

"Is it?"

They smiled at each other. "What do you do in the City, Elaine?"

"I teach and I write."

"You're a writer?"

"Yes."

"What writer had a house in Key West?"

"Hemingway."

"All right! Ever been there?"

"No. I've never been to Key West."

"You should go, if you're a writer."

"I am a writer. Do you think it would be more fitting for me to be a secretary, or perhaps a waitress?"

"I've made you mad."

"Well, I don't lie . . . unless I'm in a really tough spot."

"I'm sorry. Most people never stop talking, telling how good they are. Me, I like to check the details. That's how I can tell. And it's not every day I meet a writer. Though, to be honest, I always thought someday I'd like to write. I liked Hemingway a lot in college. *The Old Man and the Sea.* People who didn't much like to talk. Suits me."

"You could write about Danbury. It's not every day they chop down the Danbury Fair, all those great statues—or start to build a place like this on the lake."

"This is for the rich," Mario said derisively.

"With all the construction going on here, don't tell me you're not rich."

"Me?" Mario said. "Are you kidding? I just have money."

Elaine threw her head back and laughed. "Did you get that from Hemingway?"

He looked confused, but he smiled at her pleasure. "What do you mean?"

"Your friend Hemingway once said something like that to Fitzgerald. Fitzgerald was drooling over rich people: 'The rich, the rich, they're so different.'" Elaine waved her arm. "And Hemingway answered, 'Sure, sure, they have more money.'"

"Well, can't you see," Mario said kindly, "that Fitzgerald was right?"

"Hmmm."

"Me, I'm a contractor, a glorified construction worker, really. I just make money. Now, you, a teacher, a writer, you would have a chance of being rich."

"Really? Now, that's good news. Maybe I'll share it with Nola."

"Nola?"

"My stepdaughter."

"Oh, you're married?"

"Divorced. Hey, you know," Elaine said, "this is fun, but I've got to get going."

He jumped to his feet, almost defensively. Then he held out his arms to her. "Let me help you up," he said. "Where are you headed?"

"New Milford. Corning Blue Road, on the top of the hill."

"Well, come on. I'll show you the way."

So, by the time Elaine arrived at Judith and Peter's in New Milford, she had something more to think about, beyond her stepdaughter's re-entry into her life, beyond her deposit on a townhouse: Mario under the weeping-willow tree. Mario beeping his horn and extending his tanned and muscular arm from the window of his truck to direct her onto Corning Blue Road. She was touched by him, moved—but when she beeped back and waved, she figured she was waving goodbye. She was a realist. You want romance? she thought. Write another novel.

There were Judith and Peter standing on the second-floor side deck of the farmhouse they had restored. Behind them Elaine could see the big old barn in Connecticut red that Peter had turned into a studio. Peter painted and taught art at the University of Connecticut. Judith was a potter. They'd all met in Boston, when Elaine, a freshman at Boston College, took a part-time job at the Y. Judith, just graduated from BU, and just married, gave courses there. Judith and Peter used to kid about having adopted Elaine. She sure ate many a dinner with them in their apartment in Cambridge, discussing the relationship between literature and art. Now Judith had a son in college and a daughter starting law school. She'd devoted a lot of time to raising her children.

Elaine got out of her car and hollered up, "Sorry I'm late."

"Wait! Leave that there. I'll get your bag," Peter called back, untwining his arm from his wife and starting down the stairs. Peter was a big man, over six feet two. He had recently started jogging and swimming on schedule. As he bounded down the stairs, she saw he now had a trimmer body, presided over by an unweeded face.

Judith stood on the deck, big-breasted, wide-hipped, under her long patterned made-in-India dress. Still the gypsy style, still the long thick black hair, silver streaks now running through it. Her wide and sensitive eyes seemed more deeply set in the fleshiness of her face. When Elaine reached her and the two women hugged, Judith asked with concern, "Are you all right?"

"Yes, Judith. Now I am. What about you?"

"Who was that guy who beeped you onto this road?" Peter interrupted.

"Oh, so you saw Mario? He's contracting at Lake Acres. I met him there."

"Mario? Mario Two?" Peter kidded.

"Mario Picard. From Tampa Bay."

"What's his coat-of-arms?" Judith asked.

"Believe me, Judith, with arms like that he don't need no coat." The women giggled as they walked into the house.

"You don't waste much time—when it comes to men, that is," Peter said.

"Very funny, Peter," Elaine sang. "I do apologize for being late. Wait till I tell you all that happened today. But first—I reached a decision. Nola needs a van so Second Hand, that's her band, can go to California—"

"Oh, so she needs something!" Judith cut in. "Don't forget the three years she didn't need anything, Elaine. Kids can be cruel. Remember how hurt you were because she cut you out so completely. Come on, let's bring your stuff to your room."

"Well, I'm going to talk with Larry about this van. If she's going to California, and I can see in her eyes she means to go, it's important to her to have her father's blessing. You know, he's saying he won't see her if she goes. That's like sending her away with a curse, when he could well afford sending her off with a van."

"Oh my God," Peter moaned. They were in the guest room, and he'd put her bag on a chair. "Give his blessing for her quitting college and going off with a rock band! Are you crazy, Elaine? I'd do anything to stop Susan if she came up with an idea like that. I couldn't bless it, believe me, and, believe me, that's no curse!"

"But from Larry it would be."

"Why, may I ask you. Why?"

"Because he's not like you, Peter. He'd be cruel about it. He's do-it-my-way-or-be-damned. Why, Dad? Because you're my daughter. No, Peter, sometimes I'm not sure how much he cares."

"Maybe he cares too much," Judith blurted.

When Elaine stayed silent, Judith said, "Come on," and threw her a towel, which she grabbed at the last second. "Wash up, and then let's have a drink. You'll stay through to Monday, won't you? We'll catch up. You'll relax. We'll go for a swim."

"Yes, Mother," Peter said, putting his hand affectionately under the hair at the nape of Judith's neck.

Elaine looked at them. She thought maybe she'd just missed the generation that could have a marriage that works.

TWO

The red eye of Elaine's answering machine welcomed her home: blink-blink-blink-blink-blink. Five messages! Of course, five might include wrong numbers, hangups, but it could also bring news—good news. It could be as fortunate as mail could be. Friends, lovers, prizes. It's not always bills.

Blink-blink-blink-blink-blink. She actually postponed the pleasure of playing her messages.

It was early Monday evening, with plenty of light left. She had dropped her baggage, stripped as fast as she could, left her clothes draped over the chaise longue in her bedroom, taken a clean towel from the hall closet, and darted into the shower. Her skin was tingling from a day in the sun. She soaped herself generously, and when she rinsed off she was pleased by her tanner skin. She caught herself looking for a white circle under a nonexistent ring on her left hand. Paused. Put her towel around her waist, and came out of the shower ready for a cool blast against her wet skin. Natural air conditioning.

She grabbed the bottle of Lubriderm and walked into the living room. It was a big room, especially by New York standards. Its main feature was the Oriental rug in deep maroons and blues that she had inherited from her grandmother. She also had her grandmother's old Queen Someone couch. She had added a coffee table and a modern leather chair with ottoman from the Scandinavian Shop. And a large desk. Her expanse of windows overlooked the tops of the trees and a playground.

Her dining area was at the farther end of the room, near the front door and the entrance to the kitchen. She had bought a rectangular glass dining table she had second thoughts about, and had covered it with a reddish paisley. Larry had had impeccable taste. One of the boons of her new life was the ease she felt about living with her mistakes. Hell, she'd buy another table someday if she couldn't live with this one.

Behind the table, on the long wall, were three large Andy Warhol silk screens. Her ex-husband knew Warhol; they'd photographed each other. Larry had bought the *Myth Series* for her in the early eighties—all ten of them. They weren't that expensive. She had hung *Superman, Mickey Mouse,* and *Santa Claus.* They made her smile.

To the left of the table were bookcases, also from the Scandinavian Shop. They were beginning to fill up, though it was still Elaine's intention not to collect things, to be ready to move, from now on, on short notice without too many cartons. Since she'd been a graduate student, each move had meant endless heavy cartons of books. And somehow the romance of that had faded after she left Larry. Except for the volumes absolutely essential to her research, she didn't collect books. Lots of cassettes. Without Nola, she still prowled for new music on her own.

She walked into her long narrow kitchen and opened the refrigerator. On the door were funny-figure magnets, barking dogs and one-eyed gnomes, courtesy of Keith Haring and Kenny Scharf. Inside she had seltzer and half a stick of butter. She took a swig of the seltzer. Should she throw out the butter, or wrap it better? Closed the refrigerator, delayed action.

Back in the living room, she spread her damp towel on Grandma's sofa and sat, looking around, as she squirted some lotion onto her hand. How many other women, she wondered, might be living lives like hers. Sitting alone in their apartments, naked on their couches, oiling their skin.

She thought of the two widows that came before, her grandmother, her mother. Both gone now, but both in their own ways had seemed settled, content, living alone. Of course, neither of them thought that she had in any way chosen her lot. Elaine felt in many ways she herself had. She needed her independence. Sometimes she wondered, what were the compensations for one's independence?

Well, one could afford to go for it. Elaine could put down a deposit on a townhouse without having to confer. She pictured a scenario in which she discussed Lake Acres with Larry. Why, there's no way he wouldn't patronize her, call her, as he often had, a crazy lady. He was the firehose that cooled her down. "Are you getting your period, Elaine?" he would say. In her twenties and early thirties, like many bright women she had known, she could be easily convinced that doing things her way, feeling things her way, was neurotic. "Oh, God, that's it, Larry. I'm a little on edge, I don't know what it is with me lately, I'm not feeling well." Now she no longer apologized for her disposition. She could afford to be herself.

Elaine began to oil herself less thoughtfully, feeling pleasure more. What would she do tonight? Time to feast on her messages. Back to the bedroom.

(1) "Uhm, Elaine, it's Carlton Ellis. Could you get back to me?" Bzzzzzz. Chairman, Core College, Staten U.

(2) "Elaine, Nola. Give me a buzz." Bzzzzzz.

(3) Click. Bzzzzzz. Hang up. Damn!

(4) "Hi, Elaine. This is Donna. Give us a call. Anne has to reschedule lunch." Bzzzzzz. Her editor's secretary.

(5) "Elaine, Larry. There's something we should discuss." Snap!

Strange, was there dust on the tape? Larry? She picked up her phone and called Nola.

"Hey, Elaine! No. No, I haven't said anything to him about me seeing you. What? Okay. Speak with you tomorrow."

Larry. The last time she'd seen him was when he took pictures for the jacket of her forthcoming book. It was an uncomfortable situation. He insisted on doing the pictures. It brought back memories, it had to. That's how they had met. She had come to that wonderful apartment of his on Riverside Drive to have her picture taken.

She had first stepped into that living room with its combination of period furniture and contemporary art and walked right to the front windows. She had seen the Hudson River, pale blue, and the sunset over Jersey, a ball of pink.

"What a view," she had said, turning to Larry and looking at him carefully. He was slender, tall—dressed in jeans he obviously had had pressed by the cleaners. His starched white shirt was open at the neck. The neck was long and the flesh over his Adam's apple vulnerable. He was close to forty, she was twenty-five. His eyes were gray and hard to read. There was gray in his brown hair, none in his wide handlebar mustache, singular, over lean lips. An attractive man, this well-known photographer.

"What a sunset," she filled in. He hadn't said anything. Just stood there looking at her. Her enthusiasm belied her conservative appearance. Fresh from grad school and a Fulbright in Italy, she was wearing a lavender dress, sensible black Italian pumps, and two ropes of Majorca pearls.

"I'm glad you like it," he answered after another pause, and walked over to her. She was backed by the twilight. He did something unexpected. "You're beautiful," he said, and he gave her a long, almost boyish kiss.

"Now, don't misunderstand me." He took her hand and brought her over to the big, feathery couch. "The kiss was meant as a compliment." They sat down and talked.

She was flattered by the kiss. She was flattered by what he knew about her: that her dissertation on American writers and artists living in Italy in the nineteenth century had won the Hogarth Prize, that she had almost married the cousin of a count.

That she couldn't get a job. That's what the article in *Harper's* was going to be about. Five new Ph.D.s who graduated with honors but couldn't get a full-time teaching job in the tightening college-teaching market of the mid-seventies. Before he took her into his studio, he wanted to know how she felt about being unemployed.

She told him that, when the reporter had called and asked her to be one of those interviewed, she had felt embarrassed, and guilty, as if the economic situation of the country was a personal shortcoming. Then she had decided it would be good for her character to participate—to face the awful truth.

He asked her if it was so awful not to have a full-time job.

"Devastating," she answered.

He looked at her with sheer delight.

When the article finally came out, Larry's picture of her was chosen to appear on a full page under the banner headline "Brother, Can You Spare a Job?" Such public humiliation brought her a teaching offer from Maryland and one from Buffalo. Larry said, Do exactly what you want. He also asked her to marry him when his divorce was final.

She was already collaborating with him. She was doing the text for a big picture book, *Artifacts,* of the best of his early photography of art objects, work he had done before *Beautiful Women,* his first book of nudes, made him famous. She was teaching a night class in Great Books. And she had a contract with Ohio University Press for a book on *Foreign Artists in Rome and the Italian Risorgimento.* Of course, a university book contract pays nothing, an adjunct assistant professorship next to nothing. But that work, and particularly the work for Larry, was important. She shrugged off her uneasiness about not having full-time pay. Happily, she said yes to Larry.

Larry. What was it about his voice on the answering machine? Elaine felt the chill of chalk against a blackboard. Something in his voice that could crease a tape.

She dialed his number, then hung up before it rang. This is silly, she thought. I'll just say I'm answering his call and ask what's up. She let the phone ring. His answering machine. Great. "Hi, Larry, Elaine. I'm answering—"

Bzzzzz. "Elaine, hold on. Let me turn this thing off."

"Larry. I thought I was talking to your machine."

"You were. How are you feeling, Elaine?"

"Fine, just fine. I was away. Connecticut. God's country. It's beautiful, restful there. I feel fine."

"Good."

"And you?"

"I'd like to talk with you. That's why I called. Could we meet for lunch next week?"

"Well, I was supposed to have lunch with Anne Gregory tomorrow, but her secretary called to reschedule—I assume for next week. After I find out when I'm to meet Anne, I'll get back to you."

"Make it an early dinner, then. Next week, any night you say. That's uncomplicated, isn't it?"

"Ah, Larry, you're right again." Damn, why'd she say that?

"How's the book coming?"

"It's delivered with revisions. Anne seems to have big plans for it."

"Well, Joyce knew where to send it."

Joyce was the agent Larry had hooked her up with. It was she who had first given him the idea of publishing his "beautiful women" as a book.

"Are you all right, Larry?"

"Why'd you ask?"

"I don't know. Something on your mind?"

"Yes. Let's save it for dinner."

"Fine."

"Say, next Tuesday. At Teacher's Too?" he suggested.

"Your neck of the woods."

"Is that too much of an inconvenience?"

"Hey, of course not. I'm just kidding. You never did like it"—she almost mentioned the East Village, and at the same moment realized that might bring Nola into the conversation—"around here. What time, Larry?"

"You're the traveler. You name it."

"Six-ish."

"What about six-thirty?"

"You got it."

"See you then."

"Larry!"

"What?"

"I hope things are going okay for you."

He laughed. "See you, Elaine. Bye."

That laugh made her uneasy. But the coincidence of his calling so soon after Nola had re-entered her life calmed her down. Coincidences were a benevolent reminder that life is beyond human control.

Well, what would she do tonight? Order in some Chinese food. Smoke a joint. Listen to some music. Think things over. Relax. Sounds good.

Next morning: "Oh, hi, Donna. Elaine Netherlands, returning your call. Sorry I took so long. I was in Connecticut."

"Oh, good, Elaine. Anne is terribly sorry, but she forgot, can you believe forgot, the Fourth of July, the short week coming up."

"That's two weeks away!"

"I know. She's absolutely buried in work. She'd like to re-schedule lunch."

"Well, sure. When's she free?"

"Would it be possible for you to call back next week, when she'll definitely be in the office? Then I can stand over her, and we can get something concrete going."

"No problem. And how are you doing? You have a good weekend?"

Donna sighed. "Me and my radio at Jones Beach. Not to mention carrot sticks and one-calorie soft drinks."

"Good for you. You're sticking to it."

"Ten pounds so far. And believe me, after this I'm going to give up the cigarettes."

"Well, it's impossible to give up everything at once. In my case, I'm a holdout for coffee."

"Your only vice?"

"Donna, I should hope not!"

Donna giggled. "Should have known, I read your book."

"Fiction, Donna. Say hello to Anne."

"You got it."

"Hi, Carlton. Elaine, answering your call. How're things going?"

"Hectic, as always. But Myra and I are hoping for a vacation in August."

"Good for you."

"Listen, Elaine, remember your plagiarism fellow, Tom Tighe, in your 'Emulating the Americans' course?"

"I won't forget."

"Well, he's thinking of contesting the F."

"Does he know if he loses his permanent record will say F for plagiarism?"

"Not yet. I'm having Dean Smith apprise him of that."

"I mean really, Carlton, he submits a story about an aging biologist deciding whether to divorce his wife for a young Ph.D. candidate in cross-pollinization. All in perfect English, with balanced metaphors and stunning similes. This fellow doesn't even understand the extent of his contempt. What does this have to do with Hawthorne? I asked him. He hadn't the slightest idea. He's lucky I didn't bring him up for dismissal."

"I know. But he's still requesting that you change his grade."

"Well, unfortunately, I'll go all the way on this one. I mean, it's unfortunate for me. I was brought up on the lives of the saints. I know it's bad for the health to do things on principle. Fifteen of us in that seminar. I advised him to do short critical essays rather than attempting to emulate a master. I told him after his first attempt that I thought the course was too advanced for him. He's a business major, isn't he? Some of my best students have been from the business school, but usually from international banking. When he insisted he wanted to stay in the course, I helped him as much as I could. He or whoever was helping him slowly improved. He did a decent comparison and contrast of a story by Hawthorne and one by James. But to walk in with that creative-participation piece, and read it to the whole seminar, waste our time like that, shows such utter contempt of our efforts—well, don't get me started."

"So, good, you're standing by your grade."

"I sure am. But if there is a hearing, put it into the fall semester. I'm in seclusion until then."

"Working on a new book?"

"Thinking about one."

"I'll let you know how this progresses."

"Thanks, Carlton. And say hello to Myra."

"Will do."

"Hi. May I speak with Nola? Jimmy? Hi. I'm Elaine, Nola's stepmother. Tell her I'm seeing her father next week. I'll get back to her. Okay? Nice talking with you."

Saturday morning. A beautiful day, and she had a whole weekend in front of her. Now that her school term was over, she could spend, as she did this week, long stretches of time sketching out ideas for a new book. She promised herself her weekends free. But what to do?

She thought of walking to the Veselka coffee shop for breakfast. That was right in Nola's neighborhood. How long had Nola been living down around St. Mark's Place? Two months, three? Surprising they hadn't run into each other—

The phone rang. She didn't monitor the call. Picked it right up.

"Hi, Elaine!"

"Hey, Nola, I was just thinking about you. I'm going to the Veselka for breakfast. Want to join me?"

"Oh, good, you're free, then?"

"All day."

"Well, listen to this. There's a showcase at CBGB this afternoon. Maybe six, seven bands. And Multiple Monotonies can't make it. Would you believe their van was ripped off in Boston? I mean, you should see this van; the cops found it without radar. Luckily none of their equipment was in it. Then they pile their equipment in it, start down, and what happens? The piece of junk stalls, right on the highway, and some dudes crash right into them. They're all okay, but they're not going to make it this afternoon. They'll get here someday. What goes around comes around, right? But they can't make it, Elaine. Second Hand's playing. Isn't that perfect? Second Hand coming on second hand. And we're proud of it. You want to hear us, Elaine? We should be on real early. Maybe about two. Man, am I psyched."

"I don't blame you. This is great. And I'm sitting here wondering how to have fun this weekend."

"See, it was meant to be. You'll meet Jimmy too."

"Is Silas Mourner coming?"

"No. He says he can't stand noise."

"Figures. So, I'm really going to hear you sing?"

"If you want to call it that."

"Are you putting yourself down, Nola?"

"Not at all!" Nola laughed.

So Elaine scotched her plans for a long breakfast, just went to the corner deli for take-out coffee, croissant, and the *Times*. Came back to her apartment, and burrowed in for a while. Then she changed to a fresh pair of jeans, picked out a black T-shirt and black Reeboks. She put her makeup on quite lightly, and ran her hands through her short, thick blond hair, rumpling her curls into a wide Afro. She looked in her full-length mirror and passed inspection, having achieved the look she was after—minimum cool.

She had plenty of time to walk. She walked down First Avenue for a while, appreciating the low skyline created by the linked red-bricked tenements, the open-mouthed first floor of each tenement calling out commerce: Korean markets, bakers, fish stores, butchers, fabric shops. This was a poor neighborhood, Hispanic, Polish, artist, punk, and the store rents were still reasonable. Crossing Fourteenth Street, she looked up at that wide bazaar of a boulevard, which on Saturdays teemed with immigrant shoppers.

On Eighth she crossed west. St. Mark's Place. She passed the street people: men in dirty jeans who swapped silence and cigarettes on the corner that was theirs. She passed the Oriental merchants who sold more sunglasses than there was sun or eyes, more gloves than there were hands, more T-shirts than there were chests. Their shops were at basement level, and one peered down on mountainous outdoor displays of cheap and stylish stuff. The very air rang "now."

On Astor Place she gingerly wove through the bazaar of street vendors, their blankets filled with the depressing stuff that gets thrown out only to find itself back on the market, old magazines, and books and beads and shoes and radios, name it—things too tattered to have been ripped off.

She made it to the Bowery and the rock club CBGB, next door to the men's shelter and twice as seedy. The residents walked up the stairs of the flophouse, eyeing the skinheads and mohawks and chains in amazement. It was a mixed group in front of CBGB this afternoon, punks and more conservative rockers. Not too big a group. Elaine looked at her watch; it was a quarter past two.

She walked into gloom, the dark wind tunnel of the club.

"Do you know when Second Hand will be on?" she asked the guy behind the makeshift desk, as she handed him her five dollars and waited for him to stamp her hand. She eyed the CBGB T-shirts pinned up behind him on a panel.

"They're setting up."

She went over to the long bar, took an end seat that gave her a good view of the corner tables, the small dance floor, and the stage, then ordered a beer. People drifted in. She kept her eyes on the stage. That must be Jimmy on guitar. He was slim and wiry, and had straw-colored hair that was cut flat on top. He and the bass player wore jeans and T-shirts. The drummer was in Bermuda shorts, hairy, fleshy legs, no socks, running shoes. Nola? Elaine's heart began to beat fast. Jimmy yelled, "Hello, New York," struck a chord. "Let's hear it for Asia Neither Land." Nola walked out. Between one of Elaine's heartbeats and another, the music slammed on. It was so fast, Elaine found herself so nervous, that it took time to focus. The rawness of CBGB, the darkness, the dash of stage light, the magnitude of the sound.

Nola. Wearing jeans and a black-and-red tank top, no bra. Black running shoes, like Elaine. Her hair was jet-black and feathered today; she wore some black, some red extensions. Her broad face red-lipped, flushed. Not really flushed. It was as if on stage her complexion cleared up. On stage she bloomed. "She holds that mike so well!" Elaine's first thought.

Nola slammed out her lyrics, at times standing still, but bending from her waist up out toward the audience, a Mick Jagger stance. At other times she moved with the music, played the stage, but always cool and part of the beat.

Energy, energy, energy. There she stood, giving everything she had, triumphant to be there, not seeming to give a damn about being on so early in the half-filled place. She was on stage at CBGB. Famous CBGB. Second Hand played.

Elaine began to get the lyrics. "No! Neighbor! Give me the sun." It was about crack and it was dynamite. People were coming onto the dance floor. A wisp of a girl—she looked thirteen—got onto the stage, she and Nola skipped to the beat, then Nola touched her shoulder, arms from the audience stretched out, and she jumped off the stage. A boy came on the stage, and then a skinhead, then others, and Nola was able to make something out of every contact. She was fascinating, spinning a web of music and words, rhythm and beat, and the audience was drawn to her. As more and more arms reached up, lithe bodies jumped fearlessly into them, anticipating nothing but support. Elaine thought of salmon, rushing upstream. The arms were like waves, the bodies like fish. Something was going to be spawned. The music was good, but it was Nola who was irresistible. It was Nola and it wasn't Nola. It was Asia Neither Land.

"And this is for Elaine."

Elaine snapped to, her heart making one plunge in her chest; her back stiffened to contain it. Had she heard right? "I hope she's out there!"

"She is!" Elaine yelled back.

"All right."

And it was "West Side! Saturday! Afternoon!" An adolescent primal scream. Elaine heard "orgasm," she heard "Doritos." God, Elaine thought, she remembers. The song was dark, and it wasn't very flattering, but it was very real. "Am I crazy?" Elaine thought. "Is she as good as I think she is? Or am I prejudiced?"

But look at this audience. Composed of other bands. It knows music. And it wanted to call them back when the song ended and the stage went black. And they came back. "Thank you, New York!" Jimmy shouted. "Asia, Asia!" And there was Nola again, and people were applauding. And Second Hand did one quick bam-bam drop-dead finale. Elaine got up and went backstage.

"Nola." Elaine found Asia Neither Land in the black-walled,

mirrorless bathroom. All over the walls graffiti resembled war damage. "My God, Nola, you were great!"

Nola looked paler in the black surroundings. She was life-size again. Nola said, "It went over pretty well."

"Did it ever! I don't think I'm being prejudiced. You were just great!"

Nola smiled, a big easy smile. "I'm so glad you made it."

"Am I glad! What are you doing now?"

"Oh, we'll pack up and then come back to watch the other bands. You want to meet Jimmy?"

They went out of the bathroom, and Nola opened the door and walked into the men's room, then came out with Jimmy. His jacket was off. He had on a T-shirt, a towel around his neck.

"Nice to meet you, Jimmy." Jimmy was her height.

"Same here, Elaine."

They shook hands. His was shaky.

"Second Hand did very well."

"Glad you liked it. Are you going to hang out?"

"I thought I'd stay, but, I don't know, I feel overpowered, you guys were so great—" Do I sound surprised? Elaine asked herself, almost in panic. "I—I, I think I've got to go. See you soon. Nola—Asia—I'll give you a ring, okay?"

"Sure, Elaine, soon. And thanks."

The sun blasted her, and the amebic watermarks of a migraine swam in front of her eyes, pebbling the day into an unreal event. The flat boulevard of the Bowery stretched in front of her. She waited for the light, and even then took some extra seconds before she stepped from the curb. Her destination was the squeezed-in restaurant in Day-Glo pink across the way with the head of Elvis peeking from its own small window. She hadn't touched her beer. She was on her way to a Cajun martini. The interior of the small, clean restaurant, with its jammed-together tables, wall mirror, and long L-shaped bar, was cool and inviting.

The brunch crowd was lingering over fluffy light-yellow omelets and cornbread and biscuits and grits.

The bar was rather crowded, but she found a seat on the television end, near the door and the small Elvis window. On a shelf by the window were baseball memorabilia and a group picture of the bar's softball team.

"Hi," said the bartender, a young man with long black hair, a sleeveless black leather vest, a white apron around his slim hips, and a tattoo of a cross perched on an anchor on his muscled arm. He could be between sets across the street.

"Hi. A Cajun martini."

"Straight up, right?"

"Right," she said, and then glanced over toward, but didn't watch, the TV.

She and Nola at the apartment on Riverside Drive a year or so before Elaine left Larry. Larry out on a shoot, as he often was on those Saturdays. Elaine alone with Nola. Reverse Speed's newest release was blasting, "Give me orgasm or give me Doritos!" Over and over, faster and faster. "In my whole life," Elaine said to Nola, "I've never heard women discussing orgasm."

Nola, punked out and slouching on the couch, seemed confused. Did she think Elaine was discussing music? Or was the subject of orgasm so old hat to Nola that she thought Elaine was nuts to bring it up?

Elaine sitting on a chair, her stockinged feet resting on the coffee table. "When I had my first love, my first sexual love, I was twenty. And I still believe twenty, twenty-one is time enough. Life is long, Nola. Give them Doritos until you're ready. But, anyway, the first time, I began to feel this sensation, and I got as embarrassed as could be. I thought I was about to pee, and I spent all my energy holding back. I had no idea that I had been experiencing the beginning of orgasm and that I had cut it off. All I had to do was relax, go with the sensation. Can you imagine? No one ever told me."

"Piss," Nola responded.

"What?"

"Piss. No one says 'pee.'"

Elaine's drink came, and she continued to watch the picture of the baseball game on TV. The sting of the first sip of the cold peppered vodka darted down her throat, enlivening her. "And this is for Elaine." Nola was good. That it hit her as such an A-number-one surprise was the one-two. She felt panicky. Amazed that her Nola was so damn good.

She sipped some more. No way you can slug a Cajun martini.

So, Elaine, you're ready to lend her three thousand for the van—or get Larry to, which would be more appropriate. Why? Well, it seemed perfectly natural then. All that supportive self-help stuff bubbling over. It was what Nola really wanted to do. A road tour as process.

Now, that's enough, Elaine told herself. Stop being so hard on yourself. Are you this judgmental about anyone else? No. When you were young, were you supported in anything you really wanted to do?

No. No's what they said. From movies to telephone calls to friends to reading so much to men. No. No. No. Say no to youth, say no to inclination, say no.

So you greatly desired to give to Nola what you never had. A yes. Many yeses. Too many for Larry. Yes. Yes. Yes.

"Another?"

"Yeah, but with ice this time; I'm getting wimpy."

"All right!"

But, still, the major piece of the puzzle. Three thousand dollars to get it out of her system, to go through it, to have had it, and then to go on. Back to NYU. Graduate. Grad school? Career? Marriage? Life. Anything you want, dear. If you really want it, go for it. Go for it! Go for it!

Yes. But not taking the full responsibility for it. Maybe she'd never come back. Maybe she'd live to become Asia Neither Land.

Maybe she'd be discovered. Her stepdaughter a rock star. "This is for Elaine."

My God. Was this guy in California the right manager? Had she signed anything? She had to be careful now. The record industry, the music industry. Big bucks, bigger bastards. She was going to need someone with judgment. Someone she could trust. How trustworthy was Silas? Elaine had to speak with her. With Silas? Perhaps Joyce could recommend someone, perhaps Elaine could—

Whoa! Elaine thought.

"With ice. Here you go."

"Good, it'll cool me off."

Whoa! Elaine thought again. One set, one intuition, and there she was, Elaine, Stage Mother. Asia Neither Land. The Woman of Rock. Her name in lights. Her face in magazines. This is for Elaine, without whom . . .

Oh my God. She's good.

"Can I get you something else?" the bartender asked.

"No, no. I always groan in public."

"You sure?"

"Absolutely. My shrink recommends it."

He laughed.

"What are you doing, Elaine?" Nola had asked when she was small. "I'm writing. Do you want to write too? Come on, I'll give you a pad." Sitting there, pad and pencil, little girl. Looking serious, squinting her eyes slightly, the way Elaine was known to do, saying, "I think I'll write down what I'm feeling."

Oh my God, Elaine thought, I encouraged her.

She has to be careful! Do I wish she wasn't good? Or just sort of normal good. Sort of okay. Yes. Why? Because it's easier.

She's a kid. I want her to have fun.

Respect her, Elaine. Respect her.

Yes, she thought, I'm going to try to find Silas.

•   •   •

She knew Nola's address, and it was close enough to the Bowery. Just link over to St. Mark's and walk east. There was a buzz in her head, and her sweat stuck her clothes to her, but she was oblivious to the outsides of things. All she had in mind was a destination.

The building was a tall narrow one; she climbed the stoop. A new intercom on the flaked wall? Gentrification wasn't far behind. Silas wasn't listed, which didn't surprise her, but luckily Jimmy was. It was an odd system of apartment listings, double letters next to the names. But it didn't stop her. She buzzed one that didn't answer, then thought again. Ah, perhaps this combination indicated the floor above. She rang. "Yes?"

"Silas?"

"Who is it?"

"Elaine Bright Netherlands. Nola's stepmother."

"Ah, the wicked witch!"

"And who the hell are you, the fairy godmother?"

He giggled. "Come in, come in." He buzzed.

"Silas, wait!"

"Yes?"

"What floor are you on?"

"Just keep walking to the tippy-tippy top." He buzzed again.

The wicked witch, she thought and thought, as she went up the long narrow staircase. She knew how to take a million stairs. Italy, long ago, had trained her. She went at a regular moderate pace, keeping in mind that she did not want to become short of breath. It was awful to arrive at anyone's door panting.

So this was the apartment Silas had had forever. Eighty-eight Dollars and Eighty-eight Cents. New intercom. Could Silas hold out forever?

Silas at the door. His hair was now stark white, like a silent, heavy snowstorm late at night. And he kept it very curly, permanents might be one of his last vanities. He wore glasses with bright-green frames, which turned his full face jolly. His body was portly with the signs of hidden strength. An impish man, he had a violent temper when it flared. What he usually kept under control rippled through him like muscle under a surface flab.

"So here you are, my dear, after all these years. I must say you're looking better, much better."

"I had no idea that you'd remember me."

"My dear, you almost married a Bertone. And as I told Nola when she told me that her wicked stepmother was Elaine Bright, 'Why, I remember Elaine, she was a very good listener. She'd listen all night.' "

"The wicked witch, hah? That's how you referred to me?"

"Now, please, don't get your dander up. How would you like to be a fairy godmother in the age of AIDS? Thank God, I got all of that out of my system in the days when Rome was Rome. Cats are the only revenge, my dear, and staying home."

"So this is home."

Silas had led her past the tiny kitchen—the capped basin next to the sink was a half-tub—into his tiny living room, where the two back windows seemed to form an angle and touch. There were three cats evident. A fat calico, a black cat with suspicion in wide eyes, and a fatter calico. Where there were three there were more. And not the slightest smell of cat piss. Fastidious Silas. Everything was as minimal as could be. An old couch, clean, and end tables each with three thin, bent wooden legs that sang out the fifties. Nothing much else. He was a bohemian in the old style. Two or three times in his life he had made money on lyrics. Elaine knew the songs. He drank it away, he ate it away, he spent it. He was of a generation that could pride itself on living on nothing. Most of them that made it to the eighties had already been blown away. Elaine thought once more of the new intercom.

Elaine sat on the couch, and Silas sat cross-legged on a big Moroccan pillow. "There's no place like home," he said, directing the small fan in her direction. "One gets to an age when one's proud to be an anachronism. Things come to me now, my dear, right up these stairs—I don't go to them."

"Please—you played the Bottom Line a few years ago. I went, by the way. You were very funny, and rather wise."

"People have nostalgia about old fairies. I'm probably the last generation of Golden Oldies. There's a certain panache."

"You're a Pied Piper and an old con."

"Why, thank you for sharing that with me."

They both laughed.

"Do let me get you a cold drink. I don't know where my manners have gone."

"Don't get up."

"I can." He did. "I've given up liquor, you know. Thank goodness, New York has such divine water. Would you like ice cubes in yours?"

"Yes, thanks."

"It's the Catskills, my dear. Thank them. One could bottle this and make a fortune."

When he returned he said, "You've gotten younger. I can see that. Are you a Pisces? Exactly, I thought so. They have an ability to regroup. What I do remember about you in Rome was how serious you were while you listened. It was from taking too many notes in college, my dear, many too many notes. And that Bertone! She's like you in a way, you know, Nola. She's very serious for one so young. But at least she is young, or learning to be. She's trying to separate from her father and—"

"Is she? What do you mean?"

"It was difficult for her to leave his apartment. She moved in with him after you left, didn't she? She felt he needed her. So it was extremely difficult for her to move in here."

"It was?"

"Indeed. And her father came to visit and he took one look and kept repeating, 'Bathtub in the kitchen! Bathtub in the kitchen!,' and walked out. Apparently he does better with pictures than with words."

"Are you exaggerating?"

"My dear, her father's no friend of her noise."

"I hear you don't like noise either."

He smiled.

"Silas, she's very good."

"I know. They perform for me right here. Right here. And you know I make them whisper. Whisper as loud as you wish, children, but whisper. And I did have them send on a cassette to Howard Youngblood."

"Howard Youngblood?"

"A Native American hustler. Howard Young."

"That's why I came to share the Catskills with you. Is this guy any good?"

"They're all just horrible in Hollywood. You must know that. They wouldn't take an option on their own mothers unless someone else wanted one. You must know that. But Howard Youngblood looks for youngblood. He's getting them some gigs."

"Have they signed anything?"

"I don't think they've signed their lives away. They've all studied what happened early on to the Beatles. They're rather sophisticated. They're used to contracts. They're reverent about money. Money even has a magazine these days. In Italy too, by the way. Not *Il Denaro,* but *Money.*"

"Well, I just had to talk to you today. I'm glad you let the world come to you. But I'm wondering, why California? Wouldn't it be logical to make a start here? Why California first? I'm thinking of advising them."

"Oh dear. Don't do that! They don't need advice. They need a van. Nola must get away, you see. She's had enough Daddy, Mommy, and whhh—Stepmother, not to mention Grandmommy and deceased Grandpoppy."

"This is Nola's idea?"

"Absolutely. She's bent on cutting the umbilical cord."

"Is that so? Nola really does talk with you."

"We get along famously. She's a good listener, you know. Lyrics-I-have-known. We talk an awful lot about lyrics."

"You do?"

"Professionally. We talk professionally. I tell her, My dear, let it come right up. When you feel it coming, simply regurgitate. When composing lyrics, one should never hold back. In show biz you can never be too thin or too rich or too hackneyed. . . . So my advice to you is, buy them a van and let them go."

"You're good at spending other people's money."

"Practice, my dear, practice. But do respect Nola's needs. She wants to go."

A cat jumped on Elaine's lap. As she petted it, she played with a small piece of ice, which dissolved on her tongue like a wafer.

"That's what I was thinking before, Silas. I must respect her."

THREE

Larry sat at the bar at Teacher's Too, waiting for Elaine. He watched the bartender pour cheese fish from a half-gallon container into clear glass bowls. The bowl the bartender slid in front of him had an orange-yellow glow—the fish pressing against the glass, creating their own crumbs. He watched them for a long time, as he drank his first gimlet. Bombay gin and Rose's lime juice, and clear cubes of ice in a clear glass. There was a middle-aged woman in a low-cut black dress leaning over her drink on the L of the bar, and her breasts formed a deep crease, puckered. She had on false eyelashes, heavy black mascara, and a lot of bright-red lipstick. She looked at him; he was looking at her, the way he looked at cheese fish in a glass bowl. Directly, dispassionately, seeing what's there. If he weren't waiting for Elaine, he might have made a move on this woman. He figured her nipples were very brown, and that the brown formed startling wide circles. He kept looking at her. Should he make a move?

She smiled. He responded. He could leave a message for Elaine. Then he realized he was feeling well, and averted his eyes, giving himself up to something he couldn't see.

Why had Elaine walked out on him? She was the exact opposite of Delilah. When Delilah left, finally, it had been a weight off his shoulders. It freed him. Though perhaps nothing would ever equal the first two years with Delilah. She was his fantasy come true. The most beautiful of women. Red hair, sapphire eyes, incredible body. Everybody envied him. His mistake had been to marry his fantasy rather than pursue it part-time.

Delilah. He thought he would be able to look at her forever. She had offered his daughter a sloppy freedom, whereas Elaine thought she offered Nola a directed one.

He and Elaine in Milan, right before Nola's high-school graduation. They had taken a vacation "to clear the air." He certainly had tried. They were in a shop, and Elaine had pointed out that leather jacket. "Look at that jacket. It's perfect, Larry. Why not buy it for her graduation? She's done so well. Why not buy her a gift she'll really love?"

"Let's figure it in dollars," he said. The Italian girl who waited on them went for her calculator as quicky as her tight little skirt and high heels allowed. Well, he knew how much it was in dollars. He was thinking it over. "Okay," he said in the long run. He didn't say no, did he?

"A gift she'll really love!" Nola had unwrapped it, held it out, looked at it, and said, unconvincingly, "Thanks."

"Give her time."

That was Elaine. Always sticking up for her.

Ever since Nola was barely a teenager, almost as tall as Elaine, skinny, she had painted her face defiantly on the train ride in from Roslyn and loped through his apartment as if her undeveloped frame was supported, precariously, on untrustworthy stilts cut longer than they need be. She had that adolescent arrogance that proclaimed, "This is what's cool at school and you don't know a thing about it, because you're old and out of it, not to mention dumb." Then she'd go right into the kitchen, open the refrigerator, and grab one of those diet sodas, that nonfood, that Elaine stocked for her.

"Her attitude doesn't bother you?" Larry would demand. "Why the hell do you encourage her?"

Elaine would ask: How was Nola to walk into her father's apartment? How was she to show herself and share her news? It must be difficult to wend in and out of his life every other weekend. As there was separation anxiety at the beginning, so there will be at the end. God knows what courage it took for Nola to ring the bell—according to Elaine.

"What about me?" Larry demanded. "Do you ever think about me?"

She just couldn't stop encouraging her. He knew she was hurt when Nola didn't invite her to her high-school graduation. If it were up to him, he'd have spoken to Nola, insisted that she invite her stepmother. But Elaine acted as if everything was okay. He knew she was upset, because she made plans to visit Judith and Peter for graduation weekend. Okay, he thought, get a good dose of Nola's lack of consideration, you deserve it. In a way, he was damned glad.

But Nola outdid herself the week before her graduation. She stood there in the living room with Milan's elegant interpretation of a black leather biker's jacket slung over her shoulders. A gift she'll really love! She loved it, all right. She had attached heavy chains to the shoulders. When she turned her back to them on her way to the kitchen, he and Elaine were treated to a skull-and-crossbones Mystic-taped to the leather. The word "Neither" taped over the image and the word "Land" under it.

Elaine let out a short laugh.

"What are you laughing at?"

"The death of Western civilization," she wisecracked.

Nola walked back into the living room, a can of Diet Pepsi in her hand.

"That's a three-hundred-and-fifty-dollar jacket you've just defaced!"

"Oh, Larry, that's the—"

Nola whirled around to face Elaine. "You don't have to explain, Elaine! I can take care of myself."

"See?" Larry had spat out at Elaine.

"I see she's into punk."

" 'Into'!" Nola mocked. " 'Into.' Whaddya think this is, some bourgy fad? This is my life. This is me. As soon as I graduate, I want to change my name legally. I'm in a group and I'm Asia Neither Land to them. See?"

He saw red. "Asia Neither Land? Asia Neither Land! What do you mean? You hear that, Elaine? You hear that? It's your fault, Elaine."

"My fault?"

"Look at that jacket!"

"I'm looking!"

He grabbed the damn jacket from Nola's shoulders, slammed it with his fists until his knuckles bled from the chains. He threw it across the room. It landed with a thud. "She wants to do that to my name! Are you happy now, Elaine?"

"Larry—"

"Don't Larry me! Stop living through her, God damn you! Just stop living through her!"

"Me? Living through her?"

"I'm sick of it, you hear!"

"Is that what you think? I'll live through myself, then, you bastard!"

"Listen to yourself! Don't you hear yourself, Elaine?"

"I'm listening: I'll live through myself then, you bastard! I've had it up to here, up to here!"

"Stop!" Nola screamed. "Stop! Don't you talk to Daddy like that!" And she had burst into tears.

Women.

Larry looked up from his drink, and for a split second Elaine was any new woman walking into a bar. She seemed to have a moment of hesitation too. Then she saw him and walked his way.

"Hi. Hope I haven't kept you waiting," she said. "By my watch, I'm on time."

"Here's to your watch." He saluted her with his drink. Then he moved the stool that was too close to his. "Here, please, sit down."

"You're looking well."

"Am I?"

"Yes. You look good without the mustache. Makes you look thinner." She paused. "And your hair? You're coloring it? It has that running-for-office look."

He thought better of what he was going to say. "You're looking well yourself."

"Thanks." She said to the bartender, "I'll have a kir—no, make that a gimlet, straight up."

"Now you're talking!" Larry agreed. Gimlets were something they still had in common.

She smiled, a relenting smile, a friendly one. Then there seemed to be nothing to say.

"So, Anne couldn't see you last week?"

"Or this week. She's really busy, even forgot about the long weekend coming up."

"As long as she didn't forget about you."

Elaine showed some surprise. "I doubt that. She's been so enthusiastic about the book. And when we have lunch, she confides in me."

"So you two really get along."

"Yes. We're so different, though. I feel awkward around her. She's so elegant, so refined."

"So rich."

"Well, that too. Though, God knows, she's doing so well at Panther Publishers, she really doesn't need Reid's money."

"She doesn't? He's a lucky man," Larry said, and thought of Reid, whom he knew from way back. Reid Gregory came from old money, and became the black sheep early on, when he insisted on being an entertainment lawyer. He was one of those on-camera lawyers. His clients made headlines. He did too, after he wrote a series of vaguely pornographic novels under a pseud-onym—Linda Lee Linda—which earned him his own millions. Either he made a very dumb move, or, more likely, he knew the story was about to be leaked, but, "for an undisclosed sum," he came out of the closet and proclaimed his true identity in a cover story in *People* magazine.

The uproar from women all over the country was incredible. "Fantasy Interruptus" was what *Time* magazine called it. Not that it hurt sales. Elaine had a famous editor.

"She's a terrific editor," Elaine said. "Really, she's made a dif-ference for me. So many of her suggestions were just excellent. She's as smart as they come. But at lunch it's Reid this and Reid that. I tell her, Anne, I'm interested in Anne. Look at all you're doing, look at the great books you've published; nothing against your husband, but this author's interested in Anne."

"Be careful of the rich, Elaine. They are different."

"Hah! Funny you should say that!"

"Why?"

"Oh! Nothing, just a sort of coincidence."

"A meaningful coincidence?" Larry mocked.

"Well, actually, maybe. In fact, meaningful coincidences have been popping up lately. Nola came to see me the other week. At first I wondered if that was why you called."

"Nola came to see you?" Something grabbed at his throat. "What did she want?"

He watched Elaine hesitate. Get ready, he thought.

"She wants something bad enough to risk displeasing you by seeing me."

"And that is?"

"Well, you know, of course, that she wants to take off a se-mester from school and go west with Second Hand. Now, ostensibly she came to me because she wants to buy a van. But it's another type of help she needs, I think."

"I see. A psychodrama. I'd almost forgotten your gift of psychic prophecy. But it comes back. Ah, let me see, and correct me if I have my facts wrong. Wanting to change her name to Asia Neither Land and hanging around with skinheads and assorted scum—they were stages she was passing through, as I remember. It turns out she was passing through on her way to California. California! Do you know they have Nazi punks out there, Elaine?"

"Nothing passes, Larry, unless a path is cleared for it. And you're blocking."

"A path. How Hare Krishna of you, or is it Muktanandi?"

"It's common sense. And I don't like to be made fun of. In fact, I refuse to be made fun of."

"Forgive me."

"Give her your blessing, Larry. She's determined to go. Since she's going to go anyway, don't block her. Lend her some support."

"Let Jimmy support her. Have you met her young gentleman yet? Let him support her. He's a finance major!"

"A finance major? Are you kidding?"

"Would I kid you?"

Elaine shook her head and smiled. Larry smiled too. They still shared education.

Elaine said, "Well, I heard some of Nola's music, and she's good. Very good. Nola needs you now. Don't cut her off. Help her."

"Help her go to California? Over my dead body!"

"I can't believe you just said that! How many generations of dead bodies are we going to present for young people to trip over or kick aside? Are you really going to take the responsibility for sending her out into the world unfathered? Hasn't she felt enough abandonment in her life?"

"Abandonment? *I've* felt abandonment!" He needed another drink. He nodded at the bartender and pointed to their glasses. "Anyway, that's neither here nor there. 'Over my dead body' might be another meaningful coincidence." He took his wallet out and slipped a pill into his mouth, which he downed with the fresh drink.

"What are you talking about?"

"I'm not well!" Having said it, he turned away. Took out his handkerchief, blew his nose. "Allergies."

"Not well? Do you mean allergies?"

He shook his head.

"What's wrong, Larry?"

"Later." He went into his wallet, which he had carelessly left on the bar, and brought out a twenty. "We're going to our table," he told the bartender. To Elaine he said, "Let's bring our drinks."

"Do you know what you want?" Larry asked at table, as she studied the specials on the small blackboard placed on a chain for them.

Their waiter came over, and hovered.

Finally she said, "I think I'll have the swordfish."

Larry said, "And I'll have the pasta salad with broccoli." When the waiter left, he said, "Well, that's done."

"Major decisions are always easier."

"Are they?"

"Sure, you get a gut feeling for consequences, and go from there."

"You're right," he said, pointing to his darker hair. "Here's a consequence."

She looked at his hair and he watched her register it finally. He was wearing a wig.

"Oh my God!"

"Did I shock you?" He was almost enjoying this.

She put her hand to her mouth and nodded. She stared.

She took her hand away from her mouth, but she didn't go

for her drink. Her hand was shaking. "Do you want to tell me about it?"

"It's like the latest joke," he said debonairely, as if convinced, particularly with her off balance, that style could save him. "The diagnosis is good, it's not AIDS, it's probably only lung cancer."

"Is that the diagnosis?"

He shrugged. "Looks that way."

"When did you find out?"

"Six weeks ago."

"And you went right into treatment? That's good."

"Well . . ."

"You caught it right away?"

"It's ironic. I gave up smoking on New Year's Day, and a week later I started to cough up a little blood. I thought it was my body adjusting. Remember when you gave up smoking—when was it, that last trip to Italy—and you got that terrible cough and cold?"

"Yes, I remember. But what about the blood?"

"I called Sullivan, and he said, Try a humidifier."

"He didn't tell you to come right in?"

"He said, Try a humidifier. Call him when he got back. It was right after New Year's, remember. He was off to the Alps or Vermont. Some damn place."

"And the humidifer worked?"

"No, I didn't bother. I could live with the dry air."

"You just let it go?"

"Sullivan didn't seem worried."

"Sullivan didn't seem worried? Sullivan wasn't spitting blood! Sullivan was going skiing."

He shrugged.

"Why, if I had known—" And she stopped short.

"If you had known? What would you have done, Elaine?"

She couldn't answer. She gulped her water, grimaced. "Have you caught it in time?" she asked finally.

"Perhaps. I'm not dead yet. And don't look at me like that! This whole thing might be a false alarm."

"What do you mean?"

"They've located something in the blood tests, but they don't see anything on the lung. The choice was to open me up, or treat me as an outpatient. They suggested the latter. They felt that the radiation could eliminate the symptoms. And it has. I had a terrible cough, and for two weeks I could hardly talk."

Elaine looked at his eyes, carefully. "Have they put you on drugs?"

"To alleviate anxiety. I'm not in any pain."

"To be honest," she said carefully, "you seem erratic to me. Who's your doctor? Are you with Sloan-Kettering or NYU?"

"So now I'm erratic, am I? I go to Columbia County."

"Columbia County? Upstate?"

"I can stay with friends."

"Larry, this is serious! Are you taking care of yourself?"

"Serious? Thanks for telling me. I thought it was a game. Actually, it is a game. Serious or not serious, it's all a game."

"It's your body, it's your life. But it is not a game."

"You're a Girl Scout in drag, Elaine. You and your meanings. The only thing that has meaning in life is what we can save from meaninglessness for the moment."

The waiter came with their entrées. They looked at the food in front of them. *"Bon appétit,"* Larry said. The young waiter, serious about food, said, "Enjoy."

Larry continued. "Don't you think I'm right?"

"Right?"

"About the meaning of life."

"Look, I'm not going to humor you because you're sick. I don't know what you're up to and I don't know what you mean. I'm no longer twenty-five. I can't handle life like it's going to end up on an important quiz. What are you after, an intellectual discussion? Columbia County is no place to go if you have or might have cancer."

"Don't be so dramatic," he said. "I'm feeling pretty good today. Better than I have in a while. Columbia County or no Columbia County, I feel better."

"Well, then, thank God for that."

"And while I'm feeling good, there are a few things I should attend to. Particularly, I'm thinking of my photographs. When I was spitting up blood, which I'm doing less of these days, it's them I'd think of. What happens if—? I have a whole archive of unpublished work—I mean, of unpublished work I like. I could hand them all over to Joyce. But that would mean explanations I'd rather not give. You, Elaine, are now one of the five people, including my doctors, who know I'm sick. It would take a lot off my mind, if worse comes to worse, if you'd take care of the work. You have a good brain for things like that, the best. Who else is there like you? If you'd go through the photos, talk things over with Joyce, probably it wouldn't make a lot of money, but I think I'd like one more book. You've collaborated with me before. If anything happens to me, would you do it—posthumously, that is—once more?"

He waited awhile. "Well, what do you say?"

"I'm confused."

"Does that mean no?"

"I've got to think about this."

"Where the hell's your heart?"

"Huh?"

"Don't you even give a damn about my last wish?"

"Just think of all you've been telling me, Larry! For goodness' sakes, give me a chance to digest."

"Is the fish good? Well, is it?"

She looked at him. "And what about Nola? How much does she know of this?"

"Not a word. And I don't want you to tell her. It's too early. This whole thing, the way I'm feeling now, could be some sort of crazy false alarm."

"Nola should know, Larry."

"Nola. Nola. Always Nola. If you tell her, I'll kill you."

"Larry!"

"I mean it, Elaine." He smiled. "What do I have to lose?"

"I'm not going to sit through this, Larry."

"Come on, Elaine. Don't you have a sense of humor? I'm telling you, I'm not sure I have what they say. I had no idea Nola would want to speak with you again. I thought she might have, eh, loyalty. If you say anything to Nola, I'll deny it."

"You're being overprotective, Larry. She has a right to know."

"I've already told her the one thing that is her business."

"What's that?"

"She didn't tell you? If she goes to California, I'm writing her out of my will."

"Oh, Larry!"

"Don't oh-Larry me."

"But don't you see? There's something wrong, Larry. You've got to take care of yourself. There's something wrong with the way you're talking." She took a breath. "There's something wrong with your head!"

"Is there? I think there's something wrong with *your* head. And my daughter's head. What you put in it. I'm not going to contribute to Nola's going down the tubes. There's money involved, money. I made it the old-fashioned way. I worked for what I have. Maybe the finance major can set her straight. I'm not contributing to madness. And I don't think there's a thing you can do now. Any word to Nola's the wrong word." He laughed. "No matter what happens now, whether you believe life's a game or not, you're playing." He laughed again. "I don't want loose ends, anything left to slop over. I want to see something definitive at the end."

"You're crazy," she said.

"Am I? I wasn't fifteen years ago, not that I'm complaining. I wasn't crazy before I met you. I used to be a success. You sucked what you could out of me; then, when you had everything you needed, you left. You can call it liberation or any damn thing. Once my photographs were everything. Remember? When you needed things, you worked with me on a book, two books! Now you'd have to think it over. You can go to hell!"

She put her fork down. And put her napkin on the table. "I'm not going to take this. You're very cruel." She didn't have time to say anything else. He grabbed her arm.

"Larry! You're hurting me!"

"Am I, now?"

She swung at him. He loosened his grip in surprise, as people turned to look. She jumped up so abruptly that her chair toppled over. She brushed by their earnest waiter, who hurried over to the table as she left. "Is everything all right, sir?"

"Great," he said. "Just great!"

"Elaine. Elaine." She heard the voice, it was such a rich voice. The voice of a stranger, yet hauntingly familiar. She was hearing it in her dream. For she had taken a cab on Broadway and gone straight home, had whizzed past the large West Side buildings, the tip of Central Park, Rockefeller Center, the Chrysler Building. She'd like to come back as the Chrysler Building! She had closed her eyes and lit up Art Deco fins.

At home she had stripped hurriedly, afraid, almost, that, as in a bad dream, she woud not be able to loosen herself from her clothes; that they would reappear backward, and twisted, and be even tougher to take off. She didn't want to think. She didn't want to drink. She didn't want to smoke. She didn't want to know. She unhooked her phone from the answering machine, so she wouldn't hear it ring. She slipped under the cool sheets, and, in a fetal position, hugged herself into a deep sleep. Hours later she heard that distinct voice in her dreams. "Elaine." It woke her. She sat up in bed. She knew that voice. But she couldn't place it. "Elaine." Where had she heard that voice? Then it came to her quickly, and surprised her, Mario.

She played her messages.

"Elaine. Is that you? I hope I have the right number. This is Mario Picard. Tuesday night, around ten. Could you call me back, 203-555-9734? If not, I'll try to reach you again." Bzzzzzz.

"Hi, Mario. This is Elaine."

"Oh, Elaine! That *was* your number. Great!"

"Did I wake you?"

"At seven in the morning? You kidding? You got me going out the door. What are you doing up? Did Hemingway get up this early?"

She laughed. "I went to bed really early last night. My way of dealing with trouble. My ex-husband's not well."

"Oh? I'm sorry."

"So am I. . . . How'd you get my number? I don't remember giving you my last name. Pam?"

"No. I thought of that, but I didn't want to mix business with pleasure. I went up to Corning Blue Road. Your friend Judith's okay. 'Oh, you're Mario Two.' Cute. I didn't know you almost married royalty."

"Oh, please! She tell you that?"

"First she didn't want to give me the time of day. But I won her over."

"Charmed her?"

"Anything for your number. So, what about Mario One?"

"It's a long and, I must say, boring story."

"Well, I have all Fourth of July weekend and a boat. Bore me."

"A boat?"

"One of the guys is lending me a really nice motorboat. I'll take you around the lake you're investing in. I'd love to see you again. I . . . I . . . What is this? I'm like a kid. I've thought of you every day since we met. I very much want to see you again."

"I'm flattered. I mean, I've thought of you too."

"Are you being polite?"

"Yes and no. The strangest thing happened last night. I heard this familiar voice in my sleep. It woke me up. It was your voice. You were calling my name."

"On your answering machine."

"I had the sound off, Mario. I just played it now. That's why I called right away. It was such a coincidence!"

"So you heard my voice?"

"I did."

"Well, can you come, or do you have plans?"

"I made city plans. I didn't want to drive this weekend."

"Take the bus. I'll pick you up."

"I'd have to check with Judith and Peter."

"Oh; oh, sure. I'd drive you there, too."

"Okay. I mean, look, let me think. When can I call you back?"

"Usually I'm here at six. Or I can call you."

"Either way. I'll try you at six. Okay?"

"More than okay. Goodbye, Elaine."

"Bye."

"A meaningful coincidence?" Larry had said mockingly yesterday at Teacher's Too. Larry acting like that, sick. God, she was supposed to meet Nola for breakfast. What was she going to say?

FOUR

Nola Netherlands woke up quickly on Wednesday morning, and looked at Jimmy lying on his side. The early-morning sun was plying holes on the wall while Jimmy lay in cool shadows, his short-cropped hair slightly tousled, his lips just missing meeting, his arms crossed over his chest, swearing to a deep and silent sleep. She wanted to write about his peace in sleep, the sun holes, her feelings of the new day. She simply woke up into the significance of things, and that clarity alarmed her.

The displacements of her childhood, the parental incongruities, Nutty Elaine—all that was in her soul, pushing and pulling and often foggy as hell. She was certainly armed for a bull session. Parents and grandparents and stepmothers, they screwed up so much nowadays, were so busy trying to find themselves, that they were funny and weird and after a while you just wondered, What next? Unless you decided to mess up too and get wasted, or become a skinhead, or give up on yourself. Which was the way she had been for a while. Not the wasted part, but the giving-up part. Until she learned to focus on herself. And that took Jimmy's coming along. Maybe otherwise she'd still be living with her father.

She loved her father dearly, and moving in with him in her freshman year, just the 1 Train away from NYU, had been a turning point in her life. No one had argued. Maybe it was for the good, her mother said. Her grandmother made a big deal about not being consulted. Her grandmother had the green eyes that her mother had too, and that only Nola had missed out on. There was always concern in her grandmother's eyes that narrowed into wrinkles on the side. Whereas her mother's eyes were always the same, round and beautiful and cool. Her beautiful mother in the kitchen: "Hmmm? What was that, Nola? Your father said it was okay? Okay."

Her grandmother had just come home from the bank. She had worked there forever. She was dumping the salad mix from the supermarket into the salad bowl with a clipped efficiency that had nothing to do with salads. Her grandfather had called her grandmother "the boss," and used to call her mother and Nola "buddy." If he had been alive he would have said, "Good for you, buddy." He would have made a toast.

Her worried grandmother was pouring the plastic vial of dressing into the salad. Beautiful Delilah was scooping ice into her glass. Scotch always reminded Nola of her grandfather. Scotch perfume.

"Have you known about this, Delilah?" her grandmother asked after she told them she was leaving home, bye-bye.

"Hmmm?"

"I should know better than to ask!"

Everything happened to her grandmother. A lousy attitude, not the truth, but still Nola began to feel guilty.

"Oh well, I'll just have one less kid at home now. How about putting down three plates, Delilah?"

"And one less check," Delilah said.

"We've always managed somehow," her grandmother said, in a knowing way.

"Forgive me for breathing," Nola snapped, more for attention than anything else. Now she was watching her own defection blend smoothly into the brew between the two older women.

"Don't you care? Don't you want to say goodbye? If Grandpa was here, he'd make a toast."

"Sure would," her grandmother said.

"Don't start!" Delilah said. "Let the poor man rest in peace."

"Peace? Why not? He left me all your bills!"

"I wish I could go tonight!" Nola blurted.

"What's wrong with you?" her grandmother asked, suddenly looking very hurt. "What's got you upset? I'm the one who should be upset. How do you think I feel about you leaving?"

"One less check!"

"My God, Nola, after all I've— Oh, what's the use. Don't you have a sense of humor?" her grandmother retorted. "You'll go crazy in this world if you don't know how to laugh! Where would your mother and I be if we couldn't make a joke?"

Funny.

Her father had needed her. Today she knew that it was not her responsibility or in her power to give her father back what was missing in his life. It just wasn't her job. But then she moved in, even calmed down her appearance. He thought he was saving her, and she thought she was saving him. And for a while that delusion made them both heady. Still, it would always be a high point in her life, a major sound, walking in the hall past that quiet, organized, and beautiful living room, to the bedroom on the right, which would now be her own room. She was no longer a guest in her own father's home. She had outlasted the intruder. She was ecstatic that Elaine was gone. When she opened up the door to the bedroom, she realized why it had been closed. "Oh!" she exclaimed. Her father came in behind her and set down her luggage.

"Like it?" he asked.

"Like it!" she replied.

"Dorm-room modern," he said, and she laughed.

What was there not to like? Bed, bookshelves, desk, all in high-tech blacks and whites. The windows, west and northwest, had the river view she loved, and there were new dark-blue pleated shades on them—pulled up, making everything light and bright and airy. The walls had been repainted a light blue, and on the floor there was a Native American rug with a pattern in blue and black and white and orange. On the sleek wide desk she saw the Macintosh computer she and her father had talked about a few weeks ago. She walked over—printer too. And then, on the trolley in front of her double bed, a new sound system and a TV with remote control. She was walking into fairyland. The generosity overwhelmed her; her father had always been tight.

"I can't believe this, Dad. You shouldn't have. It's too much."

"I was afraid you wouldn't like it. I was afraid you'd say"—and he mocked a falsetto—"I'd rather do it myself!"

Maybe, after all, it was Elaine who had been tight. Maybe she really had kept him from his daughter.

"I love it! I don't know how to thank you."

"Keep up your grades, be serious about your studies—that's all."

He didn't even go into her hair colors and her clothes. He was trying, she realized, and unconsciously she bought into his unspoken assumptions.

"I will! I will! I'm happy to be here. God, this must have cost a fortune. Did you have a decorator?"

He looked around sadly. "No. I did it all myself. It kept me sane."

She wanted to deny he had said that; she wanted to turn it around. This was her room. Not an exercise to forget Elaine. He didn't need Elaine. Nola would keep him sane.

"What's wrong?" he asked, noticing her sudden collapse of enthusiasm.

"Nothing," she said. And then "Nothing!" again, this time as if she meant it. "I was just thinking." She walked over to him. "Thanks." She kissed him on the cheek.

"Thank *you,*" he said, making something out of the "you," her. He really meant it. It was her turn to smile again. She could see she was making him happy.

But she wasn't happy much of the time. She dragged, moped, lost energy. Her hair didn't feel right; she'd get pimples on the sides of her cheeks. She'd look in the mirror and see a big question mark in it. She'd stare and stare, trying to stare past her own eyes. She wrote poems in a flamingo-covered notebook she bought at Barnes & Noble for $3.98.

Then Jimmy came into her group as the lead guitarist, and he was the only person she ever let see that book. "These're poems, not lyrics."

"Poems *are* lyrics," Jimmy said.

But they were so close to her heart. He started to score them. "Here, you sing," he said.

"I write. I don't sing."

"You got a lot of don'ts, lady."

"Hey, you sound like my stepmother! Ms. Upbeat."

He looked at her. "I'm not Ms. anything."

"I didn't mean that."

But maybe in a way she meant that too. Even her father was after her on that one. He wasn't into her having orgasm like Elaine was, but he came out with a statement on boys' early experiences, and how nowadays, as he put it, early experiments or mistakes could end in AIDS. You could wonder about any guy, if you had a brain in your head, and she did.

They were in her room. Jimmy put on a blank tape, and he played the guitar, and she took the poem he started with and sang. They went through it once and again and again and again, and played with the tape and got the song louder and louder and faster and faster, till Nola did a jump off the bed and slammed into Jimmy, who moved his guitar and slammed into her. Then they let the tape do it while they danced. His hair was long then, a mane, shaved on the sides but not a mohawk exactly. Jimmy didn't like to follow anything exactly. That's why he was good. That's how they really became Second Hand. Because they weren't! They were the hand that didn't know what the other hand was doing. And they were the one hand clapping—loud. When you think it out, it was intense.

They ended up on the bed, hot and horny. She was on the pill anyway, because she was bleeding too much. This was the bed her father had bought. That came into her head. Then there was just the music they had taped and the two of them. She forgot about herself. For the first time, it really happened. Jimmy was so hard. He was rubbing against her stomach and it was hurting her and making her wet. He had his mouth all over her breasts and she was running her hands along his back. And suddenly all she wanted was him along with the music. They both moaned when he entered her. He didn't stumble like a kid. Right away found her out. She could feel every thrust. And she was screaming—Nola was screaming to Asia's song. The louder she screamed, the more she felt. Something rumbled in her stomach to the pitch of her voice. It was like a giant match scratched across a matchbox. It sputtered, hissed, flared. Then went out. They lay across the bed, drenched.

A few days later Jimmy said, "You could come to a meeting with me, you know. ACOA," he said. "It could help."

"ACOA?"

"Adult Children of Alcoholics."

"What are you talking about, Jimmy?"

"I'm talking about your poems, I guess," he said unsurely. He rubbed his fingers along the strings of the guitar. He bowed his head over his thoughts. He was sensitive to her privacy.

"What do you mean?"

"I guess I mean 'Scotch Perfume.' "

"What?" Then, even as she asked it as a question, she faced it as fact coming right from her gut. "Do you mean my grandfather was a drunk?"

That was Jimmy. He was her key man, her key mate. Take any of the meanings. He opened doors. As she dressed to meet Elaine, she tried not to wake Jimmy, but she did wish he would wake up. Well, she'd be quiet. She turned, took a look in the mirror over the sink, a look at him, then left, no noise. They lived in a world of sound, so she had her own appreciation of silence. And the small "click."

On the stoop of her tenement, she felt the dry breeze in advance of another hot day. She was living without air conditioning for the first time in her life and was becoming intimate with weather. This whole summer in the city with Jimmy stretched out like an adventure, leading to the fall and to the band's going on the road. As she breathed in the morning air, everything stretched out in front of her—endless, exciting, parts of it captured in song. Immortality and a New York City street.

Jimmy's apartment was on St. Mark's near Tompkins Square Park. She took a look at the park to her left, and then walked down the stairs and turned right. She was meeting Elaine at the Veselka coffee shop. Elaine wondered how they hadn't bumped into each other before. Well, she really hadn't been in the neighborhood that long, and never went out for breakfast, anyway.

She had a tug about Elaine. Why had Silas called her the "wicked witch," right to her face? That was their joke. It wasn't meant to be mean. How could she know that Silas knew her? Elaine had seemed sort of distant over the phone.

Nutty Elaine. The wicked witch. She was going to stop saying things like that. Not that it was such a big deal. But it made her feel—uneasy. As if she were trying to use Elaine. No, she wasn't like that. It was more Elaine's fault than hers that they lost contact. Elaine stopped calling when Nola moved into her father's apartment. She could have called. After all, Elaine was the one who always said yes. Not that Nola wasn't hoping for one for the van. But yes, always yes, yes, yes. Sometimes Nola used to get desperate for a no. Why did Elaine open herself up so much? Why was she so easy? Still, "wicked witch," right to Elaine's face. Why had Silas blabbed like that? It made Nola feel bad.

There were two junkies loitering on the corner. One guy looked like his eyes had been washed out with soap. She moved along gingerly. He had looked at her. But what does a guy like that see? A quarter, a half a buck?

Elaine was already at the restaurant, having a cup of coffee. She looked up from her paper. Nola waved at her, and passed the register and candy counter. The lunch counter at the Veselka was irregular. It squared around the grill and then straightened out. Tables were squeezed in around it. Four of them abutted the windows onto Ninth Street. Potted plants hung, their straggly greens dipping down close to people's heads. Elaine sat at one of the tables in the middle of the room. "Am I late?" Nola asked.

"Not at all. I just walked faster than I thought. Just look at these murals."

There were two wall-size murals, one on the wall before the windows, and one on the wall behind Elaine. Both of them depicted the Veselka, the grill, the workers, the clientele of musicians, students, and Ukrainians, the ketchup bottles, the smokers, the yellow menus, the cups of coffee, the *Post*. The murals were as alive as the place; the peculiar perspective, in which the Heinz bottles and the shape of the counter reigned, was, when you studied it, close to reality. "They're by Arnie Charnick," Elaine said. "He has a wonderful eye."

"I guess."

"Before these, he had one with a Ukrainian window-washer strapped across the skyline of New York. Would you believe, he got sick of it after a while. Whitewashed it! Didn't even photograph it. This time, at least, he put them on canvas."

"You're really into this stuff?"

"Well, Nola, the murals capture the place, don't you see. They capture the spirit. This place, this time. Us. All of this will change. But the murals won't. They're full of life. They stop time."

"Life is short and art is long," Nola said.

"All right! You know your Pater."

"I took 'PMS and the Victorian Householder,' but we ended up doing a lot of men."

"That must have been Serena Fox's course."

"Yeah," Nola said, impressed.

"Did you like it?"

"Sure. It took me three semesters to get in! I did a paper on Christina Rossetti."

"Did you plot her menstrual cycle as it affected 'Goblin Market'?"

Nola laughed. "No. But I liked her stuff. It's far out. Anyway, the title didn't have that much to do with the course. It was mainly to make us aware of the unspoken conditions then."

"Pater could have had PMS, you know."

"You mean 'cause he used to go nuts?"

"You got it. I'll tell you," Elaine said, with delight, "you can call the course anything you want, but it's all education."

"Well," Nola said, "I'm going to finish up. Honest. You spoke with Daddy?"

"I certainly did."

"That sounds mysterious."

"I'd say it's complicated, or I'm confused. I'm not sure. There are things that I want to think about. But he does seem dead set against this tour. He told me he was pretty specific with you. Is that true?"

"What do you mean?"

"Well, did he say if you go he'll cut you out of his will?"

"Sure," Nola said matter-of-factly. "That's why I came to you for a loan."

"Tell me, have you seen your father lately?"

"Yes?" the waitress interrupted. She was a middle-aged Polish woman who seemed to be somewhere else. Kraków? She looked around the room. Pencil in hand she absentmindedly smoothed out the apron at her middle.

"I'll have eggs up, tomatoes rather than potatoes, wholewheat bread, butter on the side, coffee, and the orange juice," Elaine said.

"I'll have a blueberry muffin, a side of sausage, and coffee," Nola said.

The woman wrote something down, nodded, and went off.

"As I was saying, Nola, have you seen your father lately?"

"We talk on the phone. You know, Elaine, it was very intense leaving the apartment. Like maybe someday I'll tell you about it. If it wasn't for Jimmy . . . I had to get on my own, Elaine."

"Why, Nola, that's okay. You don't need to apologize for having your own life."

"There's a lot to it, Elaine." But she really felt like saying, "Just 'cause you could move out on Daddy without a thought, doesn't mean . . ."

"Now *you* sound mysterious."

Nola clamped her lips and looked at the woman bringing her coffee and Elaine's juice.

Elaine drank her juice. Then she said, "Maybe you should go to see your father."

"Maybe. Maybe like in the old days, on the Fourth of July."

"You staying in town?" Elaine asked.

"Yeah. You?"

"I might go to the country for the weekend."

Nola looked at her stepmother. Her close-cropped blondish hair was thick and curly, emphasizing the daring break in her strong nose. She was very attractive. She had a way of looking like someone you'd want to know. Her light-brown eyes were— warm. They could be embarrassing, the way she'd flood up with a feeling or a thought. There was an annoying oversincere quality about them. They didn't hide things like her grandmother's did, or keep quiet like her mother's. They wanted more then Elaine admitted. Elaine's eyes just weren't cool.

What about a summer job? Nola thought. Maybe an early shift right here. They looked like they could use someone, for sure. Was Elaine going to lend her the money? In a way, three thousand bucks was the least Elaine could do. But when she brought it up the other night at a meeting, someone said, What do you think that woman really owes you?

A family. Elaine broke up her father's marriage. If it wasn't for that bitch, her mother said, her father would have come after them. Not that she wanted him back. She'd lost all her respect when he took up with the pseudo-intellectual, one of those Greenwich Village types who think they're smart, but they're just following one another. Fooled him 'cause she doesn't know a thing about good clothes. Just making believe his money doesn't mean anything to her, and then hooking him—what a sucker. Be nice to her, Nola, she holds the purse strings.

"What's wrong?" Elaine asked.

"Nothing."

"You know, I still haven't gotten over your gig. . . ."

"You really think we're that good?"

"You're that good. So good that I feel like warning you to give it up if you can and, if you can't, at least figure out what you can do to support your habit."

"Look, you don't owe me anything."

Elaine looked confused. "You mean the money? That's not what I meant. What I meant is that it's a hard life being an artist, Nola."

"What's so hard about your life? And you've written a book!"

"Listen, we only know each other's lives from the outside."

"But I know a lot of people's lives from the inside, and they have real problems, problems they can't walk out on."

Elaine tilted her head a bit to the side, the way she did when she was thinking. "Well, I'm not in competition for hard luck.

In that department I have no desire to overachieve. But tell me, Nola, does this mean you're in group therapy?"

Bull's-eye, Nola thought, the woman is uncanny. "In a sense, Elaine."

"Do you want to tell me about it?"

"Well, it's something you have to sort of experience yourself. I'm going to the Anonymous Rooms."

"The Anonymous Rooms? Aren't they for alcoholics?"

"There's a room for everyone with a problem, Elaine. There's a room for everyone who comes from a dysfunctional family, or anyone whose life is out of control because of their own addiction or the addiction of another. The addiction can be alcohol or drugs or people, food, spending, gambling, name it!"

"It encompasses a lot."

"There are a lot of rooms. And the miracle is, they work if you work them."

"I can see that. You came to me after all this time and asked me for what you wanted. And you seem calmer, more confident. You've done a lot of growing up."

"I've learned a lot about myself. And I've come in contact with my Higher Power."

"Your Higher Power? I guess at times we have to remember that we can only do the best we can do."

"You sound sad, Elaine."

"Do I? You should go see your father, Nola."

"And hear him talk against Second Hand?"

Elaine shrugged. "I don't know."

Okay, Nola thought, here goes. "What about the van, Elaine? Are you going to at least take a look at it?"

The waitress brought their food.

"I'm not being coy about the money, Nola. I know that van's not going to wait on you forever, but you know how sometimes I have to go slowly?"

"Will you come to look at the van?"

"Why, yes, I will."

"When?"

"I've got a bunch of things on my mind. And I want to speak with your father again. What about next week? There's the long weekend. Then on Tuesday I'm having lunch with my editor. I'll call you on Wednesday, okay?"

"Next Wednesday," Nola repeated.

"You've got it."

"I hope so."

"Oh, Nola, one way or the other there's no question of that. You do."

F I V E

Elaine got off the bus at Danbury, and stood outside the small waiting room watching people being picked up or getting into the cars they had left in the large lot. Would she even recognize Mario? Was this wise? "Oh?" Judith had said on the phone. "Sure, you can stay." Elaine wanted to, but didn't tell her Larry was ill.

Should she have checked in with Judith? She could have gotten a hotel room. Was she being too open, was she exposing herself? If she hadn't heard Mario's voice in the dream, would she be there? She had given up this kind of adventure, hadn't she? There'd been enough of them right after she left Larry.

For about a year or so she'd had adventures—until a longer affair with a young editor she'd met at her first publishing party, Ben Gary from Cincinnati. He had an unrenovated studio apartment he paid a fortune for, and all the insecurities of an uncentered but good-looking young man who was dying to make it big in New York. He spent too much time trying to figure out how that's done, rather than figuring out who he was and how *he'd* do it.

At first Ben was a lot of fun. He was exuberant and liked to party. Loved romance. She used to joke that he'd read one trashy manuscript too many. For her birthday he bought a bottle of champagne and two real glasses and took her for a buggy ride around Central Park. He'd also take time off from work to spend in bed. He bought her body oils, exotic soaps, and erotic gifts. There was something unreal about Ben's New York state of mind. He definitely played the innocent, thought it was smart. For him, she was some sort of trophy. She was older and experienced, and she had been married to Larry Netherlands.

She wasn't complaining. He was good-looking, fun, new. She saw clearly that in a way she was going along with his "as if." She didn't love him, and after thirteen months that came to bother her. Or did it bother her that he didn't love her? They were just out of sync after a while. "Hollow" was the word. No real love to connect them.

They began to get on each other's nerves. One day she got annoyed at him for being so passive about his landlord, taking all his bull about the repairs in the bathroom. The bathroom was a mess, and the plumber never came. It just began to kill her that Ben didn't stand up for himself. It was as if the whole relationship would work if only Ben would take care of his bathroom.

Poor Ben. One working day the landlord calls and Ben's out buying one of the lunches he liked to spread in front of her in bed, and she answers the phone. "He's not here, but I have a question. When are you sending over a plumber to take care of that bathroom leak? The tiles are crumbling off the wall!"

"Who are you?"

She gives her name.

He asks her to spell it.

She does!

Ben gets a lawyer's letter from the landlord. Four complaints. She's number three. Cohabitation with Elaine Netherlands. Spelled right. The landlord wants to evict him and rent that crumbling place out for more money!

That did it. It was over. What a fight.

Two months passed before he called. He wanted to take her out to lunch.

"Lunch?" she said. "Forget it. What's wrong with dinner?"

"Can we compromise on brunch?"

She had to laugh. "Okay, why not?"

At brunch he told her this was another goodbye. He had lost his job. Too many days before her, with her, and after her in the sack. But he sounded rather relieved about going home. "That way, I don't have to go through with the suit." He meant the legal battle with his landlord. "If it were just getting a new job, that's one thing. But I'll be damned if I look for another apartment!"

She said, "I'm sorry."

"And you thought," Ben said, his voice rising, despite his intentions, "you thought I was paying too much!"

Every once in a while he sent her a postcard. He was writing a novel.

"Elaine!"

She turned. "Oh, Mario!"

"You came."

"I said I would."

"There was a bus before this. Would you believe it, two from New York. I didn't know . . . It doesn't matter. You're here."

He hugged her. "You look great," he said. His arms were hard. He smelled wonderful.

"So do you."

God, what a handsome man, she thought. More than that, what a nice feeling. He was so happy to see her.

"You travel light," Mario said. They were on the white motor-boat, docked. She had slipped off her jeans, folded them, and put them over her sandals in her Sportsac. She left her T-shirt on over the top of her bathing suit, and adjusted her straw hat with bobby pins.

"That'll never last," he said.

"You're right. But I don't want too much sun." She smiled at him.

"Here." He reached into a side compartment for a neatly folded bandanna and then came over to her. "May I?"

She took the straw hat off and he fixed the red bandanna for her, tying it carefully in the back.

"Do I look silly?"

"It looks better on you than on Wig. It's his. We were out last Sunday."

"Oh, I remember him."

"All the ladies remember Wig, God help them. Not that he isn't as sweet as they come. All the guys from Quebec are as sweet as they come. It's just that, well, Wig's Wig."

"You seem quite fond of him."

Mario said, "Here we go," and started the boat up. "Wig was my brother-in-law. When I first came from Fort Lauderdale—"

"I thought you were from Tampa Bay."

"Originally. I see you check out details too. Paulette and I lived in Fort Lauderdale. When we split I came to Danbury and stayed with Wig. Now he's my right hand. In the field, that is. Has no head for business." He paused. "And I have a kid, you know, a little girl. Seven. He's her uncle."

"No, I didn't know. Do you get to see her?"

The boat was whizzing through the lake now, and he faced her as he steered. She felt the spray on her legs and arms. She put her straw hat under her seat.

"Just saw her. Took some time around Memorial Day. And I'll get back there Christmas."

"Sounds familiar." Then she said, "I bet she loves her daddy."
He looked pleased.

"What's her name?"

"Victoria."

"Wow, that's nice."

"Thanks. Do you have any children of your own?"

"No. Just my stepdaughter. And . . . It's beautiful here." She almost said something about her ex-husband's being sick.

"There's Lake Acres, see, way over there. See?"

On a far hill she did see the outline of the buildings. "It's a beautiful site."

"I like the hills," Mario said. "When I think of Florida, I keep the hills in mind. I try to convince myself, Well, Florida has no winter, but it's flat, flat, flat." His voice played with the flatness.

"You have a nice voice."

"Guess so, if it made it to your dreams."

They were quiet for a while as the boat sped through the water, circling islets. She watched the irregular shoreline, saw some of the nice houses tucked out of sight, out of harm's way.

"You're a good navigator," she said.

"Had to be, in my old line of work."

"What was that?"

"That was a while ago."

"Oh. Sorry. Didn't mean to pry."

"You weren't prying before," Mario said a few hours later, as they sat on a blanket in the midst of trees on the islet where they'd stopped. They were drinking beers, watching the lake. "It's good talking with you."

"I'm glad."

"It's just so easy to talk to you. You bring out the truth."

"That's nice."

"The truth is, I had a good business. It just wasn't enough. After Nam. I don't know. Paulette. She was wild when we hitched up. I liked that in her. Me and Paulette and Wig. Fun and games.

I'd moonlight bringing pot in. Jamaican. Top stuff. Wig'd drive it north. I needed the rush. The danger. In the meantime, I let the work go. Progressively, you know. Slow. I just wasn't there. I fooled myself that I could be a part-time bad guy. Meanwhile, I'm drinking too much, drugging too much. Then the kid comes along. And Wig—well, Wig just had to get out of there. Go back north. Straighten out. And me, I just kept getting these lonely feelings. Paulette wasn't there for me anymore. She'd say I wasn't there for her either. We had an open marriage. Those were the good old days, you know. Good old sex and drugs and rock and roll. In plain English, I fucked up royally. So did Paulette. She'll admit that. It took me a long time to grow up. Too much discipline too early, the way I figure it. Being an army brat. Taking it all the way through Nam. Never even smoked a joint before Nam. Believe it?

"Everything took me a long time. Like I was looking for something I never could find. So, instead of finding something, I destroyed everything. Let it all go. Almost didn't make it. It's here where I turned a corner," he said, and paused. "Came here, dried out, grew up. Found another crew of French guys, with Wig's help. Another try. For my daughter. For me. I spend a lot of time alone now. I keep my nose clean. It's not much of a life. But it's money in the bank. It's sanity."

Elaine didn't say anything.

"Too much talk? I made you quiet?"

"Oh, not at all," she said. "I was just thinking."

"You do that a lot."

"I seem to. I was thinking of Hemingway. That's your fault."

"You don't like Hemingway?"

"It's not that I don't like him. I just hadn't thought about him much, till you brought him up when we met. Remember? Now I'm thinking how he surrounded danger with a lot of stuff. Bulls and bull and boxing gloves. Rifles."

"Macho mania," Mario answered, for some reason surprising

her. "I'm a weekend refugee from it. Hemingway just wrote about it. I live it. Try construction."

"Do you still get the urge to play bad guy?"

"Sure."

"What do you do about it?"

"Nothing much. Hunt."

"You hunt?"

"Sometimes."

"I never did," Elaine said.

"Against your principles?"

"Oh, I'd be curious to give it a try."

"Not too bloody for you?"

"Don't know. I'd keep in mind we're all meat."

Mario laughed. "I bet you'd be curious enough to give anything a try."

"Oh, no. I know I have limitations. Would you?"

"Try anything once? I guess I have," he said quietly.

"Oh!"

"Don't look so serious. All that's behind me."

"It is? Then what do you do for kicks?"

"You."

"I'm hardly big game." She looked away.

"Why, you just told me you're good red meat."

She laughed. "I'm having a good time."

"You sound surprised," he said.

"Maybe I am." Then she faced him. "I like you."

"Good," he said.

She said. "Let's go for a swim."

"No, no. You can't escape yet. I'm going to take you for dinner, girl," he said, when they docked. "We could go by boat—it's right on the lake—but I figured you'd want to freshen up first. We'll drive; it's on the way to your friends' place."

"I'd just feel funny getting there too late."

"Well, call them from my place."

"I don't know."

"You don't have to worry about me, Elaine, if that's what it is."

He had lifted the cooler from the boat, then turned and looked her in the eyes. His muscles were still at work, his blue eyes backed up by the sky. "There's no way I'd try to take from you anything you didn't want to give. I want to say that straight out. Any way you want it is the way you'll have it. Scout's honor. It's knowing you that matters."

"Why, thanks, Mario."

"No, thank *you*. I've been in hibernation for a long time. I really didn't think it was in the cards for someone like you to come along. I just want to make that clear."

"You have."

"There you go thinking again. About what?"

"About going to dinner with you. I think I'd like that."

"Oh?" He smiled. "That's good. That's very good."

"Damn!" he said, happily, in front of the big Victorian boardinghouse. "I just knew you'd ask." They were in front of the steps to the wooden porch, looking up at the big American eagle that was affixed to its roof.

"That comes right from the Danbury Fair. Claude—you'll meet him and Mathilde—Claude bought this at the auction."

"Oh, that's right, you told me they auctioned all the statues from the Fair."

"Yes. And Claude bought the eagle. He's a real old-timer. Says he wants to go home to Quebec with his wife, the money he'll make someday selling this place, and his American eagle.

"There's a waiting list among the French Canadians to get in here. This place is a gold mine. He runs a tight ship. Anyway, let me show you my place." They walked up the stairs. "See, this first floor's theirs, but they're not in. Here." He took her through a side door and up the wooden stairs.

"Oh, this is nice," she said.

It was a small apartment with wonderful woodwork. The windows looked out over an expanse of green back yard.

"For the time being, it's all I need. I've talked with Claude about the possibility of buying in. I told you I've been in hibernation. A place like this has to be kept up. Two apartments, and eight rooms with kitchen facilities let out. You've got to be here. Stay put. That suited me just fine. Wait till you see their place. The whole first floor—it's nice. Now, now I don't know."

"Really?"

"Really. Maybe there's something more to life than making money. Here, here's a towel, there's the phone. You take a shower if you want, make yourself at home."

"I don't want to displace you."

"No problem. I've got a few things to do. I'll be back in, say, a half hour?"

"That's very kind of you."

"Just leave me some hot water."

"I'll walk you to the door," Mario said late that night, after he drove her to New Milford in his pickup. His tone was tense.

"Oh, that's okay. I don't want to wake them."

He put his arm around her. "I'll watch till you're in, then," he said. "Good night."

"Good night," she said, uncertain.

He brought her closer and looked in her eyes. He paused for a moment, and then, very slowly, met her lips with his. What began so gently turned into a very passionate kiss.

Elaine poured herself a cup of coffee on Sunday morning, popped a piece of toast, and sat for a few minutes in Judith and Peter's kitchen. It was a big room with modern conveniences, though the round table Elaine sat at was an old wooden one with claw feet. At her back were bay windows.

The kitchen suggested domesticity, the hearth, family life,

birthday parties, comfortable dinners with good friends. Years of them.

Judith had left a note out for her that began, "Peter will be up, and in his studio, before you, I will be up after you. . . ." Peter will be up, and in his studio. On the phone, Judith had said, "Sure, you can stay. Last time you were so preoccupied you didn't have a chance to look at Peter's new work."

Elaine stood, refilled her mug, and walked out of the kitchen and into the wide meadow. Cows, each with a numbered tab punkily stapled in one ear, were up against the neighbor's wire. They turned to watch her go by. Number 43 watched her progress longer than the rest.

The red barn that had been turned into Peter's studio was next to a pond. Everything was quiet. The air was fresh. She sipped her coffee, then took a deep breath. Walked over to the door and knocked.

"One minute!"

Peter opened the door. He was in farmer jeans that were too big and an old sport shirt. "Welcome, stranger!" he said. His beard, which had once made him seem on the cutting edge, and his longish hair, which had thinned on the top, now made him appear avuncular.

"Am I disturbing you?"

"Not at all. In fact, I just put my new stuff out, in order. See? It's a whole series on the pond in different seasons."

"Great!" she said.

"I mean, it's not Andy Warhol."

"I was hoping we wouldn't get into that."

"I'm not saying he's not a decent printmaker. But the guy just can't paint. His fifteen minutes of fame were over years ago. Honest to God. I don't know how you hang that stuff."

"I like him. Shoot me."

"Someone should shoot him again," Peter said.

"Well, Peter," Elaine said, "that's the downside to the fifteen minutes. Anyone can take a potshot." She was angry, but sipped her coffee.

"I've been trying to see the pond," Peter said, bringing the conversation around to uncommercial art. He pointed to the large canvases he had set up against the walls of the studio, obviously expecting her to visit. "I started in fall—the first one to the left— and they progress counterclockwise through the seasons."

"Gotcha."

Elaine walked around slowly, stopping at each of the big canvases. In the spring painting, Peter's yellows and lavenders, pinks and blues, coalesced into a pattern that could be water, lily pads, sky.

"I love these colors," she said, trying to relax into his abstractions. She wanted to be able to dive into his pond, but at the brink of each one she was stopped. She just couldn't dive into paint. The work seemed so old-fashioned; it seemed too much of an intellectual homage to a lot of great painters that had come before. It scared her.

It made her wonder about her own voice. "It's so new, it's so fresh," Anne Gregory had said of *The Passion and the Vow.* That was the title Anne suggested. Elaine had called her book *Men and Women,* but Anne said that wouldn't sell. Tuesday they were going to have lunch. Suppose the book turned out to be a disaster? Suppose everyone tiptoed around it, the way Elaine was now doing a balancing act around Peter's paintings?

Anne said *The Passion and the Vow* had a very interesting narrative voice. Well, it had taken Elaine four years to bring it together. There had been this renegade nineteenth-century Jesuit priest and minor poet, Francis J. Mahoney, an Irishman in Rome, who had been very close to the Pope. He had finally lost all of his political power and was ruined because of his fatal attraction for a young Italian girl, who was his lover for many years. Elaine had set his double life and the scandal of his downfall against a contemporary story of a married American woman who had come to Rome in the 1970s, a scholar of temperate habits. While looking for Mahoney's letters and journals, she herself becomes involved in a love affiar with an Italian aristocrat of an obsessive temperament. The two love affairs were juxtaposed through the book, setting up a mounting sexual tension. *The Passion and the Vow* portrayed the way things happen between men and women, only in the book she was much clearer about them than she was in life. Peter's life, she thought, was much clearer than his paintings. Could it be that you really do have to be a little nuts to make art? A little unbalanced by the day? Looking at Peter's canvases, she felt very unsure of herself. She hoped, she prayed, she wasn't painting ponds.

"Thanks so much, Peter." She turned finally from the canvas he was now working on. "I think the range of colors is just fine. I'm going to go outside now and really look at that pond, thanks to you."

"Good." He smiled, relieved.

She was relieved too, having said what she could, having made him smile. Hey, they liked each other, they were old friends.

But then he said, "Are you seeing that guy again?"

"You mean Mario? I have to call him later today."

She didn't like his tone.

Outside, everything was very still. She sat down at the pond's edge and set her empty cup in the long grass. She peered into the pond and tried to imagine the scene through Peter's abstracting eyes, but the pond blurred with thoughts of Mario and the good time she'd had yesterday.

"That guy," Peter called him. She liked that guy. They seemed to understand each other. They seemed to have gone through enough to really appreciate each other. And the way he looked at her! She was supposed to call him after lunch. Should she? Or should she wait at the pond? The same pond. No matter how you color it. The pond outside her window. Should she visit with Judith today? That kiss. Was she in something? In lust? In like? In . . . nah.

At that moment what had sounded like a power lawn mower turned into a roar. She stood up. The studio door opened. Was Judith being woken up as well? She saw the surrounding hills and the billowing clouds and then the motorcycle coming down the winding dirt road that led to the back of the property. She walked toward the road and at the end waved.

"Nice bike," she said as Mario dismounted. She didn't blink an eye. Nola would have been proud of her. She was so cool.

"It's not a nice bike, it's a Harley," he said. "It's Wig's. Want to try it once?"

They just stood there smiling at each other. He hadn't waited for her call, hadn't waited for her to think herself out of him. He was there to get her. She liked that.

She held out her hand. "Come, I want to introduce you to Peter."

He took her hand and they walked over to the studio, where Peter stood. "Peter Steinmartin, Mario Picard," she said. "Peter's a painter. I was just looking at his work."

The men shook hands, but they both looked wary.

"I'm going to go inside for a minute and see if Judith's up. Then Mario and I are going for a ride."

"Will you have lunch with us?" Peter asked. "I know Judith was planning lunch."

"Thank you," Mario said. "Could we make it another time? I wanted to show Elaine around, and then, Elaine, I thought we could see the fireworks from Lake Acres? What do you want to do?"

"That," Elaine said. "I guess, if it's okay, Peter, I'll hang out here tomorrow."

Peter shrugged. "Up to you."

Elaine said, "I'll be right back."

In the house, she went to the bathroom and then got herself ready for the day. Upstairs, Judith's door was closed, but she figured she wasn't asleep. She thought of knocking on the door, but she didn't.

Downstairs, on the bottom of Judith's note, she wrote, "I'm spending the Fourth with Mario. See you tomorrow? XOX, E."

"I can't believe you're being so predictable," Judith said.

It was before noon on Monday, and the two of them were stretched out on a raft on Candlewood Lake. They'd swum to it from the property of Judith's friends the Nelsons.

Elaine had the top of her suit off, but put it on as she sat up. "This lake is something," Elaine said. She was feeling proprietorial about the irregular shoreline, the smell of pines, and the buzz of motorboats. Just last night she and Mario were miles away on the Lake Acres side, watching the colors explode.

"Biggest man-made lake in the East," Judith said. "But you're still predictable."

"So are you. You probably would have signed a petition against making this lake, had you been around in those days."

"And you?"

"Everything changes."

"You sure do!"

"Okay, okay. Let me have it."

"It's just that you're being so predictable. Mario's so different from Larry."

"I've noticed. And I like it. But I'm feeling pretty bad about Larry right now."

"Oh?"

"I don't know, Judith. He's not too well."

"Really?"

"Really. We tried to have dinner together and it ended up in a huge fight. He wanted me to do some collaborating on his work."

"What's wrong? Is it serious?"

"I can't talk, but it is serious. He acted strangely. And, whatever, Nola's not to know. He had no idea I'd seen Nola. And I don't think he liked that one bit."

"Oh."

"I was very upset. Then, the very next day, I hear from Mario. Actually, that night, that very same night, I heard Mario's voice in my dreams."

"Here we go!"

"Hold on, Judith. You don't know him, and maybe you don't know me anymore."

"Touchy."

"Yes and no. Mario's quite wonderful, by the way. Maybe you'll get a chance to know him."

"I bet you're getting to know him!"

"What the hell does that mean? It's your imagination that's predictable, Judith."

"Really?"

"All Mario and I have done is get to know each other, talk."

"You have that much to talk about?"

"Sure."

"Doesn't it bother you?"

"What?"

"That he's not an intellectual. I mean, even Ben—they could have gotten you on the Mann Act for Ben—but didn't he want to write?"

Elaine looked at Judith carefully. "What is it you don't like about Mario?"

"He's just not for you."

"Well, he's not for you. Maybe he is for me. I think you're jealous."

"Jealous?"

"Of me having a man in my life."

"Hey, I hope you have a good time! Maybe, though, it would be nice for you to come up here to spend some time with us."

"Isn't that what I'm doing now? Aren't we having some delightful quality time?"

"Don't be cute! At least you could pick up after yourself!"

"Huh?"

"Like bring your coffee cup back to the kitchen. What am I, your mother?"

Judith pushed her long hair, which was drying in the front, off of her face. She still didn't shave under her arms. Her thighs were thicker and dimpled now, and Elaine could see wisps of pubic hair. She was Elaine's idea of a sensual-looking woman. Though Elaine was blonde, she shaved everything that showed and oiled up afterward. Even feminism couldn't get her to accept superfluous hair, though God knows she would have stayed with her maiden name if it weren't "Bright"!

Judith said, "Lately I begin to feel like everybody's mother."

"Well, you've been a wonderful mother."

"I'm glad at least Easy Rider didn't come before you had a chance to look at Peter's work. I'm sure if he had you would have been out the door."

"You *are* angry I went with Mario yesterday."

"I shouldn't be? You ask to come up for the Fourth. Then you get on the back of a motorcycle and take off? Not to mention you leave one of the best mugs I ever made out in the grass for me to find. David's working at summer camp and Susan's clerking in Washington, and I end up picking up after you."

"I just didn't think this weekend out carefully. He called, and I accepted, and I also wanted to spend time with you. Hell, Judith, no! You're right. I wanted a safe place to stay. I wanted to make sure I wouldn't have to get overinvolved. I wasn't thinking of you or Peter. It was inconsiderate. No wonder you're mad."

"Ah," Judith said expansively, stretching her legs out in front of her and looking at the bulk of her thighs, "every once in a while I see the value of consciousness-raising. Just so you see it, that's all a good mother asks. And how the hell do you keep in such good shape?"

"Flatterer."

"No, I mean it. Where's your flab?"

"I'm sitting on it."

"You call that an ass? You've lost weight since you left Larry, haven't you?"

"I have. Leaving burns calories, that's for sure."

"And your hair's lighter."

"It is."

"And you look younger. Of course, you *are* younger."

"Not that much."

"Enough. Peter doesn't even want me to dye my hair. He likes the gray. Maybe there's an eat-all-you-want divorce diet."

"It's effective, but lacks comfort."

"You think I'm too comfortable?"

"Why are you so touchy, Judith?"

Judith looked out over the lake. "I watch you. You left a husband. You left a good life. Maybe, sometimes, I think of what's passed me by. I mean, my children are all grown up!"

"So is Nola."

"Really, Elaine. It's not the same thing!"

Elaine was quiet.

Judith said, "Sometimes I think I'm still waiting for my life to begin. It's crazy. I love my husband. What would I do? Be like you? Walk out and then find I'm answering ads in the personals!"

"Come on! That was a long time ago. That's when I first left Larry. But I still love reading them. The alphabet land of expectations."

"But you really don't answer them anymore? No more Borrow-A-Husband?"

"No," Elaine said.

"What're you thinking?"

"How wild I felt after I left Larry. I was in the mood for sex."

"Nothing like ordering it from a Sears catalog."

"Well, Judith, I'll tell you the truth. The male-female situation out in the real world is sometimes a bit less than ideal. Sometimes you actually have to figure out for yourself how to get what you're in the mood for. Sometimes Saint Bridegroom is busy with the new crop of damsels and just doesn't whiz by on his white horse.

I figured out what I wanted at the time, and I got it. It was a learning experience. It was okay."

"Good sex?"

"Okay sex. If I had to leave Larry again, I probably could do it making less of a mess."

"That's what you said when you didn't marry Mario One."

"Oh, God. I'm about to marry a Bertone and—"

"He wanted you to iron his shirts."

" 'Elaine, *cara*,' " Elaine clowned, " 'all the women in my family iron their men's shirts.' "

"Come off it!"

"You mean you never believed that? Believe me, when he was drunk, and that was often, he asked for worse. That's so many years ago. Why did you tell Mario he was royalty? We're at Lake Acres, right over there. What a ride! He took me to Kent first, and we looked at the waterfall. My first time on a motorcycle. It was great. It was like floating through the air. Anyway, we're back in Danbury by the water. 'So,' he says, 'we have time now. Tell me how you almost married into the royal family.' He's funny. And I have to go explain how he was a Bertone and how he wasn't really a count, in fact he was a bore, which was hard to digest, and how I would have had to do his shirts. Forever and ever."

"And what did you tell him about Larry?"

"Not much. I told him what I told you. That he might not be too well."

Judith looked at Elaine quizzically, but decided not to press. "What do you know about Mario Two?"

"Mario Picard. Can you cut out this Mario Two stuff?"

"Okay, okay. But, seriously, Elaine, what do you know about this guy?"

"I know he went to college, was in Nam. He made his mistakes, he messed up a marriage. He grew up. Came north. Worked hard. Started another business. Made money."

"Thrilling."

"That's exactly it, Judith. There's something about him that *is* thrilling. He's sort of a loner. Reads a lot. Keeps to himself. An introvert who looks like an extrovert. Sort of like me. We seem to see each other for who we are, without having to ask too many questions."

"Well, he's gorgeous, all right. Why don't you admit you're just horny?"

"When I'm just horny, I take care of myself."

"You're kidding."

"No, I'm not."

"You don't mean a vibrator, do you?"

"It's not the best sex I've had, but it's far from the worst. You can quote me."

"God, a vibrator."

"Come on, Judith. A lot of married women use them."

"With Peter? Are you kidding? I mean, I'm not saying I wouldn't try it. But I sure don't need it. He's the original I'd-rather-do-it-myself man. I mean, he even objects to people doing it on pot! I can't complain. And I'm sure it doesn't compare."

"Well, it's not biodegradable. But I've never met a man yet who blushes about taking care of himself. Why should a woman?"

"Well," Judith said, "you've never met a man like Peter. That's just it. I'm glad you liked his new work. It pleases him. He expected you'd take a look a few weeks ago. I mean, his work is so much better than what's around. He should have a gallery, he really should. He should be in museums! I wish he could cut a break. I wish he'd have a change of luck."

"How would that work? Look, I gotta get out of the sun. But I want an answer." Elaine dived off the raft and then surfaced. She sat on the runged ladder then, half in the water. "I'm waiting," she said, and with her palm hit the side of her head, near her ear.

Judith looked at her intently. "You tell me. You're the lucky one. Your book's going to be published."

"Judith, what a thing to say!" She came up on the raft again, and flicked water at Judith. "Don't you give me the evil eye!"

"God, when I first met you, you were such a kid. You were so quiet. So unsure. You were really poetic. You've changed so much since then."

"In certain ways, of course! It's either that or stand still. I want to hear every new song being sung, especially by girl rockers."

"Oh, I get it. Down with men! Up with the vibrator. I wouldn't be a bit surprised if that's why Peter has such trouble getting a gallery. Too bad he can't be a Guerrilla Girl."

"Don't kid yourself. The big bucks are still with the men. I say, learn from men. I learned a lot from answering a few personals, from going out with a few married men."

"Really? Let me guess. You learned all married men cheat?"

"How do I know? I just realized one day that a lot of men have fairly defined priorities. Then it hit me, just like that, that not all of Larry's Saturday shoots had to do with work. And I realized part of his frustration about my leaving. Why he was so angry. He probably wished he could confront me and say, 'Just look at some of the women I've been in contact with and I never, never let it touch you. Our marriage was more important than any other woman, even the most beautiful women.' But how could he say that to me? It must have made him feel like punching a shadow, that I'd walked out of that marriage. He knew his priorities; no matter what his predilections, I came first. He would never have upset the marriage. Why would I?"

"So you're saying you respect your ex-husband because you've decided he cheated on you."

"I'm saying I understand his priorities. I understand how I fit in. And I've got to remember them, especially now. I can't feel guilt about Larry. I'd better figure out what I really want. I'd better be clear, if I want to get it. And that's a lesson I didn't learn from women. I learned it from married men."

"They could have been ax murderers. You were just lucky."

"Lucky? You've got to be able to see your luck, to grab it as it passes by."

"Well," Judith said, "I hope for Peter's sake his luck is coming. Sometimes I feel so, so sad for him. For me it doesn't matter at all. I can take this world or leave it. And Dylan, by the way, is good enough music for me. Don't you get to a point where you don't want to hear the kids scream? Ah, I get it! Maybe that's 'cause you didn't have your own."

"Sometimes I think I am my own."

Judith smiled. "Sometimes I agree with that. No," she said, continuing her thought, "I've been lucky, I really have. I wish I could give Peter some of my luck."

"No matter how he'd use it?" Elaine asked.

"Oh, he'd use it the right way."

"Oh, you know his right way? Now who's the child?" Elaine asked louder than she meant to, and stood up. "Come on, baby, time to get out of this sun."

"You and your friends have a good visit?"

Mario came over right after work to drive her to the bus stop.

"Yes," she said. "And I enjoyed the weekend. Thanks, Mario."

"Here's the bus."

"New York," she read, from his car.

"When will I see you again?" he asked.

"Soon, I hope."

"Do you want to come up here again next weekend?"

"Why don't we speak during the week?"

He didn't say anything. She continued. "Tomorrow I have lunch with my editor, and then I have to call Nola, and I have to speak with her father too. I'm sitting here having back-to-reality shock."

He took her hand, squeezed it. "Just don't you forget, I'm real too."

"I got to go."

"Wait!" he said, and drew her to him. His lips on hers, the taste of his mouth. It was a hard kiss. Then he let go. First.

SIX

Walking into the Stanford East Hotel, where Elaine was to meet Anne Gregory, was for Elaine an immediate out-of-body experience. The decor was more than disorienting, it was dizzying, especially when one was drifting in from a long weekend and sun. The glass-and-chrome elevator that rose from the middle of the lobby glimmered. There was a long line of waterfalls, around them large tropical trees and spreading vegetation. The jungle greenery sent up a musky odor that the air conditioning couldn't control, any more than it could the humidity in the air. The lobby was a miniature rain forest boasting carpeting as thick and as tangled as luxuriant undergrowth.

Elaine tried to focus on why she was there, which was to discuss the plans for her book. One thing for sure, she thought, trailing her way to the Plushe Roome, Anne Gregory was treating her to another expensive lunch at another exotic locale. The tab was bottom line that her publisher valued her.

Anne Gregory was already seated at a choice banquette from which she could see the entrance. She was a very attractive woman, about forty-five, and had the soft, unblemished complexion of the very young or the very rich. Her big round brown eyes shone with a mischief she was too old for. It might have been WASP breeding. A sense that she was at a very nice party with all the right people. If she wanted to, why not kick up her heels? She had an oval face, a small nose, and slender, delicate hands on which she wore beautiful rings, glittering jewels, a danger in New York. She wore her wealth smartly, simply, on her back, around her neck, on her arms. Why not? She was dazzling. Brought into Panther Publishers as a senior editor, she had just been made editor in chief, not without demanding a big raise, a five-year contract, a completely redone office, and an unlimited expense account. This was an old, conservative publishing house that not only reeled under the demand but was titillated by it. In Anne Gregory's high tone, child's voice, and need for luxury, the company saw new profits.

A lot was expected from Anne Gregory's image. Because her way had always been to stay one step behind the important male, letting him take the credit for her talents, few people realized how brilliant she really was. She had been a shy child, and a very shy young woman. She had, as Elaine's father would have phrased it, buried herself in books. She understood the world through words. And these words she knew how to spell, to punctuate, to construe correctly. There was no way she could live with making mistakes in front of others.

As an editor, Anne had great skill. She could intuit the direction an author should be taking, she could help an author refine his ideas. Any book under her auspices read better for her editing, her precise criticisms and excellent suggestions. She knew a lot of celebrities, and since she had that selfless person's quality of entering the skins of others, she suggested book ideas that often hit the mark, making lots of money. Now her talents with words and ideas and other people's sensibilities had caused her to be promoted to an administrative job. The world had lifted her to an exposed position.

"You look very good," she said to Elaine, who had awkwardly maneuvered herself through the small passageway between the tables, staying too close behind the maître d', who now almost bumped into her as he pushed the table out so that she could slide onto the banquette next to Anne.

"So do you."

"You always look so confident; I admire that."

"It must be the way my pocketbook got caught on that chair at the second table, and how I hit the guy on the next chair with it when I extricated myself."

"You carry it off," said Anne, who would have died of embarrassment if she hadn't been able to pace herself more cleverly.

"Anne, what else can I do? Isn't it good manners to walk out of your underpants when they drop, straighten your shoulders, and march on? Especially at a colonial watering stop in the middle of a jungle."

"See what I mean? I couldn't have carried that off. Would you care for a drink?"

Elaine ordered a glass of wine and Anne ordered another.

"I have a nice surprise for you," Anne said. "Take a look at these."

She handed Elaine a manila envelope. "The photos?"

"Yes. These are the five shots Publicity thought the best. It's just a matter of picking one for the jacket."

Elaine opened the envelope and looked at the shots one after another. Larry's work. He was so damned good. He made her look good. Part of his popular success was due to the airbrush. She did not object.

She chose three of the five, spread them in front of her, and then eliminated another one. She looked again. "I bet you I'm picking the one you picked," she said to Anne. "You know, it brings back memories. I met Larry when he took my picture. 'Brother, Can You Spare a Job?' Yes, that was how we met."

"I know."

"You do?"

There was an unselfconscious element to Elaine, particularly after a long weekend in the country. Perhaps it was a danger to her that she was surprised someone would know anything about her that she hadn't told herself.

"Larry's a great photographer," she said now, "so professional. I didn't think these would come out too well."

She looked at the close-up, head and shoulders. She looked at herself looking out at the viewer, intelligently, pensively. There was a smile on her face that seemed to be related to her feelings. It probably was during the last roll of film he had shot, when he had called out, "Got it!" And Elaine realized that's what makes a photographer. He knows what he sees when he sees it.

She handed the photo to Anne, who looked at it and said, "This one?"

"Certainly, Anne. It's the best one, don't you think so?"

Anne took back the other photos as the waiter brought the drinks. "Well, actually," she said, "I'm partial to *this* one. This is you. It's so . . . it's so confident."

Elaine looked at the photo, surprised. It was one she had eliminated immediately. There was no smile, and her jaw was too pronounced. "This one looks like I never get laid."

Anne looked at her strangely for a moment. Her cheeks colored. "Reid liked this one too," she said out of nowhere.

Elaine made sure she kept her mouth shut.

"Why, to me," Anne continued after a pause, "this photo is brilliant. It's you."

Elaine looked at it. She really didn't need the wine, she felt hazy enough. "Is it me?" she asked, confused by the way Anne saw it. Then she thought, Anne knows the book business. She knows what she's doing. Except what the hell does Reid have to do with it? Should this one be on the cover? Will this one sell the book? "Can I have back the one I picked?"

She looked at the two of them. Could she live with Anne's

choice? Should she? She kept looking at them, trying to convince herself her own choice wasn't the better. Should she consult her agent?

"Well?" Anne asked.

"It is my choice, right? I can have the one I want?"

"It is your choice."

She took another sip of her wine. "I hope I'm not making a mistake, Anne. But, honestly, I can't live with this one. I thought it was always better to have an author's picture with a smile. A connection with the reader. I mean, that's what Larry says." Larry? She was bringing in Larry, Anne was bringing in Reid. Great.

"It seems to me, without the smile the confidence radiates. The whole look goes beyond connection."

"Hey, Anne. I don't want to go beyond connection. I really don't. You know how much I respect your opinion, but this is the one I can live with. Not only is it me, but to my eyes it's state-of-the-art Larry Netherlands. I'll tell you, it beats looking in the mirror. I have to have this one." It was her turn to pause for a moment. "Can I be assured?"

"Just sign it, and we'll use it." Anne was finishing her second drink. "After all, it's only a picture."

"I thought one was worth a million words."

"Not in our business."

Elaine said, "I'm not totally convinced."

They both ordered lobster salads; the food was excellent at the Plushe Roome. Not at all overdone like the decor.

"I'll be going away for the summer," Anne Gregory said, as the meal progressed. "I'll be handling things from Vermont. Anything you need, just speak to Donna, and she'll know how to reach me."

"Can I get you by phone?"

"Reid's coming with me—and Cynthia too. He needs solitude, quiet, and—the way it looks—me. He always says I'd live like a hermit if he let me. It turns out, when he needs to live like a hermit, he needs me. So I don't overuse the phone."

"Who's Cynthia?"

"You mean, I haven't mentioned Cynthia to you? Is it that I simply imagine that I tell you everything? She's charming, absolutely charming. So young, so fresh. She's a boost to Reid, and, in a different way, to me. Of course she is older than your Nola, but in a way she's like the daughter I never had."

"Nola's my stepdaughter. Which often makes me the wicked old witch. We're back talking with each other, but, believe me, when we had breakfast—"

"Tell me something, Elaine. You're a sophisticated woman, you understand the world."

"Why, thank you."

"Don't you think life has a myriad of ways of working out? I had such simple ideas as a schoolgirl, and now it's so different. That's my objection to women's lib. It's so simple. Can you imagine, some women have the nerve to say to me, How can you live with that girl in your house? I tell them it was my idea that she move in for a while. They simply do not understand, and, worse, they think they have a right to try to save me from my own life. Why, since I had the idea of Cynthia's moving in— and, God knows, she has her own floor and her own privacy, if there's one thing we've plenty of it's room—I get to see more of Reid. And I adore Cynthia's parents; we had Easter together. This was my idea, you see. We create our own lives nowadays; you say that in your book. I consider that I'm living creatively."

"Well, it certainly looks like you are. For me, it would be very painful. If I had a lover, I'd be reluctant to—"

"Lovers are lovers, Elaine. I'm not talking about a lover. I'm talking about a husband. I'm talking about a marriage that lasts. It takes creativity to enhance a long relationship. The one thing about lovers is that they always change. God knows, I've seen that for years."

"It's called 'serial monogamy.' I mean, usually. Well, for me, it might be unimaginative, but it's the best I've found. I'd like something to last, sure. Who wouldn't?"

"And I'm accomplishing that. Maybe it's I who should write a book!" After a pause she said, "No, I don't mean that. I don't have what you and Reid have."

"What do we have?"

"Talent."

"Anne. You're a brilliant editor—look how you've helped me with my book. You're beautiful, you're healthy, you're rich. You've just been promoted! Take a good long look at what you have. Grab on to it. I'm interested in Anne Gregory. It's you who bring up Reid. But, believe me—I think I can speak for all your authors—we don't think of you as Reid Gregory's wife. Because we need you and adore you as Anne."

"Oh, Elaine. You always make me feel so . . . so privileged. I'm privileged knowing you, working with you."

"Thank you, Anne."

"Ah, I'm just curious, but I said before, I think of you as a sophisticated woman, and not one of those let's-just-hear-it-for-us-poor-women. So I'm sure you understand."

"Understand? Anne, it's your life, and to me you're deserving of the best. But, strangely enough, since you've asked, the only times—twice—that I've seen what you've described . . ."

"What happened?"

"Well, the Cynthias have been decoys; the husbands have been gay."

"Gay? Reid's not gay."

"I didn't say he was. But you asked me my experience. That's what I've seen. Everyone's life is different, no? Experience isn't an even thing."

Anne's face was flushed. She reached in the gold case for the after-lunch cigarette that she allowed herself. "Do you mind?"

"Mind? I'm tempted to join you."

The waiter came over as if on call. "Espresso for both of us—right, Elaine? And no dessert. Ah," she said, taking her first puff. "We still have a bit of time. Tell me, is there a new man in your life? Donna said you were a bit mysterious about your weekend."

Elaine decided to ignore Anne's tone. "Well, I did have fun this weekend."

"Fun?"

"Exactly. For me too, it's sort of a new concept. If you've been born a perfect little lady"—damn, why did she say that?—"it takes you a while to find the kid. But fun's fun," she said, trying to get off the subject fast. "Since we have a little time, tell me, has my book been presented at sales conference yet?"

"Not yet."

"No? Do you have the presentation planned? And do you know how many books you'll print? I was hoping the book would come out in spring. It has a lot of spring in it, don't you think?"

"I think it has a lot of everything; it's simply a fine, fine work. We haven't scheduled it yet. There's no particular season for *The Passion and the Vow*. It goes beyond category. But I'm making a mental note."

"Is that a good thing? I mean not having a category. What peg are you going to hang it on at sales conference? What angle will the salesmen use to sell it?"

"Angle?" Anne smiled. "Believe me, Elaine. You do not have to think about things like that. That's where I come in, that's where the company comes in. Leave these considerations to us."

"Of course. I know you know what you're doing, and I certainly don't want to butt in—"

"But you're nervous and don't know what to do with yourself," Anne supplied. "Believe me, I understand. And I don't want you worrying about these things. These are my concerns and the company's. You have only one thing to think about."

"What?"

"Why, your next book, dear. Everything else will take care of itself. Trust me. All you have to do this summer is write."

"I'm glad you liked them," Larry said over the phone. "I was happy to do them for you. And call Joyce. Tell her to follow up on the publishing schedule. Don't trust anyone's mental notes."

"That's just what I thought I'd do." Elaine was stretched out on her futon, her head propped up on pillows, twisting the cord of the phone as she spoke. The photos had given her a contact point with him. "And you say you're feeling better?"

"Hate to admit it, but the treatments seem to have worked."

"Hate to admit it?"

"Just a figure of speech."

"Oh, really."

"Please, Elaine, don't play shrink with me. I know what I mean."

"I'm sure you do. Did you see Nola over the Fourth?"

"No. Why?"

"I thought she might visit."

"I thought she might, as well."

"Larry, don't get down on her. Remember, she doesn't know what's going on."

"Don't get me started, Elaine."

"I want you to know I'm going to call her tomorrow. I'm going to take a look at that van Second Hand wants to buy."

"You mean that she wants you to buy."

"That's right. She wants me to lend her the money. There's something I didn't emphasize when we met, Larry. Or perhaps, if I hadn't had to run out of the restaurant, I might have."

"You didn't have to run. You exaggerate. It's your middle name. Exaggerate, exaggerate. Turn everything into a scene. It must be the writer in you."

"I'm sure. When I think of it, I shouldn't even be calling you. I must be dumb, really dumb. If we were normal in any way, you'd owe me an apology."

"Yeah, right."

"But what I want to tell you, Larry, is that Nola has talent. It's an important fact. She's really good. In my opinion, her lyrics are dynamite, and on stage, on stage, she has it. Charisma."

"I thought that went out with the Kennedys."

"We're not talking Camelot, Larry, we're talking rock and roll." He laughed.

She continued. "I was thinking this over. I mean, you're in the arts; what would you expect from your daughter? She comes by it naturally."

"Rock and roll, art? Oh, I see what you mean. If she has a van, and things don't work well, she'll have a place to sell tie-dye. I want her to finish school."

"So do I. But from what I gather from Silas Mourner—"

"Silas Mourner?"

"Don't you know, he's Jimmy's upstairs neighbor? Wait a minute, Larry—how often have you seen Nola since she moved out?"

"I walked up there once. Long time since I've seen a bathtub in the kitchen. None of her furniture fits. I still have a roomful of it."

"I heard you saw the bathtub. Did you see Jimmy?"

"Who?" he said, and laughed.

"Her boyfriend," Elaine said sternly.

He said, "I know. He told me he was a finance major, remember?"

"You know, I'm really surprised. This is just dawning on me. It's not right that you need an intermediary to tell you about your daughter. Silas tells me Nola feels very strongly about this tour. He's hooked Second Hand up with a manager. What I started to say is that of course it would be great if she finished school first, but that's not what she's going to do. What I think you should know is that in my opinion she's very, very good. For what my opinion is worth, she might be at the beginning of a career. And she's going to do what she has to do. And if she doesn't have a good van to go to California in, the group might buy a piece of junk like the van Multiple Monotony has, which couldn't even get them to New York."

"Multiple Monotony?"

"The Boston group. Second Hand took over for them at

CBGB. They had an old van, it stalled on the highway. Someone bumped into them. They got out okay, but they couldn't play."

"An old van? An accident? You're a sucker, Elaine, a real sucker."

"Better a sucker than a prick."

"What did you say?"

"Hey, I'm sorry, Larry. I thought I was thinking. I didn't mean to say that out loud."

"Funny as ever."

"I just want you to know— Look, Larry. Maybe Nola hasn't had the easiest time? I mean, you yourself know Delilah. And, God knows, when we were together she was just a kid. You know how kids see things. When has she really asked either of us for anything?"

"What about the leather jacket? Oh, that's right, that was your idea."

"But this isn't, Larry! Nola came to me. She asked me for support. She's come back into my life. I stayed out, you know that. But now, Larry, I don't have it in me to turn her away."

"Translation: you mean if you don't say yes to her you won't hear from her for another three years."

"That's cruel, Larry. She's asking both of us for what she really wants. I'm at least going to listen. I want to take a look at that van. She's asking for some confirmation that we hear her. I think it's much more than the three thousand dollars. It's Nola spreading her wings. I'd like to have a relationship with her, Larry. I'm not going to throw this opportunity away. I have to call her about the van, but, because of your objections, I really don't know what to say."

"Hold off. I'll call. I'll speak to her first. Don't do a damn thing till I speak with her!"

"If that's a threat, I accept."

He laughed. "Same as ever, Elaine. Always your way."

"You sound sad," Mario said over the phone.

"Timing, my friend," she said. "I just got off from my ex-husband. He thinks I always get my way."

"I bet!" Mario laughed.

"What is this, male bonding?"

"It's just funny. How's he feeling?"

"I keep wondering if perhaps he's mental, rather than physical. Oh, that sounds awful."

"I like when you're awful."

"I begin to think you're prejudiced."

"I sure am, girl. Listen, I was wondering how your lunch went."

"That's so nice of you. It went well. There's no date set for publication, but Anne just wanted to talk and talk. I picked a photo that my ex-husband did. He's a photographer, you know. Anyway, I wish I looked as good as his picture. I've got to think the lunch over. Tomorrow I'll call my agent and talk things over with her. All in all, things are fine here. Oh, I've been ordered to write another book."

"You going to?"

"I'm at the thinking stage. I'll talk to Joyce about that too. Enough of me. How's work going?"

"Really busy. Making up for that long weekend. I have a suggestion, Elaine. Would you be free Sunday?"

"I think so."

"You do, do you? I thought you might show a stranger the town. Easy enough for me to come in for the day."

"That's a great idea! What about a New York brunch?"

"Sounds good to me."

"All right. I know just the place. I'll arrange it and call you back. Okay?"

"Fine," he said. "I miss you. Don't answer."

She laughed instead. "I'll call you soon. Bye."

• • •

Her thought was of her friend Vicky, who owned The Original Dish. They had gone to St. Agnes's together, and had been the best of friends. And both of them had left Jersey after high school. That's what they called their hometown, "Jersey." The Jersey right across the Hudson River on the New Yorker's map of the world.

"But it's changing. Jersey's gentrifying now. Painters live there," Elaine would say.

"Yeah," Vicky would say with her I've-seen-everything-twice-and-wake-me-when-it's-over look. "And watch, once they gentrify that dump, the wiseguys will play godfather with the property taxes."

Elaine thought it was great, just great, that her old school friend had been ground floor on nouvelle cuisine, and Vicky thought it was great that Elaine had written a book. "Believe me, I could write one too," Vicky said, "if I had the time."

The Original Dish had a famous Sunday brunch.

"Here we go again," Vicky said over the phone. "You met him in Danbury? What the hell were you doing there?"

"Trying to get to New Milford, to see Judith and Peter. They're making a shopping mall out of the Danbury Fair, and when I didn't see the statues I lost my way."

"That makes perfect sense."

"Oh well, it's a long story."

"And you're going slow with him?"

"Exactly. I don't want to rush into anything."

"Well, that does make sense, especially now. I want to meet this guy."

"So, can you fit us in?"

"For you, anything. What time?"

"Unfashionably early."

"Great. How about noon?"

"Perfect."

"Not that it's that jammed anymore."

"Well, it's summer."

"I don't know," Vicky said. "The *Times* is killing us. *New York* magazine too."

"Come on. They always give you rave reviews."

"Yeah, but they're writing this stuff about it being fashionable to make a meatloaf and baked potatoes and inviting friends over to eat it. It's something called 'dinner at home.' Couch-potato cuisine. 'It bodes ill,' as Sister Dolores God used to put it."

"Don't forget, 'This too shall pass.' "

"Yeah, it will. Even though she was just reading it off Our Father's invisible teleprompter, I'm beginning to see that that one makes some sense."

"I look forward to Sunday. You'll like Mario."

"Looks like you're beginning to collect them. The Mario Collection, by Elaine."

"And for one moment I thought you were going to rise above the obvious."

"I think for one moment we did."

Did she mean with The Original Dish? Did she mean with her last shattered love affair? Either Vicky was addicted to crisis or Sister Dolores God was vengeful and had taken out a celestial contract on Vicky's peace of mind. Since high school her life had been a series of crises. She was always rescuing someone from something, always generous to a fault.

"Oh? What's wrong?"

"Another time, babe. It's nuts here, gotta go."

"You'll make it! You always do. See you Sunday, Vicky. Thanks."

Elaine walked past the cast-iron buildings south of Houston Street on her way to meet Mario. It was before noon, so the Sunday promenade of fashionable shoppers hadn't begun. The galleries and the stores were closed, and the streets themselves looked sleepy. Mario wouldn't be in yet, but, rather than browse, she decided to cut her walk short and go over to see Vicky.

The Original Dish, just on the edge of Little Italy, on a corner, had its bright red-and-white awning up. It wasn't the monumental SoHo style; it had the intimate appeal of Little Italy. She looked into the restaurant, whose front window and door resembled an old-fashioned storefront. Vicky was sitting at the shiny, completely contemporary bar. She saw Elaine and waved. Mario, who'd been talking with her, turned to the door. By the time Elaine entered, he was there to meet her. He was handsome in his European-cut slacks, his sport shirt open at the neck.

"Hello," he said. He put his arm around her, and after the briefest pause, kissed her cheek.

"Hello yourself. You're here early."

"So are you."

Vicky sat for a minute, watching them. Vicky was short and slightly stocky. She wore her ubiquitous jeans and Mickey Mouse T-shirt. She had short brown hair and beautiful big brown eyes.

Four well-dressed people had followed Elaine in. Vicky was not amused. She lowered her eyes, which at times could be as wide as Liza Minnelli's, and at others as world-weary as Judy Garland's. There was something about Vicky that had that mother-daughter look. "We're not open yet."

They stood there. "Cody," the older man said. "We have a reservation."

Vicky looked down the clipboard on the bar. "I have you. Twenty minutes. Wait outside?" They were perfumed and obedient. After they walked out, Vicky got up and locked the door. A line was forming behind the Codys.

Elaine noticed the Codys looked happy. "There's something about a New Yorker that loves a line," she said.

"And we're not talking coke anymore, anymore," Vicky answered. "We're talking long straight lines. Otherwise, you're out of business. Even the rich aren't happy about the clubs they can get into. Let's get you out of harm's way. Right now they're just impressed by how important you must be, but they can turn." Vicky said, "Come on," and brought them back to the restaurant.

This small room was full of light. The chairs and tables and tablecloths were white. Fresh flowers on each table. She sat them by the window. There was a bottle of champagne, in a bucket of ice. Vicky put her vodka down on the table and took the towel by the side of the bucket. "Let's have a toast!" She opened the champagne, filled their glasses, and put a drop in her drink. "To a happy day in New York." They clicked glasses and drank to that. "And to you, Vicky. Thanks," Elaine proposed, and they clicked again. "I'll try to stop by later," Vicky said. "Joe's going to wait on you. He's backstage in the kitchen practicing his Italian. He loves *Tosca*. He can't wait to try, Mario, Mario, Mario," Vicky sang, imitating Callas, as she walked away.

"That's what they did to us back at St. Agnes High," Elaine explained.

Mario asked dryly, "Does she mean there's yet a third Mario?"

"Groan. Of course not."

"*Cara,*" Joe proclaimed, sweeping in with a basket of breads. He was tall, and getting plump, another one of Manhattan's waiters for a show-biz break.

"*Caro!*" Elaine answered.

"*E questo è Mario? Madonnnnna!*"

"Joe says he likes you," Elaine said as he left.

"I figured that without Italian."

"So you didn't speak Italian at home?"

"Italian?"

" 'Mario'?"

" 'Mario' is a good French-Canadian name."

"Really?"

"It sure is. I'm a quarter French Canadian, a quarter Indian, and half Brit. You thought I was Italian Two?"

"I did." She didn't get the pun.

"What about you?"

"My mother's side was Czech and my father's side was Italian and Irish. And me, I'm light, so everyone thinks I take after the Czech side, but I take after my Italian grandmother. We're an odd mixture, aren't we?"

"No chance of being royalty."

"Bread?" she asked. "Better have some. It might be a while. What did you and Vicky talk about?"

"You mean, what did she grill me about?"

"What do you mean?"

"I think I had to pass some sort of New York test. Then we talked boats."

"You seem annoyed. Are you?"

"No, just observant." Mario looked around him, in a half-detached, half-amused way, as people began to stream in. "It's just meeting the family."

"Well, I certainly didn't think of that aspect. In fact, I planned to be here before you." She must be in a tough spot, because she was almost lying.

"Why?"

"Well, ah, just to be here."

"To help me pass the test? I'm pretty good at tests, Elaine. I did real well in school."

"Why are you angry?"

"Because you're fighting me. I could have met you at your place. And because, well, damn"—and he couldn't help smiling—"she called me a visiting fireman."

"Oh, God!"

"I said I was looking for you. 'Oh, you must be the visiting fireman!' "

"What did you say?"

"I said, no, I was Mario Two."

Elaine laughed. "Sorry," she said, "but you're right, you're good at tests."

"I better be. After all, I'm not Larry Netherlands. In fact, I had about ten seconds to figure out that he was *the* Larry Netherlands. Why didn't you tell me?"

"Is it important?"

"At Kent Falls you had a lot to say about the subconscious. Maybe it's important that you didn't tell me."

"Hey, you should have been a shrink."

"There were a lot of things I should have been. I think how I'm not so far away from forty and I've never really figured out what I want to be when I grow up. I envy you that. You write, you teach, and you know what you want. Larry's the same way, right?"

"Larry—"

"Let's drop it!" Mario said. "It's okay. Vicky just got to me, that's all. But she's okay. She has guts. I— Damn, don't look now, but Joe's heading our way."

Joe was in fact dashing over as if he'd just remembered he was a waiter serving brunch.

"Giuseppe, you've returned," Mario said.

"Ma sicuro," Joe said with a flourish.

Elaine smiled. "And you said you didn't speak Italian."

"I'm modest. Actually, I pick up on language real good."

"It's nice to be outside," Mario said as they walked along the water's edge at Battery Park. There were people promenading on the walkway all around them; the sun was dissolving their faces into patches of light and painting them into superbright clothing.

"I guess brunch wasn't my best idea."

"It was all right. I'm actually glad I met Vicky. I held off on telling her I have a daughter with the same name."

"Hey, that's right. Victoria."

"Got a letter from her this week. I'm telling you, that girl really enjoys writing. I should have brought it. You'd like her letter."

"My stepdaughter's seeing—or at least talking to—her father this weekend. We have a date next week. Maybe he'll stop fighting her about that van."

"Maybe he's just afraid of spoiling her."

"Denial spoils."

He was quiet for a while.

"Is that the ferry?" he said, pointing out over New York Bay.

"Yes. Want to do it? I think it's the best bargain in New York. Come to think of it, it could be the most tourist pleasure you can get anywhere in the world for a quarter. Round trip."

"Sounds like a good investment."

"You know, I was thinking of investments this morning, walking through SoHo; that's the whole area of art galleries south of Houston—"

"Houston?" He repeated her pronunciation.

"Right, it's pronounced like House, not like Texas. It's to let the cab drivers know who they can take. . . ."

They stood on the ferry, at the rail. He had his arm around her. There were many people pressing. The water sparkled and the skyscrapers on the narrow point of the island were gathered together like friends waiting for them to return.

They watched the skyline and then the widening of the bay. They saw the cleaned and beaconing Statue of Liberty, clear as a bell.

Mario said, "Beautiful lady."

She looked at him. His profile. The long straight nose under the head of hair. The strong chin. His eyes were focused and his handsome head was strong and powerful in the sun.

Women looked at him. She saw them do that on their walk to the ferry. She was more comfortable with the relaxed way he looked back than she had been with Ben Gary. Ben was a tit man, so, when the New York girls took off their bras and dressed for summer, the more he looked the more he starved. Tit torture. Her husband, Larry, had been the exact opposite. She couldn't read his eyes, and most often she wasn't sure that he was looking. She only sensed strain.

Mario was not starved, and he was not obsessed.

Elaine watched him watch the statue. "I'm surprised she doesn't look back at you."

"Heart of brass," he said, and kept looking.

•   •   •

In the late afternoon they found a parking space outside of Elaine's apartment complex.

"This is why I thought it better to meet at The Original Dish," Elaine said as she led him into the grounds. "It's difficult to find your way to the right building your first time here."

"Right." he said.

The anonymity of the tall brick buildings in this large complex was softened by the interior landscaping. Buildings were shaded by leafy trees. As they wended around the playgrounds, the squash courts, and walked on quaint cobblestoned paths, Elaine told Mario the history of the complex. It had been built originally for World War II veterans returning to a city desperate for new housing. The troups returned, the houses were built, and the babies boomed. Then the trees grew, the babies grew, and the complex weathered well.

"The thing about this place," Elaine said, "is that it's been kept up. Thou shalt obey the rules. Thou shalt not use the roof or sun on the lawn or play thy TV loudly, or have pets, or open thy front door to strangers. They don't even have cockroaches here—not that I'm complaining. Or else the cockroaches have such good manners that their parents teach them only to appear when people are fast asleep."

Mario smiled. "Well, it looks safe enough, which is no small thing in the city."

"This is no place for rebels. Sometimes I think it could use a shaking up. But the rent's so reasonable that I can't even think of giving a loud party! I feel ambiguous about this place. Sometimes I feel like a wild person in disguise. An invisible Steppenwolf."

"Yeah," Mario said. "I can imagine they wouldn't want any rock bands."

"Well, that's for sure."

"Oh," he said, embarrassed, "you meant the book. Hesse."

"That too."

He was quiet.

· · ·

"Here we are!" He walked into the living room, and she closed the door behind him.

"Nice room," he said. He went over to the print of Mickey Mouse. "Why," he said, "this reminds me of home."

"Disneyland East."

"Hey." He looked closer. "Andy Warhol."

"See these?" She pointed to four small silkscreens of break-dancers in Day-Glo colors, dancing on waves. "Keith Haring. You can buy these at the Pop Shop for a song. Art for the people—isn't it great?"

He went over to look at them.

"Do you like them?" she asked.

"Sure do."

"Want to see my view?" They walked over to the window. "See, I look right down over the trees and the playground. I enjoy hearing the kids when I work. I like it here."

"So do I," Mario said. "I'd like to go to that Modern Art Museum with you. I bet that would be fun."

"MoMA?" She looked at her watch.

"Not today!"

"Honest, Mario, I didn't mean today. Want a drink?"

"With pleasure."

They sat on her Italian grandmother's couch. He had a beer and she had some wine. She almost put on Prince, but decided on Joe Jackson. They smoked a joint.

"Another beer?" she asked.

"Not now, thanks. I was wondering, would it be possible to wash up?"

"Oh, of course. I'll get you a clean towel. Hey, do you want to take a shower? You're welcome to, you know. I wouldn't mind one myself."

"Great," he said.

She turned from the hall closet with the clean towels. "Here, you can use this bath. I'll use the one off my room."

"And I bet we don't have to worry about hot water."

"Just getting into it," she said. She wished she hadn't.

In her bedroom, she stripped. Spread her arms. Watched her wrists and her fingers. Then she turned the radio on to K-rock, but not too loud. She hadn't lost sight of thin walls and civic responsibility as she floated. Time circled round itself. Good pot. She turned down the fluffy top sheet on her futon, then went to the bathroom and decided on a bubble bath. Lilac. She danced to the music as the tub filled, then turned off the faucet and got into her bath.

He was in the living room when she came out, going through her Sunday paper. He was bare-chested, sitting there in his slacks. Not a speck of flab. His hair was curly, dark, and wet.

He looked up at her, in her cotton T, shorts, clogs. "You really are beautiful," he said.

"Let me get you a drink."

"A soft drink, if you got one. I'm taking it easy."

"Okay."

She brought back two sodas and sat down.

They both drank. Didn't talk. "We need music," she said, but he took her hand to stay her.

"Don't I hear music?"

She nodded.

"Elaine," he said, "do you want to go listen to it in your room?"

She was quiet.

He stood up. "Good." He took her hand. "Come on."

"Looks stupid," he said, putting his hand on his erection. "Women are beautiful, men—poof." He stretched toward her on the bed.

She still had on her T-shirt. "We have a difference of opinion," she said, putting her hands on his. "I don't think it looks stupid at all."

"I love you," he said.

"I think I love you too," she answered. She was looking at the darkness of his pubic hair, his big aroused penis, the tight muscles of his thighs.

"Think?"

She was quiet.

"Well," he said, embracing her once more, "I guess that will have to do for now." He kissed her slowly, intently, and then he reached under her shirt. She felt his big hands on her breasts. He pulled her T up so that he could taste her nipples, with his lips, tongue, his teeth. Then he pulled her shirt up over her head, but didn't take it off, leaving her arms entwined in it. He went back to her breasts, her nipples. In this state of soft bondage, her nipples hardened and she relaxed, allowing herself every sensation. He went down on her, taking off her lacy, navy-blue bikini, spreading her legs, and finding her softness with his tongue.

She thought of the condoms she had placed in easy reach—if her hands were free. For a second rationality returned and she wondered about loosening herself and going for them. His tongue was teasing her, enticing her, his beautiful head between her legs. She felt the T-shirt twisted around her wrists. She moved under him and groaned. "Are you ready?" he whispered, extricating himself from in between her legs and, at that same time, putting his hand to where his fluids and hers mixed.

She was ready.

He was above her. Spreading her legs once more, he entered her, he plunged. She could feel the swollen ridge of his penis, and he, in control, plunged again and again, still in control, feeling her response. He grew conscious of wanting to hold on, having to hold on, needing to give her more and more. She grew conscious of wanting to hold on too. He plunged deeper and deeper, feeling her wetter and wetter, but, wet as she was getting, she didn't come. He plunged so deep that he missed a beat and slipped out. "Damn!"

"Oh." She smiled, eyes closed. She extricated herself from her T-shirt, took his slippery penis, and directed him back in. She peeked at him. His head was thrust back. His eyes were closed, his dark expressive face immobile, masklike, in transport. She closed her eyes. He opened his. He watched the thrust of his groin dispassionately, put his hand flat and strong and determined on her soft belly. Moaned once to her crescendo of short cries.

"Come," she whispered.

"Not yet."

Something in each of them, beyond reason and consciousness and love, demanded to hold on to a shred of self, wanted the other to surrender first. The battle of the sexes; the field, bed.

Then it changed. Suddenly they were holding out, not in defiance, but for the growing extremity of their own pleasure. He was claiming his pleasure; she hers. And it came to each of them, wave after wave, insisting on itself. He thrust again and again, and she saw behind her eyes all the darting colors of a flower unraveling. She opened to him, every boundary past. He was no longer Mario, nor she Elaine. She unfolded, and he, feeling this, went beyond himself, thrusting into the sensation to which she was now fully opened.

They came together. They felt the wetness unite them, smelled the muskiness of their sex rising from their thighs. They drifted off simultaneously, floated past their satisfaction into dreams.

He woke up first, erect, and excited her. They made love again. Afterward, "What are you thinking?" he asked raspily.

"How good I feel. I feel I could put it all together. Everything."

"If you could put it all together, what would you do with it? Can you hold it in your hands?"

He cupped his big hands in front of him close enough for both of them to see. They smelled of them.

She moved down against him, snuggling her face in his chest. He put an arm around her.

"Mmmmmm. Mario?"

"Yes?"

"I'm a little worried."

"About what?"

"Condoms."

"Condoms?"

"AIDS."

"AIDS? We don't have AIDS."

"It's a crazy world."

"I'm all right."

"So am I," she said, "as far as I know. But anything can happen."

"We have to start somewhere."

"Trust each other?" she asked. "Trust our luck?"

"Yes. Don't you see? We're having luck—it means something."

"Lovers' luck?" she asked.

"We're having it, Elaine."

"All right!"

He stroked her hair, her cheek. "All right," he repeated. "I'm going to turn that radio off for you; then I guess I'd better get going."

"You're welcome to stay."

"Am I, now?" He traced the line of her side. "I've got to go very early; I'd wake you."

"Promise?"

"Then I'd better set the alarm even earlier. Where is it?"

"Over there. And just turn the music lower," she murmured, turning. "It's nice."

He kissed her shoulder. She was almost asleep. He waited till she was. Then he was alone in the night, glad to get up to adjust the clock and the radio, to have something to do.

SEVEN

The following Saturday night, Mario stood in Elaine's doorway. He was smiling. He handed her a button. "This is for you. I found it in Wig's glove compartment." It was the old slogan for Quebec autonomy: *Oui, à la prochaine.* Mario said, " 'Yes to the next time.' I thought that fit us too."

She looked at the blue-and-white button in her hand. "But you're so late, Mario. I was just about ready to give up on you. Well, come on in." It was ten-thirty; she'd expected him at nine.

"I wanted to grab a ride with Wig. I thought of taking my pickup truck, but, even though Wig's always late, I waited on him. You're not mad, are you?"

"Oh, no. I'm just glad you're here," she said matter-of-factly.

"I thought about you all week," he said to her.

They were standing very close to each other now, looking in each other's eyes. She put her arms on his shoulders, lightly. "I could hardly work," he said. "You were in front of my eyes.

"This is what I thought of all week," he said, and he kissed her.

She wanted it to go on and on. It was he who pulled away, put her at arm's length, looked at her again, smiled.

"Do you want something to drink?" she asked, flustered.

When she came back to the living room with the wine and two glasses, he was sitting on the couch, going through her *Village Voice*. "Have you been to The Ritz?" he asked.

"Oh sure. A few months ago I saw Marianne Faithfull there."

"I've never been. They're doing reggae tonight. I don't know the groups, except Yellowman. Do you like reggae?"

"Actually, I love reggae."

"So, do you want to go to The Ritz tonight? Party reggae?"

She didn't answer.

"Let me take you. Come on, what do you say?"

She wanted to say, Let's just stay here and make love. She said, "Are you sure?"

"It would be a pleasure to take you." She was sitting on the couch now, looking at the paper too. They kissed again. "Come on," he said finally. "Show me New York. Otherwise you're going to think I came to visit for the wrong reasons."

"I wouldn't think that."

He laughed again. "No?"

Mario had an instinct for the City. The night life around St. Mark's Place fascinated him. The punks, the tourists, the kids, the cons. They walked as far as the Bowery and had a Cajun martini at Great Jones Cafe, took a look at the flophouses, the street people, the crowd in front of CBGB's, before they circled back to The Ritz. But there was an awfully long line there.

"Maybe this isn't a great idea," Mario said. "I'd rather walk than stand. Want to walk some more?"

"Yes," she said.

The night seemed magical, and she attributed this to him. She caught herself. After all her success in graduate school, she had attributed her intellectual growth to Larry. Now she saw the New York she could show Mario as a reflection of her worth. Was she going to give her New York over? Begin to attribute its excitement to the fact that it fascinated Mario? It was almost irresistible, but she forced herself back to herself. Though there was no lack of magic.

On the way back to her apartment they passed a neighborhood club and decided to go in for a drink. A cabaret act was going on, and from their end of the bar they could look in on the back room of tables and see the small stage. A good-looking man was sitting on a stool, the mike familiar in his hand, singing, accompanied by a small group. His black hair was glossy and pushed back on the sides, and his songs were very funny. Buster Poindexter and His Banshees of Blue.

"He seems familiar, somehow," Elaine said.

"To me too."

"Oh, wait, I saw something in the *Voice*. Would you believe it, I think that's David Johansen."

"Well, I'll be. A living legend. The New York Dolls," Mario said.

"Hey, you know your music in Florida."

"Oh, in the distant past I got around."

"What a transformation he's made. This is something."

Buster was singing a song about a fat black lady who proclaimed fat was back in style. He pressed forward with a revivallike intensity and, at the same time, a lounge-lizard cool that was absolutely out of sight.

She thought of Nola. Nola had that quality that Buster had. Certainly not the polish, but the charisma, the intensity. What if Nola spends the next twenty years like David Johansen/Buster Poindexter, obviously getting better and better—just listen to him go at it!—while the audience gets smaller and smaller for audacious, idiosyncratic rock.

Was this his fifteen minutes of fame? Or would more come later to him? What about Nola? Was it a long hike to nowhere the van would be encouraging Nola to take? Larry had called, told her he was still trying to convince his daughter to wait. Wouldn't waiting be better?

"Elaine," Mario said. "Elaine," he repeated. "Mario to Elaine. Elaine to earth."

"What?"

"Where were you?"

"Listening to the music. Thinking."

"How can you do both?"

"I don't know," Elaine said. "But music does that to me. This guy's great, isn't he? And we just bumped into him."

"Our timing's good together," he said. "Alone, my luck's never been that great."

"I know what you mean."

They left the bar and, hand in hand, continued their walk. It was close to two o'clock, and a cool breeze stirred the summer dampness, the way hope can stir in the heart.

"Elaine? Elaine."

She looked across Third Avenue, and saw two figures and a hand waving. "It is her, Jimmy!" she heard.

"Who's that?" Mario asked.

Elaine said, "That's Nola—and Jimmy. Looks like they're crossing over."

Self-consciously, Elaine kept hold of Mario's hand until her stepdaughter was in front of her.

"Elaine, what are you doing here?"

"I could ask the same."

They were both taking walks.

"We bumped into Buster Poindexter. Have you heard him yet?" Elaine asked.

Nola shrugged, didn't say anything, so Elaine continued. "Mario's the friend from Connecticut I mentioned to you, Nola. I wish he had been here to hear you play. We walked past CBGB tonight, and I was telling him how great your gig was there."

"I think they might be booking us again," Nola said to Mario. "When I know, I'll tell Elaine, and if she remembers, she can tell you to come."

"Remembers?" Elaine said.

"Like in I left a message this morning. Did you get it?" Nola asked.

"Yes, I did. But yesterday was rather heavy. I talked with your father and he said you two were still discussing next year."

"Sure."

There was a pause.

"When do you think you'll be playing there again?" Mario asked.

"We don't have a date yet, but within a month. Then, come hell or high water, we're off to the Coast. We might be in a movie. This gig will help us."

"All right!" Mario said. "What kind of rock do you play?"

"Our own kind," Jimmy said. "Sort of a spin-off punk. Come hear us when we get our gig."

"Sure."

"Well, you guys," Elaine said, "I'll be talking with you. Nola, I'll call Monday. Okay?"

"Sure."

"Bye."

"God," Elaine said to Mario, "she thinks I'm avoiding her."

"Are you?"

Elaine didn't answer. She said, "I've got to see her next week."

The next Wednesday, when she was finally to meet Nola, it was difficult for Elaine to get up. It was one of those mornings when life itself dealt a hangover. Her brain was misty from . . . from the past. The van—well, she'd decide after she saw it. All she was doing was taking a look, Larry or no Larry. She'd given him plenty of time, but everything bothered her this morning. She couldn't shrug off the complexities of Larry; a rather formless anxiety about Anne Gregory and her book; even Wig entered her head, for some reason.

She struggled out of bed and into the shower, then emerged in a somewhat better mood. Still, today she'd have to face a decision. Was it one she had spent weeks avoiding? First things first, she told herself. Take a walk, get something quick to eat, make it to Avenue C. Then see the van. Don't jump ahead.

Nola was waiting for her. From a distance everything was bigger than Nola, and she looked like a little girl. There was the concrete wall, surrounded on three sides by the mesh fence. The crumbling concrete had a mural on it. Big figures of dark-skinned youths pushing back an older drug dealer were still evident in the blues and yellows and oranges that were fading under the onslaught of bold black graffiti, the tags of neighborhood kids. The work loomed over Nola. Yet she stood out among the cars, being backed by the big black van—the Econoline 200. Small, thin, alone. Preoccupied. In fact, when she saw Elaine, for a moment she seemed annoyed at the interruption. Then she came to herself, waved energetically, but she didn't smile. She took off her earphones and slipped them around her neck.

"Been waiting long?" Elaine asked.

"No. I just got here a little early."

"I thought Jimmy would be with you. This place is a little, eh, deserted, wouldn't you say?"

"It's cool. See? Carlos just leaves the driver's side open. Sometimes guys sleep in it, but no one's messed it up."

"It wasn't the van I was worried about. What are these, graffiti?" Elaine asked noting black paint on the black van.

"Tags. Names. Initials. You know."

"Yeah, I know."

"Look at the other side. There're some in white and yellow. Local color," Nola said.

"How long has the van been parked here?"

"A month."

"So far its luck's held."

"The van's luck, Elaine?"

"Maybe yours."

Nola shrugged. "I have the keys. Want to go for a drive?"

"Sure. Let's see what it's like inside."

Nola slid the side door open. She let Elaine in first. The inside of the van was carpeted in blue. And Carlos had wallpapered the sides. There were small blue and brown birds on orange and silver branches. "Isn't it funky?" Nola asked. The back window had a fluffy kitchen curtain in orange that hung askew. There was a slightly urinous, sweaty smell. Nola climbed into the driver's seat, and Elaine took the passenger's bucket seat.

Nola adjusted the side mirror and revved the motor. "Here goes nothing," she said. She pulled out into the street and drove around the decaying streets, the boarded-up buildings, the painted walls, the small gardens. "Let's get past Avenue A," Elaine said. "I've have enough of Alphabet Land for the morning."

Nola drove around Tompkins Square Park. Junkies, skinheads, old people.

"You're a good driver."

"It's the van. Elaine, this van has its own magic."

"Let's see, the mileage, is that untampered? Twenty-five thousand? That's not too bad. Do you know why Carlos is selling?"

Nola shrugged. "He doesn't need it in the city."

"What does Carlos do for a living?"

Nola shrugged. "He follows bands. That's all I know and all I need to know. And he came down from thirty-eight. I know he needs the money."

"I'm surprised he hasn't sold this quicker."

"This van is ours, Elaine! It's waiting on Second Hand!"

Elaine smiled. "I have to say it's comfortable. And it's also comfortable driving with you. Go west, young van."

Nola said, "You see! You see! There are definite vibes!"

"Maybe. We'll see. I meant west on Houston, and then turn right on Lafayette."

"Where we going?"

"To see my mechanic."

"Here," Nola said, passing her Walkman. "Want to listen for a while? It's our new tape. What do you think? Put it up loud!"

Elaine did. This is the way the van would sound on the drive to California. Filled with luggage and instruments and the band. The song raced in her ears. They were young and on the open road and making their own music. All the way to the garage, Elaine rode with Second Hand.

She opened her eyes. "We're here," Elaine shouted. "You can park right there, next to the hydrant. It's okay."

It was a big corner garage.

"Terrific," Elaine said, handing Nola back her Walkman.

"Not too shabby," Nola said.

"Not too," Elaine answered, and slid out of the van.

"Vhat's this?" Ivan asked. He was a short man with curly rust-colored hair.

They were standing near the gas pump in the middle of the large, car-filled place. "This is my stepdaughter, Nola. Nola, Ivan; Ivan, Nola."

"You're too young for such."

"You're absolutely right, as usual, Ivan."

"Of course. There's more to life than cars."

"For example, vans. Nola's interested in buying that Econoline for a long trip. I mean a long trip, Ivan. It's got to be in perfect, I mean perfect shape."

"Have confidence. Vhen you want to bring it around?"

"Now, Ivan. It's important. Could you do me a favor and check it out today?"

"For you . . . Vhere's the long trip going to, Nola?"

"Cross-country. California."

"Good for you. You're young. Believe me, vhen you're old you get . . ." Ivan looked around his place. "You get busy."

Nola laughed.

"It's not so funny," Ivan shrugged. "A minute, I'll be back."

"Elaine, where the hell do you find these guys?"

"You think it's easy? Ivan's the best! He does Jackie Mason's car."

"Whose?"

"An old-time borscht-belt comedian. You're too young for such."

Nola laughed again.

"Okay," Ivan said, returning. "For you. You come back about six?"

"Great, Ivan. Thanks. Let's see. Nola, can you come back at six?"

"Sure."

"Can we let it go at that? She'll pick it up at six, and I'll come by early tomorrow morning, see what you think, and pay."

Ivan put his finger to his lips. "Ssshhh."

"You're a doll, Ivan."

Ivan bowed slightly, smiled, and said, in explanation, with a flourish of his hand, "Beautiful ladies."

"Hi, Ivan; Elaine."

"I know."

"Nola pick it up?"

"Yes."

"I couldn't wait. How is it?"

"Excellent. A few adjustments and it flies."

"Really?"

"Not too expensive."

"Tell me, ball park, how much do you think the van's worth?"

"Say forty-two."

"Hey, great. And, while I've got you, do you know of any safe but not too expensive garages where it could be parked over the summer?"

"Nearby. Outdoors, but twenty-four-hour security. A hundred thirty, a hundred fifty."

"New York cheap. It's okay. How much do I owe you for today?"

"Nothing, Elaine. Time enough vhen you bring in the van."

"That's nice of you, Ivan. I'll get back to you as soon as I can."

"No rush, Elaine."

Nola was at the Veselka, sitting at a table past the zigzag of the counter, drinking coffee, when Elaine walked in, *Times* under her arm, and spotted her. "Hi, there. I'm not late, am I? Isn't it a beautiful day?" She sat down. Motioned the waitress for a cup of coffee. It was delivered right away. "This is just what I need," she said.

Then she put the cup down. "The news from Ivan is good. The van seems to be in top shape. Just needs some adjustments he can do."

"I know. That's what he told me."

"I have some questions. Now, you're raising the three thousand dollars. Does that mean it would be your van?"

"Jimmy's and mine. He and Lloyd, the drummer, have raised money too. That'll go for the trip and the insurance and posters— everything. We're going to pool."

"Okay. We know your father has objections to the van. What about your mother?"

"Oh, she's cool. She just thinks Daddy should come up with the money."

"Sounds familiar. I mean, I'm sort of in agreement."

"He just wants to keep me a little girl. He seems very spacy. I did what you asked, called him and told him you were going to look at the van. All of a sudden he starts asking me about what I'm doing Memorial Day. I say, Like Labor Day, Daddy, and he says, Labor Day, is it?"

"I think he's acting peculiarly, too, but he absolutely refuses to have me discuss his health with you. I don't know if he's in good health. His accounts are confusing."

"You know him. Sometimes he can use a lot of sympathy."

"I didn't realize *you* knew him."

"Don't forget, I lived with him for almost three years."

"I don't forget. Believe me. But there is something you have to be very clear about, Nola. Your father is a fairly wealthy man. You're his only heir, and he's threatening to cut you out of his will if you drop school and go on this tour."

"That's okay with me, if he really means it."

"You can't assume it's just a threat."

"Elaine, he's not going to die."

The muffins came at the right time. Elaine played with her square of butter.

"I mean, you know Daddy. He thinks of things like wills. I mean, you were in one once, weren't you? Look, I've got to live my life, Elaine. I'm real clear about it. I bring it up at meetings. Even if something awful were to happen, I have to live my life."

Elaine kept quiet. "I got a title for some lyrics," Nola said. " 'Ivan and Van.' 'Ivan and Van.' Sounds right, doesn't it? Maybe that's the whole thing. 'Ivan-and-van / Ivan-and-van / Vhat, vhat, vhere, vhen? / Ivan-and-van.' "

Elaine seemed preoccupied. "Not bad."

Then Nola said, "Elaine, I'm going on this tour no matter what—if we have to bring Carlos along and feed him and let him be our groupie. Nothing's going to stop me. It can't. It's got to be this year, it's got to be now."

"Okay, Nola," Elaine said. She stood up and reached in her jeans pocket. "Here," she said, passing to Nola a small white envelope. "And I'll pay for the tune-up or whatever Ivan thinks is necessary. And I'll also pay for a decent garage for the summer, till you leave."

Nola looked at the yellow check.

"Good luck, Nola. Nothing but luck for you and Second Hand. I hope you knock them dead. I think you will."

There were tears in Nola's eyes. Had Elaine ever before seen tears in Nola's eyes that weren't angry ones?

"It's different," Nola said. "It's different, being right here in my hand. I guess, I guess we're really going."

Elaine felt a stab in her heart. My God, Elaine thought, she's so young.

Nola put the check back in its envelope, and placed the envelope in her jeans. "I can see the road." She wiped her eyes. "Even through tears." She laughed. She took Elaine's hands from across the table, and hung on tight. "It's scary, isn't it? I guess we're really going to go."

"Oh, Nola," Elaine said. And she squeezed her stepdaughter's small hands.

Two days later:

Bzzzzzz. "Elaine, this is Pam Delaney, Prospect Realty. It's twelve noon, and I just think you'd like to know. I have a check in my hand for a deposit on a Lucerne model in the next stage—Twelve. The Lucernes are now going for two hundred and seventy-five thousand dollars! Congratulations, you made a good deal—and a great location in Eleven. The best, really. This should cheer you up if you're not already cheery! Have a good day. Congratulations again."

"Wow!" Elaine said, replaying the message. Seventy-five thousand dollars higher than what she had reserved at, less than two months ago. Incredible! Means something. Can't mean nothing. A significant coincidence. She had to be doing something right! It was at that moment, early on an afternoon in late July, having lent Nola money for her van, with real-estate values accelerating and Mario in her life, that Elaine Bright Netherlands realized she had had a change of luck.

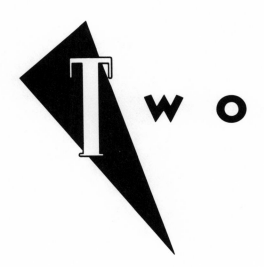

PART

TWO

EIGHT

In late August, Nola is driving to Columbia County to visit her father. Last visit before California. She knows he isn't thrilled about the van. Her first impulse is to take a train. So she brings it up in the rooms. It's an Anonymous Room meeting of adult children of alcoholics, the child in them always hoping to please. She gets to the meeting early enough to sit around the central table. She tells them she'd been thinking of taking a train, having him meet her. Please him. People-pleasing, parent-pleasing.

"But I have wheels now, and I don't want to spend fifty dollars for the train. So I tell him, No thanks, I don't need the money, I'm going to drive up.

" 'In the van?' he asks, like I'm taking poison.

"And I'm proud of myself, like I don't act out? I don't fall for his act, I just focus on me, on what I want to do, and, calm, and real nice, I say, 'Yes, Daddy, the van.' So what's he gonna say to this, like start a fight? All he can say is 'See you Monday.' Thanks for letting me say that."

Her father's spending a month at Chatham, at Bunny's place. Can you imagine a grown man going out with a Bunny? Sure, Bunny's a painter and all that. It's like he can't go out with a woman without somehow showing Nola that her own mother isn't up for a Nobel Prize. Bunny has to be in the city Monday through Wednesday, so that's when Nola's visiting. Bunny would have probably left for a weekend too. The women in her father's life are always your world-class codependents, always showing him what really nice people they are and how great they think it is that he has a daughter. Like they'd want her to live with them or something if they marry her father. At least her father's no longer getting married. But these women make her sick. What do you think of Tiffany, Carolyn, Sandra, Twitty, Pee-Pee, Bunny? he'd ask. "I've already had a mother and a stepmother, Dad." That always made him laugh. She doesn't go as far as saying that she hasn't yet had an older sister. Nola just knows she'll grow old naturally. Act her age. No big deal.

So there she is driving to Chatham. No more Hamptons. Too pricey. Her father's friends are into farmhouses now, and no place to swim. She finds herself, hands on the wheel, transposed to Montauk, walking out on the pier with her father. Suddenly she feels she's left something behind, but can't fix it. Montauk. Salt air. At night fluorescent fish. The lighthouse. Maybe someday she'll write an old-fashioned love song and make a killing. Silas did. This is dedicated to my dad, when he liked oceans. She starts singing, as she drives, over the rap she's listening to. Moons and Waves and Stars and Lobsters. Over My Big Black Caddy! she's crooning. This on the Taconic. The Deathway. Beautiful winding roads, hills and vales and trees, and cars coming on at right angles. Wheee!

Off the Deathway, she has to concentrate on her father's good directions. Mr. Precise. Sure enough, country roads take me home and three red barns. She takes a left and parks where the dirt road turns to grass. Her father's on the porch of the old farmhouse. And what's that with him? Her father with a dog. Down, boy? Oh, man, what next.

"Cute little terrier," she says, out of the car and meeting him halfway between it and the old farmhouse with the wraparound porch.

"Jasper."

"Hi, Jasper," she says, automatically using the welcoming tone of the Rooms, just as if it had been Jasper's turn to share and the group was responding to "I'm Jasper."

"Part poodle," he says. Then she looks Nature Boy in the eye. "Hey, a rug, Dad? What's up?"

Her father looks embarrassed. Puts his hand to his hair. "Is it that obvious? . . . Obviously."

"It's cool. What is it? Added protection against being invaded by a skinhead?"

He laughs, swings her bag over his shoulder, and leads her into the house. She thinks, Hey, not a bad start.

He shows her around the old place and leads her upstairs to her little old farmhouse bedroom. Pegs on the wall. A quilt over the narrow no-one's-ever-gotten-laid-here-be-nice bed. "Cute," she says. He drops her bag, and it's back downstairs. To ye olde farmhouse kitchen.

"French bread," he says, "and farm-fresh eggs. They were warm when I got them. Cheese. See? Jarlsberg, I know you like. Stilton, I know I like. Chèvre. And I thought we'd go out in the back and pick our salad. Wait till you see Bunny's garden."

So that's okay. An activity. Something to do. Keep the kid busy. Maybe Bunny comes out at night and nibbles on her own lettuce.

So he takes her out to the back of the house. "All right!" she says. The bright, tilted patch of the garden, floppy with growth, is surrounded as far as the eye can see by meadowland. She takes the overview first, then closer to where they stand and to the right—a round wooden table and four wooden chairs under a wide-spreading tree, near an old stone hut. It's really pretty. She wishes she had her earphones in, but there were things you couldn't do around Daddy. And that's okay, if it makes him happy. You only got one da-da-daddy. And today he's in a good mood. He's standing close to her in the back of the house; he seems glad to see her.

She points to the garden. "Do you have a plastic container and a scale?"

"Huh?" Not too quick.

"You mean this isn't a salad bar?" She gives it away.

He runs with it. "Do you see croutons? Do you see bacon bits?" he asks.

"No, no. Oh, this is awful! It's so confusing. Don't you people eat veggies around here?"

He puts his arm around her. "Come on. I'll show you how it was done in the old days."

As they enter the garden, he bends down and picks up a straw basket. But in his pressed jeans and polo shirt and new rug he doesn't look like a farmer. He's tanned, though. Usually he's afraid of ultraviolet and stays out of the sun. He's throwing caution to the wind, she's thinking. Imagine thinking that. Jasper's acting like a dog and jumps off into the meadow in a hurry. For more than three years she's been used to city dogs that are cooped up all day and get depressed.

She walks between the overgrown rows of the blooming garden. She snaps some tender lettuce off at its white stalk. She doesn't see Bunny's teethmarks. There are some beautiful yellow-orangy peppers, the kind that come from Holland and cost $4.99 a pound in the city. Her father's picking too, and she goes over to him and puts her stuff in his straw basket. He looks up at her from the vine he's praying before and smiles, his eyes shut to the sun.

"What's this stuff?" she asks, slightly embarrassed by his mellow kindness.

"Zucchini," he answers.

"No kidding!" She crouches down next to him. She looks at the long slim zucchini, covered in soft baby skin, a lighter green than at any salad bar or in any market. At the end of the one she is examining, a flower about to burst, an orange flower, polleny. She touches it. "No kidding," she repeats. Her father, crouched on the other side of the vine, picking, says, "Oh, remember not to step on these vines or the zucchini's had it. And tell me, dear, what's there to get so excited about?"

"Tell me, dear"? Is he sick? That's exactly what she's thinking: Is he sick? She doesn't know if she should say it. She is touching the sticky flower, perfectly happy in Bunny's patch. "The flower of the zucchini," she says. "Elaine used to tell me about them. How in Italy they stuffed them with cheese and then breaded them and fried them and they were this big delicacy. So this is what she was talking about. The flower of the zucchini. Ever try to picture a flower on a squash? Unreal."

"Ah, I see," her father says, but not unfriendly. "Another saga from Elaine's grad-school days."

She gets goose bumps. Like here they are on this pretty day in Bunny's garden and suddenly they're somewhere else together. A place called the past. Among the zucchini, she gets a sun-and-dirt whiff of loss. Soon after, she'll call it a premonition; much later, a memory.

Actually, it's fun in the kitchen, making salad from scratch. Everything's so tender from the garden. She prepares a big wooden bowl just crammed with good stuff, and her father, like he's really in this Columbia County mood? She's in the refrigerator looking for some bottled dressing, and he calls out, "Take the Poupon jar on the left. It's the dressing. I just mixed it." He's making dressing, which is new; what isn't new is his specialty, scrambled eggs.

She goes out and sets the table under the tree. And then brings the salad out, and the bread and cheese too. Scrambled eggs. He often tells the story of how he learned to do them, very slow over the fire, in a pan well buttered, using a soup spoon from the edge to the middle, piling up the fluff. It seems it was his first girlfriend that taught him how to make eggs. "Jenny," he'd say. Always that look in his eye. "She made a photographer out of me." (Substitute "man"—even Nola as a kid figured that one out.) "My first photos, Jenny." Later she figured naked photos, though he never would show her Jenny. "Lost," he said.

As she came back into the kitchen, the screen door creaking and slowly closing behind her, she could see him thinking it to himself again. It was his attitude over the stove, the concentration on slowly piling up wet eggs. She could see it in the slope of his back. Straitlaced as he was, her father had never gotten over girls.

"Here we go!" he says triumphantly, taking the black pan off the fire and turning around. "Everything set? Thank you, Nola. Let's bring these out just like this. They shouldn't be moved. I'm telling you, there's only one method for real scrambled eggs. Farm eggs, Nola. Warm when I bought them." He has a raccoon mitt on, and the pan is in his hand like a trophy, and she opens the screen for him, bows low, and says, "After you, chef," and follows after him as if the two of them and scrambled eggs make a procession.

They sit down to this meal that they've pulled out of the ground, not to mention chickens' behinds, and it really is like something they created. They're both hungry and eat. Her father hums. And she thinks of the two and a half years they lived together. He obviously does too. Because, out of the blue, and after he's gone in to start the coffee and take some pill he says he needs and been back awhile, he looks out over the farmhouse and the barns and says, real emotional like, "We're getting along. Just as we did on Riverside Drive. Why did you leave, Nola?"

She held her own. "Why do you have to say that, Dad? Do you want me to feel guilty?"

"No, of course, you have to lead your own life. And there is your young man. I wouldn't think of competing with Jimmy. But you know, Nola"—and suddenly he's a pity package—"it wouldn't have been for that long."

It was a nice lunch, but, no escaping, Nola came from a dysfunctional home. Her grandfather and her mother drank, and her father had always expected something from her that he'd never found in women.

"We always did all right," he says out of nowhere, "when they left us alone."

Bad moment. She notices he has these swings: he's up, he's down. But a lot of the time he's up.

Tuesday night, after a $2.50 movie in ye olde Art Deco movie house in ye olde town, it's chilly, and back on the farm he has his excuse to make a fire. Both of them cart extra wood from the weird old cellar to the big fireplace in the living room. He brings out a bottle of French brandy and does a little sipping. She lives it up, has a beer, then a Coke. The flames are flickering, and Jasper, a real dog who's leapt in fields and obviously has fun memories that wag his tail, is stretched out in front of the fire like he's family. "Watch this!" her dad says, and with the brandy downs a pill.

"What are those pills you're taking?"

"Mine to know," he says, and then—she swears he really says this—say ten, maybe fifteen minutes of flicking fire has gone by, she's thinking of the video of the Yuletime log and is really into it, and he comes out with, "Would you have a tape of any of your music?"

"Huh?"

"You heard me."

"Sure, I have a tape. I have some rap too, and the sound track to *Repo Man*."

"No, your stuff, I'd like to hear it."

"It's not mood music, Dad. Even Silas makes us whisper it."

"Oh, yes. Silas Mourner. Elaine told me about him. She says he suffers from having too many talents, too many things he could do well. A lot of people are like that. I've seen it. They start out like shooting stars—"

"Supernovas?"

"You could say that. A lot of light, and just as much fizzle."

"Shooting stars never stop. . . ." She began to sing.

"Is that your song?"

"No, Dad, be real. That's Frankie Goes to Hollywood."

"Well, excuuuuuse me."

They both laugh.

She gets her tape, maybe because she's a sucker for punishment, and he puts it on, and Second Hand and Asia Neither Land burst louder than a crackling fire.

He tries to look understanding. He says, "I hear Israel Horovitz's kid is into this stuff."

"The Beastie Boys, Dad?"

"I guess. What's so funny?"

"Nothing." She gets off the couch to try some brandy. Pours it, then wonders what she's doing.

"It's very quiet without the music," he says, after the click.

"Elaine says the music changes the quiet."

"You've been seeing a lot of her, I hear."

"She lent me the money for the van."

"I know."

There's a pause; then he says, "He didn't change his name, did he?"

"Who?"

"The Beastie Boy. Horovitz's son."

"I don't know him. I mean, they're a famous group. They're the Beastie Boys."

"Well, I do know. I asked his father. And he finished school. What are you going to do about school?"

She takes a deep breath. "Well, Dad, it wouldn't make much sense to start, 'cause in late September the band's off to California."

"Asia goes to Hollywood."

She doesn't know if she should smile. "Second Hand goes to Hollywood. I'm not the biggest deal in this band."

"Then who is?"

"The band is. We're the band."

"So," he says, "you won't be finishing school."

"I will, Dad. Next year. I promise. But this is something we've planned, and we have the van now, and we have to do it. We're just taking a little more time. We have some gigs in the city. We'll make a few bucks, maybe."

"Maybe. I would have liked to see you graduate."

"You will."

"Will I?"

"Sure. Just another year."

"Just another year."

"Don't get down again, Dad. It's so nice when you're up. It's fun!"

"Fun? Here, Jasper, here. That's a boy. Fun."

"One thing I want to ask. When you take me out of the will, does that mean you won't be paying for my last year at school? Or do you have to do that? Don't look at me like that, Daddy. It's practical. I'm being practical. I just wanta know."

"That's what taking you out of the will means to you? It's a clause to you? *When* you take me out of the will! That's not practical, Nola, that's dumb! Fight for yourself. The world's tough. *When* you take me out of the will. Don't be such a wimp."

"A wimp? What are you saying!"

"And don't yell. Jasper will hear." He laughs sharply, and in the light of the fire she finally sees the lines on his face.

She calms down. "You want me to fight for the right to be an heir? It's your will, Dad. It's your right to change it."

"My will?" he says. "What am I going to do about you?" And again he's down in the dumps.

The rug, the mood swings. And he might be on a diet. "Tell me, Dad, are you in love, or are you doing drugs?"

"In love? I gave up love after your two mothers."

What a strange thing to say. "Drugs, Dad?"

"Don't be dramatic, Nola. Prescription drugs. Legal. I'm sick."

"You're sick?" And of course she knows right away he is. Elaine always says we know a lot more than we think we know. And then all of Elaine's hints—Have you seen your father? and, after Nola had all these phone conversations with him, How does he seem to you?—come out of storage. His tan is hiding it. He just looks like he's getting older. And she's now the daughter of a father who's sick. She turns to the fire. It's all suspended. Even her mind doesn't take it in. It's out there. Crackle. The background music of the Yule log.

Her father's patting the dog while the overstuffed chair and the brandy and another pill are taking care of him. "Let's not pad it," he says, like he should add "son" or something. "I'm in remission. But it is cancer. And most probably it has affected the lung."

Lung cancer.

Like on the surgeon general's report.

Like you read about.

Since she was a kid, hadn't she told him not to smoke? She shoulda tried harder.

"Nola, are you okay?"

"Yeah. I just seem to be sweating. I don't feel too good. Excuse me. It's the beer."

She goes to the bathroom out in the hall, but nothing comes up. She gags over the sink and something that just hits the base of her throat feels bitter. She's got to come out. He's calling her. She screams, "I'm okay!"

"It's the beer," she says when she comes back. "And then I tried that brandy. I don't like to drink. Grandpa was an alcoholic. Your first wife too. Did you know that? I always wanted to tell you that." And she starts talking about drinking and, whatever she's saying, she just wants to talk, to talk forever, but underneath it she doesn't know what she's saying, she's just out of there.

"I'll beat it," he says. He's smiling. "Stop worrying. Go on your tour if you need it." Like sure, bye-bye, Daddy. "Do anything that makes you happy." He's into it now. "That's the name of this game. Do your own thing, right?" He's humming now, without a plate of eggs in front of him.

Her two mothers. Drugs. He's high. With all that she knows about addiction and . . . It's not just the brandy, it's both days. He's flying. Another one floating out over the horizon.

"I'll lick cancer. That's what John Wayne said. And I'll do it. If John Wayne can do it, Larry Netherlands can do it!"

"Dad. Stop it! Stop it, for goodness' sakes. John Wayne is dead!"

Maybe she should stop singing and go into diplomacy. It was not what she wanted to say, not what she had wanted to stop. It was too late.

"Why didn't you tell me he was ill?" Nola sort of bursts in on Elaine. Her stepmother's packing for a week in Danbury. Elaine has one of those honey-colored tans that look wild with her blond hair, and she's allowing her hair to grow out into a wider Afro. She's wearing a sweatband around her forehead and she looks cool. This time her eyes don't betray her. She says simply, "Nola, I will not allow you to put this on me. I told you Larry didn't want me discussing his health with you; I told you to go to see him, instead of just talking on the phone. I appreciate that you must be feeling very bad about your father; but don't you dare load it on me."

Nola doesn't.

She's shaky. "I don't know what to do."

"Well, he's on an even keel, isn't he? We meet over the phone occasionally, and he says he's doing okay."

"But cancer, Elaine, cancer?" She hears herself say the word. Cancer. "I always told him not to smoke."

"Did he use the word 'cancer'?" Elaine asks her softly, really curious.

She nods.

"You sit there. Let me get you a Pepsi."

"Diet?"

"Sure. Oh, the phone."

"Get it. That's okay. I just need to sit here."

Nola looks around Elaine's living room, lets time pass, as Elaine talks on the phone in the bedroom. She's ready to stand and go for her own drink when she sees Elaine shoot across the room saying, "Sorry."

"I wonder what life was like without the phone," she says as she comes back to the living room with two sodas. "That was my editor's secretary. I wanted her to convince me that Anne Gregory hasn't been sold into white slavery. It seems she's simply been whisked away to serve her husband. I wonder what it's like in Vermont with a sex guru—and his girlfriend. Obviously enough to keep you away from work."

"That's Reid Gregory's wife? Daddy knows them. I always thought he was a creep. 'Have you had your first boyfriend yet, little girl?' Yuck!" They're quiet for a while.

Elaine gets up and goes over to the stereo. Nola sees her pick out Joe Jackson, and then reject it. Everything gives you cancer. Instead she says, "Have you heard this rock compendium of Weill and Brecht? Lou Reed does an incredible 'September Song.'"

"*Lost in the Stars?*"

"You got it. I'll put on his side first."

They listen to the music. Elaine is sitting opposite her in one of those big old-fashioned chairs she got from her grandmother. Was it in her grandmother's will? Elaine looks—healthy. "I got Mario into Weill," she says, and then goes off with the music to remember a moment that's passed. Her stepmother, her father— they just go off to other lives. Sometimes they display themselves like snapshots of trips they've taken. Elaine with her new boyfriend in Connecticut. Her father crouched in Bunny's garden.

"He says he's in remission," Nola says.

Elaine nods.

"And he's telling me to go away and have a good time, as if I'd go right now."

"He agrees to California?"

"You got it. He's very agreeable. He has a dog, and he makes eggs and thinks of good old Jenny, and, da-da-da-da-dum, he asks to listen to my tapes! He's Mr. Mellow. Sex and death and rock and roll. He's on painkillers or something. He's flying."

"That's exactly what I thought when we had dinner at Teacher's Too. But he wasn't Mr. Mellow."

"Maybe things weren't going well with the Rabbit."

"He doesn't have a Volks."

"Bunny."

"Oh. It's serious between them?"

"Yeah."

"Well, it's good he has someone."

"He has me."

Elaine nods.

"He doesn't want me to leave."

"He doesn't?"

"No. He's feeding me guilt. Go have a good time while I have cancer."

"You said he's Mr. Mellow. Illness can change people. He might very well have meant what he said. We only have one life. Maybe now he desperately wants you to have yours."

Nola gets up to flip the record.

"You like it?" Elaine asks.

"For what it is, it's good."

She turns and faces her stepmother. The beat of Berlin, the cacophony of times past, and sadly, seem appropriate. Right now Nola feels like Marianne Faithfull's cracked voice. She's being sent a widow's veil. "I'm going to wait a semester. I'm going to call him up and tell him. I can't leave right now."

Her stepmother looks at her. Doesn't say a word, just looks right through her.

"What do you expect me to do? I can't leave my own father. You knew he was sick when you lent me money for the van."

"Yes, I did."

"So I'll pay you back, and we'll start parking in the street."

Elaine puts her hand up. "I'll keep up the parking lot. You bought something you really valued. Now you have to protect it. Protect it from what comes out at night in this city!"

"I thought you loved New York."

"New York's for the tough," she says sharply.

"Are you mad at me?"

Elaine sits forward and makes a fist. "It teaches you to hold on to what you have. How do you think the Chrysler Building must have felt, standing there only three months, when the Empire State Building went higher? Did she crumple? No, she stood there proud as she could. Stood as tall as she could. Still stands, proud of her fins. No other building has fins."

"Elaine, what the hell are you talking about?"

"I think, Nola," she says, loud and precise over the music, "I think I am talking about life!"

She must have been having a severe outbreak of Nutty Elaine. Nola doesn't leave feeling much better.

And her father's reaction hadn't been exactly gangbusters. She gets him right before a dinner party at Chatham. "What's that, Nola? Oh, I see. Well, you'll have to wait on the tuition check awhile. Get me the cutoff for late fee, will you? One second, Nola. Hold on! Okay, now. What? Of course I'm happy. I'm feeling fine. Look, sure, this is what I think you should do. But, you know, last-minute, Nola. What, Bunny? One second, Nola. Okay. Don't forget the cutoff date. Sure, sweetheart. Bye." She's in the apartment, and when he clicks off she feels as she used to feel as a child—alone in the house. But then the emptiness lifts, and she feels safe.

NINE

Wig's sitting on a stool at the wooden bar of the French-Canadian club by the lake. It's a shack of a place—must be "quaint," Wig thinks, because right after this Columbus Day weekend it's going to be torn down. Raymond's is going to have to relocate, so someone is always offering a round when Raymond himself isn't saying it's on the house. Wig bought rounds on Friday. But by Sunday he's broke even without getting to New York.

Wig spends his money. The States—what are they to him? A series of construction sites. Raised ranches. Office buildings. Townhouses. Malls. Florida. Connecticut. Not home. He could be a rich man ten times over by now, like a few of the French guys. If he wanted to settle down and count money. But why? He's strong, he's not afraid of work. He can always make more money.

And, money or not, there're always plenty of girls. They're looking at him right now.

"Come on, want us to pick your stick?" one calls from the pool table.

"Later." He just isn't in the mood.

He'll get up soon. Show his ass, show his muscle. He's good-looking, and they go for that. He's slim, compactly built; the blue veins stretch along his strong, lean arms, defining tendon and muscle up to the capped sleeve of his T-shirt. His face is long, angular, weathered. His eyes narrow, and he has a black mustache over lean lips. He's looking at himself sideways behind the bottles. Elaine told him he looked like that French painter—Gauguin. Maybe. He watched Gauguin on a special. They must have had good dope in Tahiti. His kind of guy.

He told that to Elaine. Elaine laughed. Mario got himself an educated woman. Not screwed up like the American girls who hung out at Raymond's. They look alike. Underneath their tight jeans, their fat asses and their wide hips bulge. Their short sleeves expose fleshy arms. Some have tattoos. Wrecks, overweight and wired. Looking for one of the good-looking French guys they think are stupid because their English isn't great. Extra holes, the guys call them. Wig doesn't. He thinks, Those girls are smart enough to know where to go to get laid. And by a French guy, who, alone with her in the dark, knows how to be grateful. Live and let live.

Wig looks toward the door of the bar. Where are Mario and Elaine? He's lent Mario his Harley for the day. Maybe the last ride of the season. A beautiful day. If the Danbury Fair were still up, the roads would be packed with cars going there these ten days. The Fair was gone, but the weather was still beautiful. That's what they used to say. Fair Days, Fair Weather. Still true. It's getting dark. He looks out the back window, down to the lake.

He might as well play some pool. Pick up a few bucks for later. Meanwhile, Jean Marie is at the bar; he was born in the same town as Wig. Remembers when Wig was the strongest kid in Beauce—by legend, that is. Remembers what Wig wants to forget. How he hurt his father and left home. Jean Marie isn't thirty, but he knows. Blond, short, compact. A good-looking kid. Drunk, he is insane. He has never registered a car in the States, though he has totaled two. The third he went to Florida to get. Wig went with him. There are a lot of French Canadians outside of Fort Lauderdale, where his sister lives. Sheetrockers, tapers, roofers, siders, just as in Danbury. Their bar is the Rumba, just as in Danbury it is Raymond's. They get awfully good coke at the Rumba. Well, the best blow doesn't compare to New York. Next weekend, he figures he'll drive Mario to New York.

Pauli Girl's at the bar too. All six foot six of him. When he and Wig used to do piecework together, they could frame and Sheetrock a house in a day and a half. Still can. Pauli Girl's okay. In the States he lets everyone know who he is. He's big enough to dare them to say a word. Not like in Quebec. In those small towns everyone's a cousin. Wig can't get over how big a deal they make of cousins in the States. Count them—first cousin, second cousin. Poof! As strange as colds! Grown men take off days from work in the States because they have colds! Well, no one knew about colds in Quebec, and even at six foot six you didn't come out of the closet in a town where everyone is your cousin. Pauli Girl's okay. He gives good parties, plenty of coke, dirty videos.

Still, some of the guys don't want to hang around him. Why? What are they afraid of? Fags don't rub off. Live and let live. Who could put up a house like Pauli Girl and him, before Mario got them all in harness, doing industrial work?

Wig's very proud of Mario; maybe you have to be in this country a few generations to get brains. Not that Wig thinks he's not sharp. But he always feels sort of out of place. He likes it at Raymond's. He likes it in his car on the Lower East Side with Trisha. He likes it alone, all alone, with his coke and his right hand. His right hand's getting tired lately.

He's thinking of Mario, and there he is, opening the door for

Elaine. They're flushed from the long ride, they look at each other, and then come in holding hands. He knows from the way they walk that they've just had sex. Probably right there, in the back, in the grass. Now that it's dark. "Wig, hi," Mario says, and Wig can smell it.

"Nice ride?" Wig asks.

"Nice ride," Elaine says. She looks down the bar. Waves at Pauli Girl.

Wig says to Mario in French, "Looks like you've found a new mistress." Mario laughs. A younger Mario used to tell Wig, "I only have one mistress to whom I'm true." That's when his marriage to Paulette was breaking up. That's when they shared the same mistress, the same highs. Before Wig had to leave Florida, before Mario joined him but lived alone, stayed away from drugs, saved his money.

Mario answers him in French, "I leave that other mistress to you. But you treat her too well."

"What are you two talking about?" Elaine asks.

"The past," Mario answers.

"Sex and drugs and rock and roll?" she says.

She's close; she often is.

Wig finishes his beer and Mario orders. Raymond puts up his hand, then pours shots all around. He's a big man, in his fifties. Veins break across his short nose and full cheeks.

"Have you found a new place yet?" Mario asks in French.

Raymond says, "Maybe. But maybe I go home."

"You're lucky," Wig says.

Raymond says, "I save my money."

Wig shrugs. He didn't leave home for money. In fact, he never planned to come to the States. No place was as beautiful as Beauce. When he went home for his father's funeral, he walked out of the big white old-fashioned church that stood on top of the one hill and looked down at his village. All those small houses below him. Flat land, modest homes on either bank of a slim, meandering river. No trees. That he noticed the lack of trees showed how long he'd been away. Why, when he first saw Danbury, the trees amazed him. Why were there so many trees?

Beauce had no use for trees. They were the reminder of the Maine woods and the mosquitoes. The men were away all week, chopping down trees, so that they could afford a clean, well-ordered village to come home to on weekends. So they chopped down the trees of Beauce. Good riddance!

At the time of his father's death Wig was working on the siding of a half-million-dollar house in Ridgefield, Connecticut. It was there that he first heard the word "quaint. . . ."

"A penny for your thoughts," Elaine says, smiling at him.

"Quaint."

"Well, that's worth a penny."

How can a town like Ridgefield that houses rich businessmen, lawyers, doctors, be quaint? No, his mother is quaint. Her small, clean house and constant ways and absolute frugality with money are quaint.

"My father used to tell me how lucky we were, living in the village," he explains to Elaine. "He had ten sisters and brothers. On the farm they insulated windows with snow! Now, that's quaint! Not Ridgefield, Connecticut."

"You've got a point there, Wig," Elaine says.

When his father beat him, he'd yell, "You don't know how lucky you are." He had to whip sense into him. His father used to get an orange for Christmas. Wig got underwear. Each Christmas, when he unwrapped the toy he'd been allowed to pick out, it just never looked as big as in the catalogue. His father was right. Wig knew deep in his heart that he couldn't feel thankful enough. He said he was, but his father saw straight through him with his strap.

"It's a great bike."

Wig looks at Elaine. "The Harley? It's a piece of shit," he says, matter-of-factly.

"Huh?"

"Any Japanese bike is better."

"Then why do you have a Harley?"

"Because it's a Harley. A Harley's a Harley. I left school, I went to work in the woods with my father to buy one."

"You did?"

"My father said, 'You want a Harley, go to work like a man.' "

"Were you a man?"

"I was sixteen. I left school. I was high in my class too."

"But that's terrible."

"Terrible? My father left school at eight. Me, I had a choice. You want something, you work for it."

"Learning's work! He could have offered you a Harley as a graduation gift—to keep you in school."

Wig laughs. "I like the way you don't make sense. You don't make sense like a good woman. Mario's lucky."

"I mean, Wig, being encouraged to leave school? And to leave it to buy a motorcycle?"

Raymond pours another round. He and Mario and Pauli Girl are talking. Real estate? Who's Pauli Girl kidding? He only knows work.

"Your father sounds awfully negative," Elaine says.

"He's dead now. I went home for his funeral. But he was right. He warned me not to go in the woods. Said it was for men, not for boys raised on warm milk. Always said my mother spoiled me. But me, I had to go to the woods. And, you know, they put me on the tractor right away. Oh, was he mad. He said I was too young. But all the French guys tell the foreman how good I am with machines. It's the Maine woods, you know. You live there five days a week, in camps. Like dogs. It's cold. The food's crap. No women. All the men working too hard to get hard. My father was right."

"I guess you didn't like it."

"Like it? Hey, I didn't last two weeks. The second week, I bring some hash in. In those days we get good hash in Quebec. They don't search me at the border, because I go to work with my father. I'm on the tractor, and in front of me I see a Harley, waiting for me. A Harley with a halo around it. That's what I'm seeing. I don't know what happens. I know I have to take a leak, so I get off the tractor. There's also this big branch on the road. I figure I clear it by hand. What I remember is taking a leak, turning back to the tractor, and I hear this crack of thunder! Next thing I know, I'm flat on my back and I'm telling you—excuse my French, Elaine—it's like I've just been fucking a tree. But really into it, you know. Like I can't get up, I can't get away. Arms all over me. But I do sort of fight the tree and get to my feet.

"Next thing I hear is 'Moron! Mr. Big Man!' It's my father; I think he's yelling at the foreman, but he actually got the American foreman by the arm and brings him over to me. 'See? I told you it was too soon for him.'

"I look around. My father's pointing to the fallen tree. There's no tractor. There's just this uprooted tree. 'You'll pay for this. I don't care how many years. Mama's boy. Good for long hair. Should have been a girl like Paulette. Warm milk . . .'" Wig stops.

"And?" Elaine asks.

Wig shrugs. He does not remember hitting his father. But they say he hit him hard. They say the American foreman tried to stop him. His father on the ground. The foreman, blood dripping from his nose . . . His father out of work for two weeks. Wig at the bar in Beauce . . . "And," he says to Elaine, "I came to the States."

"But you left something out!"

"How do you know? Mario tell you this?" Mario turns at hearing his name.

"I mean, you're so protective of your father. But, Wig, it must have hit you that you just missed getting killed."

"Yes! At the bar, at Beauce, they say that a lot. I know from then on I live on borrowed time. At first I don't realize it. I mean, I'm sixteen years old, and I destroy a tractor."

"You didn't destroy it. A tree did. And it must have hit you, on some level, that your father seemed to care more for the tractor than the fact that you just missed being killed."

He is relieved. He takes her hand and brings it to his lips. "Ah, Elaine," he says, "you don't know the whole story. Thank you for taking my side. But it was very bad what I did."

"Hey, kissing my girl, are you?"

"Wig was just telling me about how he came to the States."

"Has he gotten to Danbury yet?"

"That was strange," Wig says.

"How?"

"Oh, you're going to love this one," Mario says, getting up to go for a leak.

Wig watches his friend go. He could use another round, or something. Maybe borrow a twenty till tomorrow? Maybe play some pool. Thinking of his father's death. Beauce. The church. The tractor. He looks at Elaine. "It just happened, you know. I was in the bar one night in Beauce. My father was home and I was staying out. And I get into my car to visit my girlfriend, and instead, hey, I have my working papers from the woods, I got some clothes in the trunk, all of a sudden I'm driving. I figure, the border's only sixty miles, if I get 'cross, I'll just see. Usually, alone, sixteen, they stop you. But I have my papers, and who knows, maybe it was Sunday night or early Monday morning and they believe I'm going to work. I was going to work all right." He stops. Looks at his empty shot glass.

"Do you want another?" Elaine asks tentatively.

"Maybe a beer."

"Okay. My round."

"I just drive, drive all night. I want to go to Danbury. I think it's Danbury, New York. I already got maybe three friends there. So I know the name. Maybe I see the sign, I don't know. I'm so tired, I just get the car off the road and go to sleep.

"Then, when I wake up, oh my God! I'm tilted, you see." He shows her, putting his body at an angle. "But I got to get out of this car. Yet everything's on an angle. Like this. I'm not sure I see what I see. But I get out of the car, I start walking, following. I'm in this huge field. It's foggy."

Wig points to Pauli Girl. "I look way up. I'm in front of a lumberjack, twice as big as him, maybe more. The mustache like that, checked shirt like that, big boots. Only difference, Pauli Girl could walk between his legs. But he looks so nice too, you know. Very gentle. A giant lumberjack. I figure it would be good to work for him.

"Then I see a big saint, as big as the lumberjack but in blue with a red cape. Big 'S' for 'saint' right on his chest. Red, like Christ's blood. I'm beginning to pinch myself. I see a bunch of pigs, but I feel my own flesh, so, no matter what I've done, I'm still a man. There are bigger pigs than me. I'm so thankful that God hasn't turned me into a pig for my sins that, right there, I get on my knees. And I haven't been in church since I'm fourteen. But I cross myself. 'Forgive me, Father,' and I say the whole thing." Wig downs his beer. Pauses. Then he puts his arms out, part shrug, part cross. Brings his head closer to hers. "You guess where I am, Elaine? Sure! The Danbury Fairgrounds! But you see? Before I know I'm in the United States, I know I'm in purgatory!"

Is it Wig pissing him off? Mario wonders. Wig's driving him to New York, and Wig's cough has just cut through the music. "My cough," Wig says in French, turning to him and away from his driving. "It's all this smoking."

"Well, your mother will make you tea with honey in Beauce!"

Wig gives him a look and goes back to his driving. So what if Wig's going to spend his first Christmas in how many years in Quebec. Mario's just used to him and his brother-in-law going to Florida, to visit Paulette, visit the kid.

"Why don't you come with me?" he asked Elaine, Thanksgiving weekend. She had fixed a turkey. Vicky and her girlfriend came; a former student of Elaine's who lives in Paris now, and his wife; Silas Mourner, along with a woman writer who is famous in

England; and Nola and Jimmy joined them, late, for dessert. Nola complimented Elaine on her choice of music. And they all ended up in a rendition of "We gather together to ask the Lord's blessing."

So, when they were alone, he invited her to go with him to Florida. And the funny thing was, he hadn't planned to. He figured he could use some time on his own. He figured the hell if Wig wasn't coming. He'd go to the Rumba. Hang out with the guys. He was almost sorry he'd spoken. Until she hesitated.

"Well?"

"I really appreciate your asking me. I really do. I'll think about it. I really will."

She'd think about it?

"Don't you want to meet my parents? We could drive to Tampa for a few days. Maybe take Victoria with us. Don't you want to meet my daughter?"

She looked uncomfortable.

"It's not that. You have family, Mario. Not me."

"What does that mean?"

Elaine shrugged.

"I'm asking you to be part of my family," he continued. "You'd love Victoria. She's so bright."

"I'm sure she is," Elaine said as if it were a joke played on her.

"What are you planning to do while I'm away?" he asked.

"That sounds like you're suspicious."

"God forbid! I know every woman wants to spend the holidays alone. It's a new form of women's lib."

"I'm not saying I want to. It's, oh, I don't know, it's the holidays. Let me think."

"Think. That's the way to handle it. Think!"

Well, damn it, what was he supposed to do? Rush to her tonight to find out she didn't want to be with him for Christmas?

It opened a floodgate in him. Made him shaky. Restless. "Remember that night?" he asks Wig in French. The night he and

Wig and Paulette were in a bar in St.-Georges—high and wild, and Paulette threw her glass against the top shelf, then everyone else did too. That's when he really fell in love with her. Home to meet her family. Young and crazy and wild. Would Elaine ever start a riot in a bar? She'd think about it first. She is in her apartment, thinking, now. He himself, Mario Picard, feels like starting a riot. What is wrong with him? Working too hard? Too much pressure? So much work before Christmas. All his French guys, his Sheetrock guys, his tapers, all will be spending the holidays at home. They are so close to the country they left that they end up nowhere most of the year. He knows how they feel, in a way. He's jumpy as hell.

He reaches into Wig's glove compartment and takes out a rolled joint. He needs it to calm down. They share it.

"I'm restless," he says to Wig.

"Why don't you come with me for an hour or two? You'd like it. Meet Trisha."

"What is it about this Trisha?"

"Everything. Wait till you see her. She's beautiful. And this black girl she's with, she knows the ropes."

"I know. Trisha gives the best head, and the black girl cops the best crack."

"I can't complain," Wig says, and means it.

What the hell, Mario thinks. A change of pace. So he'll be a little late. A little late to hear Elaine tell him she wants to think for Christmas.

And Wig must have read his mind. He gets off the FDR Drive and heads to the Lower East Side. Of course, usually Mario would say, "Here's where you let me off." This time he doesn't. Wig drives on, and, on East Houston, starts cruising. "Wait till you see her," he says. "She's Greek."

"Treesha!" Wig calls. She turns around. Wig's like that with women. He can spot one at a distance from behind. She motions to the black girl, and they both come toward the car. "Get out!" Wig says impatiently, which surprises Mario, but he moves out and gets into the back seat with—Iodine.

"That's right," the tall thin black girl in the miniskirt says, her eyes in front of her, her blouse opened. "The name's Iodine."

Trisha's as noncommittal. With all Wig's talk of how she gives head, Mario figured that she'd be like a regular girl in that respect, crazy about him. But she's a whore and doesn't seem at all impressed.

"I'm Mario, Trish," he says. Wants a look at her. She turns around. She's swollen above the eye, and the left side of her face's bruised. There's caked blood on the side of her lip.

"My God, what happened to your face?" She's young. At the most nineteen. A kid.

"I'm all right," she says as if he's a creep. Is she even eighteen?

This is more than he bargained for. He wants out of this. They're driving, and it's on the tip of his tongue to tell Wig to let him off when Wig stops the car and Iodine is sent to cop. He watches the girl walk down the street and nod at the three guys by the fence near the housing project. "You've got to try some," Wig says in French. "Iodine's good."

"That'll be the day," he answers. "That will be the day, my friend. I got to get going. I'm late."

In English Wig says, "Will she yell at you if the tea and honey is cold?"

When Iodine returns, they find they have only one pipe, Wig's, so he and Trisha start. What the hell is he doing? Mario wonders. He's in the middle of a mistake. "How old are you?" he asks the petulant Iodine.

"Twenty-one," she says. "Everyone's twenty-one."

Then she figures he wants conversation. She gives it: "It's Pete-zoom. Good stuff."

They pass the pipe back to them. "I think I'll stick to pot." Mario takes a joint from his wallet. Lights it. Passes it to Iodine. "You sure?" she says. After the toke, she puts her lighter to the vial and at the right moment takes a toke of the crack. She smiles then. Surprise! And holds it out.

"What the hell!" he says. "If it makes you happy."

Iodine's esctatic. She holds the lighter carefully, working over his portion like somebody's mother. "Here," she says. And then, like a New York waitress, "Enjoy." Mario takes a toke.

My God, he thinks, I don't believe this.

Trisha's head's no longer in front of him, and Wig's moaning. "No," he says, when he realizes Iodine's unzipping his fly. He moves to his side and takes out his wallet again. Hands her a twenty. "Get some more."

Iodine says, "Boy, welcome to heaven."

Heaven? It has to be paradise. Rush after rush of Pete-zoom. Sheer light.

Later, when the girls get out of the car, Mario gets out too. He takes Trisha aside. He presses a new twenty from the cash machine into her hand and whispers, "Take care of your face." She looks at him. He sees her tongue press inside her upper lip. He takes another twenty and gives it to Iodine. He's a cash machine himself, standing there in Alphabet land, handing out twenties.

"I thought you had an accident!" Elaine in the hallway. She's been in bed: "But not sleeping! I thought you had an accident, and now I almost wish you had! How the hell can you be so damn inconsiderate! Where the hell have you been?"

"With the boys. Come on!"

"I was so damn worried. I had a joint. I took a Valium. I mean, it's two o'clock."

Was it? "Well, if you're so worried about me, why the hell don't you come to Florida over Christmas? No end to the trouble I can get into there!"

"Is this what it's about? You're mad at me!"

"I am not!"

"Oh, Mario, it's okay to be angry."

"But not to keep you waiting. Is that the deal?"

"I didn't say I won't go to Florida. It's just that—well, look, let's sit down and talk."

"Talk?" He finds himself picking her up. "Talk? I'll show you talk."

"Mario!" He's carrying her into the bedroom. He's surprised at himself. She's a feather. He tickles her. She begins to giggle. He tumbles her on the bed, and he's right there too, on top of her. She says, "You're nuts."

"I'll show you nuts."

"I'm still upset."

"Want to bet, lady? Want to bet?"

He can't get enough of her. He just can't. She fights like hell to make him stop, so she can put on music. He lets her go. But then they groan above the music. Oblivious, finally, to the thin walls.

A crystal-clear early-December morning. Mario can't sleep. He gets out of bed quietly, and is dizzy when he stands. His insides churn and he can feel his spirits sink. He sees black in front of his eyes, and zigzag patches of white. His life is rushing downward, from his head, from his heart, from his groin, putting too much pressure on his legs.

He walks into the living room and raises the blue shade; he opens the casement windows, and looks out over the tops of trees. There are still some brown leaves catching the sun and blowing off in the chill wind. His mouth is as dry as his feelings, and he tastes his sticky tongue as he waits for cool air, for the day itself to revive him.

He wonders if he should take a long, long walk. . . . No. He heads into the kitchen to make himself something he usually only drinks early on Monday mornings when he has brought his pickup and has to drive back to Danbury, instant coffee. This too tastes extremely bitter. He wonders where Elaine keeps sugar. He should at least go across the street, get a good cup of coffee from the Greek, and the *Times*. Greeks. No.

He finds some sugar in a bowl, caked from disuse, and stirs a clump of it into the coffee. Round and round and round goes the spoon. He brings his coffee to the living room, puts it down, stretches himself out on the old-fashioned couch, resting his head on its arm, and looks out the window to the light, the brick buildings, the branches. Then he gets up, turns around, and faces the word processor on Elaine's long desk. The computer printout paper, the dictionary, the cardboard tops of her diskettes. Her life.

He closes his eyes, and when he opens them, Elaine is in the living room, looking down at him. She is wearing a long blue robe. Her eyes are wide and vulnerable. Somehow his mother comes into his mind. She was a tall, elegant woman too. Always dressed the part. Lace edges to her slips. Coming into his room when he was a child, explaining away the loud nights. Had they happened?

"Comfortable?" she asks.

"Couldn't sleep."

"Want something to eat?"

"This is fine." He motions at his cup.

"I'll get you some more."

"Sugar?" she asks from the kitchen, surprised.

"Yeah, throw in some sugar."

She comes back with two steaming cups, puts them on the coffee table, and sits in the chair across from the couch, her bare feet resting on the table. She reaches for her coffee. Sips for a while. Finally she says, in a calm husky voice, "Mario, I think we should talk."

"I'm sorry I was late."

She takes a breath. "You know, we've always been honest with each other."

"Yes."

"I couldn't sleep either."

"You were asleep. Trust me."

"Was I? Listen, Mario, you came in at two in the morning from a night out with the guys. Okay. And you were speeding, weren't you?"

"Are you complaining?"

"Don't get defensive. I just want us to talk."

"Talk."

She looks into his eyes. He doesn't turn away. He feels restless and at the same time excited.

"I know you're upset because I've hesitated about Florida. I've hesitated for a few reasons, and I want to tell them to you. In terms of work, Christmas vacation is a chance for me to write. Joyce keeps saying I should start something new. I need some time alone to get into a new work. I mean, that's my logical reason. The other, I guess, is deeper. I mean, eventually, sure, I want to meet your daughter. But it's almost like a joke in a way, Mario? I mean, I know we're not married—"

"That could be remedied."

"Could it, now?" For the first time that morning they smile. She continues. "I'm just not ready to go to Florida yet. I'm not ready to meet your family. I'm not ready for another stepdaughter—"

"You'd love Victoria!"

Now she smiles ironically.

He sort of understands, just like that. "Then are you ready for a kid?"

"At my age?"

"Hey, you still got that biological clock."

She laughs. "Sometimes, for the first time, I even hear it ticking. So I need some time alone. Do you understand? It always takes me time to sort things out."

"Did you and Larry try to—"

"No."

"Why not?"

"I had my work; he had his daughter."

"I'm not Larry."

"I know. It's really . . . With you, I mean, it's the first time I ever thought seriously of— Do you think I'm crazy?"

"No," he says, and suddenly he feels on top of the world. "Not at all. Take your time. It's okay. If you've got to think, think."

She sighs.

"That was so difficult for you?" he asks.

"Yes."

"Do you want to know about last night?"

"I think I know. You went out with the guys, got a little high. Did a little coke. I don't trust coke myself. I've seen people get pretty wasted on coke."

"What about crack?"

She looks at him. "Are you kidding? I read the papers."

"Ah, they just make a big deal about any new drug."

"You're not telling me you did crack?"

"Wig likes it. So I gave it my once. And that's it, believe me. That stuff's a killer. It's too good. You know, I woke up thinking about it?"

"Mario!"

"Hey, I felt like a real nobody last night. I thought you were sort of slipping away from me. But what you told me this morning . . ." His wallet is on the table. He reaches over and takes out a joint. "Let's relax, okay?" He lights the joint, takes a toke, and passes it.

"I think I need this," she says. "Are you serious, Mario? You actually tried crack? Next thing you'll tell me is that you're going to do a little heroin."

He laughs. "I'm not a fool. I told you the truth. I've wanted to try it since I first read about it. And then Wig kept talking about it all the time. And last night, because I didn't think I had much to lose . . . Well, once is enough. That's for sure. But what you're saying this morning—Elaine, you make me feel good, so damn good."

He passes the joint again. Elaine says, "I can't believe it! Wig's on crack? On crack? Why, he's not a fourteen-year-old kid in the ghetto! I mean, you tried it once. I mean, I don't think that was smart at all—"

"Hey, you want the truth? I gave it to you. I don't do hard drugs anymore. You know that. And I won't do crack again, unless you want to try it once."

"I think I'll pass."

"Okay. That's up to you."

He can see her trying to understand. He's surprised she doesn't. He says, "I thought you might like to give it a try, that's all. When you're not thinking, you like an adventure."

She looks at him pensively. "I'd be afraid."

"Afraid?"

"I would be. I'd be afraid once I started—it all starts with once—I might not be able to stop. Like they say in the papers. All those kids in Harlem. All those mothers no longer watching those kids. What makes me any different from them? How do I know I'd be able to stop. No, it makes me scared."

"Scaredy-cat! Wouldn't even try it once. I tried it once, and look at me. Hey, don't look at me like that. I promise you, never again. Come on, Elaine. What about a bath? A bubble bath to warm us up?"

"You think so?"

"What's wrong?"

She shrugged. She got up. "I'll call you when it's ready." She leaves.

They face each other in among the bubbles. "I'm glad we talked," she says. "But I'm upset by a lot of what you had to say."

"Sometimes that's the way the truth is."

"I know."

"Come on, smile, babe. You know, Wig still hasn't canceled

his plane ticket. I'll buy it for you. You could think in Florida. Write too. I'd leave you alone all you want. What do you say?"

She perks up a bit then, and he thinks, Why am I pushing it? It might have been okay, a few weeks alone.

"Next Christmas, I promise you," she says.

"Next Christmas?" That's all he says. His happy feeling? Fled.

TEN

Four shopping days before Christmas. Elaine saw a dusting of snow on the bare trees and the grassy ovals of her apartment complex as she went out to move her car to the right side of the street. She sat in her car, waiting for the legal time for it to be there, drinking her cup of coffee from the deli, and listening to music on her headsets. Rather than leaving notes to thieves proclaiming NO RADIO, she relied on their intelligence to see there really was no radio to steal.

It was a very clear, icy-cold day, as vivid as the holiday wrapping paper visible in the shopping bag next to her. She'd wrapped twelve small packages—all of them ornaments for Nola and Jimmy's tree. Neither the weather nor the cheerful wrappings nor having found a space easily thrilled her. In the season of perky elves, she seemed to be susceptible to small dark demons.

Elaine looked at her watch. Time. Other people were getting out of their cars and locking their doors in understated triumph.

She got out of her car, then leaned over to the passenger seat and grabbed her shopping bag. She was walking over to Nola's. It would be the first Christmas in, she counted, five that she'd spend any time with her stepdaughter. Every year, in accordance with the dictates of the season, they'd exchanged cards. This year Elaine had expected one from L.A. But Second Hand was still in New York. They had gigs, and Asia Neither Land and Jimmy Along had a tree. Elaine didn't.

She was on First Avenue now. Trees were being sold on every other block, and their fragrance was in the air. A lot of the sellers were down from Quebec, wearing their ubiquitous red-and-black-plaid flannel shirts and wool caps. They lived out of their vans for this season, guarding their trees, making their American dollars. Probably washed up in the coffee shops where they ate. Or did they bring food down with them and just go in for coffee? No one ever writes them up in the *Times*. Another silent group of foreigners working their asses off . . . She walked farther.

". . . coke?"

She shook her head. Looked cool. Just your garden-variety dope dealer—young, open-laced running shoes, good-quality jeans. He, his beeper, and his friends were in her neighborhood. Not only on the corners that had phones. It looked like a yard sale on Tenth Street. She thought of what was happening to Wig and had a moment of rage.

She got to Nola's place, rang, and was let in. She did her steady walk up the flights of stairs. She heard music. "Hi, Elaine. Merry Christmas."

Nola at the door. The tree, Jimmy, and, of all elves, Silas Mourner behind her.

"Looks like I'm not too late for the trimming. Had to repark the car. Here, these are for you."

"You're cold," Nola said, taking the package.

"It's cold out. Jimmy. Silas. Merry Christmas."

Jimmy surprised her. "Elaine." He put down an ornament and came over, embraced her warmly.

"Silas." He kissed her on both cheeks, in homage to their old Italy. With his snow-white hair, green-rimmed glasses, and rosy cheeks, he looked like Santa. "You look like Santa."

"Father Time, my dear. Father Time."

"Well, then, to the New Year."

"Do you think it will be good for business?" he asked Jimmy.

"I hope it's good for Second Hand," Jimmy said, ignoring the rub. Then he turned to Elaine. "Nola tell you we have a manager, Elaine? From Hempstead. Long Island loves us."

"So I've heard."

"Look at this!" Nola said, diverting the conversation, not without guile. She had unwrapped one of the small packages. "Come on, you guys, help me open these." She was holding a pear made of fractured and reflecting glass.

The most fun Elaine had had that week was picking out trimming. There was a Santa on a wooden sled, a purple translucent ball from Norway, a crystal bird with a big beak hovering over a small nest. Nola and Jimmy opened them one by one and figured out where to hang them on the tree. Silas was busy using his talents to turn glimmering wrapping paper into a glittering chain. "I can use this!" he said, appreciative of Elaine's eye for wrappings.

Elaine walked around the room, bopped a little to the music, looked out the window. Then she said, "It's nice to see a tree."

"You mean, you don't have one?" Nola asked. "You and Dad always had the greatest trees."

"They were for you. Didn't you get it, Nola?" she answered. "I think I'll get myself a soda." She went to her stepdaughter's fridge. Then she said, "Christmas."

"Look at this!" Nola held up a small golden baby angel. "A . . . a *putto*!" she said, recalling her stepmother's nomenclature from across the years.

"I always liked *putti*." Elaine moved back into the room.

"Roma!" Silas proclaimed. "I'd still be there if it weren't for my bed. I had this superb brass bed. The police—not the group, children, but the real article—had a station on my block. And, with all the violence of the seventies, and the kidnappings, and with the ears and fingers and bodies popping up here, there, every-which-where, in letters, in packages, in cars, well, it was just too much. It simply got on my nerves."

Nola peeked out from behind a branch. "Your bed, Silas? What did the violence have to do with your bed?"

"Everything, child. My brass bed transmitted all those damn police calls right through its pipes. At first I thought it was a series of nightmares. But I actually was being woken up nightly to every crime in Rome. I was enveloped in a brass tabloid."

"You shoulda gotten another bed."

"Ah, Jimmy, Jimmy, you're such an American. I looked at it from a different point of view. If Rome was coming right into my home, and making me give up my extremely comfortable, ornamental, and at certain times nostalgic bed, I might as well give up Rome. Logic, Jimmy. We were a generation that lived by logic."

"And comfort." Elaine laughed. "Show me an expatriate and I'll show you someone who found an especially pretty place and figured out how to get someone else to clean up for him, cheap."

"Such a cynic, Elaine. Anyway, I'm an ex-expatriate now. In a six-story walkup. Atoning for the excesses of my youth."

"Your logical youth," Nola said, darting away from the tree, stepping back as far as the small room would allow. "That's great, Jimmy," she said, approving his placement of Elaine's ornaments. "They're the best," she said to Elaine. "Yours always were."

"Here, Jimmy," Silas said. "I think this chain is long enough." He handed an end to Jimmy, and the two of them distributed it around the tree; nicely, considering it would have been better to put it on first.

Elaine and Nola watched. "Silas Mourner's logical youth," Nola said.

"You better watch out, Silas," Elaine said, "or you're going to end up in a song."

"One I should be singing in California?" Nola asked, moving toward the men.

"Where did that come from?" Elaine asked. She hadn't been thinking of Nola's postponed trip, but now of course she was. She felt uncomfortable.

"Everyone else is happy we're going to graduate before we go," Nola said.

"Well, so am I," Elaine said. "You guys only have one more semester now—"

"Now?" Nola said.

"Look, I think it makes a lot of sense. For goodness' sake, I'm not against your finishing school!" Elaine took a slug of her soda. "And I'm happy to continue to pay the parking for the van. Merry Christmas."

"What are you doing for Christmas?" Jimmy asked, coming over to her.

"Jimmy!" Nola demanded.

"Don't mind her, Elaine. It's 'PMS and the Rock Star.' "

"Ha-ha, Jimmy."

"I'm not going to do anything special. I planned to work, but I seem to be having trouble getting started."

"Why didn't you go to Florida with Mario?" Nola asked.

"I didn't want to at the time. Maybe I should have."

"Couldn't you still go?" Nola asked.

Jimmy said, "You should do something Christmas Day."

"I will be. My friend Judith's coming in for a visit."

"All right! I don't think it's a good time to be alone," Jimmy said, taking one long look at the tree.

He was a good guy. A sensitive kid. Nice face. Intense eyes. Relaxed body language. Elaine wondered if he really would end up in finance. Maybe Nola and Jimmy would marry and settle down and have kids. And Elaine would visit on holidays, with a shopping bag full of excitingly wrapped presents. And she'd bump into Delilah at times, and Larry—

Larry. His voice on the phone lately. "Bunny would like to

meet you." She would? Well, she'd have her chance this afternoon. "Have you heard from Anne Gregory?" She had a call in. Anne had decided to join Reid in Thailand for the holidays. He was on a trip "all alone," as Anne phrased it over the phone when Elaine finally got through to her, Anne's intonation X-ing out Cynthia. Another triumph of creative marriage. Was Elaine being too creative? Should she have gone with Mario? Mario had a daughter to visit. And at the last minute Wig had decided to go see his sister and his niece after all. Should she be there as well?

"Beautiful tree," Elaine said out loud, taking a good long look at it and pulling herself away from her uneasy thoughts. It was beautiful, not too big, well proportioned. It didn't crowd the small room. It was her height. Silas had actually bestirred himself to kneel down and plug in the lights. Suddenly wild neon lights shot on and off, darting through the pine needles, and red chili peppers lit up. Nola and Jimmy's first tree together.

"You want to grab a bite with us, Elaine?"

She looked away from the tree. "Thanks. Not today."

"You feeling okay?" Nola asked with new concern.

"Me? I'm fine. I never even get head colds, do I?" She cooled it. "What I need is some time to myself. Great tree, you two. Superb chain, Silas. And I love the lights."

"Are you sure, Elaine?"

"Really, Nola, I am. And I'm busy this afternoon. I have something to do."

"Thanks for the ornaments," Jimmy said.

"Yeah," Nola said, walking her to the door, smiling, and, Elaine thought, rather relieved that she couldn't stay.

Elaine spent the late afternoon in Saks Fifth Avenue. The inside of the store was decorated with white branches strung up high over the counters. Infrequently, small white lights blinked from them. She wandered from cosmetic counter to cosmetic counter, noticing the brands and, when she could get close enough, trying out shades of lipstick. She was in from the cold clear day with a crowd of shoppers whose luxurious topcoats and scarves and furry hats were warming up, and whose bodies and clothes were sending off clean scents. Among them stood stunning, overly made-up women verging on thirty and meticulously handsome, fey-looking men offering squirts of perfume. They carried straw baskets of gifts for those who were buying gifts. Fragrance Models.

Christmas was the excitement of a New York department store. She remembered the first time her grandmother had taken her to Macy's. The long line, the success of sitting on Santa Claus's lap and whispering desires she made up as she went along. She had started to tell him of gifts for other people until her father's mother told her that was not the way it was done.

Milling around, smelling the scents, she watched wealthy women (all women looked wealthy in Saks) shop. They had long red nails and cleanly plucked and penciled eyebrows, and she could hear the swish of their long leather and fur coats as they bent over counters. She watched them exchange credit cards for merchandise. Seeing their big shopping bags fill up with items that came wrapped in red and gold cheered her. She should have come here sooner. She wondered about the people who complained about the commercialization of Christmas. For her, a kid from Jersey, Christmas started on Thanksgiving Day with Santa being brought to Macy's, preceded by the galaxy of cartoon characters floating through the sky. When she first heard Sister Dolores God talk against that, she thought she was crazy. Even a studious and melancholy kid like Elaine couldn't understand why Christians being thrown to lions and martyrs being stoned to death were more appropriate to Christ's birth in a barn and visitation by camels than a giant Superman or Donald Duck that had to be blown up in Hoboken and transported across the river. Now, in the sweet-smelling warmth of the crush, she could kick herself for having been so down at Nola's. She should have claimed her own Christmas first, before attempting to walk into the room of others'.

What was Christmas but the most elaborate smorgasbord of heart's desires to be bought, wrapped in glittering paper, tied round with beautiful bows, and presented to people you love? It was the gift itself, all wrapped up and under the tree. That was the beauty of it. Once it was opened—then it took its chances. But wrapped up . . . She should move on.

What to bring Larry and Bunny? Nola had told her of ye olde farmhouse. Something for a country kitchen? She went to the third floor, and decided on a very beautiful long, oval cutting board, with different stripes of inlaid wood. She wanted it gift-wrapped, which the harried saleswoman told her would take another half an hour, since they had to call for boxes for that shape. Elaine went to the women's room, freshened up, and then browsed some more. It was only when she was out in the cold, carrying too big a package under her arm, hoping she'd find a cab before some con man eyed her as one not at the moment able to guard her pocketbook, that she wondered once more about Christmas cheer. She shook her head as a scrawny Santa approached her, cheeks too red, white beard askew, holding out a basket, ringing a bell, and saying to her, "Ho, ho, ho. Give dough." Ho, ho, ho, yourself, she thought, hailing a cab in the clear air.

"You shouldn't have," Larry said, taking the package and leading her down the long hall to the living room like a guest.

"You're looking good," she said. He was thinner, definitely, but in a good mood.

"Look who's here," he called out. "Bunny, Elaine; Elaine, Bunny," he said cheerfully, depositing the gift among the others in the fake Art Deco fireplace. Elaine took off her coat and hung it, familiarly, on the iron railing that separated the oval foyer from the two steps down to the big room.

"It's so nice to meet you," Bunny said, extending a hand.

"I've heard a lot about you," Elaine said. She smiled at the younger woman.

Bunny was wearing a beige wool skirt and a matching jacket,

short-waisted, with shoulder pads. She had long thin brown hair pulled off her face, and was wearing a very red lipstick that added some panache to her plain, high-colored face. Her cheeks protruded, and her brown eyes were small. The big smile on her face, like her entire allure, was out of a forties movie—maybe a girl serving enlisted men coffee at the USO. Elaine noticed the one big cloth-covered button sprinkled with rhinestones on the jacket, and the loop that encircled it. Everything was from a vintage-clothing store. It was a style that just missed dowdy.

"Let me get you something to drink. Do you want to try my eggnog? It's potent." Bunny smiled brightly.

"Sure," Elaine said. Ugh, she thought.

"Sit?" Larry said, and the two of them found themselves on the big feathery couch once more.

"No tree," Elaine said.

"We have one in Columbia County. That's where we're having Christmas. Didn't Nola speak to you about it?" Larry asked.

"No. She's too discreet."

"Is that what you call it?" Bunny said. "We asked her to invite you. Really—" Bunny cut herself short and was out of the room precisely and heavily, grounded to duty in her textured stockings and granny shoes. She came back with an enormous tray. "No, that's okay. Here," she said, as Elaine moved to help her. She brought the tray to the coffee table in front of Elaine and Larry.

"How pretty," Elaine said. Bunny had filled a martini shaker with the eggnog, but brought out the three glass punch-bowl cups to drink it from. On an opaque round dish she had an assortment of Christmas cookies. Bright green and red sparkles shining from tree shapes and Santa shapes and reindeer. "You made these?"

"Larry and I."

"How sweet."

Larry laughed.

"It is sweet," Elaine defended herself. "It's the holiday season; it's nice."

Bunny poured. Elaine picked up one of the small red linen napkins.

After she poured, Bunny got up from her chair facing the table and the couch and walked over to the big windows. "Sunset is so early," she said. "You just missed it, Elaine."

"I know." Bunny wasn't twenty-five, the way Elaine had been when she first gravitated to those windows. She might be thirty.

"You are welcome, Elaine," Bunny said.

"Huh?"

"For Christmas dinner."

"Thanks. I made other plans. Judith's coming in," she said to Larry.

Bunny said, "Sure, by now you would have. And here I've been waiting for your answer. Well, if you want to do something right, do it yourself," she said, and looked at Larry.

"You're a painter?" Elaine changed the subject. "What are you working on now?"

" 'Painter' isn't exact. I was doing more painting before, but now I combine it with photo montage. In fact, Larry and I are thinking of doing some work together."

"Really?"

"Well, it's from the book," Bunny said imprecisely, the windows behind her, the eggnog cup in her hand. "While Larry is . . . recuperating, while he's undergoing this new treatment, we've been bringing together a lot of his unpublished work. It's fascinating, Elaine. You know how good the work is. I know he wanted you to help him. But, anyway, second best, I guess, but I have the job, and—"

"Some of the photos seem to have an effect on her," Larry said. "So I'm printing what she likes, and she's been incorporating them into her canvases. Why don't you show her the one we're going to hang, dear?"

"Yes," Elaine said. "I'd love to see one."

Bunny looked wary; then she shrugged. She walked over, put her cup on the tray, and left the room.

Elaine avoided Larry, concentrated on picking out a cookie. "New treatment," Bunny had said. They were three civilized people, so she knew immediately not to intrude on Bunny and Larry's two words.

"Very interesting," Elaine said of the collage, in which various photographed body parts and faces were separated by painted barriers.

Instead of responding, Bunny looked at her watch. "Whoops, it's time for your pill."

"Leave it out, dear," Larry said.

Bunny shrugged. Left the canvas against the wall and went out of the room again, then returned quickly with pills and water.

"We did our own Christmas cards too," Bunny said cheerfully. As Larry downed the pill, she allowed her face to go sad, but her voice stayed upbeat. "Did you get yours yet? No collage, that one. All Larry's work."

Elaine remembered that she had made gingerbread Santas during the first Christmases of her marriage—for Nola, natch. And though she hadn't abandoned her own research, she put all of her ability into her collaboration with Larry. Together they'd done two books. He's found another one like me, she thought. For all the physical disparities, watching Bunny cater to her now ill ex-husband was like watching a younger version of herself.

She wondered if Bunny had come across Elaine's old lavender dress and her Majorca pearls in a vintage store yet. That's what she had worn the day she met Larry, in this very room. She pictured Bunny wearing her once so-proper grown-up clothes.

She actually took another cup of rich cholesterol and sat herself back on the plump couch and watched the two of them talk. It was then that she realized she hadn't had anything much to eat. Bunny was sounding him out about the photos he had done in Venice in '77. "You were on that trip, weren't you, Elaine?" Bunny asked.

"Yes."

"The richness of that work . . ." Bunny went on about it, but Elaine, who knew how to keep quiet, simply smiled.

Bunny was radiant, ready to overcome any obstacle, any jealousy even, to be true to Larry's talent, to be careful of Larry's waning health. Elaine was jealous.

Was it real people we fell in love with, flesh-and-blood real people? Elaine wondered. Or certain types? It was an amazing experience to sit on a couch and watch herself in Bunny. It was as if she had never existed. By watching Bunny and Larry together, she realized that a part of her own self-esteem had stayed in the very safe keeping of Larry's loss of her.

"What do you hear about the book?" Larry asked.

"Nothing right now. Anne's decided to play Ping-Pong in Bangkok. Reid's there, boning up."

Larry laughed. "No plans for the book?"

"Oh, yes. Anne says they're planning some ads, and a book tour too. The publicity person is supposed to contact me right after the New Year. Spring publication. So I hope it's a good year . . . for all of us."

"Oh, I'll be okay," Larry said. "Bunny's giving me a second wind."

Bunny, sitting opposite them, picked up the plate of cookies, offered them to Elaine once more. Was it her rouge or was she blushing?

Second wind, Elaine thought on the bus. Was she crazy taking a bus this season? Well, she had a seat from which to watch the traffic jam. She looked at her watch, seven-thirty already, what else did she have to do? Second wind. She should be—yes, should be—very happy that her ex-husband was getting a second wind in his besieged lungs. What she felt was rage.

Jimmy had been hinting about Christmas dinner before. It was painfully clear that Nola hadn't wanted her there. So what? Even if Nola had extended the invitation, Elaine would not have driven to Columbia County on a holiday. Maybe Nola would have suggested they all go in the van! Remember high-school graduation! She hadn't been invited to that either. So what? She could kill, she was so mad. Who? She looked around at all the shoppers and tourists on this rather safe bus. She saw the headline. Middle-class person mows down her own! Why? 'Cause Nola didn't invite her to a place she wouldn't go?

The bus bogged down in holiday traffic on Fifth Avenue; only the horse-drawn carriages, moving in and out of the four lanes as if they were motorcycles, were getting anywhere. And they were all going to the Christmas tree at Rockefeller Center, straight ahead. A carriage drew up next to her. Inside were a smartly dressed young couple, a white blanket pulled up to their knees, champagne in a bucket in front of them; they clicked real glasses and drank. Well, she'd done that once with Ben Gary of the leaking bathroom. She'd taken her turn at being part of the postcard. The carriage whizzed by.

Forty-five minutes later she got off the bus at Twenty-third Street. She saw a crosstown bus right there, but no, she found herself walking. Walking fast in the cold, clear night. Gaining energy that replaced her earlier rage. She jogged from Park Avenue South to Second. Then she ran to First. There she steadied her pace and turned the corner. Again, she wasn't thinking, simply moving, walking now two blocks to the supermarket, in front of which there was a line of Christmas trees.

"Hello," she said to the vendor. "Are you from Quebec?"

"Yes," he said, with his Québecer's nice smile, steaming coffee in his gloved hand.

She went to the tilted trees and took a long look. "How much is one like this?"

"Fifty-five dollars."

"Fifty-five dollars?"

"Seven feet."

"Do you deliver?"

He nodded.

"I don't want to pay fifty-five, but I want one about that size."

He shrugged and went to the tied trees, which in the night light looked somewhat like fragrant rolled carpets.

"A fresh one!"

"Here," he said, coming back with a big one. "This one good."

"How much?"

"Fifty-five with delivery."

"Take forty?"

"For forty." He pointed to a smaller one.

"No. Here," she said, "like this." She and the Canadian bumped the trunk against the pavement. She didn't see too many needles fall.

"Fifty," he said.

"Cut off the bottom?"

"I put a . . ." He showed her the X he'd make too.

"Okay. Can you deliver tonight? Great. In an hour. I have to get to a cash machine, and I have to get a stand. Here." She wrote the address down for him and explained how to locate her building.

She went to the cash machine, the variety store, open late, and then home.

The Canadian came on time, and he helped her put the tree up. "Oh!" she exclaimed when he cut the cords around it, and the branches unfolded into storybook shape. Before she had time to think, the apartment was filled with growth and fragrance. It was as if the living room were alive. Her heart filled with the spirit of pine.

During the next days she did not work on her writing at all. She cheerfully went her rounds. She bought ornaments for herself. She bought lots of kids' gifts, things she would once have liked to receive herself, and deposited them in big cans and under plastic trees at the two neighborhood banks that were collecting gifts for New York's homeless children. She looked at all the other toys other people had given. Together it added up at least to a little. Some kid, somewhere, would find something to like.

"A tree," Judith said, sitting in Elaine's living room, "and a roast in the oven?"

"A goose."

"A goose?" Judith said in disbelief.

"A small one."

"That should do wonders for my waistline." Judith was wearing a red sack dress, the red fine against her dark, gray-streaked hair and expressive face. "This season, I swear, even if you don't celebrate it, the parties alone can ruin you. I came here to avoid the season with you. I thought that was our deal. And I find a tree and a goose. Always surprises."

"I was feeling sorry for myself," Elaine said, champagne bottle in hand, "before I put up my tree."

"And then you turned into the spirit of Christmas?"

Elaine popped open the cork and poured.

"L'chaim," Judith said. And after she drank, "I always feel sorry for myself at Christmas. Do you know what these trees did to my life when Susan and David were young? They'd come home from school and tell us all about their friends' trees. Not only their Christian friends—Jewish kids too. I say I felt sorry for myself, but I felt bad having to say no to them. You know what it's like to say no to Christmas in this society?"

"Couldn't you have had a nondenominational tree?"

"The good old Chanukah bush?"

"Exactly!"

"I wish I could have, Elaine. But I just didn't buy it."

"Why?"

"It's another compromise in the land of compromises. I just couldn't compromise the fact that I'm Jewish."

"Christian, Jewish, what does it matter? Why can't we pick and choose among religions, take what we need?"

"That's too easy."

"Does it have to be difficult? I mean, in the summer sometimes

I go up to South Fallsburgh, to the ashram there, and hear Guru Maya. She sits and sings and tells us God exists in us as us, and I believe that. And this week I was feeling low. I went up to St. John the Divine. Have you ever heard the Bishop speak? He's inspiring. They believe in the New Jerusalem on West One Hundred Tenth Street." Elaine paused and then said, "Last night I went to Midnight Mass for the first time in a long time, and I prayed for my parents."

"My goodness, what are you having, some Born Again attack?"

"I'm taking what I need."

"But you're so eclectic! You just can't go around suiting yourself like that!"

"I just have."

Judith looked at the tree. "What were you feeling low about?"

"About being so alone. About not having a family."

"I'm telling you, this time of year can kill you."

"Well, I'm proud of myself. I didn't let it. The minute I put up this tree, everything changed. I was picking out the ornaments—I mean, I haven't had a tree in years—and I kept seeing those that said, 'Our first Christmas together,' 'Our fifth Christmas together,' 'Baby's first Christmas' . . ."

"And?"

"And," Elaine said, "I wondered if I were ahead of a new market. I thought, If I were really to commemorate this Christmas, I'd have to find an ornament that read, 'To my first real Christmas on my own.' "

"A million-dollar idea!" Judith joked. "Knowing you, by next year you'll have it in production."

Judith looked over at the tree bursting with lively figures and then to the rectangular table set for dinner. "Those candle holders of mine hold up, don't they?"

"They're great."

"Who knows, if I worked harder, if the kids hadn't come along . . . We all have trade-offs, Elaine."

"Translation?"

"You know what I mean. I had the kids, you sure have had more of the world. None of us has it all."

"Are you sure? It's still not too late for me."

Judith said, "If you mean for kids, I hope you're joking."

Elaine didn't answer. Poured more champagne. "I think that roast must be just about ready. But let's have a toast. To our friendship, Judith, and to the New Year."

"And to the new ornament," Judith said. "What shape will it be?"

"Maybe in the shape of a full heart," Elaine said. "A new ornament for a very old tree."

ELEVEN

Bzzzzzz. "Elaine, where are you? Miss you, baby. You're my lady. See you soon."

"To this year with you," Mario said. They were in the living room; he was pouring the champagne. The tree had begun to droop, not to mention shed, but she wasn't quite ready to discard it. It was two weeks into the new year. "To health, to love, to luck. To us. To Lake Acres. To completing the mall. To your book," he said. He had a slight tan and a big smile. "And to next Christmas," he said, "together. Wait!" He grinned even wider. "And to New York, New York. It's great to be back." Clink!

"Hi, Donna. Wasn't I supposed to hear from the publicity person this week? Okay, thanks. Sure, Monday or Tuesday is fine. Will Anne be back by then? Okay. You have good holidays? Oh, you were? Me too. Well, here's to the New Year. Talk to you soon."

"Hi, Marla. Is Joyce free? She didn't get back to me yesterday. Oh, I see. Okay. Tell her I called."

With every phone call Elaine made to Panther Publishers or to Joyce at the agency, she became more timid. Every time she got Donna on the phone, or Marla, she felt a little shier. That was the word, "shy." As if she were doing something tactless before publication, making an unsubtle nuisance of herself. She had been raised to be polite. To identify other people's feelings and to be careful of them. When she had wanted something her mother wouldn't give her, her mother had always said, "How do you think I feel? Think of someone else for a change. I'm the one who has to say no." There was something she wasn't being given. She couldn't identify what it was. All she had was the feeling that she should be sensitive enough not to embarrass her publisher. But she couldn't bring herself to question what there was to be embarrassed about.

In the bubble bath with Mario. They were stretched out at either end, her legs on top of his, her Achilles heels feeling his hard belly. Each with an arm dry to share the joint. It was very late at night, actually early Sunday morning. They had made love. He hadn't been able to sleep. Gone out for a short walk to shed his anxiety. When he came back, he woke her up to love. Then she was wide awake, so they drew a bath. Both had worries. She wasn't the only one. There were some big drainage problems at the Danbury Fair site which had slowed construction. And at Lake Acres, because it was a warm winter, there was too much mud. He had started smoking cigarettes again.

And Wig. "He's hooked," Mario said, tracing her calf with his wet hand. "When he works, he works like a superman, but it's harder and harder to rely on him. It's going to cut into our weekends, love. I got a payroll to meet, and you were right, I can't really depend on that guy. He was a wreck in Florida. I said, Wig, get off that stuff."

"Crack?" Elaine asked.

"You got it. And you were right about that stuff. I'm af—"
He cut himself off.

"Afraid of what?"

"You're going to make too much of it."

"It's my prerogative. I'm a writer. Or I think I'm a writer."

"You are a writer. What you should do—"

"Come on, Mario. Don't get me off the subject. What are you afraid of?"

His smile faded. "That he'll bring that stuff back to Danbury. I've made him promise to keep it away from the men."

"Oh, Mario!"

"I don't want you to worry about it. And I don't want to talk about it. I'll take care of it. It's my problem."

"But I can see you're worried, Mario. You hardly sleep."

"Things seemed easier last summer. The money seemed to be pouring in."

"Everything got very easy last summer." With her toes she touched on why. "Now mud's holding you up in Danbury. Imagine wishing for a colder winter! And me, I can't get my editor on the phone."

"Look, when I have a contract and the delivery isn't on time, like now, when they're giving me some crap about money I know I don't owe, I get on the phone and I demand to know what's going on. I counterattack before I'm attacked. Get it?"

She took a final toke and gave him the joint. Then she slid farther down into the water. "I don't want to call anymore. Hello, Donna. Hello, Marla. All I get are the assistants. I'm embarrassed. Everybody's always busy."

"But you've got to find out what they're going to do about your book."

"Don't you realize, Mario," she snapped, "that they're not going to do a damn thing about my book!"

She untangled herself from Mario and sat up straight. Said nothing. Just listened to her own words. Mario's eyes shifted from her, and he didn't say anything either. He seemed surprised.

•   •   •

"Hi, Donna. Is Anne in today? She won't be back till tomorrow. What time? I want to see her. Oh, she'll call? At what time? I need a definite time. Eleven? She'll definitely be there at eleven. You want me to call if she doesn't? Does that mean she won't call? Really? Tell her eleven, tomorrow. Really, hah? That much work? You mean she couldn't get it all done in Katmandu? Yeah, I know she didn't go there. You tell Anne Gregory that I'm coming to the office at eleven o'clock and I'm staying in that damn office until I speak with her. Angry? Why should I be angry? That's right. Eleven. Fine. Oh, it's okay? I'll be there."

"Yes, that's exactly what I told her, Joyce. Wait on you? This is the first time I've gotten to speak with you in a month. Yeah, a major shit fit. That seems to be what gets people to answer the phone. Oh. You have tried? You couldn't get to her either. I don't know, Joyce. I don't know if I can, I'm furious. Okay, okay, I'll try to be politic. Ask her what? Okay. Okay, I'll write it all down. I'll try. Okay. Okay. You're going to call now? That's how you see it? Okay. Okay. Yeah. Okay, I'll ask everything I want to know. Calmly. Yeah. Okay. Okay. If you say so."

Joyce said Elaine now had Anne Gregory on the defensive.

At ten to eleven on Tuesday morning, Elaine arrived at Panther Publishers. They had recently been bought by Cantilever Rigging and had moved to the Homemakers of America Building, which Cantilever owned. Panels of the lobby walls were floor-to-ceiling mirrors, and Elaine veered round a potted plant to take a full-length look at herself. She tried to act as if she weren't really looking, so that the elevator guard, if he noticed, wouldn't think she was vain. She was wearing her three-quarter-length leather jacket, which she had bought on her big advance; her suede boots from Milan; and the long green skirt with the slit. She was carrying a big leather pouch of a bag over her shoulder, inside a notebook for the notes she'd promised Joyce she'd take. She had to stay cool. She had to ask specific questions. Do I look okay? she wondered. Do I look like a writer?

It still amazed her that the banks of elevators in these New York skyscrapers carried everybody, that they didn't eject you if you didn't look like you belonged. But once on, and going vertically, no one looked like he'd ever taken a subway.

Through the lavish mirrors she watched this particular crush of people going into the up elevator in the bank that had its light on. There were messengers, and harried-looking men in business suits. There were well-dressed secretaries, along with people who had appointments and a breezy we-gotta-get-where-we're-going air. There were no workers on the elevator, or punk kids, except for the messengers. And who the hell was that? Anne Gregory! In a beautiful flowing fur-trimmed coat. She got in the elevator last, turned around, looking too preoccupied to focus on anyone else. She glanced at her watch. The door closed. Seven minutes to eleven. Anne Gregory was going to work.

Two minutes to spare. Elaine had planned to be in the office at five to eleven, and at five to eleven that's just where she'd be. She was not going to be polite and give Anne Gregory time to settle in. She resolutely turned from the mirror and, at the sound of the beep and the sight of the light, she walked into the very next elevator going up. She was let off in front of the imposing doors to Panther Publishers. She walked in.

The receptionist looked up. "Yes?"

"Elaine Netherlands, I have an eleven o'clock appointment with Anne Gregory."

She picked up a phone. "An Elaine Nettermans to see Anne Gregory?"

"No, it's an Elaine Netherlands."

"She'll be right with you," the receptionist said, as if Elaine had just barely passed muster. "Please take a seat."

It was a large room, and it contained two people, Elaine and the receptionist, who had nothing to say to each other. Elaine looked at the couch and then at the large display cabinet of books. She unbuttoned her jacket and went over to the display. She examined the books. There were mysteries and children's books and cookbooks and Loretta Irone's latest, not yet on the market.

Donna entered the room. She was a pleasant-looking young woman, wearing black slacks and a long sweater over her stomach and hips. She had a round face, slightly anxious, and dark eyes, and wore bright-red lipstick and big goofy earrings in consecutive circles of red and black. She was an earthy person. A contrast to her boss. One could imagine that she sweat.

What Elaine saw on Donna's face was the burden of balancing everything. On how much money? Elaine thought. Did she make twenty-five thousand doing most of Anne Gregory's dirty work? "Good to see you, Elaine," Donna said. "Anne will be right with you. Come on in."

The enormous room had been sectioned off into cubicles. Donna's was in the middle tier, and Elaine, following her there, watched young men and women come and go from cubicle to cubicle. Donna introduced her to two assistants, one from the publicity department.

Everyone looked busy. So had that receptionist who had described her as a commodity: Hello, there's a hundred and twenty pounds of human being out here, want me to ship it in to Anne Gregory? Everyone looked busy, yet Elaine's publicity was not done. Elaine had not yet met her PR person. Her book tour was up in the air. Her publication date had been delayed till early summer and she still did not know how many copies of the book they planned. Everyone looked busy, but she wondered what was getting done. She remembered she had promised Joyce not to get mad.

What about ironic? She was probably as welcome as a new Chrysler with questions about its fuel efficiency would be in Lee Iacocca's office. She was a product that did lunch! A commodity that asked questions! A walking, talking Brillo box showing self-interest in shelf life. She was not part of this office.

Donna motioned her to the seat next to her desk, in her airless cubicle, and then picked up the phone. "Elaine's here, Anne!" she called cheerily. "Anne'll be right with you. Want some coffee?" she said, putting down the phone.

"That would be nice."

"Cream? Sugar?"

"A little milk."

"Elaine, dear!" The voice was Anne Gregory's. She swept in. Elaine could smell the perfume, and she couldn't help admiring the beauty and the grace: The style of the red and white silk blouse and the white wool skirt. The pearl-and-ruby necklace at her throat, and the rubies and diamonds on her fingers. It was as if two bearers with trumpets—the type of servants you probably could hire and attire for nothing before World War I—announced her arrival, one blaring "MONEY," the other whispering "taste."

"It's so good to see you. It's been so long."

Elaine stood up, and Anne led her into her office.

"I'll bring in the coffee," Donna called after them.

The large corner office had windows on two sides, giving panoramic views of the skyline of Manhattan. Anne Gregory even had the Chrysler Building in this lifetime. Elaine looked out at the miraculous curved fins slanting upward: at this height she could see the gargoyles clearly.

"I see you still like the view," Anne said.

"It'll do."

"Please, sit down."

After she sat down, she opened her bag. By the time Donna had brought in the coffee and put it on Elaine's side of Anne's desk, she had her notebook on her lap. Suddenly she was shaky and had trouble grabbing a pencil. God damn it, she thought, if you cry, Elaine, I'll kill you. She'd wait a minute before she attempted to pick up her cup of coffee. She closed her eyes for a second and envisioned the smell of pine.

"You seem upset," Anne Gregory said gently.

"I might have reasons to be, Anne."

"If I've done anything to upset you—"

"I have some notes here. Perhaps we can start with them."

The phone buzzed. "One second?" Anne said.

Elaine sighed, put her notebook on the desk near her coffee, and stood up. She went to the bookshelves in this room and looked them over. Yes, there they were, lots of copies of the books she'd seen in the display cabinet. Piles of Loretta Irone on a table, ready to be shipped out to important people. Then, on the bottom shelf, she saw two copies of *The Passion and the Vow*. As Anne answered another call, Elaine bent down and picked out a copy of her book. The green-and-blue cover was shining and attractive; she flipped to the back cover and the smiling picture she had chosen. She wasn't smiling now.

"No more calls," Anne said brightly. "Come, sit down. Doesn't the book look handsome?"

"All two copies of it?" Elaine asked.

"Oh, that's not the book, just the jacket."

"Where's the book?"

"Hasn't Lisa contacted you yet?"

"Lisa?"

"Lisa Kayle."

"My PR person is supposed to be Judy Epstein. They didn't give me the head publicist."

"Oh, well, what I meant is that Lisa still is overseeing your book. Judy works very closely with Lisa. I'll check this out." Anne jotted a note to herself.

"How many books are you going to print? There's no way this book will sell if it's not in the stores!"

"I'll check this out," Anne said, making another note.

"Anne, are you telling me you don't know the size of the printing? From what I see around here, at least it's two!"

"Elaine, it pains me to see you so upset." Anne Gregory leaned forward. She looked upset. "Excuse me for a few minutes, I'm going to find out about this." She got up quickly and left the room. Anne was flustered.

Elaine grabbed her notebook and wrote: "Thought Lisa K was my publicist. Forgot that I was given her assistant instead. Won't tell me and/or doesn't know size of printing."

Elaine looked over what she wrote. Anne came back. "I've given them hell! But is my face red. The truth is," Anne Gregory said, settling back in her leather chair, "that publishing is more and more a very difficult business. Since we've been taken over by Cantilever Rigging, certain things have changed. A few years ago we would have been at liberty to take a flier with this book. Now we have to tread more carefully."

"Take a flier, Anne? You implied more than once that you were committed to making this a best-seller!"

"Oh, but Elaine, dear, didn't I tell you to leave this to us and just work on your next book? It's the writing that's important. We're interested in taking a look at the proposal for your next book. What's done is done. Move on. We have to be realists. The book clubs didn't select your book. You didn't get a book club."

"I didn't get a book club! Aren't you paying attention?" Elaine blurted out. "We've known that for months. Joyce says decisions by the clubs are so arbitrary. I mean, you can't win them all."

"Well, that changes our sales prospects."

"And the printing?"

"We are just forced into a smaller printing."

"How much smaller?"

"Leave that to us."

"I've left enough to you. At least I chose a picture that doesn't make me look like a dumpster."

"You have strength, Elaine. Strength. Believe me, dear, you'll go on. Why, I remember when Reid—"

"What has Reid to do with this?"

"But it's through him that I understand the agony of writers."

"Agony, is it? How many copies of my book are you going to print? If you don't know, can't you call someone up?"

"Ask Joyce!"

"Joyce knows?"

"Joyce will know. Let's go through channels here. She's your agent. I'd rather talk to her about these things, and then let her talk to you."

"I bet."

"What can I do to please you? I really feel I've not been a good editor, if you react like this."

"To please me, you can tell me the truth."

Anne looked at her. "The truth? The subsidiary-rights person has had trouble with the book."

"I thought Helen loved the book! She was the one who said there was a real chance for the book clubs to pick it."

"But, dear, Helen's been gone for almost a year. When Cantilever took over—you know they own Symond Press as well—we got Saul Prince from Symond."

"Saul Prince? But Symond's all murder and lust and swooning virgins."

"Saul knows his business. And, dear, he didn't think your book was commercial. He predicted it wouldn't get a club. And, perhaps you should know, he's not so sure he can sell paperback rights."

"He predicted that? Let me digest this. You mean that the man who sent my book out to the book clubs predicted I wouldn't get a club before he sent it out? He predicted he couldn't sell it and he didn't sell it? Now he's predicting he can't sell paperback rights? Will he be right again? He must be a genius. A corporate giant. He predicts he can't sell books, and, lo and behold, he can't sell books! He should get a bonus. I'm sure he did!"

"This is why I'd rather discuss these things with Joyce. You're the author. You're in no frame of mind to—"

"I just want to know what's going on with my book. Panther

has always been known for quality, right? I'm not dreaming that up. Isn't your motto 'In the long run, literature lasts'?"

" 'Lasts,' not 'sells,' dear. And we don't deal that much with the long run anymore."

"I'm beginning to see that. But you're making one disappointment—not getting a book club—and Saul Prince's opinion an entire defeat. That's not the way to accomplish anything. We have to be positive."

"Elaine," Anne said with a sigh, "you are forcing me to be very, very honest with you." Her tone was full of regret. "I'm afraid Saul Prince feels your book is literary."

"Is that bad?"

Anne, after a pause, nodded.

"Well, I'm sorry it's literary. Is there no upside to that?"

"Don't be upset."

"Don't be upset! You're telling me you've changed your mind about my book because of the takeover, because of Saul Prince. You always said you had faith in my book. You said it could be big. Why didn't you stick up for it? Why didn't you ask Saul Prince what happens when *The Passion and the Vow*'s reviewed? After all, 'literary' is not a dirty word to book reviewers. Won't good reviews help sales?"

"If it's reviewed."

"If? Anne! If?"

"The Sunday *Times* is backlogged. Really, dear, nothing against you if they don't review your book."

"Oh my God!" Elaine sat up very straight. "But what if they do review my book, Anne? They've reviewed my collaborations with Larry. The *Times* even reviewed my book on foreigners in Italy. Don't you remember? Joyce sent you the reviews."

"Why, of—of course, dear."

"We've just got to be positive. My book will be reviewed! I believe that, I really do. The question is, will my book be in the bookstores? Are the salesmen out there, getting books on the shelves so that WHEN the book is reviewed people will be able to buy it? Or have they decided no one's going to buy it, so they've decided not to put it on the shelves? What do you think you're going to do? Tell me I'm a literary writer and that's why you can't sell a book Saul Prince scotches? You've made a corporate decision to abandon my book. And if your neglect ruins its chances, you're going to pin it on me. What does a writer know about corporate politics? The writer's not part of the game! Well, get this straight. This writer reads *Money* magazine!"

"Oh, Elaine—"

"Now, you tell me, and I won't leave this office, I won't leave this chair, till you tell me. How many books are you printing?"

"You leave me with no choice, Elaine. We ourselves had no choice. We must go along with the market. I've checked. We'll be starting with five thousand copies, but we can always go back for more."

"Five thousand copies?" Elaine put her notebook in her pocketbook and stood up. She stood up very straight. "I guess I can translate that to thirty-five hundred at the most."

"Dear, if it's well reviewed, we'll go back for more."

"By the time you go back for more and get more on the shelf, my book will be yesterday's news. Anne, you've killed my book."

"Oh, Elaine. I feel just dreadful. It's nothing personal, dear."

"Joyce, yes, I kept my cool. I'm calling from the lobby. I'm deciding whether to go to a movie or bomb this place. I wanted to tell her she was a dangerous hypocrite, that deep down she hates writers. Who wouldn't, married to Linda Lee Linda? I wanted to tell her she personally, through complete incompetence and lack of loyalty, killed my book, by not sticking up for me or overseeing Saul Prince. But no, what did I say? My back was to the wall. I start sounding like the crazy writer they want me to be. But I said it, and I go by it. I believe it. I told her I thought my book would be reviewed. That it's their corporation that's made a mistake! You think so too? Really?"

Bzzzzz. "Elaine, it's Nola. Dad's at University Hospital. He's doing okay now. Room 3246. I'm going there now. Gotta run."

"Nola. Me. I'll be there tomorrow morning. If you need anything when you get this message, call. I'll leave the machine on."

She walked out of the elevator and then down one of the long shiny white corridors of University Hospital, to Larry's private room. It was a corner room, and before she saw her ex-husband, she saw a terra-cotta vase filled with an overabundance of colorful long-stem flowers. She focused on it as she went to the half-closed door and knocked lightly in case he was asleep.

"Come in."

Larry was sitting in a chair on the opposite side of his bed, near the windows. Gaunt. He hadn't shaved; he was growing a beard. He was not wearing his wig.

"Don't get up, Larry."

"Why not?" Slowly, he stood, as she walked over.

"Hi," she said, touching his hand. He smelled of unscented soap. She turned immediately to the window. "Wow! What a view." But she didn't mean it. She just had to look away.

The pedestrian East River. Across it, brownish low-slung buildings and storage vats. A garbage barge floated by, followed by a flow of seagulls. There was also a huge white boat in the river. Not a graceful one, but enormous. It looked like a by-product of the military-industrial complex gone to sea.

"See that big white ship," Larry said.

"Can't miss it."

"It's Donald Trump's yacht! I have about the best view. The nurses, doctors too, come in to see it!"

"Really? Huh, Trump's yacht."

"I'm told it's been there three days."

They both looked out the window at it. Then she turned, walked past the bed, and took a seat by the flowers. He went back to bed.

"Do you want the bed lowered? Do you want to rest?" she asked.

"No, I'd rather sit up." When she faced him, she had the impression that his eyes had lightened, turned to water. The hair on his head, wisps going sparsely in either direction, seemed as frightening and crazy as his being deathly sick. Other than that, he looked thin, elegant, in control, and brave.

"What happened?" she asked.

"I couldn't get my breath. I'm better now. What happened . . ." He paused. She could tell he was trying to understand his words. "I got very weak, Elaine. Very weak. My crit, my blood count. It was bad. They had . . . they had to give me blood."

"Oh my God!"

"In my case," he said ironically, "contracting a disease with a long incubation period is the least of my worries: I'm not afraid of blood transfusions in the age of AIDS. Though Bunny, she's like you. She's out today looking for virginal donors, in case I need more blood. I told her it's like looking for a wise man." He closed his eyes.

"Can I get you something?"

"What?" he dared her and opened his eyes. "I'll be all right. This is temporary. I'll be all right." In fact, as if to prove it, he sat even straighter in the bed, reached over to his tray, and sipped some ginger ale from a straw. "Want some soda?" he asked. "My night nurse—I had to hire a night nurse, just to ensure Bunny would go home and get some rest. She—the private nurse—knows all the ropes. She worked here for ten years, before she went on to private duty. She showed me how to order from the menu. I have more ginger ale in that drawer"—he nodded over to the one under the flowers—"than I've consumed in my life-time."

For something to do, Elaine moved her chair and opened the drawer, took out a soda. "Here," he said, pointing to his tray. "There's plenty of ice. And there are clean glasses too."

She stood up and went to the window side of the bed to prepare her drink.

"So what happened yesterday with Anne Gregory? You had a fight?"

"Hey, the word travels fast! How'd you hear I was there."

"I spoke with Joyce."

"Joyce!" Elaine said. "I hadn't realized you were that close with Joyce."

"Oh, that was long ago!" Larry came out with. Inadvertently he had answered her question.

"You mean—? Larry! Don't you think you should have told me?"

"Told you what?"

"That you and Joyce were once lovers!"

"Don't tell me you're jealous? You knew she was in the first *Beautiful Women* book!"

"To tell you the truth, Larry, while we were married, for some reason, I had the naïve idea that you got all those women to strip for art. I never thought you fucked everyone in that book!"

He laughed out loud. "You are jealous!" He began to cough.

"Be careful!" she yelled as if he were coughing on purpose.

"You always were a Florence Nightingale," he whispered hoarsely. "I didn't fuck them all. I wish I had!" he mumbled in spite, like a kid with a sore throat, and then he coughed again.

The coughing controlled her. She kept quiet. Got up. Handed him his ginger ale. It subsided. He closed his eyes again and she averted hers. When she turned back, he was watching her.

"What's on your mind, Elaine?"

She took a breath. "Here you are sick, and I'm so angry—"

"About what?"

"About being duped. I certainly wouldn't have given my book to an agent who had or was having an affair with you."

"Long ago, Elaine. You know those things never last. Look who you're with now."

"You have some nerve."

"Okay, it's a meeting of true minds."

"We have different ideas about what constitutes a lover."

"No, we don't. We have different ideas about what constitutes a marriage. Passion never lasts."

"It doesn't?"

He turned to the window and Trump's yacht. "For me the record was three and a half months, and that was years ago."

"With Jenny? Ms. Scrambled Eggs, loose?"

He smiled weakly. "Yeah."

Then he continued. "If you're lucky, you end with a friend. Joyce is an extremely intelligent woman. We're friends."

"She took on my book for you."

"She took on your book because she could sell it."

"And I'm beginning to see why. I remember Anne Gregory saying, 'Oh, Elaine, I'm so glad you write under your married name, even though those women with unshaved legs don't.' And what did I answer? I was so unconscious. It was our first lunch. I tell her the trouble I had at St. Agnes's 'cause my name was Bright. I never thought it was your name specifically that she was thinking about. How much of the sixty-thousand advance did your name buy me? What would my advance have been as Elaine Bright?"

"If it was a factor, it was a small plus. Anne Gregory knows how to promote a book."

"And how not to. Saul Prince, from the biggest shlock house in New York, says he can't sell my book, and Anne Gregory watches him do it. Her faith in the book was like spit in the wind. Damn! You should have told me about Joyce—"

"We were still married when you finished that book. I was doing everything I could to help you out, to show you I loved you, to get you back!"

"Don't excite yourself! It's done. It's done. You want to know how much they're printing? The first printing of *The Passion and the Vow* is somewhere between two copies and thirty-five hundred. She said five thousand, which was the highest she could lie. They've killed my book. And I stood up for it! I said they were wrong! I proclaimed it would be reviewed. How many people have you laid on the *Times Book Review*? Maybe it still has a chance."

She sat down.

They were quiet.

"Don't lose your confidence," he said finally. "Believe in your work."

"It's hard to be the only one who has confidence."

"You're not the only one."

They looked at each other. Outside, the East River, Trump's yacht, the wide world. Inside, two people who had tried to make it together and hadn't done so well. When he could control the tremble in his voice he said quite clearly, "I believe in you."

Bzzzzzz. "Elaine, it's Joyce. Have courage. I'm pressing for a larger printing. I'm giving them hell."

Bzzzzzz. "Hi, babe. How's Larry doing? Hope okay. I won't get down there till Saturday, late. This mud is killing us. I love you."

Things went haywire in February, one night when Mario and she were coming back from The Ritz. It must have been about two in the morning. They'd just caught Icehouse, the opening band. It was a clear night and, once again, unusually mild for the season. They were walking with their arms around each other. They could see the full moon. Mario talked about the mud that accompanied this strange, postmodern weather, which in effect hindered the Danbury projects. Elaine said she was grateful Larry was out of the hospital even though he needed a lot of help at home. The mud and her own problems with her book would take care of themselves, given time. They passed the playground behind her building and heard "Hey, Mario! Over here!"

They looked into the yard. There was a dark figure sitting on a swing.

"Wig?"

"*Salud.*"

"Mario, what's he doing there? They lock this place."

"I climb."

"Well, climb out!" Elaine whispered loudly.

"No," Wig said. "Some kids, I climb with, open it for me. From inside. Come in."

"Come on, Elaine," Mario said.

"Get him out," she said. "This is really bad."

"Come on, Elaine."

"Mario, you don't know how many rules they have here. They can throw me out."

"So you'll live with me."

They walked into the yard, shadowy in the moonlight.

Wig was sitting sideways on the swing, his neck and head tilted up, resting on the chain of the swing. He and Mario spoke in French. They went on as she got more edgy. "You climbed in here with some kids from the complex?"

Wig looked at her. "You excuse me? Mario just tell me it's against the rules."

"You're lucky, Wig. This place is patrolled. You could have been arrested. Mario, let's go!"

Wig looked at Mario. "Arrested? Oh boy!"

"Come on, old buddy," Mario said. "Let's get out of here."

"Good swing. I swing and swing," Wig said.

"I know," Mario said. "Let's go."

"Look," Wig said. And his handsome face was drenched with exquisite appreciation. "The moon."

"Yes, it's beautiful," Elaine said. If they were caught in the children's playground after two— She tried to act cool.

"She a lady, the moon," Wig said. "A woman. A beautiful woman. Hard to come on. Like you, Elaine."

"Come *by*, not *on*, Wig. You're being quaint—or cute, I'm not sure."

Wig said, "I try."

Soon after, the three of them sat in Elaine's living room. "No more crack!" Wig said proudly. He was cutting lines of coke on Elaine's hand mirror. She watched his absorbed concentration, a religious intensity that he brought to no other area of his life. He had his long hair pulled into one braid at his back. His skin was so tight over his bones that one could look right to the structure of his beauty. His prominent cheekbones added depth to his slightly slanted eyes.

"None for me," she said.

Wig looked up, concerned. He hadn't heard the disapproval. "A little?"

"No. And I'm not so sure there is such a thing as a little."

"You right about this stuff," Wig agreed, having concluded his tea ceremony. "No good." He snorted, then pointed to the bulge in his pants. "Strange, hah?" he asked Mario as he passed the mirror. "Guys take coke to party, to find a girl, and then— poof!—can't get it up. Not crack."

"But, Wig, it's horrible stuff!" Elaine said. "Crack, even coke— it hooks you."

Mario divided one line between two nostrils, snorted unconvincingly, as if to be polite. And passed the mirror back to Wig. She was relieved to see this.

"Hey," Wig said, rolling the bill tighter, "somedays, Elaine, I say I'm going to stop. No more crack, Mario, that's for sure. Tonight ends that for me. But this, Elaine," he said and then snorted, "this I can get in Danbury. I say I'm going to stop this too. Then I don't. Sometimes I think people out for me. Paranoia. I read about this. I'm getting paranoia," he said with great interest.

Wig looked at her, astonished. "And cost! Ask Mario. I make

good money. Even with all the mud. Poof, it's nothing." He passed to Mario again. "Go ahead. Good stuff, hah?"

"I pass. And you have enough to keep you up for the ride back," Mario said to Wig. He winked at Elaine. "You drive carefully, buddy. I'm planning on getting me some sleep."

Wig said something in French.

"Tabernac'!" Mario responded. He had told Elaine that French-Canadian curses had to do with the Mass, not sex, so Elaine knew Wig had upset him.

"What did he say?"

"Nothing but problems," Mario answered. "I might have to ask you for some—"

Mario was cut off. Wig began to talk again, faster and faster, his head turning from Elaine to Mario sharply.

Wig stood up abruptly, knocking against the coffee table.

Mario stood up too.

"What's not his fault?" Elaine asked, having strained after a few words of the dialect. "What's he talking about?"

"Get me some Valium for him, Elaine."

"Valium? Is that wise?"

Wig was still trying to explain something to Mario. Talking, gesturing. She saw him become a girl. Amazing. With just a hand on his leg and the way he straightened his neck and brought his head to the side, he could interpret a woman. Then he was Wig again, responding to the woman he'd just been.

"Get out of here, Elaine. Get the Valium, quick!" He put his arm on Wig's shoulder, but Wig resisted. His head jerked as he talked.

"Hurry!" Mario shouted.

Elaine went to the bathroom in the hall. She heard a scuffle, loud voices in French, a crash.

When she came back, Wig was cowering at her front window. The vase on the sill had fallen. There were shards of alabaster and yellow straw flowers all over the rug. Her grandmother's vase. She felt guilty thinking of the vase first.

"Give them to me!" Mario shouted.

He took the glass of water she had brought and the pill. "One? Get me the bottle."

"Mario—"

"Hurry. Here, old buddy, here." He held the glass of water in one hand and the yellow pill in the palm of the other. Wig was shaking, his head bobbing.

She didn't want to see any more of this. Went back to the bathroom, began to obey Mario, but couldn't. Would too much Valium combined with all that coke kill Wig? She had the idea of lying, telling Mario she only had one more. But that seemed like butting in, insisting on her way. Manipulating. Of course, if he OD'ed and the police came to her apartment . . .

"This will have to do. All I have for him is two."

Mario took the pills and brought them to Wig. Just swallowing pills seemed to calm him.

Wig spoke to her then.

"What's he saying, Mario?"

"He's saying he's sorry. He wants a beer."

"He wants a beer? A beer with fifteen milligrams of Valium, Mario?"

"Do me a favor," he said. "Get him a beer."

She did what she was told. At least he had calmed down. When she came back, he was sitting back on the couch, his face drained of color. Wig drank his beer. Mario sighed, got up, and went to the hall closet. He came back with a pillow and two blankets. "Why don't you stretch out?" he asked his friend. He looked at Elaine. "I think he should sleep over. Is that okay? I'll watch him, and clean up this mess."

"Of course," she answered. But she had no idea if it was okay, or where her responsibility lay. It would be wrong to send this crazed man out on the streets. She felt she had to do whatever was best for Wig at that moment; there was no time to indulge in what was best for her.

She didn't sleep all night. Wide-awake. Mario stayed out with

Wig the longest time, and then it was his turn to come to bed and toss. He finally slept. After a few hours, it was dawn and she gave up the pretense. Got out of bed quietly, dressed, and tiptoed into the living room. She took a look at Wig. He was dead to the world. Naked, twisted in her blanket.

His skin was ash-white, sickly. His flesh seemed to be chipped away to his bones. His shoulder blades and spinal cord stuck out, exposing a hideous vulnerability. She was appalled.

She needed a walk. Went over to the Veselka for a cup of coffee. Bought sticky rolls for home, and came back an hour later with them and the *Times.* The men were both up and dressed. Mario was making coffee. "Good timing!" she called out with fairly phony enthusiasm. "I brought sticky rolls."

They both liked them a lot. She couldn't eat. She was upset. The house smelled stale with their smoking, and she hated that. It was as if her soul were stale. Mario had had a few cigarettes, Wig was chain-smoking. What was she to do? Tell them no smoking in her house? She was actually glad when Mario took her aside and told her he was going to take Wig back to Danbury himself.

"He needs help," she said.

"Don't I know it."

Wig said, "I stay with you here. I stay with Mario there. I cause trouble. I'm sorry, Elaine. It's the coke."

"Then why don't you stop using, Wig, before it's too late?"

"Stop?" He looked confused, then amazed by the suggestion. "I can't," he explained.

"I'm sorry about this," Mario said, standing by the door.

"It's okay."

Was it? The door closed after Mario and Wig and left a void. The apartment was empty. She felt, suddenly, a stranger to herself.

She didn't know what to do with the day. Go to a movie? Walk over and browse at Tower Records? Still undecided, she went to her drawer to take out some cash. She was very surprised to see that, of the four hundred she was sure she had left there, only sixty dollars were left. She took some Valium herself, and went to bed.

"I didn't tell you?" Mario on the phone that night. "No, no, don't worry, it wasn't Wig. It was me. I thought I told you I was borrowing some. That asshole had to meet a man. Yeah, I know something's got to be done. But what, sweetheart? I'm sorry you had to see this. I get it all the time. No, no, he hasn't moved in with me. He's just staying with me for the time being, till he finds a new place. I'm trying to convince Claude to rent him the attic space in two weeks. No, just for the time being. Someone's got to take care of him. And I'll pay you back as soon as I see you, plus. No, no. I insist. Plus. I love you, Elaine. Stay the course, babe? I love you. You know that."

I love you, Elaine thought. She called out for Chinese food, and asked for three fortune cookies with her takeout. She sat on her futon, TV on and ignored, tray in front of her, and cracked the cookies open:

You should be able to make money and hold on to it.

Whether you choose love or fame you'll be able to handle either or both.

Luck is coming your way.

Driving to her classes the next day, she tried to file away her problems. Staten University seemed an oasis of tranquillity in her life. The well-landscaped campus, the new buildings, the swell of students. The campus buzzed with the final idyll of youth, those four years when the surges of the body have time and place and the mind is free to roam.

She taught as part of Core College, the experimental humanities program at the university, where she was free to compose her courses and the students were free to take what they wanted. She never lectured, taught only through discussion, and had a talent for drawing students out. She liked her students; they were intelligent and eager to learn. This semester she was giving a course in the "Poetry of Rock Lyrics" and a course in "Heroines of the Italian Risorgimento." Both overenrolled.

She parked her car and, taking her briefcase, got out and walked to the Core College office for her mail. She had a half hour before her first class. Another mild day. Through the rolling greens of Staten—mud. She sighed. Smiled. Said hello to young faces happy to say hello. And suddenly it hit her just like that: on this problem of Wig's, she'd go to Nola.

TWELVE

"So, what's up?" Nola asked. She and Elaine were having breakfast at the Veselka. Elaine was noticing her stepdaughter's square chin and her clear gray eyes. God, she resembled Larry. With one hand Nola pushed her hair away from her face. It was longer than usual, and bleached blond, but purposely kept dark brown at the roots. No makeup, just a pale wipe of lipstick. Another look.

"What's new with you, first?"

"Me? I'm playing guitar now. Just picked it up, and I'm playing. Got a teacher too." Nola paused. "I'm getting serious. I'm real glad I didn't leave town yet. Really. I gotta get it together, if I'm gonna get anywhere as a girl."

"Did you have a fight with Jimmy?"

"It's gotta have to do with a man, Elaine?"

That startled Elaine. She shrugged.

"What's wrong, Elaine? You look sad."

"Maybe nothing, maybe everything. This is between us, right?"

"Sure." Nola looked interested.

"Those meetings you go to . . ."

"You in trouble?"

"Maybe Wig is."

"Wig?"

"Mario's ex-brother-in-law. His foreman."

"So, he's in trouble. What about you?"

"I'm okay. It's Wig, and his effect on Mario."

"Well, if you're okay and Wig's not, how come you're looking so down?"

"Because I'm worried about him. I think he's in a very bad way."

"The meetings I go to, we learn to focus on ourselves. I mean, you're powerless over Wig. If you're as psyched as you were over the phone, or as unhappy as you are sitting here, I say, take care of yourself. You're powerless over other people."

"Powerless? I want to help the guy, and help Mario. He's in trouble, maybe, and I want to help. I'll worry about myself after."

"After what?"

"After I'm sure Mario's okay."

"Oh."

"I mean, he might be okay. This might all be in my imagination. I didn't know what to do. The truth is, Wig is strung out, Nola. I don't think he keeps a cent he makes, and now he's staying with Mario in Danbury. He came over the other night. He was in a bad way. Very bad. You can see the bones through his skin. His body looks like a concentration-camp victim's."

"What's he on?"

"Coke, and . . ."

"And?"

"You're not going to believe it, Nola. Crack, till Mario got him to stop it."

"Why wouldn't I believe it?"

"He's not a ghetto kid. He's a grown man, used to making a good living."

"There's lots of grown men on crack, Elaine. And no one person can make another person stop it, no matter how good the intentions. Go to one of the Anonymous Rooms, go to a meeting. Get yourself some help."

"Me? I'm not talking about me! I'm talking about Wig. If you think it would help *him*. Right now I'm not that interested in me!"

"That's why you need help."

"Please, Nola. I've been through therapy. I know what I need. And I'm in no mood for mind games."

"Okay," Nola said. "Me, I'm an adult child of an alcoholic. I lived with my grandfather, who was an alcoholic—"

"But he worked every day of his life, Nola."

"Sure, Elaine. But that doesn't count all the days my grandmother called in sick for him. She's the original enabler. Not to mention workaholic.

"And Mom. She thinks she's okay. She takes pills, she drinks, she goes through men. And my job is to be her mom, though I never could do anything right. I reminded her of Dad and of you. When she'd drink, she'd call me Nut—she'd say I was like you. Like I let her down."

"I was always letting my mother down, but she didn't drink."

"Who did drink?"

"No one . . . Well, her father. Her brother. But in the old days. All those old men . . . Eastern Europeans. I don't know. . . ."

"That's right, you don't." Nola tried to say it matter-of-factly. "Mom thinks she's a functional drinker and an occasional pill taker, but she's an addict."

"Delilah? Aren't you exaggerating? I don't know your mother, of course, but what I do know . . . You'll excuse me, she just seems a bit of a child. A bit self-absorbed. She's not very grown up."

"That's what I'm saying. I'm the adult child of an adult child. Dad, he couldn't take it. I used to blame him for not coming after us. Maybe I still do. He never saw what was really going on. He took her mood shifts to be some sort of terminal shallowness. He couldn't face that she was simply out of control. She still is. I can accept that today. She didn't do better without him, the way you did."

"The way I did?"

"Sure. Remember, I lived with him after you left. Then he needed me. You did okay. It was he who was in a bad way. Me, I'd still be there if it hadn't been for Jimmy. I mean, I felt it was my fault, somehow, you leaving him. 'Cause I used to wish you would! Yeah, I did. But wishes don't make it true. They're just feelings. I felt responsible for him after you left. Like I had to take care of him. I've got to remember that I'm not his Higher Power. That his not giving up smoking was not my fault. I'd still be there, I mean full-time, Jimmy or no, if Jimmy hadn't told me I was ACOA."

"What's that?"

"An adult child of an alcoholic. Ready to try to make everything all right for everyone else."

"Oh . . . I guess we're all adult children to some degree. Anyway, I'm glad you admit I'm doing okay."

"You? You always land on your feet."

"Better than on my head."

"See what I mean?"

"That's just being practical. And I wonder—don't get me wrong—but I wonder if you're making too much of all of this. Saying it's me who needs meetings. And Delilah—after all, everyone drinks."

"You gotta be there."

"I didn't mean to put it down. Obviously the meetings have helped you. I was just wondering if they'd help me help Wig, or help Mario help Wig. . . . I don't know."

"Look. There's a network of Anonymous Rooms. Go get a listing and see for yourself. There's a room for everyone."

"Yes, you told me that once."

"It's true! There are rooms for addicts and alcoholics and relatives and friends of both. You're a friend of an addict, right? Go to one of those rooms. There are rooms for overeaters and overspenders and gamblers and people who are simply codependent, busy fixing everyone else. You can start with a meeting for friends and relatives of alcoholics or drug addicts. It hardly matters which. Everyone's cross-addicted today," she added nonchalantly. "Check it out. If you're looking for ways to help Wig, maybe you should. And, you know, they're free. Not only do they work, they don't cost anything. Just call up the AR hotline, or walk me home and I'll give you lists of meetings. I got loads of the stuff. It's as simple as that. Help Wig. Help yourself. I shouldn't tell you what will work for you."

"You're powerless over me, right?"

"You're a quick read, as usual."

"Thanks, Nola. I'll think about it. Maybe I'll give it a try. See if we can get something going for Wig. I really don't know what else to do."

"You have to really realize you're powerless. It'll make you feel better, it really will."

"Sure. It's great watching someone destroy himself. It's Mario who should be listening to you. Mario's trying so hard to help that I think he really is hurting himself."

"Maybe you're hurting yourself trying too."

"Nola, come on. This is terrible stuff. I've got to do something."

"Maybe that's your drug of choice."

"What?"

"Others. Trying to do something for others. Yeah, maybe that's it. Even me. I never zoomed in on it before, Elaine. Maybe that's your addiction. Hey, you really should go."

Elaine shook her head, looked at Nola. "Somehow," she answered, "I don't feel any better."

When Elaine picked up the pamphlet listing the Anonymous Rooms, she discovered a new world in her own neighborhood. Hour after hour, day after day, in hospitals and churches, there were meetings going on.

She kept reading the listings, the dates, the times, wondering if she should give it a try. She knew she didn't want to go with Nola; she wanted to do this, if she did this, alone. So over and over the list she went. Then she centered on a notice for initial meetings, for concerned relatives and friends, at Village West Medical Center. Getting Help, it was called. And as she had told Nola, that's exactly what she wanted to get. Help for Wig. Which would be help for Mario too.

She was no stranger to outreach groups. She lived in a city in which help was offered in a myriad of courses, discovery courses where you could do everything—learn to tie a scarf, fly a plane, strip for your boyfriend, converse over a pasta dinner with professionals of all ages; real-estate courses, and condo-conversion courses, and Alexander Technique, and financial planning for singles; Tai Chi and body sculpting; introduction to Mandarin, and Go Fly a Kite. How to meet people by meeting people. There was always something to do. And this is not to mention all the therapy groups, and the anonymous groups that Elaine was encountering for the first time, and the encounter groups. People talking with one another at the end of the century. Articulating things that had always been kept quiet before. Who knows, Elaine thought, perhaps we will be able to self-help ourselves to sanity.

She sat in her safe living room and thought of the explosion of the pushers on the streets and the proliferation of these secret meetings going on around her. She walked to her window and looked out at the windows like her own, feeling all alone in an ominous situation. Did she want to be all alone? She wouldn't mind a weekend or two in Danbury, if Wig weren't at the apartment. A week, for God's sake. Here she was close to spring break and locked into too much time alone. Too much time with her book in limbo and Larry sick and herself— What was that Nola had thrown in casually? She used to wish they'd break up. She got her wish. When she was a kid, she must have prayed for it. And Elaine, she hears it and simply lets it slide.

Well, now she was alone. All grown up and all alone. An outreach program on something this serious? What could anyone tell her that she didn't already know? That crack was absolute stupidity? That Wig was killing himself and just had to stop? She went away from the window and back to her list. She decided on Getting Help. And she knew damn well who needed it.

It turned out that Getting Help was an experimental meeting that Village West Medical Center had pioneered two months ago. It allowed people from the community to sit in on a meeting that included families who had patients currently in the hospital's detox center. Elaine found herself in an empty conference room on the first floor. Chairs were set in a circle. She chose a seat and while she waited, she read the material informing her that everyone connected with the direction of this program was a recovering addict, alcoholic, or codependent. It made her scan the face of Ginger, the facilitator, who came in first and offered her a bright and enunciated hello. Ginger was a tall woman, thirtyish, with long dark curly hair and red lips. Her skin was pockmarked under her well-applied makeup. She wore a black business suit and a dazzling white blouse. There was something very pleasant about her chipper brightness. It was not phony, it seemed caring. And certainly, if the pamphlets didn't lie, it was well earned.

The other facilitator, Soren, came in next. He was a trim, light-haired man, of medium height. He said hello, but without Ginger's outgoing zip. Had he been an alcoholic? she wondered. He was wearing a dark-blue suit, a white shirt, and a red tie. His brown shoes were slightly scuffed. He seemed quite professional as he opened his briefcase, but he had a remoteness that, whatever its cause, seemed terminal. He was handsome, Scandinavian-looking, with a short nose and light-brown eyes. At the most he was thirty-five.

Then other people rushed in. They had come from an earlier meeting. Was she the only outsider? They sat in their circle and introduced themselves. She began. "I'm Elaine. I . . . I have a friend in trouble and I thought I could get some help." "Hi, Elaine," Ginger and Soren greeted her. Ginger said, "I'm glad you're here."

A short, plump black woman spoke next. She had a careworn face, and was dressed in the white pants and top of a hospital attendant. Her name was obscured by her accent, and Elaine couldn't read her badge. She seemed to be one of those hard-working Island women who had left the poverty of home determined to make American dollars. Now trouble brought her here.

The other blacks were an exceptionally elegant couple. The woman well dressed in an emerald suit and light-blue blouse, the man extremely tall and thin with unusually long and expressive hands. He wore charcoal-gray slacks and a pastel-and-gray Italian-knit sweater. Gucci loafers. She was on Wall Street and he owned a business. They were very uncomfortable. This was the last place on earth they'd planned to be.

There was a family from Chester, Pennsylvania. Parents, a grown daughter, and a daughter-in-law. The latter two were in their twenties, the daughter-in-law a sultry redhead with a slight French accent. The father was a good-looking middle-aged businessman, in shape. He wore the ubiquitous green pants of the suburban upper middle class, a jersey opened at the neck, and a look of concern in his clear but small brown eyes. His hair was abundant, though graying. His wife looked older than he. She wore a gray skirt that tugged at her plump stomach, and a short white sweater with a pocket over her ample left breast. White tennis shoes and short white socks over her nylons. She had a determined look, a square jaw, and white hair. Who did she remind Elaine of? That's it! Elaine realized when she gave her name. Barbara looked like Barbara Bush. Barbara and Charles.

Then the door opened and another middle-aged couple appeared. She was blonde with nervous brown eyes, short, wearing polyester slacks and a blouse. He was about five ten, compactly built. "We're sorry," she said. "Abe hadda—"

"Ah," he cut her off, "what's the use?"

They sat down. "Okay," he said. "I'm Abe, she's Tama."

Ginger didn't miss a beat. "Hi, Abe. Tama?"

"Me?" Tama asked. "Oh, I'm Tama."

"Hi, Tama."

They were from Jersey.

Ginger sat, relaxed, in her chair, smiling at everyone. "I welcome all of you who have your patients here, and those of you who don't but are concerned about another. This is the preliminary meeting for family week. The detox program of Village West is four weeks long, and during the patient's third week he or she meets with family and friends in a supervised situation. On the first day, family and friends meet to discuss their patients and to develop a set of guidelines for their own behavior, based on what they expect when the addict or alcoholic completes the program and returns home. Tomorrow morning, those of you who have patients here will meet with them and other facilitators, and you will tell them of your feelings and of your guidelines for the future. The patients will listen but will not respond. In the afternoon you will meet for another hour. The patients will give you their drug and/or alcohol history and afterward tell you what they expect from themselves and from you on their completion of the detox program. I also welcome those of you who are here as part of our new program, Getting Help, which allows you not only to sit in but to be part of this meeting. We are happy to see you.

"Today is your day. The Medical Center's program is for you, the codependent, as much as it is for your patient in the hospital.

For, as you saw in the films and talks this morning, addiction is a disease. A dreaded one that affects the family member as well as the addict. It is a family disease. Its disease status is recognized by the medical establishment, and as a result your insurance is paying for this specialized treatment. Those of you who have friends or relatives who might be interested in entering the program should be aware that the insurance limitation for a hospital stay is four weeks. You might want to speak with someone about this at the end of the meeting.

"But the main reason we are here today is for you. For, certainly, your lives have been interrupted in the most painful of ways, and it's your pain and anger that we will be addressing this afternoon."

Ginger went round-robin, starting with the family from Pennsylvania. Elaine particularly noticed the daughter-in-law, so pretty, so young, twig-thin, and fashionable, her abundant straight red hair and long bangs hiding half her oval face and all of her high forehead. She seemed distant from the family and more hidden and frozen as her father-in-law talked. "Well, I should be in Seattle today," Charles said. "Do I have pain and anger? And tomorrow I had business in Detroit. I don't think that qualifies for pain and anger. It's an inconvenience. I shouldn't be here. But if it can help Gerald get well . . . !"

"But you have the right to your feelings."

"Feelings," he said, and shook his head. He clenched his hands. "Is there a feeling left that all of us haven't been through?"

"Do you want to share some of them with us?"

Charles looked at Ginger, as if to explain. "He's a fine boy. Strong, handsome, smart. Every company he's been with, he's been aimed toward the top! The opportunities he's had! Why, at twenty-five, he's commanded a salary that it took me twenty years to approach! Look at this family. Look at his wife."

"And he has a baby!" Barbara came out with.

"Please, Barbara," Soren said, "you'll have your turn. There's no cross-speaking today. But does anyone want to comment on what Charles has shared?"

"They've all had opportunities," Abe said, his flat Jersey accent adding a homegrown reality for Elaine. "They're all beautiful and charming and they come from good homes. And all they want is that garbage, to shoot that garbage up their arms! Feelings? You want feelings? What do feelings have to do with anything? Her mother and me, his mother and me—we got two, you know. My daughter's here, God knows where my son is. Her mother and me, we got feelings. I used to tell a joke, you know? I don't tell jokes anymore. Or, when I do, it's a joke I'm telling a joke. Her mother and me, we just don't have feelings anymore."

"Let Tama speak for herself. Do you have anything to say, Tama?"

"He doesn't think there's any hope. He's been through a lot. He's done everything."

"How do you feel?"

"How does a mother feel?"

The hospital attendant, in halting tones, spoke of her son. He lived with her half the time, always needing money for crack. If he didn't stay clean this time, she was going to sell her house and go back to Santo Domingo.

"But what are you going to do before you sell your house?" Ginger asked. "What if he doesn't stay clean and comes and asks you for money?"

"I give it," she said. Her look was cautious in front of this white girl.

Ginger explained: "But wouldn't that be enabling him? In other words, each time you give him money, he has a way of getting his drug of choice. He won't hit bottom. Often it's only after a person hits bottom, realizes the people who love him will not give him a thing—out of love, not out of a sense of punishment—that the patient learns he has to come to some realization of the effects of his disease."

"He here now." She shook her head. "He go back on crack, I sell the house, go home." She looked convinced.

"But, Eda, it takes time to sell the house. He'll need a lot of money if he goes back on crack."

"I know. I sell the house."

There was no other answer for Eda, and the teacher in Elaine sympathized with the woman who had worked so hard, raised children, bought a house. She knew what kept her from learning the lesson Ginger was trying to teach. The concept of "enabling" was alien. If a son asks, a mother, if she has it, gives. Would she go home? Elaine wondered. Would she sell her house? Would she lose all her money?

Ironically, the upper-middle-class black couple were as adamant as Eda.

"Of course we'll give," Louisa said. "We'll give rather than see him on the streets."

Her son had OD'ed at Bowdoin, in Maine. Had whirled like a dervish in the quadrangle, screaming obscenities. He was big, like his father. A basketball player. They couldn't control him. He didn't sleep for three nights. He was wild. They called his parents. He collapsed before he could be sedated and sent first to the hospital in Bangor, until arrangements were made here.

Her fine hand touched the big round pearls over her light-blue silk. "My son's not going on the streets."

Roy was quiet; his long hands were active, rubbing each other, spreading out, palming a ball, saying more than he did.

"Is this Roy Junior's first time out?" Soren asked softly.

Louisa didn't understand, so Roy said, "Yes."

"I know he's only nineteen," Soren continued, "and it might seem to you now inconceivable to let him go. But part of the disease is that the patient is often looking for a weakness in others, an out. If Roy Junior knows he can depend on you for money, what is there to keep him off his drug of preference? What does he have to lose?"

"He's going to lose Bowdoin," Roy said. "He's lucky now if they let him back in school."

Louisa said softly, "It's better he come home."

"Oh boy," Abe blurted out. "I feel sorry for you people."

"Why?" Ginger asked, ignoring that he had cross-talked.

"Because you people musta worked hard to get what you got and where you got and, take it from me—we got two—we sold our house for the first one and spent all of it on the second. We live in an apartment now. I take every hour of overtime I can get, their mother's working for the first time in her life. That's what you got comin!"

"We work hard," Louisa said with dignity. "Who doesn't? And so did our parents and our grandparents. Do you think we are going to allow our son out on the streets?"

"What power do you have to stop him?" Soren asked.

"Money," Roy called out in rage, "the power of money!"

In the silence that ensued, Ginger asked if anyone wanted to speak to that.

"I hate to tell you this, Roy," Charles from Chester, Pennsylvania, said, as if the two of them were on a plane in business class working on a deal. "But, no matter what you have, it won't be enough. There's not enough money in the world to stop these boys once they get going."

"Roy," Barbara said, "let me tell you something." Her powerful jaw showed strength and anger. She rose above her white socks and tennis shoes. "Charles and I have a nice home. You know what my prayer is? One day, to go out to the back porch and stretch out on the hammock and feel peace. Just stretch out for a half hour, listen to the birds, the lawn mowers even, and feel, We're okay, we're like everyone else.

"At least, Roy, we still have our home. And Charles makes a good living. But we don't go on vacation. You know, we collected Hibel pieces, music boxes, what all, for over fifteen years. Beautiful things. We paid good money; we loved them. What did he get for them? Five dollars apiece on the streets?" She pointed to her daughter. "Sally's wedding? He was there. We couldn't invite Marlene, because the two of them were separated then. Couldn't invite Marlene or our little grandchild." Barbara looked at her daughter. "Tell Roy, if you want to, honey."

Sally nodded. She was as pretty as her sister-in-law, but with brown hair pulled back, a fuller face, and with the freckles the redhead should have had. An innocent face. A high, moneyed voice. "I was so sorry, Marlene, that I couldn't have you as matron of honor. What could I do?" Her voice was pitched toward tears. "I had to thank God that my big brother had a new job and was well again. My big brother, Jonny's best man. My wedding. Isn't it supposed to be the happiest day of your life? At least we had our honeymoon. I didn't find out till we came back. Gerald was best man, and he had a new job. We weren't going to insult him. He was supposed to take care of the money after the wedding. That's part of everything! It's traditional. The best man takes care of the money. We wouldn't think of insulting him.

"He took care of the money, all right. He stole it. Over seven thousand dollars he was supposed to deposit. We came back and he had taken every cent of our wedding money. All of it. Every cent. That's what I think of when I think of my wedding. The day that should be the happiest in my life. Now I don't even look at the videotape. It's ruined for me, my wedding day. I don't want ever to think of it again. We were close, like this! He always used to buy me the best gifts! And he stole my wedding money." She put her hands over her eyes and sobbed loudly.

Barbara said, "You have other children, Roy? Think of them. I blame myself that this happened to Sally."

Sadie had been quiet. She was another single, who'd come in late. When Soren had asked her, she said her husband was an alcoholic in an advanced stage of liver disease. She was in her sixties, plump, well dressed. Elaine noticed her good Italian suede boots. She too was a working woman, but from the Hamptons. She'd never broken with her husband; she'd just made a life on one side of him. "Particularly now," she said, "that the children have grown up. I go on my own trips. Oh, we used to travel." She gave a look as knowing as Sally's was dazed. "I'd instigate it. Trips with the kids. The family, you know. It took me a while to admit, only his body was there. Who were me and the kids to him? What was Texas or Arizona? He was at the wheel thinking of his bottle. Not that he wasn't a sweet man and a good provider. Just that he was always thinking of his next drink. That's where he was. Didn't give a damn about the state of Florida."

"Well, Sadie," Ginger said, "what are you going to do if your husband starts to drink again?"

"It doesn't matter what I do anymore. The doctors have told him he'll die if he takes another drink. So he's not drinking now, but I think he should sign himself into the program again. He's been to our hospital, but he should come here."

"But if he doesn't readmit himself and he does start to drink—"

"I told you, Ginger," she said, "I won't have to worry about that; he'll be dead." She smiled slightly, as if she heard the irony of her words and knew the irony of her life and his.

"It takes time to die," Ginger replied.

"Nah. What it does take a lot of time to do, and God knows I've watched it, is to kill yourself. It used to scare the kids. He's a lucky man, though. They still love him. Call all the time. How's Dad? they want to know. They still love him."

"Why, Sadie"—Tama spoke up—"if the children still love him, you must have kept things together. That reflects very well on you."

Sadie looked surprised. Then she nodded her assent. And suddenly big tears formed, but did not fall from her eyes.

"Elaine," Ginger said kindly, and Elaine grabbed on to her seat, "you don't have a patient here either. Would you like to share any feelings with us?"

"I'm feeling sad."

"Is that all?"

"I'm afraid."

"Of what?"

"This is all so new to me. I have a friend who's in trouble. My boyfriend's ex-brother-in-law. That's all. I mean, I feel funny even being here with all of this grief."

"But you can't measure grief. You said you're sad. Don't you think you have the right to your own sadness?"

"Of course! I've been analyzed. Five years of analysis. I know what I feel! Can I just listen for a while? I'm a good listener," she said, and laughed like she'd made a joke. But she knew her laugh must have sounded crazy.

Soren said, his remoteness cutting past the politeness, "What are you afraid of? You said you were afraid."

"I'm afraid the whole country is falling apart. All those politicians talking about drugs eating into the fabric of the American family, into society. Do they care that what they're saying is true?"

She looked around her and thought, This is really happening. It's as concrete as dollars and cents. All over the country, families talking like this. She remembered what she had overheard on the subway, going to Larry's last Wednesday.

"Who's your man?" she heard a black high-school student say. He was with three of his friends. They were unruly, as all kids seemed to be on subways and buses. But experience told her these were good kids, awkward, gangly, teenagers, hormones whirling, life what they see. "Tony," one answered. "He the one with long hair?"

"Nah, you don't know Tony. He's my main man. He'll gun you down if you miss a quarter." They talked half jive, half admiration, as they discussed the style of the individual drug dealers on each street. Tony with the gun was their hero, their role model. He was a big man. And they were teenaged kids.

"What are you feeling, Elaine?" Ginger asked.

"I told you, I'm feeling afraid for society."

"Yes, you've said that. But what are you feeling for your friend and for yourself?"

Her heart was pounding. "I was raised Catholic," she said. "And it brings it all back. I'm afraid of the devil."

"You should be!" Marlene spoke suddenly. "That's what it is." Barbara looked surprised to hear her daughter-in-law's accented voice. "I kept it a secret from them," she said, pointing. "I have no one to tell. I go back to Chantilly and everyone says I'm so lucky—a good marriage. And what should I tell them? That my husband mixes heroin and cocaine and shoots it up his arm? Speedballs—that my husband shoots speedballs? That I have a child to support and have to work every day of the week to make a little bit of money? It's better than starving. I'm starving in the United States and they are thinking I'm so lucky. Did I ever think once this is what my life would be? How did this happen? What did I do?

"I stole for him, you know. Yes. I stole jewelry from my girlfriend's apartment, so he could buy us food. But he went to New York and didn't come back for three days. He did not care if his baby had milk! I was dry, all dry. Nothing to eat. And his parents call, and where is Gerald? They think there's something wrong with me. I can't keep Gerald home at night.

"He was always so clean, so neat. You should see. He loved to dress. He had an Izod shirt of every color. All neat. All systemized in his drawer by color. They see him unshaven. Smelling. I don't bathe him, perhaps? Don't they know? Can't they see? Only after he takes their music boxes—then they know! Then I'm alone and he steals all of Sally's money. I'm Catholic too. You're right, Elaine. It is the devil! I am so ashamed."

There was an amazing transformation in Marlene. The long red hair was swept away from her lovely face, and she shone through, finally, a human being suffering.

"I'm sorry," Elaine said.

"Be careful, Elaine. You have a steady job. You don't have to worry about kids. Give up your boyfriend."

"It's my boyfriend's friend."

"But you said it yourself. It's the devil."

"The disease," Ginger said, "is tricky, devious, and will attempt to beguile the patient. And it beguiles the friends and relatives too, into attempts to support the unsupportable. Now, I want you to take these books. One is *Women Who Love Too Much*—"

"Just what I need," Abe said.

"It works for men too."

"Maybe that's what my daughter needs, when she works the streets!" He looked around, stunned. And then closed up, silent.

"The AMA," Soren said, "has certified alcohol-and-drug addiction as a disease. It is a progressive disease. Chemical abuse breaks down the body and the mind, and leads, inevitably, to institutionalization, jail, or death. The practical result of this is that insurance companies will pay for four weeks of hospitalization. Remember, it is a disease, because, left untreated, it will lead to institutionalization or death. It is a family disease, because, as you can see this afternoon, each of us is affected. The second book we want to give you is about living life one day at a time— a book for friends and relatives of alcoholics, one used in the Anonymous Rooms. At these free, anonymous meetings, which go on in your communities, you can get the support you need to focus on yourself, to realize that you are as powerless over your loved ones as your loved ones are over their disease, and that you, like them, can share your experiences. Through these meetings you can all help yourselves and find yourselves in recovery, one day at a time. We'll now take a half-hour break. Those of you who do not have a patient with us, feel free to speak with us about the detox-center program. The rest of you, please meet back here in a half hour, and we'll discuss the expectations you'll have of your patients when they are released. You will be presenting them to your patients face-to-face, in a meeting tomorrow."

Elaine made a decision a few days later. She called Mario early, left a message on his new machine. "Hi. You in the shower? Coming up today, babe, want to speak with you and then with

Wig." She'd found a way to help. She gathered all of her material from Getting Help, and got into her car.

She was in the mood for soft rock, and rotating the stations on her headset, she came to a twenty-minute block. An office in the West Fifties had faxed in a blanket request for music about the sunny side of New York.

"Somethin other than street people and pushers. All right!" Sy Piggy called out cheerfully.

Billy Joel. That sparkling, bright, baby-booming Long Island voice came motorcycling over bridges and through tunnels to the weekenders' fair city. She liked Billy Joel's voice. She wondered what Nola would think of that. It cheered her up. It was the New York of the old black-and-white films: expensive champagne, sophisticated romance, and a melody. A lucky voice that made her feel she was still doing well with the moon and New York City.

On the hour, she turned to the college station. She had a perverse enjoyment of hearing rookies roll-call the news. The young woman's voice sputtered on. "Andy Warhol died today. The Popmaster . . ." What a terrible joke! "He entered New York Hospital for routine gallbladder surgery. A private nurse was on duty when the fifty-eight-year-old maker of soup cans passed away in his sleep."

Disgusting, she thought, and turned the station. "New York Hospital declined comment today on the death of Andy Warhol. . . ."

Oh my God!

She saw Andy in front of her eyes. That thin frame, his pale, pockmarked face, those noncommittal eyes looking straight at what he wanted to see, the weird white hair—you could count the thick strands of it on his outlandish wig. She saw him with Larry. A shiver went through her. Andy. Larry. Each photographing the other. She bore left at the Brewster sign. She drove on.

She entered Lake Acres and drove until the road itself turned to dirt near the top of the hill. She saw Mario's crew, and Wig, in a long-sleeved thermal top with a T-shirt over it, balanced on a roof. He had seen her first, it would seem, for he was already waving to her, like a topsy-turvy Chagall, as she got out of the car.

She waved back. But she didn't see Mario. "Mario?" she called, and Wig motioned. "Wait."

He was by her then, wire-thin but quite handsome, his narrow eyes appraising her with that eternal Québecer niceness mingled with a certain French caution.

"Andy Warhol died today," she told him.

He shrugged. "Like Lennon?"

"In a hospital." Then she was sorry she had said that. She wanted him to go to a hospital.

"Your pictures," he said. "Worth more?"

"Maybe. But his work is all worth more. Always was. A lot of people underestimated Andy. And now . . . Now he's gone." She said, "I thought I could talk with you after work. Is Mario around?"

He shrugged.

"I guess I'll try the Fair?"

"Maybe," he said, his eyes elsewhere.

"You don't know where he is?"

Wig looked around.

"See you," she said. He was high, damn it. High and working on a roof.

"Elaine," he called as she walked away. She turned to him. "Maybe Mario got a cold."

The enormous acreage, the oval of the Fair, was a bleak swamp of brown on that mild winter day. It was devoid of statues and was surrounded instead by the neighboring hills, staked by trees whose branches scratched against the palatable gray of the low sky. Through the trees Elaine could see patches of townhouse roofs. The landscape was lonely. The mud had made it necessary to throw down paths of planks to the construction, and she saw big machines idle. It was lunchtime. The skeletal outline of the mall, in steel green, punctuated by glass, had a big-top quality to it. The architects were encorporating the ghost of the Fair.

The mud may have slowed progress, but Danbury Fair Mall was certainly going up. She got out of her car and walked on a plank, a long walk amid damp brown fields on a gray day, to an almost completed structure.

Inside, it seemed colder than out. Groups of workers were eating, talking. They looked at her, then looked away. No one called to her or stopped her. She heard the competing soft rock of their radios. She wondered how many of them were high. Then there was another music. The music of carnival. She remembered that Mario had said they were having trouble around the setting up of the carousel, on the second level.

She turned to the left and walked up the stationary escalator stairs, ignoring the sign that forbade it. It came to her that this was the type of sign everyone would have obeyed when she was a child. On the second level she turned left once more and followed the music that was coming from the far end. In the distance she could make it out, the new Italian replica of the old carousel.

That entire end, where Mario was subcontracting, was to be the food pavilion. She remembered the Fair of her childhood excursions. The spun cotton candy, hot corn, foot-long hot dogs, shaved ice. The ghost of that would be echoed in franchised food stands, Sheetrocked, taped, almost ready for paint. The First Name Cookie Pavilion and the Unspellable Ice Cream Stands, and the Bagels of All Nations. Foods of the world unite! The Danbury Fair is dead, long live the Danbury Fair Mall. Burp!

The carousel, being set up at the far end, was a two-decker. Brilliantly painted horses on the first level, cozy carts on the upper level. Backing it a wall of glass overlooking Danbury's impressive tree-lined hills.

The music was blaring, though the carousel was stationary. The first person she saw whom she knew was Pauli Girl, who got up from the carousel's platform and his lunch and walked to her. "Hello, Elaine."

"Hi," she said, looking up. "It's moving along." She pointed.

"Inside, yes. The mud slow us down. Mario say go home. He get your message."

"Oh, great! See you."

"Goodbye, Elaine."

"Bye, Gaston." No one other than the guys called him Pauli Girl. She wondered if he was bigger than André the Giant.

"Well, say something, what do you think?" Elaine asked. She and Mario were in his kitchen. Pamphlets from Getting Help were spread over the table. He had brought home pumpernickel-raisin bagels with cream cheese, a new hit in Danbury, after he got the message that she was coming. He had, as he said, decided to leave the job, come back, and straighten up. Two guys in a small space—even when both were neat. She was drinking coffee. Mario smoked.

"What do I think? I think now I know what you're doing here," he said.

"Well, I wasn't looking for a girl in your bed."

His blue eyes squinted tensely. "You know, sweetheart, I might take that as a compliment if you were checking up."

"You would, would you?"

The muscle in his forearm quivered as he took a drag. "Yes. It would be sort of normal. It would be a comfortable, dependable feeling. But this run's for Wig."

"Mario, you saw how he was at my place. He needs treatment."

"You saw him today. Does he need treatment today?"

"How'd you know I saw him?"

"He beeped. How'd you think I knew you were here?"

"I called."

"Oh."

"I'm surprised he got it together enough to beep. He looked sky-high to me."

"Babe, that man's been Wig for a long, long, time. Why don't you let me worry about Wig, and you worry more about me."

"I do worry about you."

"Really? You spent a whole day on this." He waved his hand over the pamphlets on the table. "You don't know Wig."

"I know he's living off of you. He's right here in your apartment, for goodness' sake."

"Listen, he's family, and I owe him."

"You always say that, but what exactly do you owe him?"

"When I left Florida, I came here. He set me up with the French guys."

"That's it?"

He looked at her carefully. "There's always more."

"Why did you leave Florida?"

"I left the state of Florida to Paulette."

"Okay, don't tell me."

"Why do you think there always has to be a reason, Elaine? Why can't it be that I just wanted to start over? There was money to be made here, and, with the way these guys can work, I made some. Do you think they'd have trusted me without Wig? What do you think I'm going to do while he goes to detox? Mud isn't bad enough? You want me to lose my foreman? I need Wig right now, you get it?"

"But he's high!"

"For Christsake, Elaine, look around you. Who isn't?"

"I'm not. You're not—or at least I hope you're not."

His eyes snapped with an anger she had never seen. "You insulting me? Look, I better get out of here. I have work to do."

"Wait! I apologize, Mario. I really do."

"Well, good. Let me explain something to you, Elaine. It's Friday, I have crews in two locations, and I'm sitting here with you. Not only that, I have to pay my men this afternoon. On the books, off the books. I know it's not glamorous, but I have a business to run. And these months have not been too good."

"Because Wig's a drain."

"Get off my back about Wig, damn it. Thanks for your help, but no thanks. Maybe you need help, being so damn helpful."

"You sound like my stepdaughter!" she said.

"Well, go help her. Go help Larry!"

She motioned to the material from Getting Help. "I thought it was such a good idea. What a day!"

"What a day and what a week! You know what keeps me sane? Thinking of the weekend with you. Thinking of getting out of Danbury. There's Manhattan. There's life after Danbury. I don't want you talking with Wig. Believe me, I know the guy. The important thing is for him to stay put. And that's exactly what he'll do this weekend. I'm going to finish the afternoon, and then I'm driving to the City with you. Okay?"

She didn't say anything.

"Look, you can leave this literature right here. He's a big boy, he can read it himself."

"Okay," she said with no enthusiasm.

"Damn it, Elaine, I'm an ordinary guy, in a world of ordinary men. There's just so much I can take. It's you who make my life special. And getting out of here. Seeing you in New York."

"And what makes me so special? You talk as if I'm not an ordinary person. It's you who have a thing about me!"

"A big thing," he said. "A real big thing. But that too will pass if you hit on me like this. Let me live my own life, Elaine. That's one thing you just got to do."

"And that's what happened," she said in the Rooms. "I went there to help his friend and we ended up back in New York, leaving his friend the apartment—and the detox information. But he's not interested, even though he's fully insured. It was then that I realized I had no power over the friend. What about me? I'll be on spring break in New York, though I'd rather be in Connecticut with my boyfriend. I got confused, but suddenly I really did realize that I'd better start focusing on myself. So I said to my boyfriend, I want to spend spring break with you. You say our friend is your business; fine, do what you have to do. But I'd really like to spend a week or so with you in Danbury. It would be very good for me to get away. I would like your friend to be out of the apartment, because I want to be there. I just focused on myself. I put my needs out there; not the needs of our sick friend. And my boyfriend called tonight and said, The coast is clear. Come on up, if you want to. It wasn't the greatest invitation, it wasn't perfect. But it's okay. He heard me. I can't manipulate the results of putting myself out there loud and clear. Thank you."

Larry sat on the feathery couch where the two of them had once courted. Sickness showed in the parched cast of his skin. He had shaved; with his beard went all pretense about his drawn and wrinkled neck. The loss of weight made his white teeth too regular; when he spoke she couldn't miss the grin. He wore well-cut black cotton pants and a checkered sport shirt opened at his vulnerable neck. His clothes were clean and pressed and he sat erect. He eyed her as if he were saying, Look at this.

Picking an invitation off the long glass table in front of them, he did say, "Look at this."

She read. "Oh!" Larry had been invited to St. Patrick's Cathedral for the memorial service for Andy Warhol. That Wednesday, that very day.

"You want to go?"

"What time's the Mass?"

"I think you missed it. I didn't think you'd really go."

"Really? Thanks for thinking for me."

"He was religious," Larry said. "I wish I were."

"Maybe you are," she said.

"And don't know it. Oh, Elaine."

"Did you read this?"

"Oh, that?"

Five hundred homeless and hungry New Yorkers will assemble on Easter Day at the Church of the Heavenly Rest, on Fifth Avenue at 90th Street. They will be served a delicious meal, and they will be treated as honored guests by some eighty volunteers. They will also be saddened by the absence of one who, with dedicated regularity, greeted them on Thanksgiving, Christmas and Easter. Andy poured coffee, served food and helped clean up. More than that he was a true friend of these friendless. He loved these nameless New Yorkers and they loved him back. We will pause to remember Andy this Easter, confident that he will be feasting with us at a Heavenly Banquet, because he had heard another Homeless Person who said: "I was hungry and you gave me food. . . . Truly I say to you, as you did to one of the least of these, my brothers and sisters, you did it to me."

"That's really moving," Elaine said.

"I hope they serve plenty of chocolate at the Heavenly Banquet, for Andy's sake."

Elaine giggled. "But it is moving, Larry. Charity," Elaine said. "Maybe he was ahead of his times again."

"You think he was ahead of his times?"

"Definitely. Charity," she said, "maybe Charity is going to make a comeback, along with a capital 'C' and an exposed breast."

"Ha! That's good."

"I'm flattered."

"I've always appreciated you, Elaine. Perhaps too much. I hope Mario does. What's wrong? Did I hit a chord?"

"No! I was thinking of Andy."

He put his head back, as if he was suddenly very tired.

"You know, I won't be coming next week. I'll be in Danbury for Easter. I spoke with Nola. She said she or Bunny will cover."

"Goodbye, Elaine."

"I'll be back."

"Perhaps we'll next meet at the Heavenly Banquet."

"Come off it, Larry. That's manipulative."

"So's photography."

"Yes, I learned that myself."

"I taught you a lot."

"Yes, you did. At times you still do. I think you should go to bed, Lar."

"No, today I'm sitting up. You go. The nurse will be here in a few hours. I'd like the luxury of a few hours to myself."

"You're angry I'm going to Danbury?"

"Angry? Why would I be angry at you?"

Elaine said, "You can't forgive me, can you?"

"Get me my pills before you go."

She looked at the label. "Strong stuff."

He nodded.

"Let me stay."

"Not today." Then he said, "He walked among us."

"Are you speaking of Jesus?"

"No," he said matter-of-factly. "I'm speaking of Andy Warhol."

"I am staying."

"No. You're going," he said. "I'm going to spend a few hours alone."

He took his pill, then put down the glass. He looked at her intently. He smiled, exposing those teeth.

"You must be in pain, Larry. Let me stay. Talk to me!"

He kept smiling.

The stone façade of the Gothic cathedral was white and clean, rescued from the grime of traffic some years ago, when the Pope had visited St. Patrick's. Some of the police barricades had not been removed, though the Mass for Andy Warhol was long over. It must have been quite a crowd. She walked up the center stairway. There was activity. People coming and going after work or after shopping. Tourists too. Incense from the opened doors. Imitation Gothic, the best. Nothing in ruins. Inside everything was warm and light and inviting. She went to the font and then walked down the center aisle and was overwhelmed by the beauty. The altar was banked with wisteria and tulips. It was a sea of spring. Each of the massive stone columns that led to the altar had at its base a spectacular arrangement of calla lilies. And stained-glass windows looked down over everything. An entire cathedral decked out in Easter hope. Lilacs. Pinks. Yellows. Whites. For the dead rising.

She genuflected and then sat down and thought of Larry. Just pictured him in her head. Just allow space. The spirit will enter the space.

She pictured Larry.

She pictured Andy.

She closed her eyes to the beauty around her and let words circle as they came. The Lord is my shepherd; I shall not want. He leadeth me away from evil and toward righteousness. He restoreth my soul. My cup runneth over. Hail Mary full of grace. Blessed art thou and blessed is the fruit of thy womb, the fruit of thy womb, thy womb. Surely goodness and mercy and Mary full of grace and sheep and shepherds and cool waters and right-eousness . . . Over and over, the mantra. She was crossing herself with cool waters until there was nothing left but hope, and love echoed in prayer.

P A R T

T H R E E

THIRTEEN

A new Waldbaum's had opened in Danbury, and the night sky was cut through with laser beams in celebration. Elaine and Mario sat on the porch of Claude's, watching the red and the blue lines streak in either direction and then crisscross in the heavens.

She had walked up the wooden stairs before, to Mario's quarters, and found everything in place, the sun streaking through the old windows, the small apartment looking as neat and ordered as a Swiss chalet. Wig was gone, just as Mario had promised. This evening they had had a cup of coffee with Claude and Mathilde. Claude's immense stomach, his red face. Mathilde's heavy corseted body. The pride with which she still called her husband "my man." Two old-timers. Now Mathilde appeared on the porch in her robe.

"Are we disturbing you?" Mario asked.

"No. Stay out as long as you wish. I take a look."

Mathilde walked to the edge of the porch and looked up. Elaine saw her sturdy back, the crossing of lights, the full moon. She could feel the woman's pride of ownership, as if the part of the sky she could see, as well as the covered porch and sloping lawn, were Claude's. "Everyone's talking about the salad bar," she said. "A dollar ninety-nine a pound. Imagine! I guess it's okay, though. I guess a dollar ninety-nine's cheap if you don't like work. I hear they got everything real beautiful. Tomorrow I take a look. Doesn't cost nothing to look." Meanwhile, she watched the laser beams spread out across the heavens.

When she went in, Mario said, "The coast is clear now," in a mock whisper, and lit a thick joint.

They shared it in silence. Mario took her hand in his and said, "I'm glad you're here."

"Me too."

She had been right to focus on herself. It had helped Mario as well. Just having Wig out of his apartment appeared to have lightened his mood. He tugged at her hand now and, without words, they got up, went inside, and climbed the stairs to his apartment.

Mario closed the door behind them, and, after they took their jackets off, he threw both on the chair behind him. He did not want to let her out of his sight. He pulled her toward him and kissed her, his tongue finding hers. He kept kissing her, her tongue, her lips, and then her eyes, her cheeks. At the same time, he unbuttoned her blouse, feeling past her lacy bra. She responded to his excitement, then he responded to hers, and it was as if they were carrying each other further into passion, finding out for themselves the happiest secret: they could still go further.

After they made love, they sprawled naked on Mario's clean-smelling sheets. The night air mixed with the subtle dankness of orgasm. The blue and red laser beams arched through the sky. Mario smoked a cigarette, she watched the smoke rising. The smell did not bother her at all; nothing bothered her at the moment. She had returned to her element, water. He, raised on his elbow, smoking his cigarette, flicking it absent-mindedly, drawn to the laser beams too, was remembering fire. And that polarity was exciting, even now, when both of them were spent.

"Yes," Pam said. Elaine was sitting in the Lake Acres office, across from the woman with the pleasant face who had sold her an option on her Lucerne model. "Even with the new tax laws, Lake Acres is booming. You certainly got in at the right time. And a super location, really. We've had quite a few calls about your location." Elaine looked past the glass sliding doors. Completed townhouses as far as the eye could see. Spring had done its painting-by-number act—patches of yellow daffodils, purple crocuses, and lime-green grass dotted the well-built complex, turning real estate back to land.

"I must say," Pam continued, "Stanley Howard is a persistent man. He really does want to talk with you about your Lucerne. I told him this has nothing to do with Prospect Realty. In fact, this complex never encouraged speculation. Lake Acres is a family place. But, you see, he's a Danbury resident. And an empty-nester. He'd like to sell his one-family on Westhill and move here, and he knows exactly what he has and exactly what he would get. He's a good friend of an associate of my husband's. So, if you'll allow me to give him your phone number, I'll do that as a friend. Or if you want his—"

"Yes, I'll take his. And you can give him mine in the city. I'll be here for a week, or two. Maybe I'll call. No harm in meeting the man."

"That's exactly what I thought," Pam said. "I thought there was no harm. Here," she said, handing Elaine a business card with Stanley Howard's name and number on the back.

"Thanks. Well, Pam, I'm off. Shopping. Want to hit the new Waldbaum's."

"Wait till you see their salad bar!"

· · ·

To Elaine, the salad bar was a salad bar. The Korean markets in the city did just as good a job. She took a look at it and then rolled her shopping cart down the farthest aisle to the produce section. That's what wowed her! The plethora of lettuces and broccoli and scallions and peppers, all mechanically misted, the bins of garlic and onions and different types of potatoes, the flat Italian parsley and curly French parsley, the dill and bouquets of basil. To see so much fresh produce displayed on either side of a bright new boulevard of space! She couldn't stop tearing off plastic bags from the roll and filling them with fresh lettuces and vegetables. She knew she was overloading on greens. But, what the hell.

The fish section was sensational as well, and the displays of red meat! The cheese aisle with samples! She took a toothpick and jabbed some wine cheddar and some Armenian butter cheese. She decided against the Canadian crackers. She had some scented pepperoni too. You could eat your way through this market. Opening week especially. She needed paper products and olive oil and vinegar. So many varieties. Which were the best? By the time she got to checkout, an hour and a half had passed. She picked up *People* and *Money* magazine as she waited. She couldn't believe she spent $89.63! The high-school girl packed five bags for Elaine.

And all she had to do was roll her Waldbaum's shopping cart out the electronic door right to the parking lot—half expecting management to come out screaming for the cart—open her car trunk, and unload her bags. It was almost an out-of-body experience, the ability to shop so much and take it all home herself. And that night, though he came home late and discouraged, she cheered Mario with a very good meal.

The week passed in a blur of small pleasures. The weather was beautiful, buildings were going up. Elaine was sure that Mario's business problems would diminish. Just roaming Danbury assured her. Should she call Stanley Howard, or should she wait?

Maybe the townhouse would be a place she and Mario could live in together. Each day she'd sit for a while at the makeshift desk Mario had set up for her and try to write.

On Friday, after going out for breakfast, she spent time in front of the porch looking up at the American eagle that Claude had bought at the auction of the Danbury Fair. It was a beautiful sculpture, powerful and soaring. The type of eagle winging through Overnight Delivery ads on TV. Only this one hovered, wings spread, on the peak of a covered porch. Its connections with the States meant something to the usually literal-minded Frenchman, who often bragged he'd sell his boardinghouse now that it was worth so much, and go home with his wife, his money, and his eagle. His American eagle.

The spring day smelled so sweet. And it was quiet in Danbury. She heard the birds chirping. She walked up the stairs and into the house and took the stairway to Mario's quarters. When she opened the door, she saw the sunlight slant onto her desk. She sat down.

She thought of her father, who had owned a lumberyard and had worked hard. He got sick early. She thought of his thin face and his Stetson. He looked a little like Humphrey Bogart— maybe he did act a little like him too. Bogart must have been a hero of his generation. Perhaps part of the appeal of Mario was that he worked hard and was intelligent and sensitive, like her father. But much more upbeat—and much more muscle. Her father seemed crushed by life somehow, bitter about—what missed opportunities? she wondered. He held his intellect like an extra hundred tucked in the back of his wallet. Though, Lord knows, he didn't cash in. His health gave out, and he acted as if life owed him something. He was a very decent man, and he seemed to expect some payback on that. He thought life should be fair. How naïve, she thought. She wondered about that World War II generation.

They had returned from the war, and most of them had found jobs to do, bought houses, made compromises with their wives, raised families, had an occasional night out with the boys, and often, with a bowl of potato chips in front of them, turned on the TV and dosed. The feelings they had, they kept to themselves. What the light-rock stations of the eighties referred to as the "Fabulous Fifties."

She thought of her mother, saying no to everything because she was so afraid. When Elaine came home from a date, usually right on the dot, there would be her mother, thin, small, unhappy, invariably holding a cigarette between two stained fingers. The nicotine marks would contrast with her brightly painted nails, but be in concert with her shaky hand. Her mother would never ask, "Did you have a good time?" Always, a drag of the cigarette, the nervous squint of her eyes, and then the exhale: "I couldn't sleep, so I waited down here."

She felt her mother's fear suddenly, sitting at the desk in Mario's small apartment. The old feeling of not being able to help her mother, of not being enough for her mother, came back. An unfortunate generation of women. A bridge from the old times to the new. Raised to find their lives in others. Sure, they wanted to give, to be generous, to be unselfish. But how could her mother give what she didn't have herself? At the desk Mario had prepared for her visit, she finally began to write. . . .Until—

"Hey, babe!"

Elaine started. "Oh, you scared me, Mario!"

Mario stood in the doorway, a happy grin on his face.

"What are you doing home at this hour?" she said, mocking a wife. It was only three in the afternoon.

He laughed. "Wanted to scare you. Anyone under the bed?"

"Far from it. I've been writing." She had turned around in her chair to face him. "I can't believe I'm using a pencil—how primitive." She tossed it over her shoulder onto the desk.

He came over, took her hand, and kissed it.

"You're in a good mood," she said.

"Why not? You're here. Thank God it's Friday. The ground

is dry. It looks like I'll be able to make the payroll. You bring me luck!"

"You bring me luck too."

"Well, then, stay another week."

"Really? I won't say I haven't thought of it. But I'd have to keep writing with that tree stump. What a decision. But, for you, yes. Though I'll probably drive in to see Larry next Wednesday."

"The city. The hour-and-five-minute drive to the City!"

He reached out his hands and, taking hers, pulled her from the chair. "Enough work," he said. "Rest till Monday. Trust me. Give your weekend to me and you shall see! Though I'll tell you, girl, I sure am glad to see you writing. Can I read it?"

"I have to look it over first. But I like it. Claude's eagle got me going."

"Great. That means you have to stay for inspiration." He took her in his arms and they went dancing around the room.

"What's going on, Mario?" she said, laughing.

"I'm trying to charm you. It's as simple as that. Remember Carlson?"

"The guy who didn't pay you?"

"Well, I got him. Twenty thou, covered. I just checked at the bank. He's got it. I deposited it."

"Bravo, Mario! That's just great!"

"Look." He stopped, reached into the pocket of his work shirt, and held the deposit slip up. "It's right here. Hallelujah. I'm going to finish up; then you get dressed—best jeans—I'm taking you to Chuck's for happy hour."

"Oh, great."

They were smiling in the middle of the room. "Things are going to be okay," he said, more seriously. "Listen, can you draw me two checks for five fifty made out to cash? I got two guys I'm paying under the table. I'll swap checks, till the big one clears."

"Hey, that's no problem. You're good for it. I'll wait till Carlson clears."

"Well, there's still that three hundred from Wig's great entrance that night. I'll add that too. Next week I'm clearing up old debts."

"Hey!" she said, leaving his arms and going to find her pocketbook. "No problem. I'm so happy for you! See, I told you the mud would dry. Didn't I?"

"Yeah, you told me I'd get over."

"Getting over? It's more than getting over. Ouch! This pen! I'm getting a bump on my finger."

"You should apply for disability."

She smiled. "To cash," she said. "There. Okay. Here you go."

"Thanks, babe. Let's see. I'll be back by six."

"Good."

She went back to her work. Read it over. She had all next week to develop it. She felt very good.

On Tuesday, Larry took his own life. Or died of an unintentional overdose.

"He didn't leave a note," Elaine said to Nola. "It must have been an accident."

"Do you believe that?" Nola was very pale, the way she had looked as a child before she got a bad sore throat. There were tears streaming down her face, but she wasn't actually crying. She talked in a normal voice to her stepmother, who had come straight to St. Mark's Place very early Wednesday morning.

Nola said, "I unlocked the door. I walked in. I swear it was quiet. Like something wasn't there anymore. Not ripped off or anything. Just not there. 'Dad? Dad?' He was on the couch. Oh, man, he didn't look like he was sleeping. His mouth was open, his eyes . . . His neck was funny. But he wasn't there. I knew it already. Just like you say, we know things. Thank God he wasn't there, to see himself look like that."

"Where was Bunny?"

"It was Tuesday, Elaine. Tuesday afternoon. Bunny was out.

He wanted me to find him. Monday it would have been Bunny. Wednesday, you. Daddy wanted me."

"Oh, God," Elaine said. "Dear God." She sat down in the tiny living room, on Nola's worn-out couch, put her face into her hands. She was exhausted and felt dry.

Had he done it? Had he really wanted Nola to find him?

"Stop living through her!"

"Elaine!" Nola cried out in alarm. Elaine had jolted and gasped.

"It's okay. It's okay."

"What was it?"

"Nothing. Nothing. Hearing things. I heard your father."

"What did he say?"

"Dear God," Elaine said, "he yelled at me." She began to cry.

She was so disoriented a few hours later, when she was again on the street, walking home, that she saw a car like hers and a driver that looked like Mario pass by and she found herself calling out loud, "Wait!"

After that she thought she should take a cab, but she continued her walk. When she turned onto her block, she saw her car safe and sound.

Mario had not let her come in last night. He had held her in his arms and said no. He took over. Made arrangements. Drove her down at six this morning, left her at Nola's front door. Then parked her car and grabbed the bus back to Danbury.

Damn! she thought as she got closer. Mario had made a mistake, parked the car on the wrong side of the street. This too! But, then, she could see she hadn't gotten a ticket. She unlocked the trunk and took out her luggage. As she walked to her apartment, she couldn't believe she had had a moment of anger at Mario when she saw that mistake. After all his support! What a life, she thought. What a life. All that happens, and she can still get upset about a stupid ticket. No, about the possibility of a stupid ticket.

"Yes, would you believe it, Mario? I thought I saw you," she said late that night on the phone. "I know it's nerves. I wish I were in Danbury with you. You even bought gas?" She laughed for the first time that day. "I think I'm going with a saint!"

He was a saint that weekend too. He couldn't come down till Saturday night. She wouldn't leave town—in case Nola needed her.

"Not that I'm needed," she said at midday Sunday. She was on the bed in her XXL T-shirt; Mario was naked. The *Times* was all around them, the lunch tray Mario had prepared on the floor. They were listening to a Talking Heads tape. She said David Byrne was good in an emergency. They had the TV picture on. Some of Reagan's men were being questioned on the trade deficit. But that Sunday she couldn't concentrate. Even the *Book Review* hadn't tempted her. She'd looked at the pictures.

"You're needed," Mario said, getting to her past the mess of papers, holding her in his arms. "Want a massage?"

"Mmmmmm."

He reached for the lotion.

"Where should I start?"

"Somewhere neutral."

"That'll take some thought."

She sat up. "No. Let me do you. Come on. You're the hero this week."

"Some hero."

"The check cleared?"

"It sure did. Hey, let me write you one."

"Later. Relax. You're back on track. That's one good thing this week."

"You convinced me." He stretched out on his stomach. "My back. My aching back."

"Your beautiful aching back," she said, warming the oil in her hands.

"God, that feels good."

"I never understood him," Elaine said. "I lived with him for almost ten years. At the end, all I wanted was out. Don't ask me why Larry Netherlands, who just got a picture and three columns in the *Times,* bored me, infuriated me, bullied me. I was happy to leave. I never looked back."

"Maybe he couldn't give a good massage."

She put more oil on the back of his arms.

"Not," he continued, "that I've been able to get it up."

"Come off it, Mario. Didn't you ever hear of being tired?"

"Looks like I'm living it."

"One night? Grow up."

"Grow!"

She laughed. "You're too thin. I gotta get back to Danbury and feed you."

"When can you come back?"

"Soon, I hope. When I feel it's okay. He might have killed himself. Nola has to live with that. I do too. I can't stop thinking about it."

Then she was shaking, and Mario had to come to the rescue once more. She was in his arms.

"I got a temperamental masseuse," he whispered.

"He let me down."

"I will too."

"No."

"Why not? Why not Mario Two? I'm a man, aren't I? They let Elaine down."

"That's unfair. Why, you've been wonderf—"

"Sure, sure," he said, getting off the bed. "Want a drink?"

"Okay."

He brought the tray out with him and came back with two screwdrivers. "Sorry," he said. "I'm edgy."

"I can drive anyone crazy."

"No, it's me. Maybe it's you, a little. You were brought up not to believe in suicide, and you don't believe in suicide. Just like me. And good old Larry, that brick that's been round your neck and mine for months, they don't come any smarter than good old Larry. He knows I'm a nobody. No, don't try to deny it. I didn't have to meet him. I could hear it over the phone. I could hear it in what you didn't say. He thought you were slumming. I had money in the bank, sure. And a business. But I'm no count, and I'm no photographer. I'm just your ordinary guy, right? I didn't know Andy Warhol. That's just what he wants his ex-wife to hook up with. An ordinary guy. I'm not going to get a picture in the *Times* obit. That's a big deal to you, isn't it? I could hear it in your voice: 'He got a picture and two, no, three columns.' Does that make him any less dead? Larry knew you couldn't take suicide. It was just one more plus that it would bug the hell out of you. It must have bugged the hell out of him, that he'd die and you and Bunny and Nola and Delilah, you'd all fuckin live. No, don't get upset. Drink your drink. I'm going to dress and go for a walk. I've been a saint too long. I need some air. You stay here, okay? I'll be back in an hour. Promise. One hour, that's all I need. Just let me out of here for an hour."

"It's okay, Mario," she whispered. "It's okay. I'll be here."

And in an hour he was back. With flowers. And she was dressed, with care. "Want to go out?" she asked.

"I've been out. I'd rather stay in with you."

"Well, then, let me go out for a while. I need some air myself. I thought, if you wanted to stay in, I'd go get a video and something for dinner. Just hang out. I'll cook."

"Burgers?"

"Ordinary burgers—for an ordinary guy."

"Touché." He was smiling. "A dirty video?"

"Two dirty videos."

"How can I resist? You look beautiful, Elaine. I'm sorry about before."

"Don't be sorry. I was getting you down. Getting us both down. I'm thankful you're here. Let me just put these in a vase and I'm off. Purple and yellow. My favorite colors."

"I know."

FOURTEEN

Elaine stayed in the City until the memorial service, which Nola had decided to have soon after her father's death. There had been no funeral, as Larry had stipulated in his living will. He had also stipulated cremation. Elaine wondered about his real will, but didn't ask any questions. As ex-wife and stepmother, she had decided on her own ritual. It was to stay out, but to be there in case Nola needed her.

She did stay out. For example, had Nola asked her, she would have advised having the memorial service later, after Nola graduated. She did offer to help with arrangements, but was told, politely, that Silas was helping with that. Okay. Elaine concentrated on finishing her spring semester at Staten and in writing more of *The American Eagle*.

The phone rang just as she was leaving her apartment for the memorial service. "Hello, Mrs. Netherlands? This is Stanley Howard."

"Oh, Mr. Howard. I had planned to call you some weeks ago, but something came up." (Why in God's name was she apologizing?) "And now I don't have time to talk." ("I'm going to my ex-husband's memorial service." She couldn't say that. She kept thinking of how to get off the phone as he spoke.) "Five thousand dollars?" she heard herself say. "I really can't think of that now. . . . Seven? Look, give me your number again, and as soon as I have a free moment . . . Oh, in cash? That's nice of you. Look, I'll get back to you when I can."

Nice of you? she said to herself as she left the apartment. She was in such a rush. She never should have picked up the phone.

She took a cab that got snarled in traffic. Her heart was pounding. She was really late, and it was impossible to cross to the West Side. Should she get out of the cab and take a subway? She knew better. Once things get screwed up, quick changes don't unsnarl them. Stay the course, she thought.

The first floor of the Ethical Culture Society reminded Elaine of a well-kept old school. There was a sign that said "Larry Netherlands, third floor." The woman behind a small caged-in area directed her to the elevator around the bend. Elaine took it. The service was going on when she entered the big, airy room, and saw the two gorgeous assortments of long-stemmed flowers, one in an enormous purple vase on the piano, and one on the left side of the fireplace. Centered over the fireplace was an enlargement of the photograph of Larry that Andy Warhol had done. It was a quadrangle, four pictures of a Larry smiling more broadly than Larry usually smiled. Looking, Elaine realized, really happy. Elaine thought it would have been better simply to enlarge one of the quadrants, to see one Larry. She stood in the back of the room, signed the register, glanced at the coffeepot and luncheon tables already set up, and then took a seat in the back row, on the aisle. She figured there were over two hundred people present. She herself felt more in control, having slipped in. No one had turned; attention seemed riveted on the speaker. She had a glimpse of Nola and Jimmy and Silas and Bunny in the first row;

no Delilah. Nola had said she was glad Elaine would be there, but had made no attempt to meet her beforehand or ask her to sit up front. That was okay. She was there for herself.

The speaker was a tall man in his forties. He had a chiseled face. He was bone thin, haunting-looking, with deep-socketed eyes. Each cheek seemed to have over it a blush of white. This must be the "minister of no faith," as Silas had labeled him and Nola had reported: "Silas says everyone says he's the best." Elaine looked at backs and sides of faces. She thought she picked out Joyce. Could that be Anne Gregory next to her? It was a well-dressed crowd. Perfume in the air. Not without irony, she thought, Many beautiful women.

"Government," she heard.

Government?

"Yes," the minister continued, "we are bitter. Yes, there is anger in our community and in our hearts. We have died with dignity, but now's the time to ask, did we have to die? Or are the drugs that can prolong our lives held back by a government, a bureaucracy who does not care. But this is not the time or the place. Because, as we've exhibited time and again, we die with dignity, with bravery. We die proud.

"Often I wonder what it would be if it were another segment of our society that were subject to this scourge. Dear God, I believe there'd be riots in the street. But we have lived as Larry Netherlands lived. We have upheld our heritage, our Western tradition. We have believed in the values of this tradition. We have been the artists and scientists, the professors and teachers, the dreamers and the doers. The photographers. So, admitting anger, we face tragedy, and die as we have lived, embracing the Judeo-Christian, Greco-Roman tradition. As the brilliant writer and my dear friend Robert Ferro put it, 'We chose to be Edwardian.' We die before our time, we eulogize knowing we are soon to be eulogized, we die as Larry Netherlands died, bravely. But with dignity, but with pride. Thank you."

There was a hushed silence. No one stirred. A pale and handsome young man stepped to the piano to play. Elaine looked down at the program she'd picked off her seat, opened it.

She was too stunned to think.

After the music, Nola got up.

"I am Nola Netherlands by birth," she began, "and Asia Neither Land, I guess, by profession. And I am here to remember my father. I am thankful for Bruce Hartigan's words, and with him share sympathy for those who have died of AIDS. But before I offer my tribute, I want to say that my father died before his time of . . . It's hard for me to say the words. Lung cancer. It's very difficult still. Lung cancer. There," she said, through shining eyes. And then she said, "He smoked."

Dead silence. Nola brought the microphone to her. One could hear the scrape of it through the room. Her head bowed, her arms hugged her guitar. She began to sing. Of the lighthouse in Montauk, and lobsters. Of a doctor prescribing drugs. Of a summer garden and what she called "zucchini flower/earth 'n' memory." "Da, Da, Daddy," she sang, never allowing the refrain to broach lament. "Da, Da, Daddy," again and again. Then the song cut off abruptly and she spoke. "Goodbye, Daddy."

"Amen."

There was a surge in the room. People clapped away confusion. And Elaine was far from the only one who cried. "I think it went quite nicely," Silas said. He was standing with Elaine and Nola. "This is Bruce Hartigan; Elaine Netherlands, Nola's stepmother."

"Pleased to meet you," Elaine said, shaking his thin, determined hand.

"I'm sorry about the confusion," he said.

Elaine shrugged.

Nola said, "I don't think it mattered that much. What you said was important."

"Thank you. And I think you cleared it up well."

"I just said what came to mind."

"It was a beautiful tribute," Elaine said. "Your father would have been proud of your song."

"Think so?"

"Yes, I really do."

"It's America, you see," Silas said when he and Elaine were alone for a moment. "I was away too long. I miss a beat, somehow. Everyone I spoke with spoke of Bruce Hartigan, and I thought I had explained the situation to him. It was quite delicate. This line between natural causes and perhaps not waiting for natural causes . . ."

"Did you do it on purpose, Silas?"

"Oh my dear contessa, absolutely not!"

"Do you realize," Elaine whispered, "that there's a consequence here? Everything is now unalterably altered. Added to the fact that we'll never be sure if Larry took his own life, we now have half of New York, or by tomorrow we'll have half of New York, sure he died of AIDS. Rumors never go away. I think havoc's your trade, Silas!"

"Elaine," Bunny interrupted.

"Oh, Bunny." The two women hugged. "Accept my condolences," Elaine said.

"I thought he was doing better," she said. "But . . . Well, could I speak with you for a moment?"

"Sure."

The two women walked into the hall. "I wanted to arrange the memorial," Bunny whispered. "But Nola was adamant. She insisted on taking care of everything. It was her father! I didn't feel I could take things in my own hands. I've let Larry down. I can't stand the way people are looking at me!"

"Elaine!"

"Joyce. I thought I saw you." Elaine was impressed anew by Joyce in the flesh, her trim and buxom body, draped in light jersey. "Joyce, Bunny; Bunny, Joyce."

"Oh, yes," Joyce said, "we've spoken on the phone. Beautiful service. That daughter of his, she has presence."

"Yes, she has," Elaine supplied.

"Well, I've got to get back to the office. Bunny, once things settle down, we'll be in touch. I'll call. Elaine, did you see Anne Gregory?"

"Actually, I thought I did."

"Of course she'd come. She wanted to make sure you knew her husband would have been here if he was in town. Didn't she get to you? Well, there's such a crowd in there."

"Quite a turnout."

"For a very important man."

Bunny looked at Elaine after Joyce left. "She didn't say anything about . . . the minister's mistake, did she?"

"Not a word. Perhaps it's joined the collective unconscious," Elaine said. "Look, what's done is done. The best thing is to go back in there and think of Larry and let this whole thing slide. People are going to remember what Joyce remembers, the beauty of Nola's tribute. And she cleared the rest up as simply as possible. I think she's even okay about Bruce Hartigan's tribute. There's a lot of suffering out there, not just what happened to her father. In a strange way, maybe it's a consolation. The dignity with which so many people have died. Maybe we do have to hear that. Let's turn this thing around. Maybe in some way Nola had to hear those words."

"Nola?" Bunny asked. "What are you talking about? This is what happens when you leave things to children! Larry did nothing but worry about her. These ideas of hers. Here you have an outcome of one. I never should have given way to her. I should have insisted on doing this the way Larry would have wanted. And you, you could have said something. You could have done more than send me a card!" She was crying now. "Poor Larry. This is supposed to be his memory. Is this his memory? What does it have to do with him? I let him down. He was always so orderly. And she made a mess. That's what his daughter did. 'Amen,' she says. Not if she has anything to do with it. And that weirdo voice of hers. And she sang he was on drugs—didn't she? Junkies get AIDS too. Maybe people are believing that! Couldn't let him rest."

"No, Bunny—"

"Oh, I've been warned about you!" Bunny went on. "You're going to take her side! You probably helped her with this. A beautiful tribute, a beautiful tribute, only Larry Netherlands didn't die of AIDS. She helped kill him! His memory. What's left of him. What he left me! I'm his executrix, not you, not her. I'll take care of him from now on. Where I came from, daughters respected their fathers. Where I came from, families stuck together through thick and thin. I'll take over from now on. We'll do things the right way. With respect. Like where I came from."

Elaine didn't know what to say. Her eyes were wide. "Where did you come from?"

"BROOKLYN!" she yelled. People turned. Bunny began to sob.

A hand on Bunny's shoulder. "May I be of some help?"

Bunny blindly rushed into the outstretched arms. Elaine got away quickly, leaving her for Bruce Hartigan, who was dying himself, to comfort.

"No, I'm not making a word of it up," she said to Mario over the phone that night.

"You sure?"

"I'm positive. That's exactly what happened. Who knows? Maybe half the women in the room rushed out for blood tests."

"You always make him out Don Juan. Are you jealous?"

"I just never did understand him. You know how you can think of great answers too late. When Lottie Spencer came over to me and said with those phony actress eyes—yes, *the* Lottie Spencer—'Elaine, I hope you're well'—can you imagine?— rather than saying, I'm fine, I should have said: I don't have to worry, Lottie. We were married; you can't have safer sex."

Mario hooted. "There you go!"

"Well, the whole thing is crazy. And you know who I had on my answering machine when I got home? Anne Gregory. Condolences galore. So sorry she missed me in the crowd. Her husband was simply crushed he couldn't get a flight. Wants so badly to speak with me. I've been through so much. Wants to do lunch. It's New York, you know. I've just become part of a famous rumor."

"Then use it to your advantage, kid."

"Ha! That's funny. That's just what Larry would have said."

"Well, he'd be right."

"He often was. You know, he deserved better."

"Wake up, Elaine. He's not alone there. Who doesn't?"

"I guess you're right."

Nola didn't go to her own graduation. "I didn't have the heart for it," she said.

"Oh," Elaine said. "I just figured you didn't invite me."

"Elaine!"

"Had I known, I would have given you a pep talk. I saw them setting up the purple colors and the chairs around the fountain at Washington Square. . . . It's a great setting."

"Yeah. Jimmy and I passed by. They'll mail us the diplomas. It's okay. I keep remembering Daddy saying how he'd miss my graduation if I took a year off and went away to California. And he missed it anyway."

Nola shrugged. It was a beautiful summer day, and Elaine had invited her to lunch at a café on Eighth Street. It had an outdoor garden and good spinach salads.

"You seem tired," Elaine said.

"Do I?" Nola looked up at her. "I've been working hard. I'm bass guitar now, Jimmy's on lead, and we're using this dynamite girl drummer, Michelle. She's going to play with us at CBGB next Friday. Wanta come?"

"I'll be in Danbury."

"You're spending a lot of time there."

"My new book proposal's coming along, and Mario and I are doing okay. We seem to like being together."

"He staying out of trouble?"

"Of course! He's up to his neck in work."

"I dig that. This producer Silas knows is really interested in us. We need a really good demo. If we can get a label, he figures he can book us. Save you the parking on the van."

"Great, Nola, that sounds good! But be careful of Silas, a bit. He doesn't have the best judgment."

"He knows everyone, Elaine. This Caroll Gug's a winner. He manages Hot Fott, Wilding, and Schlepp."

"I'm impressed."

"Listen, Schlepp's hot."

"And Hot Fott is wild?"

Nola laughed, then said, "Very funny."

"I thought so."

"But, anyway, I don't know."

"How do you mean?"

"I gotta start looking for a job. I could waitress, or there's this really good training program to become a stockbroker."

"You mean, I'd get a break on commissions? I've been selling some stocks."

"You're selling in this market? I mean, like Jimmy has two friends, two years older than us, and they're millionaires!"

"I know. I read about these kids in the papers, and you know what I think? I think, don't trust anyone under twenty-five."

Nola laughed. "Including me?"

"I exclude girl rockers. And you're not greedy. I've decided to take the seven virtues and the seven vices more seriously, since I realized the next century starts now."

"Now? Huh. Did you hear about Dad's will?"

"What about it?"

"He didn't seem to trust anyone under thirty-five."

"Oh?"

"He set up a foundation for photography, and he left me like a hundred and twenty-five thousand dollars in trust till I'm thirty-five, and some other stuff."

"Well, by then it will certainly be worth much more. And by then you'll be a little more specific about the value of 'other stuff.' Not a bad security net, Nola."

"Everything's at Bunny's 'discretion.' Like the way Sam Hannah explained it to me—I like him, he really liked Daddy."

"He's a good lawyer and a good man. I was sort of sorry I couldn't use him . . ."

"Finish it. You mean, when you left Daddy."

"That's right. Since I didn't ask for anything, I thought he could be lawyer for both of us. No dice."

"Sam tells me 'discretion' means I can hit Bunny for some money, if she feels it's in my interest. And—get this—she can use her discretion as to whether or not to consult you about me."

"Me?"

"Yeah, that's what Daddy said."

"I'll be. My guess, Nola, is that she won't consult with me. I threaten her. It's as simple as that."

"You're right. Want to take a guess if she'll let me borrow from the trust for a demo?"

"Unfortunately, I guess she said absolutely no."

"For my own good."

"Oops, I forgot about your own good. Is she also doing it for you?"

"You got it."

"I can lend you some money. Give you some time to see if Second Hand takes off. I think your music's really good. And maybe it's the time for girl rockers. You and Ms. Dynamite on the drums. Why not? Give it a shot. That's something you can't do at thirty-five. But another year or two won't make you too old to be a broker."

"Just like that, Elaine? Wouldn't you need to think it over?"

"I already have."

"You really want to lend me more money, just like that? I might not be good for it until I'm thirty-five."

"You'll be a comfort in my old age."

"I mean, Elaine, maybe you're still being too quick. What will you think in retrospect?"

Elaine smiled. "We're not there yet."

"Don't you like Bunny?"

"I don't trust her judgment. Speak to Sam Hannah. Tell him what you'd like to do. Ask him what he'd think of the deal."

"Okay, I will." Nola took a crouton with her fingers, popped it in her mouth, and crunched it. "And your book, when's it coming out?"

"Momentarily."

"You're sort of a girl rocker yourself."

"I wouldn't mind hiring the Plasmatics to drive Panther Publishers off a pier. Do they play anymore?"

FIFTEEN

"What a quaint idea," Anne Gregory said.

She and Elaine were seated at a small table in the IBM court-yard, having croissants and coffee that they had bought from the concession; they had waited in line and carried their own paper trays back to the outdoor table. The courtyard was parklike and cheerful; there was a summer breeze.

Anne Gregory looked wonderful, as usual, a light-pink silk dress, splashes of big jewels in complimentary shades at her neck, her fingers. Her eyes were intense, her soft brown hair with its blond highlights fell against her face, seemingly without design, and her complexion caught the pink of her outfit. She might have been blushing under her blush.

"Reid and I had hoped to take you out today. We will after the summer, when we get back. He's really sorry you couldn't join us for a proper lunch."

"Tell him another time gladly," Elaine lied. "I'm so busy with my new proposal that I don't want to take a long lunch break."

"You authors! Well, when are we going to see the proposal?"

"You'll be away. Do you mean, when will Donna see it?"

"Now, Elaine, don't tease me."

Elaine looked at Anne Gregory. "Am I teasing? Actually, Joyce will be handling the proposal. I want to thank you for letting us out of the option clause. We're going to go to auction."

"Auction?" Anne did blush. She had forgotten. "Well, Panther Publishers will certainly be there! Here's a little surprise for you! This just came in." Anne took two clippings from her file. "Your first reviews!"

Elaine kept quiet. She didn't tell Anne that Joyce had sent her the starred *Kirkus Review* and boxed *Publishers Weekly* over two weeks ago. She remembered Joyce's telephone pep talk: "Just listen to what she has to say. Don't react. Leave that to me. Just listen. The IBM courtyard! Really, Elaine."

"Aren't these reviews wonderful, dear? This bodes very well. We're very happy at Panther. We'll build on them slowly and carefully. Don't forget, dear, this is a first novel. What we're looking for is a literary success. We'll build on that for the second book."

"A literary success? I guess that's one step better than a literary book. Why not a commercial success as well?"

"You authors! Don't rush so, dear. Rome wasn't built in a day. Leave that to us. It's your career we're concerned with, over the long run."

Elaine stared at her, tried to stay cool. Didn't Anne realize she was saying the exact opposite of what she had said in the office?

"I do have one question, Anne. You know publishing so well, perhaps you can help me out with it."

"Yes?"

The *Kirkus* and *Publishers Weekly* reviews are excellent—"

"Raves! You could have knocked us over with a feather when they came out! Oh! Not that we didn't know the book was worth it, dear. But review space is so limited, and first books . . . ! Why, in a sense, it would be better not to publish first books. They tend to get lost so easily."

"That's an interesting marketing strategy. Anyway, these 'raves,' as you call them, are for the trade—bookstore buyers read them? Well, if bookstores want to order my book, will there be enough to go around?"

"They have ordered your book. That's what's so exciting! It's as if they read these reviews before they came out!"

"Anne, these reviews have been out for weeks."

"Oh! Oh, of course."

"How many of *The Passion and the Vow* did you print?"

"You know we were on the conservative side, dear. We printed five thousand—"

"Damn, Anne. You mean you only printed thirty-five hundred!"

"I said five."

"I know what you said."

"Well, it was a short run, but it will be five thousand."

"You mean you're printing five thousand more."

"Five thousand together. Oh dear, you're ruining my little surprise. We've gone back for fifteen hundred more!"

Elaine slumped back in her chair and groaned.

"I don't understand you, dear. Doesn't anything please you? I know you've been through a lot. Poor Larry. I was just remembering what good friends he and Reid were. I was just remembering when they went to Las Vegas together—in the early eighties, wasn't it?—for *Esquire*. I couldn't remember. I know I couldn't make it. Reid and I have a policy statement on work-related activities. But I couldn't recall—you, dear, did you go along?"

"I don't recall."

"You don't recall?"

Elaine said, "No. And, oh, any more business?" She looked at her watch. "I have no time for girl talk today. I really do have to go . . . dear."

. . .

Elaine walked home, looking forward to reporting to Joyce. A second printing of fifteen hundred. It was clear to her that Panther Publishers had bungled her book. But the shock of that had passed, and she was turning over her disappointment. The pre-publication trade reviews had been very good, and that meant something. Joyce told her to write out a proposal and sample chapters of *The American Eagle* as soon as possible, and she'd do her damnedest to place her better. That's just what Elaine would do.

It's really strange, she thought. What a disparity between the fantasy and the reality of having written a book. Writing the book was its own reward. Hope incarnate. A letter to everyone, to life. She hadn't thought of her book as a product with a shelf life. She hadn't realized that publishing was just another industry being leveraged along with the rest. Next time, damn it, she'd have to think of that too.

It was a warm Saturday night. Mario and Elaine were sitting on the shore across from Lake Acres, sharing a joint. Elaine motioned across the lake. "Do you think, if I keep my option, we might buy the townhouse together—share it?"

"You mean, live there?"

"Just a thought."

He had his arm around her. He took a last toke and then flicked the roach. They watched it spark, then land in the sands. "Never. It's like being in the City. We have New York. Hell, who knows, maybe we'd buy our own place together, farther out. Get a piece of land that's not sky high—farther out even than those friends of yours, Judith and Peter—and build our own place. Exactly as we like it. I got the guys for that. I got the guys who can build a place right."

"That's what you'd like to do?"

"Sure would. Soon. Do you like the idea?" He held her tighter. "We get along pretty well, don't we? Even if, like everyone else, it seems we do fight."

"We do. Get along, I mean. And I do like the idea. I like ideas with you."

"Look, Elaine, we met each other right over there. Sometimes I go over to that tree, and I think that it was a crazy crapshoot that we'd ever meet. Not to mention knowing it when we did meet. A lot of people, they'd fight their luck. Not go with it, the way we did."

"Hey, I was thinking almost the same thing, driving up!"

"Again? We do that all the time. It's something, isn't it?"

"My father always fought his luck. You have to know when something's happening easy."

"Like watching you walk down from Pam's and sit under the weeping willow."

"Like Stanley Howard dying for my option."

"God, Elaine, are you romantic!"

She giggled.

Elaine went to see Stanley Howard on Sunday. He was offering her twelve thousand dollars for her option on the townhouse. That meant he'd be able to buy it for eighty-three thousand dollars less than the asking price. In the last month the future Lucerne hadn't gone above two hundred and ninety-five thousand. This read like a mini-slump.

Did Stanley Howard know something? Pam said he was an empty-nester, whose parents had honeymooned at the Lake Acres hotel that burned down in '28. But was that true? Did he have some inside information? Was it possible that, when they were built, the townhouses would be worth three hundred and fifty, four hundred thousand dollars? Maybe she'd make fifty thousand, a hundred thousand—more? She saw hundreds of thousands of dollars coming her way. She was holding out and holding out and getting richer and richer.

Her Italian grandmother came to her in the middle of this attack. Grandma Elena, whom she was sort of named after, was a generous woman, but careful about her money at the same time. Small, sturdy, always keeping the vitality of tough early years. A strong woman. Absolutely devoid of self-pity. But her voice would become fraught with nuance whenever she discussed the horrible possibility of having to "Dip into Principal." And as she got older, it was a possibility she always seemed willing to talk about, even with relatives who had much less than she. Still, she was generous, she was charitable. What would Grandma Elena say about twelve thousand dollars in hand on a two-thousand-dollar investment? Something old-fashioned?

Stanley Howard lived in an old Dutch Colonial. In the real-estate ads of the day it would read "Charm Galore: Grandpa's house with original wood details, Grandma's kitchen, back yard with apple trees, four-car garage, all on level land." Mr. Howard was a tall man, white-haired, and in his sixties. His wife was plump and kept her hair blond. They were on the back porch that the Howards had added. Mrs. Howard excused herself.

"Look at all those apples," Elaine said.

"Every one of them falls," he replied. "Don't get me wrong, I'd never cut an apple tree down. But there comes a time—"

"When we've had enough of apples," said Sally Howard, bringing iced tea and cookies on a tray.

"That smells so good!" Elaine said.

"Fresh mint. It grows like the devil."

"So you're really going to sell this place?"

"Or we can rent it out," he said.

"Like that one." Sally pointed to the house way on the right.

"Oh, you own that one too?" Elaine said.

"We like good neighbors."

"But you're ready to move?"

Sally said, "We're ready for a vacation from work."

"How come you don't buy a unit that will be ready sooner? There are a few."

"It's the location," Sally said. "The end one, where yours will stand—why, that's a beautiful location. You'll see all the way to the Fairgrounds."

"With the Fair gone," Elaine said.

"Remember the Fair?" Sally said with relish. "The traffic! My goodness. Well, we need a mall."

Stanley said, "You know, my parents had their honeymoon there, at the old hotel. When I heard they were going to develop that complex, I said to Sally—"

"Spilt milk," Sally said. "I couldn't get used to the idea of a condominium then. And who ever heard of prices like that in Danbury!"

"We could have bought a unit like yours for a hundred and five."

"And I thought that was expensive. It was!" Sally said. "But now, I guess, there's still time to speculate."

Speculate! So there it was, Elaine thought. "It's beautiful here," she said. "If I were you, I'd find it hard to move."

"Well, you know," Sally said, "it won't be tomorrow."

"That's true. My unit won't be ready for more than a year," Elaine said. "A friend of mine's contracting there."

"That's what I heard too. A year or so," Stanley said.

"To be honest," Elaine said, "I don't know what to do. I like the location too. I don't think it would hurt to wait."

There was silence.

Elaine took a breath and continued. "But I don't want to keep you hanging either. So what I want to know is, what's your final offer? Just give me your final offer, your very best, and I'll say yes or no. Nothing to think over, just yes or no. Does that sound fair to you?"

Stanley Howard looked over at his apple trees. "Twenty-two thousand."

Elaine heard herself say steadily, "Okay, it's a deal. Yes."

.   .   .

The next Friday, Elaine came back to Danbury to sign papers. When she got to Mario's quarters late that afternoon, the place was clean but looked slightly askew.

Stale, she thought, opening the window. Maybe she should turn on the small air conditioner. Get things moving. Twenty-two thousand. Ten on signing. She should feel great. She was going to hang her clothes up, then undress and take a shower. Make dinner. Just her and Mario.

When she got out of the shower and back into the living room, she had the strangest feeling, as if someone had come in and gone out again. She looked at the window, the air conditioner, her bag on the chair. Strange. She went to it. Had she left it just like that? She looked in. Her wallet was there. She went to her discarded jeans and felt in the pocket. Her money was there. She couldn't stifle her sense of an intrusion. She wondered if, while she was away, Wig had been living there.

"What are you, a witch?" Mario smiled at her over dinner.

"It's possible," she answered. "But I just had a feeling when I got back that it wasn't the way I left it. I don't know. The Tone soap was new. The place smelled a little stale. I just was wondering if Wig had stayed here."

"Yeah, he was here for two glorious nights. I even thought of calling Paulette. Maybe she should call her mother. Maybe he should spend the rest of the summer in Quebec. I don't know."

"It's the crack?"

"Nah, he's not on that anymore. Just your everyday Danbury variety of coke, cut down to the nth degree. Harmless."

"Are you joking?"

"About what?"

"About the cocaine."

"Nah. What you get here couldn't hurt a baby. Only Wig's into industrial doses."

"He can get that here?"

"This is Coke City."

"You're kidding."

"I kid you not. Snow City."

"How are you doing?"

"How do you mean?"

"I thought you were off that stuff."

"Hey, Elaine, don't let's start, okay? You go away for a week, I have a few nights out with the boys. That's all it is and you know it, and I'm not going to apologize."

"But it's addictive."

"Crack's addictive. Coke's clean."

"Like Wig."

"Wig's different. And I think he's holding out on me. I think he's freebasing. He can't control himself. And he's not the only one. You want to hear it? I'm having trouble with some of the other guys. French guys who forget to come to work? I'm not saying there isn't trouble out there. But let me handle my business, okay? I mean, all that detox stuff and the Anonymous Rooms, it's great, it's great, it's there if you need it. But you gotta have some faith in me, Elaine. I'm thirty-eight going on fifty when it comes to this world. I'd like you to trust me and know I can take care of myself."

"I do, Mario. I do."

"Good." He smiled. "So, let me tell you something funny. You know how Pauli Girl prides himself on his nose? Well, he gets this great rock—I mean, like a real buy—and what does he do . . ." Mario went into a long story, which Elaine actually could have lived without, about how Pauli Girl ruined a crystal of coke.

Late Saturday afternoon the phone rang. "I have an emergency at the Fair."

"I just got up from my desk. Want me to come over?"

"Not unless you're good with a screwgun. Work on a best-seller. I'll be home soon."

"Hurry."

"I will."

She went back to work. Got involved in ideas about the second chapter. Her concentration was steady. And when she looked up it was six-thirty. She worked some more. Seven-thirty. Then gave it up. Poured some wine, spread some Ritz crackers with peanut butter. Eight-thirty. Nine.

The phone rang again at ten. "Where the hell are you?"

"I'm trying to pay back a bank loan, babe!"

"This is nuts. How much can you work on a Saturday night? I thought we were going to celebrate my sale. You could have let me know. I could have driven over and celebrated with Judith. I still might."

"Hey, hey. There are emergencies in life. Come on. Think I want to be here? Think I don't want to be with you?"

"Oh my God, Mario, someone's at the door!"

There was the sound of the key in the latch, and the door opened.

"Wig!"

"Is he there? I've been looking all over for him. How the hell did he get there? Let me talk to him."

Wig stood in the middle of the room. Dark eyes shone in his emaciated face. There were white skulls printed on the black bandanna that was pulling back his wild hair.

"He has the key!" she shouted. "I knew it! I knew it!"

"Let me speak to him."

"Mario's on the phone."

She extended the phone; he walked over to her and took it.

He slurred out words in French. She turned away.and went to Mario's small kitchen.

"He come home. Wait." Wig delivered that message and slumped into a chair.

"I'm making coffee."

Wig tried to light a cigarette. She put on water and got back in time to help him. "Here," she said, and lit it for him.

Get hold of yourself, she thought, going to the stove again. Coffee for both of them. Three teaspoons of instant each, in not too much boiling water.

"Drink!" she said.

He was dead white. Hands shaking, he put the cigarette in the ashtray and tried to do what he was told.

She wondered if she should take him to a hospital. She tried to stay calm. On the one hand, he might OD and die right in front of her. This was a possibility. But if she called the hospital or the cops . . . She couldn't do that. No matter what, she couldn't. Where was Mario?

"Do you want to lie down?"

Then she thought of Claude downstairs. Not now, no. But he was someone she could call.

Wig looked at her. But he didn't seem to understand.

He had a cigarette in his lips again. An ash was forming. His eyes closed. Before she got to the cigarette, it had dropped. She picked it off his lap; his black jeans were stained, and he smelled. His white T-shirt was dirty under his long-sleeved checkered shirt. The impeccable Wig, with the woman in his soul, who did his own ironing.

His eyes were closed. His mouth was slightly open. He was breathing.

She went for some more of the coffee. She found her hand shaking as bad as Wig's.

Mario burst through the door. Thank God! She ran into the living room.

Mario in the middle of the room. His eyes were wide and wild. His curly hair circled his head like sparks of fire. He looked like a madman. "Open your eyes!" he yelled at Wig. He turned to Elaine. "He's okay! Why the hell didn't you tell me?"

"Tell you what?"

"That he was okay. I thought he was OD'ing. For Christsake, he's just nodding."

"What? Just nodding?" she screamed.

He put a finger to his lips. "Sssssh."

"Sssssh!" she spit. "Nodding?" she repeated loudly. "Nodding? That's heroin? Heroin?"

"No, no. Just mixing a little of it with coke, that's all. Smoking it," he said to her, as if letting her in on a confidence.

She didn't buy it. "You're using," she screamed. "I can see it! You've been lying to me. Liar! Liar!"

His eyes turned to ice. He grabbed her left arm, twisting it, and brought her to him like a rag doll.

Her head jolted; she felt her neck snap. Then slowly she moved her head. It still moved.

"Please let me go," she said steadily.

He looked at her, surprised he was holding on to her. "Well, be quiet," he said, rationally. "You know I'd never hurt you."

"But you just have," she said.

"You're making things worse. He's the problem."

Mario paused. Suddenly he was his brother's keeper and in control. "Look, let him nod off. Then he's out of here—I swear. In the meantime, you and I, let's go somewhere. Celebrate your sale. Come on, it's Saturday night."

She didn't answer.

"I mean it," he said. "I know this is no fun for you. But that's where I've been all night," he said, pointing to Wig, "looking for him. You think I'm on something? I'm not. It's him. Believe me, Elaine. I've been over half the world looking for him tonight. I've been to New York, for God's sake. Yes, I have. You know, this guy could end up in jail. What the hell am I supposed to do? Let him—"

"You've been to New York? Just like that?"

"That's right. Just like that. And where is he? Screwing things up between us. I've had it up to here!" He turned from her and walked into the bedroom. "I'm going to take a shower."

How often had he been to New York? Her face was hot, and her arm was hurting, and she was beginning to experience a stiffness, not in her neck but in her shoulders.

But maybe it was she. What strain he must be under to grab her like that.

He really couldn't be fool enough to be smoking crack, smoking heroin! Speedballs? Mario? She wanted to talk with him, to reason. Wanted to make it all right, wanted to forget the throbbing pain. After all, maybe they should go out, talk all this over. He'd admitted Wig was the problem. She'd make him see Wig needed a type of help Mario couldn't give. Yes, everything in her heart knew Mario was not a man who would hurt her. That was a moment in which he had been out of control. That was not the man.

"We'll go out?" Mario called, and went into the shower.

"Yes," she answered.

She loved him. She'd talk to him. She'd help him. She looked over at Wig, dead to the world. Dear God, what was happening to her? What was she allowing, what was she excusing? Hadn't she heard it over and over in the Anonymous Rooms, one lie leading to another, one push leading to one slap to . . . ?

She had to get out of there! She grabbed her bag, went to the desk, and, with trembling hands, stuffed in every page of her manuscript. She should have taken her car keys out first.

It took her forever to find that zippered pouch she kept them in. She took them out and zipped her bag.

Slowly and without a sound she opened the door. And then she came back, she had to. She went into the bedroom, and to Mario's pants that were thrown on the bed. Thank God. That's where they were, in those pants, her apartment keys. Back to the living room as in a slow-motion dream of horror. Out the door. She heard the click.

She was down the stairs, on her toes. Off the porch. Around the back. Unlock the car. Throw the bag in. Close the door. Start up quick. The noise.

She didn't put her lights on till she made a right onto the road. Concentration took her past her pain.

•　　•　　•

Judith wiped the sleep out of her eyes and said, "No, no, that's okay, come in."

"Thanks."

She followed Judith into the kitchen, where Judith turned on a light. "Want some decaf?"

"Fine."

Judith was wearing an old blue terrycloth robe, which she tied tighter around the waist. She opened the fridge. "Brewed decaf."

"Don't trouble."

"No trouble." She turned to Elaine and smiled. "God, you make me feel young!"

"Do I?"

"Like when you decided not to go back to Italy, and came up to Boston in the middle of the night. Or when I was in college myself and things happened late. Now I roll over, or maybe go to the bathroom, or maybe listen to Peter snore. Not that that will last forever either."

"Oh, I'm sorry," Elaine said, sitting down at the round kitchen table.

"For what?"

"Well, I've burst in on you, and you sound like you have problems."

"No," Judith said, putting the filter in the coffee maker and adding the decaf. "You just caught me too close to dreams. What's wrong, Elaine? You talk to me." Having switched on the machine, she drew up a chair and sat across from her friend.

Elaine stared at Judith. Awake now and ready to listen. But the eyes still drawn to sleep. "What are you looking at?" Judith asked, turning to see if the coffee was dripping.

"You."

"What about you, Elaine? Do you want to talk?"

"I do want to talk."

"Wait, I'll get the coffee."

"All the way over here," Elaine said—the coffee poured, the two women facing each other once more—"I kept seeing my life in front of my eyes. I couldn't think of Mario directly, I just couldn't. Saying his name, even, shakes me. It's hard for me to say 'Mario' in front of you. Mario. Mario. Mario."

"There, you've done it," Judith said.

"I've done it, all right. I've done it over and over. My whole life makes absolutely no sense to me.

"You know, I thought of Mario Bertone too on the way over. Do you know what I think of when I think of him? I think of ironing his shirt. I actually did iron his shirts. It wasn't a joke. I meet an Italian cousin to a count who's going to be a neurosurgeon; I go back to Italy with him. I research my doctor's thesis in Rome. I live in a cold and charming apartment and have a terrace that looks out over the Eternal City. I hear the bells and love the rooftops and meet fascinating people and learn new ways. I have a cleaning lady who cooks. But I iron Mario's shirts, because he loves the way I do collars. He'd sit and watch me. I swear to God, they were part of my sex life. Doing his shirts made me good enough for him to do me! I submitted to his shirts. Take me, take me! I said to his shirts. I think I was some sort of fantasy to him. As close as he could get to screwing a chambermaid. He really did look down on me. If he screwed an American, at least she should have some money. I was worth one Fulbright. That was it. And my family? They thought I was out of my mind going with someone from the old country, even if he was related to a pope.

"I used to have mini-breakdowns over that ironing board when I was alone. Not because I was doing shirts—because I thought I'd never do them well enough. I'd have attacks of nerves. I'd put the damn shirt on, go to the hall mirror, stand in the draft, see another wrinkle. Take the shirt off, run back to the ironing board. I'd practice. It was awful! And I peeled his fruit. I did. The knife in my hand, the curl of the peach skin . . . It makes me crazy just remembering the things I did for that man!"

"A slave of love."

"Well, I thought I was in love. Maybe I was in love. Twenty-two, twenty-three years old. An Italian Somebody. I thought that was pretty special. Life was like a book for me in those days. Books were going to save me. We were going to get married after I came home and defended my thesis—"

"And you never went back. You decided that in Boston with me. Sometimes, Elaine, I think marrying Larry was some sort of a policy statement."

"I cared for Larry. The passion went very quickly, though. I thought it was me, at first. But it was both of us. We had companionship, work. I know I wasn't in love. That didn't last long."

"What do you think marriage is? A honeymoon?"

"I have no idea what most marriages are. They all seem mysterious and unworkable to me. I wondered for a long time if I even knew how to love."

"What about Nola?"

"Nola? I always felt for her. I always thought she was great."

"Why?"

"Just because she was Nola. That's all. Whatever she wanted to do, however she wanted to dress, she was being Nola. I never wanted to change her."

"What does that sound like to you?" Judith asked.

"It used to sound to me like I was too distant, too cold."

"So what does it sound like to you now?"

"Love," Elaine said, as matter-of-factly as she could. "I guess what I didn't know then was that love was so easy."

"Are you okay?" Judith asked after a while. "Here." She handed her a paper napkin.

"Now, for me, Judith, love is too easy! I just can't talk about it."

"Talk about what?"

"What's happened to Mario!"

"What about a drink first? What the hell? How does some *vino fino* sound?"

"Sure, why not."

Judith went to the fridge. "It's jug," she said, "but it's cold."

"You got a bargain?"

"Of course."

"Wineglasses are pretty," Elaine said out of nowhere.

"They are the best revenge." Judith seemed to slap them down on the table, uncorked the jug, and poured. They clicked glasses.

"Tastes good," Elaine said.

"Naturally. God, I slugged that." She poured some more.

"Do you mind?" Elaine asked. She reached down to her bag and took out a joint.

"No. I'll have some too. I could use a good giggle. Wait, I'll get an ashtray."

"Not bad," Judith said.

"Not bad? Organically grown Sens, cultivated by mature hippies under the California sun? The best for what it is."

They were quiet for a while. Judith coughed after the third hit and motioned no more.

Elaine said, "I'm thinking, maybe I shouldn't be doing this. I always thought it was good for me. Mind-expanding. Maybe 'cause I didn't do it at all till I was out of school. I hung out with you guys, remember? All that judgmental stuff that I was raised with, this is the way I learned to get beyond it. Getting high. Really listening to what a person had to say. Without qualification. Without conditions. Without judgment. Oh, this is what Judith says. Oh, this is what Mario says. Simple? So simple. It opened me up to a lot of life and a lot of music. It added in. I've cut down, but I'm beginning to think I should give it up completely. I can't enjoy it the way I used to. It's not the same."

"Well, if you don't do it too often . . ."

"It's still not so hot on the short-term memory. Sometimes on pot I lose a connection. I sort of enjoy that, you know? Losing the middle of a thought! I could never do that if I weren't high. I just couldn't." Elaine laughed. Judith giggled.

"Ah, it's not that funny. Do you know what I'm thinking? I'm thinking maybe I'd better give this up."

"You said that already. Always something new with you, Elaine," Judith said raspily. "But I'm glad we're friends."

"Me too. Me too."

"What's going on, Elaine?"

Elaine said, "It's Mario, it's Wig. It's bad."

"What do you mean?"

"It's . . . coke, crack, speedballs, name it. It's anything, it's everything." The phone rang.

"Oh, no!" Elaine said. "Get it. Be absolutely convincing that I'm not here."

"Mario? What? No. Listen. I'm sleeping. Call tomorrow. What? I don't know what you're talking about. Goodbye."

Judith sat down.

Elaine pointed to her arms, above the elbow. "See, Judith, it's a little red. In a few days it will be black and blue. He's dangerous, I think. Out of control. I think I can lose my arm and my money and my sanity. I have plenty of examples."

"You do?"

"I've been going to the Anonymous Rooms because of Wig. It turns out I've been going to meetings to save myself."

"You're able to talk to strangers?" Judith asked incredulously. "I could never do that."

"We're not strangers," Elaine said, regaining some of her spirit.

"Well, you and I are friends. You can always come to me."

"I know. Here I am. Thanks. I had to get out of there. I came this way rather than home. I needed to talk. I'm afraid, if I don't say it out loud to someone I know, it won't be real. I'll excuse it this time and next and next. . . . And before you know it, I'll be . . . a slave. What's happening now, I'll tell you the truth—in a million years, I never thought this would happen to me."

"What is it that's happening? I mean exactly."

Elaine looked at her. "I can't help the person I love. I see what's happening, and there's absolutely nothing I can do. I watched Larry and I knew there was nothing I could do but be there for him. But Wig, and I guess deep down I knew Mario too, has something only he himself could stop. And all I can do is watch Mario get thinner and thinner like Wig and act the way he never acted before. And I encouraged him to take out a bank loan! I remember I said, 'The banks are having money sales— big signs saying that—maybe it's the time to buy.' And he looked at me a long time. God knows what he's up to. All I can do is watch our love go down the tubes. I can't help him, Judith! I can't! And, God help me, I don't know if I have the strength to help myself. I feel I'm living in hell. I saw it tonight. But somehow I've known it . . . known it since we began to fight. And then I think, I'm not in a ghetto. The same horror. Do I have a better chance to get away? I better have the guts to try. The devil's all around us, Judith."

"The devil?"

"Yes," Elaine said, wiping her eyes with her hands.

"You believe in the devil?"

"No. I don't believe in the devil. I believe in God. I know there's the devil."

They were quiet.

Suddenly the pot kicked in. Elaine's mood altered. She felt her run was over, that in bolting from Danbury to New Milford she'd fixed things for herself. She wanted to tell Judith that everything would be okay. But when she opened her mouth to speak, she forgot what she was going to say.

"I've come to tell you the truth," Mario said. Elaine stood on Judith's deck, a coffee cup in her hand. No makeup on. Disheveled hair. Hardly any sleep.

It was he who looked good. White shirt with the sleeves rolled up and opened at the neck. A small pad and a pen in its pocket. Newly pressed black chinos. Newly shaved face. His shaving lotion smelled like a promise.

"First take this." He handed her a check.

She looked at it. "Twenty-five hundred? You don't owe me this much."

"Don't I? It adds up. Anyway, I rounded it off. Take it. It's yours."

"Thank you," she said softly and slipped it in her jeans pocket. "I'll get you some coffee. I want to hear the truth."

They sat at the table on the side deck. Beautiful Sunday morning. Mario looked down at his coffee cup. With his thumb and forefinger he traced its handle. She watched his bent head.

"Wig's in a bad way. I spoke with his older brother in Beauce. He's taking over. That was Paulette's suggestion. I've done what I can. He's gotta shape up or ship out, before he ruins my life. I took his key back and I noticed—maybe I misplaced it in all the confusion—did you take your keys back?"

She nodded.

He looked up at her, hurt. "Don't you have any faith in me at all?" he whispered.

"The truth, Mario? I'm waiting to hear the truth."

"The truth is that I made a bad mistake."

"Which was?"

He looked down again. "I started smoking a little crack. That's the truth. Only at night! Only when I was alone. Let me talk first, okay? I got very lonely after Christmas, Elaine. I can't explain it. The work slowed down and I was worried about that and . . . I was wondering how much you really loved me. Wig was always on your mind. I know how women fall for Wig, and—"

"Wig? You thought I liked Wig? You smoked crack because you thought I liked Wig?"

"I know. I'm telling you the truth." He looked her straight in the eye. "You want to hear it, or you want to jump on me, call me a liar, like last night?"

She pointed to her upper arm. The bruise. His marks.

"Jesus," he said.

There was a pause.

"Want me to warm up that coffee?" she asked.

"No. Look, Elaine, I'm not perfect. I was stupid. You know I haven't gone near a hard drug since I left Florida. Just a few beers, a joint once in a while. I don't know what happened, but since you wouldn't go to Florida with me over Christmas, I don't know, I just didn't feel right. It was like the honeymoon was over. Like something was wrong. And suddenly I'm in my apartment smoking—"

"Speedballs?"

"Are you kidding? I'm not crazy like Wig, mixing in heroin! Just crack."

"Oh, that's reassuring. The day you brought me to New York, after Larry died—I thought I saw you driving my car, hours after you were supposed to have left. Was it you?"

He shrugged. "I don't know. I did make runs downtown—from here, even. Back and forth in two hours, if the traffic's right."

"Oh, Mario, my heart is breaking."

"Mine too. I can't lose you, Elaine. I swear to you—no more. Look, I stopped. I swear to God, I stopped two weeks ago. That's the irony. I stopped cold turkey. You never would have had to know. And then Wig goes out. I've stopped before I'm out of money. That's why the check I gave you is so important. No better proof than money in the bank. It's Wig's problem that's coming between us. It's always Wig."

"You stopped smoking crack, just like that?"

"Yes, I did. Now it's in your hands, Elaine. You've got to believe me, you've got to have some trust. We're not children. There are ups and downs between people. This is really down, I know. But I love you. . . . You've got to give me a chance to show you. And I don't think it's so hot that we live apart. Maybe that's part of it."

"I was thinking of the day we'd live together, if not all the time, a lot of the time, here in Connecticut," Elaine said. "We're not children, but I, I was even thinking . . . Well, not now."

"Look, I want you to give me a chance to prove myself. You can take as long as you want. And when you see this episode is over—that Wig's not with us—that we're enjoying life again—when you see that for yourself—why, then, girl, maybe you'll ask me to marry you."

"Mario—"

"I'm not joking, Elaine. I'm dead serious. Part of this whole mess is that you run shy of commitment—"

"Me?"

"Absolutely."

"Maybe you have a point," she said, slowly. "Maybe I helped to make all of this worse."

"No, you tried your best. These Anonymous Rooms. I read the stuff you left for Wig."

"You did? Why didn't you tell me?"

"Because then I would've had to tell you about the other stuff. I've gone to a few meetings. I'll go to more. There's one tonight in Newtown. Come home with me. You'll see I go. I don't have to do it all myself, the way I did last time. I'm getting to be humble, like they say. Maybe I shouldn't isolate, or become a hermit, like I did the last time I got sober."

"Oh, Mario, that's good news."

"Don't cry. Just come back to Danbury with me. I've got to have my arms around you, Elaine. I've got to have you in my life. Trust me, Elaine. For both our sakes, trust me."

He went to his meeting that night. Monday he went to work and she left a note on the bed. She drew a big heart, and in the center of it she put her keys.

The next weekend in New York brought them even closer together. All they did was get honest, talk. "I don't know if we should keep on smoking," she said in bed.

"One thing at a time," he said. "I can't do everything at once."
She took a final toke and laughed. "Neither can I."

His check bounced the following Wednesday.

"What? That's impossible," he said over the phone. "I'll give them hell at that bank and get back to you."

When he came down that weekend, he gave her a new check. "Deposit it on Wednesday," he said. She did what he told her. But on Friday she called his bank. He had a delinquent account.

That weekend she didn't hear from him. "I have to face this full on," she said in the Anonymous Rooms. "I have to face this awful pain."

On Monday she had her lock changed. She also took a musky-smelling baggie out of her drawer, wrapped it in aluminum foil, and took it out to the hallway, to the incinerator. She threw her pot away.

S I X T E E N

Perhaps what we interpret as irony or even tragedy in life is part of a higher comedy, and eventually there's a celestial punch line followed by a good laugh. The following Wednesday, Joyce sent Elaine an advance copy of next Sunday's *Times Book Review* by messenger. Elaine had brought the envelope to her couch and was getting past the masking tape when she heard a scraping at her door. Attempt after attempt. Keys that didn't fit. Then her doorbell rang. Her heart began to pound. She kept quiet.

In the silence that ensued, she carefully pulled the *Review* from the manila envelope and saw her picture right there on the front page—Larry's picture of her, the picture she'd chosen herself—and the notation that there was a review on page 7! Her heart continued its surge as she went to page 7 and saw a full-page review! She was reading the first paragraph: "In a brilliant debut as a novelist, Elaine Netherlands, once the wife of the deceased photographer, has given heart to the idea that love is a subject that can draw its—"

"Elaine! Are you there?" Mario rang again, and then he pounded.

She went over to the door, then quietly, her back to the wall, she sat on the floor of the entryway, her *Book Review* in her hand. She closed her eyes, and prayed. "God grant me the serenity to—"

"Damn you! Are you there? I know you're there!"

"—accept the things I cannot change, the courage to—"

Bzzzzzz. "Elaine, hi, it's Joyce. Did the messenger get there? What'd you think of them apples? Busy at your computer? Great! Get that proposal to me yesterday. I have a call in to Panther about another printing. Call me as soon as you can. On my second line. Here's the number. . . ."

"Damn you. Elaine! Elaine!" Bang, bang, bang.

"—change the things I can—"

"Sorry, ma'am. I didn't mean to disturb you. I can't believe this. What? Sure, sure, I know she changed her lock. She lost a set of keys when she was with me. Can't be too careful today. I got all the way to my car when I realized I'd left my wallet on the table, and you can see I picked up the wrong keys. Elaine must have slipped out. Could I leave a note with . . .

Bzzzzzz. "Elaine, Donna. Good work! We're all excited here. Could you . . ."

"Here I am bidding for my first job in the City. The skating rink. That's right. Donald Trump. Mr. Trump himself. That's who I'm going to have to walk to meet. Can't even get into my car. Sure, it'd take my crew six months—not six years, like it's taken the City to do nothing. They'll be skating in six, seven months. Oh, you can? That's too kind. I can't. Why, a twenty's beautiful. Bless you. The note? That's okay. I'll be back. You tell her . . ."

"—and the wisdom to know the difference."

Bzzzzzz. "Elaine, Vicky. What's this my singing waiter tells me? His boyfriend's on the *Book Review,* and he says you got four stars. Better buy more place settings—the hungry washed will be coming."

Bzzzzzz. "Elaine, Nola. We're opening at Tut-A-Comin' for Basic Black tonight. Basic Black! Tut-A-Comin'! Yes, you heard right. All right! The media will be there. Para Adenoid all got food poisoning on that Montana flight. How's that for timing? You gotta be there. See you out front tonight! I'll leave a message in Danbury, just in case you're there. Don't want to miss you. Demo City, here we come!"

Elaine opened her eyes.

She didn't get up. She had prayed for serenity and now tried not to picture Mario rushing out into the streets with twenty dollars in his hand. Still sitting in the hallway, she looked at the review in her hand, and began to read.

Bzzzzzz. "Hello. I hope this is the voice of Elaine Netherlands. I have just read the impressive review of your book in an advance copy of *The New York Times Book Review,* which is flown to me weekly. I would very much like to know, do you think Western civilization as we know it will last on into the twenty-first century? Please think about this carefully. You don't know me, but I'll be calling back. Don't worry, I really will."

Tut-A-Comin' was the hot club that season. It had opened in the spring in a deserted salt mine—one of the warehouses with a huge underground area where the City stores the salt it uses during the winter months on icy streets. This one had originally been a produce warehouse built with WPA funds, and still had Mussoliniesque lettering to that effect on its block-long front. It had been abandoned as a salt mine because of all the bad press about the young boy prostitutes, the homeless teenagers from all over the country, who were using the rat-infested underground to score, to shoot up, to smoke, and to sleep. The City's latest solution for coping with the accelerated drug problem, which all of America was sending, as usual, straight to it, was to destroy crack houses, literally razing them to the ground, and to empty out the salt mines. It was an understandable act of avoidance and panic, but puzzling in a City that had such intimate life experience with the tenacity of the cockroach.

Be that as it may, part of the spirit of the late twentieth century was to give a party over any disaster, or a satellite rock show. There was no lack of positive energy, good people banding together for a cause and a good time. So there was a celebration when the City sold this salt mine to the Billings brothers with the clause that ten percent of every night's gross receipts at Tut-A-Comin' would be given toward an eventual city shelter for homeless youth. The mayor smiled, flanked by the Billings brothers. All three raised clasped hands for the camera. They took their photo opportunity, and the Big Apple continued to rock.

Hawki-Itaki was the architect. The outside of Tut was kept as wretched as it always had been. It took quite an eye to see that all the graffiti on the outside walls bore tags of galleried graffiti artists. Elaine joined Vicky to the side of the long line. "Thank you for coming with me," she said, hugging her Jersey friend.

"Are you kidding? I wouldn't miss it. So this is where all the young trendettes are. They've formed a new line."

"Basic Black's very hot."

"Good break for Nola."

"Hope so. Here're the passes. Let's go in."

"What's wrong, Elaine? You worried about Nola?"

"Vicky, this isn't a case of what's wrong, it's a case of what's right. Second Hand's my gleam of light. Let's rock."

"What about your review?"

"Oh, that too. It's just that it doesn't come with arms and legs and a fresh face and a young heart."

"But it makes noise, all right."

"It does," Elaine agreed. "You should hear some of the messages I'm getting. I think I'll package my tape."

"Now you're talkin, kid. Jeez, people really go to places like this for fun? It's scary."

"What an old fart."

"I was born an old fart," Vicky said, lowering her weary voice and her weary eyelids. "You know, the Billings brothers used to eat at my place at least once a week."

"I didn't know this was going to be a nostalgia trip."

"Jezus, what the hell's this on my feet?"

"Come on, I'll tell you over there."

Out of the gloom of the creepy room into a big dance space, Elaine said, "That was the simulated rat room."

"Oh, please!"

"Postmodern adaptation of real space."

"Did we have to go in that way?"

"That was for the cognoscenti. I just couldn't resist."

"Thanks. Hey, this is more like it. Come on, I'll buy you a drink."

After the drink, Elaine said, "Let's dance."

"You're kidding."

"Come on, come on."

Vicky got on the crowded dance floor like a reluctant husband, and Elaine danced around her. The strobe lights and the good rock beat blinked out PARTY, and Elaine danced and danced. Even after Vicky groaned and said, "Meet you at the bar," Elaine stayed with the music, dancing, part of everyone else, and by herself.

"All right!" she said, finding Vicky by the bar. "Hey, you better go easy. Too much liquor and this type of scene don't mix. It can make you dizzy. At least it makes me dizzy. Diet Coke," she said.

"I don't get it," Vicky said, drink in hand, staying as close to the bar as possible. "Don't they use stages anymore? Where's Nola going to stand?"

"She won't be singing in this room, Vicky. Let's see. Want to take your drink? The stage is down in the mines."

"More rats?"

"No, no. Tut's tomb."

"Yuck! Mummies?"

"Of course mummies. And Tut's golden head."

"Does he give golden head? Give me a good old-fashioned leather bar any day. That, at least, I understand."

"Vicky, you're such a traditionalist. Hey, give me your opinion, do you think Western civilization as we know it will last?"

"Western what?"

"May I quote you?"

"Quote me."

Tut's tomb was an enormous underground space, flanked by bars. There were two levels. Elaine thought the best position was upstairs, where there were even some tables. Since they were early, they could sit. From where they sat, they had a good perspective down onto the stage.

"What time will they go on, do you think?" Vicky asked.

"Soon."

"It's not that crowded."

"It might not be. It's a mixed blessing, opening for a band like Basic Black. We'll see."

"Don't you want to go downstairs and dance?"

"I danced."

"You nervous?"

"Yes."

The downstairs had filled up by the time, an hour later—a long hour later—that Second Hand opened. This time Jimmy didn't set up, calling out "Hello, New York." The four just walked on stage. Asia Neither Land on guitar, Jimmy Along on bass, Ms. Dynamite Michelle on the drums, and Mixmaster Formerly between keyboard and percussion. Girls as well as boys, and a former rapper, not exactly whitebread, Nola's band. She took center stage, looked around, nodded; they started.

Her whole look had changed with that long wavy blond hair

and grown-in roots. She wore jeans and a white T with cut-off sleeves.

"What the hell is that?" Vicky yelled. "Jeez, I hope it's a decal."

Elaine's eyes strained. Maybe it was an optical illusion?

On her upper right arm, Asia had a bright new tattoo.

Asia Neither Land played her guitar like a weapon as she shouted out urban wrongs. Ms. Michelle truly was dynamite, and Mixmaster Formerly was brilliant. Jimmy, no longer lead, seemed to be going along. In the middle of the sound, Elaine saw that Asia's picking up the guitar had been Nola's change of luck.

Elaine was not as comfortable as she'd been in CBGB. The songs Nola was composing were harder. And when they came out with "Salt Mine/Gold Mine" Elaine realized Asia was capable of trying to build Rome in a day.

Asia sang "Da, Da Daddy": "The good doctor does provide / That you die a junkie." The only real oldie Elaine recognized was "West Side! Saturday! Afternoon!" "Doritos . . . orgasm," et al.

The people this music galvanized went close to the stage. Others were milling around in the background. It was a unique mix, this kind of raw girl and boy energy, this kind of statement to the world, this black-and-white composition, this eccentric rock. It was honest, uncosmetic, tough; the players were exciting and the music was opposites attracting. Would it ever fill Tut-A-Comin', would this kind of rock ever be really popular? Elaine noted that Asia filled the stage. But that tattoo!

The band's energy was swelling and relentless, playing to a mainly restless room. Elaine's spirit, hard enough to get up that day, came crashing down, and for the oddest reason. Asia Neither Land was on her own.

"Long time no see," Vicky shouted.

"What?" Elaine turned from the stage.

Mario had his finger to his lips as he sat down.

That was all Elaine would remember of the set.

She stared at Mario. Her heart leapt.

"Hi," he said.

"Hi," she said.

"Well, you guys." Vicky stood. "Can I get you a drink before I go?"

Elaine shook her head. "Could you do me a favor, Vicky? Could you get backstage after this set and tell Nola I'm here?"

"If I can make my way, I guess I can. If there're no rats. After all, what are friends for?"

"Can you give her this too?" Elaine had taken the light-brown underliner from her small bag and on a napkin had written out "Brava, Bravo, Bravi! XOX, E." Handing it to Vicky, she said, "Thanks so much."

Vicky waved the napkin. "You kidding? It's my passport out of here."

"I was listening from downstairs," Mario said. "They're good."

"How'd you—"

"They left me a message to come."

"Oh, in Danbury? Two trips in one day."

"So you were there! I knew you were home."

"I was there. You owe my neighbor a twenty. You're working for Trump."

He smiled. Like an angel. He was clean, well dressed, happy. Was he high? "I had to say something. All's fair in love and war. Here, I'll give you the twenty to give to her."

"Okay."

"I don't believe this!" he said, looking in his wallet. "Forgot it's a fortune to get in here."

"Get a refund. You were on the guest list." She looked at him knowingly. He smiled back. "I got a rave review in next Sunday's *Book Review*," Elaine said.

"Girl, that's great!"

"You win some, you lose some."

"Lose some?"

She looked into his eyes.

"What are you looking for?" he asked.

"You."

"Here I am."

"Here you are."

"You changed your lock."

"What would you expect me to do?"

"You think, no matter what, I'd ever take anything from you?"

"Your check wasn't worth the paper it was written on, Mario."

"Wig fucked me up. I wrote you a letter. He's out of his head. What he did to my bank account, I can't even talk about. I can't forgive myself. I fired him. It will never happen again. But you should have trusted me. You shouldn't have changed your lock."

"You fired Wig?"

"Yes."

"I wish . . ."

"Go on."

"Nothing."

He put his hand on her shoulder. "Second Hand's okay. A little weird, but okay. How's about we go home."

She shook her head.

"What are you saying?"

She could see he was getting mad. She looked around. Lots of people. Thank God.

She was as careful as she could be. "Mario," she said, "I need some space. Please try to understand."

"How much space?"

"I need to be alone for a while."

"Why are you beating around the bush? What are you trying to do to me? You think I'm high, don't you? Admit it! You're accusing me. My word is nothing to you!"

"I'm not accusing you of anything. Listen to me carefully, Mario. I'm not saying you're an addict. I'm telling you that, for me, just for me, I think, Elaine thinks, you're acting like an addict. And I can't deal with that. I can't cope with that. So give me some space. Let's go slow."

"I can't believe you'd think that of me. I can't believe it. Where's all that love you have? All that love?"

She put her hand over her heart. "It's right here. Where it always was. Right here."

"Don't cry," he whispered.

"I won't," she said.

"I love you, Elaine."

"I know."

"But you're saying not enough?"

"I'm saying I know."

"So what are we going to do? Are we sitting here all night?"

"I'd like you to go now."

"I can't go. Don't hate me. I won't make a scene. But I can't go. I've got to prove to you you're wrong. Hell, a good review. How many columns? Just kidding. Come on. Let's go together. I'll walk you home. Then, if you still want me to, then we'll discuss it."

"Mario," she whispered. She put her hand into her jeans pocket and took out a twenty. She put it on the table, under her glass.

He looked at her. "So this is saying you really want me to go? That's what you really want!" She didn't answer. Instead, she looked down.

"Okay, then, as you wish. No scene. Don't worry. No scene. You're a free agent. You love me, but you don't trust me. Nice combination. Read my letter when you get it. I'll pay you back every cent!"

She waited till he had left the room, and then, heart pounding, she prayed. Prayed it was still there. Prayed against all odds. She looked under her glass. The twenty was gone.

She turned to the stage. The set was over; lights played against a screen. Taped music blared. Big tears were rolling out of her eyes. She couldn't correct them.

Dear Mario,
    This is the fifth letter, and I wonder, if I write it, will I

send it. I got two of yours this week, and I hope you are serious about what you said over the answering machine. Yes, if you go into detox, I will be there for you. I'm your friend. I'm here for you now, but as I've told you on the phone, I have to separate from your disease and take care of my own. Mine is to want to help you. To stop my own life to take care of you. To give way. To lose myself in your addiction. Anything other than to face my own pain. But I'm facing that pain now. I have to. Without pot. I believe I'm going to get through all this, without euphoria. I am ready to face myself now, want to face myself now, come what may.

Let me say, the most difficult thing I've ever done in my life has been to say no to you.

I fell in love with you at first sight, actually, though I couldn't admit it. Maybe I should have written you this letter before. My style is to play hard to get. Underneath, I was easy. Trust me.

Yes, I remember how generous you were when we first were together. How you insisted on paying for everything, even though I told you it wasn't fashionable. Yes, I realize you don't want to owe me money. And I do believe that, if you go into the hospital and then into recovery, you will pay me back. But that's in the future. One day at a time.

Suddenly I'm so angry. If you were here, I'd shake you so hard. How many pounds of you are there left? You seem proud to tell me how thin you've gotten. How the hell could you go through all your money? You say it in a letter. Sixty thousand dollars in two months. And what haven't you told me? I get some of your creditors on my machine! What the hell did you tell them? And how could you have ruined everything we had? How could you make me say no to my heart?

I've got to get out of here. Go to a meeting. Do something for myself. There are no quick fixes to this, no quick answers.

I pray to God you'll find it in yourself to go for treatment. I've got to get out of here now, before I go crazy. Crazy with hope. Crazy with despair. You're on your own, dear Mario. So am I. And yes, I do know that you really do love me. I love you too.

E.

"Elaine! Why, come in. Want something to drink?"

"Sure. Sorry not to call first. I was out walking and—"

"I'm glad to see you. I was beginning to think I had bad breath. Me or my Oriental dragon." Nola flexed her upper arm.

Elaine averted her eyes. "You don't like it, do you?" Nola said, going to the kitchen.

"No. It's beautiful. Red and gold, green and black."

"Yeah, the colors are great. Adrian is known for them. He's a real artist."

"I'm sure."

"But you don't like it," Nola sang.

"I do think I'd rather it were on a wall." Elaine sat down on the worn-out couch. Nola brought out two glasses of soda. She was smiling. Her broad face mobile and happy. Her cool eyes filled with interest. Elaine noticed the light powdering of makeup. She must be feeling good, because her face was clearer than usual.

"Is that a criticism?" Nola asked. "Do I sense disapproval?"

"Well, a tattoo's for life. Though on 'thirtysomething' the other night, they were saying something about there's a way of getting them removed."

Nola laughed.

"You're happy that I hate—dislike it?"

"I think it's great! Finally something about me that you come right out and hate!"

"Oh, Nola, get off it! I didn't mean 'hate.' I misspoke. And I don't need nonsense right now."

"It's not nonsense, Elaine. I'm glad you're being honest."

"How's Second Hand?"

"Coming along. We're going to do that demo. I'm waitressing at The Original Dish. It's sort of slow, but the tips are good. And Vicky's cool. She gave me the lunch shift, and even if it's not my station, she tips me off on who're producers."

"Do you have any gigs?"

"Long Island's simmered down. But they like us in Hoboken. And . . . we got a new guy. A Korean dude. He's doing percussion, and he's good on bass. He's a Juilliard dropout."

"Bass? What about Jimmy?"

"Jimmy's thinking of law school. He's been accepted at Hofstra. And in Cleveland. He might actually go out of town."

"Oh? Hey, that's news."

"I don't know how we'll do without him. He's our voice of reason."

"What about you, Nola? How do you feel about it?"

She looked at Elaine. "Scared."

"You've never lived alone, have you?"

"I always thought I was alone when I was a kid. Till the two and a half years with Daddy, and more than a year with Jimmy. I'm hoping he goes to Hofstra, but I'm trying to zipper my lips. He's got to do what he's got to do."

"But certainly you can share your feelings."

"They're confused."

"Does this mean you might end up the only one left of the original band?"

"Yes. I've thought of it too."

"You're staying with it?"

"What does that mean? Now you don't think I should?"

"Your stuff is getting more and more original. That means the going might get tougher."

"I thought you wanted me to be the Chrysler Building!"

"Since when do you do things I want you to do?"

"Do I detect anger?"

"I shouldn't have said that."

"Why not? Why can't you just say what you want to me? Why do you always have to make sure you don't sound like . . ."

"Sound like? Come on, say it!"

"A mother!"

"A mother? Not a wicked old witch? Because I'm not a mother, that's why! Do you want me to say 'after all I've done for you' and stuff like that?"

"Is that what you want to say?"

"No, damn it! It's the last thing in the whole world I want to say. I heard enough of that myself when I was young!"

"It didn't seem to do you any harm. You're doing okay. I read in the *Post* about the auction of your book."

"Yeah. Good reviews, and Joyce salvaged the wreckage. Panther Publishers didn't distribute *The Passion and the Vow* worth a damn. They didn't even think of going back for a third printing. Told me their salesmen were busy selling the next list. And the subsidiary-rights person sold the paperback as a charity. But I'm doing okay. I'm teaching this fall semester, and then I'm taking half a year off. I've got a lot I want to write."

"Well, that's good news. What about Mario?"

"He's in Danbury, I guess. Writes me he's thinking of detox. Claude, his landlord, called me. He sold the boardinghouse. I don't think he has the heart to kick Mario out. I think he's leaving it for someone else to do."

"And Wig?"

"Wig? I thought I saw Wig the other day. Or his bones. Just a few blocks from here. At first I denied it. He used to be so handsome, Nola. So sweet. I don't know if he saw me. My God, a bum on a street corner. But it was Wig. All that hair of his."

"Do you think of Daddy?"

"Of course I do. Sure, I think of him. You must a lot?"

"Every day, and when I'm alone here . . . You know, after the memorial service, about five days later, when Jimmy had to go home?"

"Oh, that's right, he comes from Cleveland, doesn't he?"

"Yes. Anyway, I was really alone for the first time? And, you know, I started to cry and I couldn't stop! For a whole day and a whole night. I don't think I slept, Elaine. Maybe an hour? I don't know. But for a whole day, all I could do was cry. It wasn't that I was making noise or anything. I did for a while, but then I didn't have the strength. But the tears, they just didn't stop. I was like a fountain. The tears just came rolling out of my eyes. I isolated too. I mean, I know Silas is always upstairs. I didn't even go to a meeting. I couldn't. I just cried and cried and cried. I still do, but it's inside."

"Nola Netherlands," Elaine said, softly.

"That's what I'm thinking."

"What?"

"With this"—she flexed her arm again, took a look at the Oriental dragon—"I think I should stick with 'Asia.' But I was thinking of calling myself Asia Netherlands. I think Daddy was actually hinting about that in Columbia County, and I didn't get it. And I thought he was slow about the salad bar! I'm thinking of going back to my last name. In memory of him. And if Jimmy does leave too, well, I was thinking, with two girls, a Korean, and a black, maybe we should regroup as Neither Land. I think I'd like that more than Second Hand. What do you think?"

"I think you're getting yourself up a new band."

"And you don't like it?"

"I don't know it. It's yours. It's going beyond me."

"I take that as an accomplishment."

"Then I take that as a compliment. What I mean is, in the words of Anne Gregory, I don't know how commercial that's going to be. I do know it's literary. I do know it'll be good."

"Maybe that's enough for us? Maybe, for music to be good today, it can't be as big as it used to be. I don't need to live like Elvis, and I sure as hell don't want to die like him!"

Elaine chuckled. "Good for you!"

"Remember how Daddy yelled at you: 'Stop living through her!' "

"How could I forget?"

"Did that have a lot to do with the divorce? I mean, it seemed to me things got bad between you right after that."

"That was simply the straw! I'm sorry to disappoint you."

"Huh?"

"Well, I know now how much you wanted us to break up. I didn't then. And I broke up for me, not for you."

"Boy, you have a lot of anger."

"Oh, why shouldn't I? I helped you with algebra and didn't get an invitation to your high-school graduation."

"Hey, you didn't ask for one."

"Damn right I didn't! You didn't invite me and I didn't go!"

"You could have asked!"

"For scraps!"

"This is great. You're really mad!"

"What's so great about it? Tell me what? That I supported you as much as I could? I took you down to Free Being when it was on Second Avenue and disappeared so you could look cool buying records. And I stood up for you when you were into—yes, I said 'into,' and don't correct me—into chains on the shoulders and crossbones on the back of your three-hundred-and-fifty-dollar leather jacket. Lucky you didn't get a tattoo then! You could have done a skull-and-crossbones in that awful bluish color and really looked like a sailor!"

"Ha! You really hate my tattoo."

"Yes, I hate it. I think it looks slutty!"

"And my leather jacket and my orange-and-purple hair."

"That was different. You were a punk!"

"Daddy didn't think it was different."

"Nola! Why the hell are you pushing my buttons?"

"Because it's interesting. Just like I was always interesting to you."

"Of course you were interesting. *Are* interesting. You're young, growing. I wanted to help you all I could, without expecting anything back. I didn't want you to have a guilt trip about me. And it was fun to watch you grow. I thought you were a terrific kid. So smart. And into new things, even though you bridged and tunneled it to Manhattan. I didn't want to expect anything from you."

"Why?"

"Why?"

"Yes, why, Elaine? I mean, why didn't you ever expect a thank-you? I kept waiting and waiting. Why didn't you ever say no to me? Why was it always yes, yes, yes?"

"I said yes because you seemed perfectly capable of handling what you wanted. That's why."

"What about thank you? Why didn't you ever expect a thank-you?"

"It wasn't necessary."

"Wasn't it? You wanted to go to my graduation. I didn't know that then. I thanked God you didn't ask. You know that?"

"I believe it."

"But do you know why?"

"You didn't want me."

"I didn't want you to show up Delilah. That's what I didn't want. She had a real thing about you. You made her feel like a fool. I was protecting her! I felt lots of guilt about your not being at my high-school graduation."

"And what about not inviting me for Christmas dinner when Bunny asked you to? Do you remember that? Do you feel guilty about that?"

"Yes."

"Good! I'm glad! . . . Oh my God, did I just say that?"

"Yes, you did, Elaine."

"My God. I guess I wanted too much from you, without ad-mitting I wanted anything. Wow. That's it, Nola. I didn't ask you to say thanks because I didn't think you would. I was afraid you'd reject me. Let me stand back from that one and look."

"Boy, did that use to piss me off about you—how you could stand back and look at things. Why couldn't Delilah do that? Daddy could. He was like that, but not with me."

"They couldn't because they were your parents. They did what they could, but they only had so much to give. So did I. But I always knew it. I always knew the limits of what I could give. I knew I'd be a terrible mother."

"A terrible mother? Maybe you wouldn't have been great. God knows, Delilah wasn't great either. But you really were—are—a hell of a stepmother."

"You think so?"

"Yeah."

"What about the wicked witch?"

"You are a wicked lady, Elaine, you really are. Oh, come on, you're not going to cry."

"Me? Cry? What about Nutty Elaine? Don't you think I'm nuts?"

"Yes."

"Oh, really? I'm so nuts that I have a guy who calls my machine every day asking me if I think civilization as we know it will last until the twenty-first century. But I'm too sane to pick up the call."

"Why don't you? You could get rid of the guy in one shot."

Elaine wiped her eyes. "Because I don't want to break it to this guy that we are in the twenty-first century already. That he can answer his own question by looking around. That maybe this isn't the time for questions, but the time to start answering. We could be in for a change of luck, you know. But we have to start being more realistic. We have to stop mourning about Western civilization and crying about the past. We don't have the time for that. We have to realize there's no time for a decadent turn of this century. All that's the past; the future is now!"

"Hey, that's good. The future is now! Vintage Elaine! Let me get my guitar."

"You're kidding."

Nola got up and did come back with her guitar. She put a clean tape in her cassette.

Then Nola sat on the couch. She said, quite distinctly, and not without effort, "Thank you, Elaine, for all you've done, all you do for me. I love you."

"I . . . I love you too, Nola."

"Even though you hate my tattoo?"

"If it were smaller I—"

"Elaaaaine!"

"Even though I hate your tattoo."

"All right! Let's hear it for countdown 2000. Let's hear it for the future, girl rockers!"

And Asia Netherlands began to sing. She was inspired.